THE
2012
CODEX

GARY JENNINGS'

THE 2012 CODEX

ROBERT GLEASON
JUNIUS PODRUG

 A TOM DOHERTY ASSOCIATES BOOK

NEW YORK

This is a work of fiction. All of the characters, organizations, and events portrayed in this novel are either products of the authors' imaginations or are used fictitiously.

THE 2012 CODEX

A Forge Book
Published by Tom Doherty Associates, LLC.
175 Fifth Avenue
New York, NY 10010

www.tor-forge.com

Forge® is a registered trademark of Tom Doherty Associates, LLC.

ISBN 978-0-7653-2260-9

First Edition: September 2010

Printed in the United States of America

0 9 8 7 6 5 4 3 2 1

For Joyce Servis

ACKNOWLEDGMENTS

The work of many people is necessary to bring a book to fruition. We particularly wish to thank Sessalee Hensley, Tom Doherty, Linda Quinton, Christine Jaeger, Eric Raab, Whitney Ross, Ashley Cardiff, Jerry Gibbs, Elizabeth Winick, Hildegard Krische, Steve Jones, and Maribel Baltazar-Gutierrez.

LAND OF THE MAYA: A.D. 1519

XIBALBA

I am Pakal the Storyteller, and I walk in the Place of Fear. I have told the tales of this Underworld of terrors many times over camp-fires and before the tables of kings. Now, however, I shall suffer the demons of Xibalba's Lords of Death as they rise up from ooze, slime, and poisonous swamps, sucking the blood from my heart and the life from my soul.

Xibalba lies in the center of the land of my people, the Maya, but deep beneath the surface. Ruled by twelve Lords of Death, it is the abode of the dead. Called the Place of Fear by our people, it holds terror for those of us who will be cast into it after we depart the living.

Only a warrior's death in battle and the passing of a woman during childbirth are rewarded. Rather than being flung into the Under-world, these women serve the gods in the afterlife, and the warriors act as guards for the Sun God as he leaves his cave of darkness each morning and journeys across the sky.

Those who do not die with such honor have suffered what my people call a straw death, in which they are struck down by the demons of incurable sickness and fatal misfortune, whom the Lords of Death have sent to prowl the upper world.

For those whose life ends without honor, dying does not take them beyond the pain and sorrow of the life they have led. For them, Xibalba holds new terrors—a dark, deep, unearthly netherworld with six caverns, which my people call *stone houses*. Each stone house contains a terrifying trial for those who have suffered a straw death. The first is the House of Gloom, a cavern in which a murderous terror without a name lurks in the murky shadows of a maze. You must find a way through the labyrinth and not fall victim to fanged and taloned demons, or your journey ends in eternal pain and damnation, forever doomed to wander in the darkness with the beast's hot breath behind you.

Beyond Gloom is the House of Cold, a place of bone-chilling cold and dagger-shaped hail. Bitter cold is alien to my people, who enjoy eternal summer and wear few clothes. The third is the House of Jaguars, filled with hungry jungle animals, then the House of Bats, whose teeth pick the flesh off people until nothing is left but bone; those who have survived this far must traverse the House of Knives, where razor-sharp obsidian blades fly like birds of their own accord. The sixth is the House of Fire, filled with brimstone and blazing heat ignited by the gods of fire and lava.

Those few who survive the grueling trials of the six stone houses no longer have to suffer—the Lords of Death turn their souls into dust that is scattered on a field of maize.

My path to Xibalba has been a long one, a journey of many years during which my feet took me to far places where my eyes saw the greatest wonders of the One-World.

I was a green youth when I fought the One Who Kills with a Single Blow. At such a young age, I didn't understand that an act of the briefest moment would take me out of my village and put me on a journey in which my feet felt the dirt the length of the One-World.

There were moments when my heart hammered with fear and times when it beat with the joy of love—and, yes, even lust.

When I fought the One Who Kills with a Single Blow, I was

Pakal the Quarry Worker. My village was a day's walk from the great city of Mayapán, where the king of all that I knew sat on a golden throne and spoke to the gods.

Now, however, I come to Xibalba—not as a common laborer but wearing the quetzal feathers of a great lord. Entering the Underworld on my own two feet, I have a sword in hand with which to face the dead even though the demons of sickness and misfortune have not dragged me down to the houses of stone.

Instead I came to Xibalba on a mission, carrying treasures more precious to me than the riches of kings.

I entered Xibalba from above ground in daylight at the temple dedicated to the Lords of Death, going through a passageway forbidden to all but the priests who tend the temple fires and obtain the sacrificial blood the gods demand as sustenance.

Standing at the top of a stairway, I stared down at the last chamber of the priests. Beyond that was the gateway leading to the first house of stone and the challenge it would present.

The stairs and the vast cavern before me were carved out of limestone, the stone that lies just beneath the dirt throughout the land of my people. I have traveled far, from one end of the One-World to the other, and never have I heard of a land with so much of it.

The land has few rivers and lakes, and most of our water is in caverns—not unlike the one I am in now—vast hollows in the layers of limestone. I know this stone well, having been a lowly stoneworker before I ate at the tables of kings. Underground, the rock is still soft and malleable, which simplifies the hollowing out of caverns and quarries and facilitates the carving of stones for buildings. After stone blocks and slabs are taken to the surface and exposed to the warmth provided by the Sun God, the stone becomes rock hard and unworkable.

As soon as I enter the Underworld, the smell of the dark, dank cavern assaults me. Beyond the putrid stench of rotting decay—not unlike the stink of turning meat—the cavern holds a stench of death that turns my skin cold, clammy, and fills my soul with terror and dread.

Shrieks come from somewhere in the darkness below, howls of pleasure that I have arrived, cries of ecstasy from those who smell my blood and undulate to the thunder of my heart.

I grip my sword tighter. The weapon of a nobleman and seasoned warrior, it makes me wish I had the muscular power I'd once possessed as a stoneworker.

Longer than my arm, the sword has a blade of razor-sharp obsidian embedded on each edge. The fire-mountain gods vomit obsidian out of their fiery volcanic maws. The sharpest material in the One-World, it is used to create the deadliest weapons.

A single swing of the sword can sever a head or limb of anyone—anyone, that is, who breathes air and walks on two feet.

I take the steps down slowly, warily, not knowing from which direction the attack will come, knowing only that it will. Slimy green moss and watery rivulets make the steps slippery.

The flickering torches barely impinge on the cavern's darkness; much of the cave is still lost in murky shadows and the black void. A cold draft chills the back of my neck, flickering the torches, throwing eerie trembling shadows on the walls.

Blood stains the bottom steps. The people hacked up here were not slain in combat but butchered, the flesh ripped off their bodies by fang and claw.

Eyo! The demons of the Underworld are angry and thirsty. Those above have forsaken the temple, and Xibalba's demons for some time have not tasted the blood that feeds them.

The entire land of my people is under the punishing wrath of the gods.

Having violated the blood covenant—the promise that our people will give the gods blood, and they in turn will give sun and water to fructify our crops and feed our stomachs—the gods are visiting their wrath on us. Their anger has made our land a living hell.

A few drops of my blood—from a nick on my leg or on my penis—will not satisfy them. They will want more—all my blood.

I stop at the bottom of the stairs when I sense something lurking in the darkness—a thing that smells my blood.

I grip the sword with two hands but know it will not cut anything that walks without its feet touching the ground.

Another stench fills the chill air in the cavern, fouler than the breath of the great jungle predator that I once fought and slew with nothing more than a staff—the jaguar.

I know what is waiting for me.

It is a drinker of blood.

LAND OF THE MAYA: PRESENT DAY

1

From a high escarpment just below the cliff's rim, Cooper Jones studied her team resting on the trail below: Rita "Reets" Critchlow—a fellow archeolinguist—flanked by Hargrave and Jamesy. All three wore dusty fatigues, camouflage T-shirts with the sleeves cut off, heavy boots, and sweat-stained dirty-white baseball caps. Reets' and Coop's caps bore the Diablos Rojos del México's team logo, while Jamesy's and Hargrave's caps rooted for the Leones de Yucatán.

Mexico City Red Devils and Yucatán Lions, Coop thought grimly. *Right now I feel more like a heat-sick Gila monster.*

No shade protected them from the blistering sun, and Jamesy was pulling his shirt off. Both men's bodies were graphic studies in macabre violence—specifically, knife and gunshot wounds—but Jamesy's chest and back scars were an unnervingly turned-out oeuvre. The first time she stumbled on him bathing in a stream with his shirt off—and had seen the knife slash diagonally traversing his chest, the barely healed bullet hole entering and exiting his broad right shoulder, and the wide white stripes of some long-forgotten prison hellhole disfiguring his back—she'd understood the kind of men he and Hargrave were.

Not that she'd needed scars to garner that insight. Their eyes said everything—eyes that neither asked nor gave, and stares hard enough to crack concrete.

"Eyes that diced at the foot of the cross," she'd once told Reets.

"And slogged the long road back from Stalingrad," Reets had said.

"Hard enough to crack concrete," Coop had concluded.

Then, of course, there were the mirthless grins that never reached those eyes.

Men she and Reets now trusted with their lives.

❧

. . . Reets had summed up their situation two nights before:

"We're hunted by the most sadistic, pistol-whipping, water-boarding mercenaries north of the Rio; by Mexico's most sadistic, gonad-electrocuting, mordida-stealing, child-pimping federales; by the most sadistic, prodigiously powerful drug cartel in two continents—the Apachureros."

"You mean we're hunted by . . . sadists?" Hargrave asked.

"No," Reets said, "cloistered nuns."

"We're not in some kind of trouble, are we?" Jamesy asked.

"Not unless you call drawing and quartering, hot coals and knives, followed by death of a thousand cuts . . . trouble." Reets replied.

"They have their side of it," Hargrave countered.

Reets nodded her assent. "After all, we've stolen some of their homeland's most historically important, preposterously priceless relics."

"The '2012 Apocalyptic Codices,' as our intrepid president describes them," Hargrave said. "You can understand why they want them back and us dead?"

"I blame the president," Jamesy said. "Some hijo de puta on his staff's ratting us out."

"Telling the Apachureros, what those codices are worth and where to find us," Hargrave said.

"Codices we now control," Coop said.

"And which our bandit buddies want," Jamesy said.

"There's also those dozen or so of their bullet-riddled friends we so carelessly left on our back-trail," Hargrave threw in.

"Someone in Washington put a bounty on us," Jamesy said coldly.

"Those Pach want us muy malo," Hargrave said.

"So they can steal the stuff we stole," Reets said. . . .

. . . *Well, onward and upward*, Cooper Jones thought. At the top of the jungle-shrouded cliff waited a man who she hoped had the last of the Quetzalcoatl codices.

The inestimable Jack Phoenix.

The bravest, cleverest, most outrageous archeologist the gods ever made—his detractors often added *psychopathic* to those adjectives— Jack Phoenix was also one of Coop's and Reets' two closest friends.

"One of our two *only* friends," Reets once remarked after eight tequila shooters.

They'd begun pooling resources almost a decade ago and they now trusted him with their most confidential findings. Through a covert communications network of seemingly innocuous weblogs, they passed information critical to their work and careers—so much so, they encrypted their e-mails to keep other archeologists from ripping off their findings.

Phoenix typically sought her and Reets' help in translating indecipherable pre-Columbian glyphs, knowing that Coop, in partic- ular, was preeminently, almost preternaturally gifted in such linguis- tics. In exchange, he passed data on to them, describing unpublicized digs and sites, which he himself had often uncovered but kept secret.

His last posts contained information that had shaken them to their souls.

At his Chiapas meeting place—an unexplored site deep in Apachurero country—he believed they'd find their missing codex.

Coop allowed herself another quiet sigh. Working her way up to the cliff's rim, she pulled herself up over the boulder-strewn, out- wardly jutting cliff top. Crawling over rocks, through brush, over fallen trees toward the ruin, she surveyed the terrain, looking for intruders.

Until a blast of harsh laughter stopped her.

Hiding behind a log, she spotted the source—a group of rau-
cously drunken bandits.

She counted at least ten of them.

Grizzled inebriated Apachureros in phony *federales* uniforms,
they were armed to the teeth with automatic weapons and pointing
at Jack Phoenix's partially excavated temple.

Waiting for Jack Phoenix to emerge from the subterranean tunnel
entrance he had written them about.

Waiting for their friend.

2

Beneath the half-buried temple ruins, Jack Phoenix crawled on his
belly through an endless labyrinth of dank sandstone tunnels barely
three feet in diameter. More than one thousand years old, the dark
narrow passageways hid both deceased royalty and their personal
treasures from grave-diggers. The designers had done their job well.
With a Mini Maglite clenched between his teeth, Phoenix worked
his way through the maddening maze, coughing and gagging on the
dust—just as he'd done every day for the last three months—still
finding nothing. Every inch of the labyrinth appeared undisturbed.
Phoenix saw no indication anywhere that anything or anyone had
trespassed those depths during the past ten centuries.

Nor had he discovered the skillfully concealed wall compartment that, he believed, contained Quetzalcoatl's final prophecy.

According to the codex—which he had tracked down in
Guatemala, then smuggled into Mexico—it did.

While Phoenix was rounding a sharp turn—which he'd probed
and combed at least a hundred times before—his flashlight suddenly
went dead, the tunnel turning dead black. Cursing his Juárez knockoff
Duracells, he searched for two more AAs in his cargo pockets. After
locating the positive and negative tips by touch, he shook out their
predecessors and fumbled the new ones into the Mini Maglite.

He was about to twist the light's handle and turn it on, when the high-pitched buzz of *Crotalus atrox*—otherwise known as the diamondback—froze him to his marrow.

He did not need the Maglite to see it. Even in the tunnel's total dark, the viper's eyes blazed, vicious and yellow, its vertically distended pupils stopping him cold.

When he twisted the Maglite's head, its beam detonated in his eyes like a thousand suns, and for several interminable seconds all he could see was searing fire.

When his vision returned, he was sorry it had.

He was now staring into the snake's gaping jaws —at its two dripping, five-inch fangs lazily unfolding from the roof of its mouth, its thin bifurcated tongue flicking in and out, in and out. Thick as Phoenix's forearm, the scaly reptile's ten-foot body twisted and undulated toward him with infinite lassitude and indolent grace.

Until the snake abruptly halted and coiled . . . two short feet from his face.

Paralyzed with terror on the tunnel floor, Phoenix could only stare fixedly into its fiery orbs—at the bony humps protruding above the sockets, at the spade-shaped head levitating above the writhing coils, and at the segmented tail banging against the tunnel floor . . . all the while shuddering at its vibrating *whirrrr!* Zig. Zig. Zig. Zig-zig. Zig-zig. Zizzz. Zizzz. Zzzzzzz. Zzzzzzzzzzzzz.

Do something!

Phoenix kept a Randall Bowie with a thirteen-inch blade in his boot, but how do you knife-fight a diamondback in a three-foot-wide tunnel? Even worse, the Maglite in his teeth—as if taking on a life of its own—was now bobbing up and down, mesmerized by the snake's own levitating head.

Christ, the damn thing is charming me.

Get with it. Shake off your stupor, you somnambulant bastard.

Suddenly the beam from his Mini Mag began to flicker, dim, fade.

Those goddamn Juárez batteries.

He kept a small flat .32-caliber Beretta shoved beneath his belt in the small of his back. Phoenix had to reach for it. He had no other options—even though a pistol shot in these close confines could easily blow out his eardrums.

His hackles horripilated at the thought.

Quit whining. You'll probably miss the son of a bitch. What are your choices, anyway? You miss it, you die. You don't shoot, you die? If you kill it and live, maybe you go deaf.

So what? You never hear anything worth listening to, anyway.

Do it!

His gaze still locked on the burning orbs, he slipped the automatic from the back of his pants and the bowie out of his boot. As nonthreateningly as he could, he gripped the knife blade between his teeth and leveled the pistol at the snake's weaving head. Easing back the slide, he gingerly pressed the trigger just as the snake hissed, reared back, and—and—and—*sprang!*

At his face.

3

Crawling up one at a time, Coop's friends joined her at her new observation post behind two massive boulders. Behind a V-shaped crevice where the two rocks touched, Jamesy immediately positioned himself with a pair of binoculars.

"I count ten of them," he said.

Taking Jamesy's place in the crevice between the two boulders and peering through the binoculars, Hargrave said: "In uniform."

"In fake *federales* uniforms," Coop pointed out.

"With automatic weapons," Jamesy added.

"I spotted two outliers," Coop said. "Sentries, maybe . . . though they seem more focused on their friends than on their perimeter."

"Friends who are waiting for Phoenix by the tunnel," Reets said.

"They have AKs *and* sidearms," Hargrave said, handing the binoculars back to Jamesy.

"They're better armed than the ones in the Chiapas canyons," Jamesy said, focusing the field glasses. He was referring to their last Apachurero firefight.

"And there's more of them here," Coop said.

"Too many," Reets said.

Putting down the binoculars, Jamesy turned to her and stared. "You want your friend walking away from that ruin?" he asked.

Now it was Reets' turn to stare.

"I assume you still want that codex?" Hargrave said. The question was rhetorical.

"Reets has a point," Coop said, taking up for her friend. "They have a lot of firepower."

"This time we have grenades, and except for the two sentries, they aren't spread out," Hargrave said.

"Sentries," Jamesy said contemptuously.

At the word *sentries*, he slipped the Gerber Mark II combat knife from the sheath strapped to his outside right calf. He was staring absently at its 7.5-inch, dagger-shaped blade; its knurled, foil-molded grip; its two-inch-wide oval cross-guard; and the rounded ball at the butt's tip—then he resheathed it.

"Jamesy and I will work our way around," Hargrave said, "and flank them on the side."

Hargrave took the two combat shotguns out of the packs at his feet—both of them SPAS 12-bore semiautomatic Franchis, each with the short illegal eighteen-inch barrel and the folding stock, which could be locked at a right angle and braced under the forearm. The stock then allowed the shooter—if he was strong enough—to fire it from behind cover with only one arm exposed. Their bodies—obviously much larger targets—would still be concealed behind cover.

Which, given the Apachureros' superior firepower, might prove to be the decisive factor—their final margin of survival.

"The ones we don't get will position themselves behind the deadfall," Hargrave said, pointing to some fallen trees.

"They'll also head toward that stump to the deadfall's right," Jamesy said.

Hargrave studied the bandits' prospective cover, then separated out a box of hot-loaded 000 depleted uranium shells out of the backpack.

"That DU buck is titanium hard," Hargrave said.

"Harder," Jamesy said.

"Shoots straight through engine blocks," Hargrave agreed.

"And hits like a .90 caliber," Jamesy added.

"After we hammer them with the grenades," Hargrave said, "we'll come in close with the triple-aught."

"After mounting the spreaders on the muzzles," Jamesy said.

Spreaders were devices that, when screwed onto the shotgun muzzles, would scatter the 000 in a pattern several feet across almost as soon as it left the barrel.

What do they need us for? Coop wondered to herself.

Hargrave then took two gun-launched grenades out of his own backpack—one of them fragmentation, the other flashbang. The two men then began shoving their hot-loaded DU triple-aught buckshot into shotgun magazines.

"Position yourself slightly to the left so you can see us. When we reach that clump of trees," Jamesy said, pointing to a stand of pines seventy-five yards away, just to their left, "we'll give you a sign. Then you two distract them."

"We'll waltz right up to them and ask if they've seen our friend," Reets said.

"But don't get too close," Hargrave said, his eyes fixing them intently. "Those grenades throw a lot of shrapnel."

"And the shotguns will spread like claymore mines."

"Got your gear?" Jamesy asked.

Coop was already digging automatic person defense weapons out of their bag. Made by the Knight's Armament Company, the KAC

PDW was popular among bodyguards and other mercs who relied on concealed weaponry. Less than twenty inches long, weighing only 4.5 pounds, it was easily hidden under sport coats and fatigue jackets. Coop planned on stowing them beneath tan wool ponchos, which they'd used as sleeping bags and which Hargrave had fortuitously fireproofed before the trip.

The two men helped them load their box magazines, each one taking thirty 6×30 mm rounds. They then loaded four extra magazines.

The women slung their PDWs from their right shoulders. Even as the two men were on their knees, crawling toward the tree stand, Coop and Reets were slipping the ponchos over their shoulders and pushing their heads up through the center holes.

4

Jack Phoenix had a high pain threshold. . . . Two decades of digging through ruins in the third world's most depraved danger zones had tested his capacity for physical suffering all too many times, from his point of view. Nothing, however, had prepared him for *this*. His problem was not so much the throbbing ache in his ears and skull— that agony was slowly subsiding.

Now he faced something far more menacing—imminent death.

True, the bullet—which hit the diamondback just below the head—had killed the snake's body. The brain, however, had lived long enough to drive five inches' worth of venom-dripping fangs into Phoenix's left shoulder muscle. Jack knew enough about diamondback neurotoxins to understand that a bite that close to the heart and head—while perhaps not instantly lethal—had to be promptly cut open, the venom sucked out, and diamondback antitoxin vaccine immediately administered . . . if the victim were to survive.

His only hope was Reets and Coop. He prayed they would arrive in time to treat him. Otherwise, he was a dead man.

That contingency filled Phoenix with a wall-banging, head-butting rage so all-consuming, he could not contain himself. Roaring like a gored water buffalo, driven mad by feral fury, he hammered the butt of the .32-caliber semiautomatic against the right side of the tunnel.

Three times.

With the third blow, the tunnel wall, to his eternal surprise . . . *shattered.*

One thousand years' worth of stale air rushed out.

He pointed the flickering Maglite into the gaping cavity, now swirling with dust. The foul haze slowly dissipated, and Phoenix was staring at the compartment's single occupant—an oblong ceramic urn, its wide stoppered mouth tightly sealed, its crimson surface embellished with a brilliantly painted, jet black likeness of Quetzalcoatl, the Feathered Serpent. His coiled, plumed body scintillated surreally in the whirling dust motes and in the Maglite's eerily flickering beam, his gaped blood-dripping jaws fearsomely fanged.

It was the most stunning rendition of the great Mayan god Phoenix had ever seen.

Unfortunately, the portentous portrait also reminded Phoenix of his recent encounter with Quetzalcoatl's featherless cousin, the thought of which caused Phoenix to shudder convulsively.

Still, he could not take his eyes off the urn nor could he contain his awe. He was staring at the greatest archeological find perhaps of all time and the fulfillment of his life's work.

The codex, which he'd "appropriated" in Chiapas, had described everything in detail—the vermilion urn, the lurid depiction of the Feathered Serpent, the location of the ruins, and the entrance to the subterranean tunnel maze.

The urn could contain only one thing:

The last of the 2012 Codices—Quetzalcoatl's final revelation of the Mayan End Time.

As he wrestled the urn out of its crypt, his shoulder shrieked agonizing hymns of hell's horrors, as if all Hades' demons were now trapped inside it and kick–clawing their way out. Pulling the urn under his chest, he commenced his long, torturous crawl to the first stope, where he stopped and turned around. He then began dragging himself back through the tight, cramped tunnels toward the opening.

On that return route, he had to crawl back through the passageway where he'd fought the snake. Picking up the dead diamondback by its bloody head, he dragged it through the tunnel with him.

After all, the serpent was Quetzalcoatl's cousin—for all he knew, his bastard son—and it had located the urn for him.

True, he was taking his life, but what was that compared to the incomparable, imperishable gift he had given him in return?

A mere pittance.

Even dead, Quetzalcoatl Jr. deserved his day in the sun. The pinioned snake had given life for the sacred codex as well.

With the red ceramic oblong urn clutched under his arm and the divine diamondback in his fist, Jack Phoenix crawled up the tunnel.

PART I

1

"Tell us a story, Pakal," my friend Cuat said.

I shook my head and kept hacking at the brush. My friend knew the time for storytelling was at night around the meal fire, in those hours before sleep, when the Sun God had returned to his cave on the other side of the Great Western Waters.

All daylight hours were spent in work, whether in the women's gathering and preparation of food, or the men's stonecutting labors. Only after our stomachs were warm from maize and beans did the storytellers entertain us.

Gray Dawn, our village headman, gave Cuat a warning look. This was not a time for frivolity. A great lord from Mayapán, the city of the king, had come to our village of stonecutters, and we must ensure our worthiness in his eyes.

Lord Janaab was the king's architect. He must approve all buildings, palaces, temples, and even city walls and roads, including the stone we cut, which was the primary building material for those projects.

My people worked the stone—that was their central task—and this day we were clearing brush in order to show the king's architect an unusually colored outcrop. If the stone pleased Lord Janaab, we would dig below and exhume it in slabs.

We cleared a path to the site in the dense jungle brush, so the lord with many quetzal feathers could walk freely to the outcrop. We then cleared more brush, so he examined another section.

The builder wanted not only the brush cleared, but the snakes and black spiders also removed. *Eyo!* If he were bitten by one of the Death Lords' poisonous pets, everyone in our village would be painted red and turned over to priests to be sacrificed.

I had never seen a great lord before, though as the village story-teller, I told many tales about them. I assumed my position as the tale-teller after the old man who had told tales since before I was born passed to Xibalba, the Place of Fear.

Though I had never journeyed more than an hour's walk from my village, I learned many tales of kings and wars, gods and demons from him and others who had come to the village. For reasons I could not fathom, Itzamná, the God of Maize and Cacao, who also gives us the gift of remembering tales, gave me the ability to recall more stories than anyone else in the village.

All of us villagers, except for the headman, were barefoot and wore a single loincloth—a strip of cotton as wide as a hand, wound around the waist and passed between the legs. The headman wore a cotton cape over his shoulders and a loincloth and told us what to do rather than clearing the brush himself.

Lord Janaab's loincloth was of the finest, softest cotton—dyed green and embroidered with feathers at the edges. His *pati*, shoulder cape, was yellow, and his sandals were of the finest deerskin while my "sandals" were the soles of my own bare feet.

The great lord wore the most stunning accoutrement of all—his magnificent headpiece. Bearing the jade face of the Creator God, Cacoch, it was festooned with the feathers of blue and gold macaws as well as the golden green and scarlet plumage of the prized quetzal.

Even the lord's servants and guards were garbed in finer loincloths, capes, and sandals than the headman of our village. The tips of the spears carried by his four guards were flint, and each man carried an obsidian-bladed dagger.

I was lifting a thick stout tree limb, with which to strike and clear the brush, when the roar of a startlingly close jaguar froze me. It crouched in a tree no more than twenty paces from where I stood, its torso almost as long as a man's but more massive.

And it was white.

Incomprehensibly rare, it was the most sacred of all the beasts of the jungle.

We stood perfectly still for the briefest moment—until panic drove our feet.

Then we ran—all of us, racing in full rout from the great beast, which weighed twice as much as a grown man and could kill with a single blow.

Hearing a scream behind me, I glanced over my shoulder. The big animal had brought down Lord Janaab.

I will never know why I did it. After spinning around, I ran back without thinking, knowing that I was no match for the animal but not willing to let it murder the lord without a fight. The lord was on his back, pinned to the ground by the heavy beast. The man had tried to block the jaguar's bite with his forearm, and the animal clamped on to it. Except for the heavy limb with which I cleared brush, I had nothing to kill or drive the beast away.

As I came up behind the struggle, I realized there was one thing I could do with my brush-clearing limb. I jumped on the animal's back. As it reared up and let go of the man's arm, I shoved my thick pole under its throat.

Eyo! His huge paw came around and swiped the side of my face. He nearly threw me off, but as I rolled to the side, I got my feet under me and pulled back on the piece of wood with all the strength I had developed from years of lifting heavy slabs of stone, with all the power the gods gave me as they fed my panic.

I heard a snap, and the beast collapsed beneath me.

Rolling off, I gasped for a breath. For the first time I thought about what I had done.

Jaguars were the greatest killers in the One-World—sacred beasts with whom kings claimed kinship.

By the gods, I had killed one.

I met the eye of Lord Janaab. Neither of us spoke, but I saw amazement in his face.

And relief.

Blood covered my chest—dripping from where the beast had clawed the side of my face.

2

"Paint them red," Lord Janaab said.

Lord Janaab had ordered those guards—the ones who'd run from the jaguar—to be painted a garish crimson, and they cowered in fear. The scarlet stain was a death sentence, and the men would be turned over to the priests for sacrifice at the main temple of the gods when the High Lord returned to the city.

We stood in the village center. Respectfully silent, all the villagers had gathered and were there when the king's builder gave commands.

Lord Janaab's arm had been treated with healing salves and bandaged with medicinal leaves. The powerful jaws of the jaguar would have crushed the lord's bones, had it not been for the large silver bracelet he wore.

My own face felt hot, and my wounds pulsated with pain. After I washed up in the cenote, I stared at my reflection. *Eyo!* My face would bear the claw marks of the jaguar for the rest of my life. I was not considered a great beauty among men, and the savage slashes would bring even less praise about my appearance.

After he had doomed the five guards Lord Janaab turned to me. "Come, here."

I went, and when I kneeled, he told me to stand.

Eyeing my body, he nodded. "You are tall and muscular."

"Yes, my lord."

"I can see why you were able to break the beast's neck. No ordinary man, not even with a piece of wood under the chin as you placed it, would have the power to break a jaguar's neck. That you were able to stay on the animal's back when it reared is a miracle. That took not only great strength but poise and balance as well."

"I'm the strongest man in the village," I said simply.

The hard work quarrying stone made men either exceptionally strong—or it broke them. I was also taller than any of the other men.

"You are wrong."

"Wr-wr-wrong?" I stammered.

"You are no longer of this village. I am placing you in my guard."

"I'm leaving the village?"

"I see more fright on your face now than when you wrestled with a jaguar. I am told you are not married, that your wife went to Xibalba during one of the great sicknesses the gods torment us with. If there's a woman of the village you desire, you may bring her with you."

"No, it's just that, I—I have never . . ."

"Never been to the world out there—the Great Beyond. The Vast Unknown frightens you more than the most powerful beast in the One-World. Good. I will deal with the Unknown. It disturbs me not in the least. My most deadly enemies are known foes—those are the ones my guards must battle—and I need guards I can trust implicitly. I need men like you. When you leave this village, you will leave behind your life as a lowly stoneworker and wear the uniform of the guard of a great lord of Mayapan."

"Yes, my lord."

"From this day forth, your name will be Pakal B'alam."

A gasp rose from those who had heard the statement, and one of the sharp intakes of breath was my own.

B'alam meant "jaguar," and it was a name of great honor, one often borne by kings. My knees felt weak at the thought that I would bear the name.

"You need not be so surprised. None of the great lords of Mayapán—myself included—would take the jaguar name, for fear of provoking the king's and other lords' ire. You are not the first to single-handedly kill a jaguar but perhaps the first to kill one without driving a spear into its heart.

"But there is no record of a man killing a white jaguar. Only demons sent by the gods have killed them. The king himself does not have a white jaguar skin. There is a tradition that permits even a lowly stoneworker to assume the name. Do you know what it is, Storyteller?"

I nodded. I knew the legend. "B'alam was a warrior who took the shape of a jaguar to battle the bat-demons who were devouring people."

"Very good. Your headman tells me you are the village storyteller. I can see you deserve the title of storyteller *and* jaguar. Anyone who single-handedly kills a jaguar has the right to bear the name. From this day forth you may call yourself Pakal B'alam," he repeated.

My knees still trembled, remembering the honor.

"Your village headman also says you are something of a seer."

"No, my lord, I do not foresee events."

"He says you once awoke the village to danger in the middle of the night to ward off an attack by a band of robbers."

"The crickets told me they were coming, not the gods."

"You speak to crickets?"

"No, my lord, but I awoke in the middle of the night, and they were silent. They stop their chirping only when strangers are about."

"I was also told about a snake you realized was in the bushes, and no one else saw it."

I started to say I was merely more observant than others, but he held up his hand to stop me.

"It doesn't matter." He waved his hand. "Bring the skin."

Two of his servants came forward with the skin of the jaguar.

They had skinned the cat in one piece, its head, arms, legs, and claws still attached.

"Jaguars belong to the king; they are of his House. The hide will be presented to the king when we return to Mayapán. He will be greatly pleased that it is white. However, the hunter who slays a jaguar is entitled to keep a claw for his feat. This is your claw."

A servant stepped forth, and around my neck he placed a narrow silver band with the claw attached.

"Wear it always." He indicated the raw wound on the side of my face. "You carry the mark of the beast, and when people see the claw, they will know that you are the one who walked away from the battle. The story will be well known by the time we reach Mayapán, and your name will be sung in the streets as *B'alam*."

I was overwhelmed. Tears of pride swelled in me, and I fought them back. A man does not shed tears, especially one who has slain a jaguar with his bare hands and a single tree limb.

"Now that we have honored your feat, we must get back to work." He smiled at me, more a feral sneering grin, which reminded me of the jaguar. "There is one last task you must do as a stoneworker before you assume your new life as a guard in the house of a lord. The limestone outcrop that was being cleared is of exceptional quality. It will be the centerpiece for a monument at the great temple in Mayapán. It must be recovered in one piece. As the strongest man in the village, your strength will be needed to bring it out of the ground so it can be prepared for transport to the king's city."

3

The next morning when we gathered to cut out the stone Lord Janaab desired, I realized how much my world had changed. The villagers whom I had known since my birth treated me differently— not so much with respect but with caution. They seemed fearful of me even though I tried to act the same as before. But the world was different: I had killed a sacred beast that gods, priests, and kings invest with magical powers. And one of the great lords of the land— an architect of cities they had never seen, of roads they had never trod—had honored me.

I knew I would miss my village, my people, but more than any of the people I knew, I was drawn to the Great Beyond, and had always wondered about what Lord Janaab called simply "the Vast Unknown."

I was not actually born in the village, though in a sense I had spent my entire life in it. After my people had quarried the best stone in our surrounding area, the lord who owned our village moved my family and everyone else to our present area, which was rich in the dark stone.

In a few years, when all that stone has been harvested, he would move my people to another location.

Our land was warm the year around—an eternal summer whose

climate ran from tepid and moist to hot and wet during the year. Requiring little—often no—shelter, we constructed our huts from the tree limbs, leaves, fronds, and brush gathered in the surrounding jungle. We kept little inside the huts except for hammocks hanging from the pole rafters and the few clothes, tools, and other possessions each of us had.

Most of our time was spent outside. Eating around the cooking fires or working, sitting at night in a circle around a fire to talk about the day's stonework or crop harvest, and listening to the tales I had memorized—that was the extent of our socializing.

The only other thing necessary to establish a village besides an abundance of high-quality stone was a water source. The gods had provided few rivers and lakes in all the land of the Maya, even though Chaac, the Rain God, sent down great deluges during some months of the year.

Rainwater did not stay on the ground, but ran off into holes, where it gathered in natural sinkholes and caverns underground, which we called *cenotes*. Water was drawn from the cenotes for drinking and cooking the year around.

Life was the same, day after day, waking and eating. We stoneworkers walked to the quarry, and those who worked maize, beans, and peppers for our meals went to the fields.

4

Lord Janaab had selected a section of limestone and ordered us to clear the top layer of ground over it. That work done, we were ready to carve out the slab of limestone that he desired. The corrosive air had not tarnished the stone and it was still damp, soft, and malleable. Only after it was exposed for months to the rays of the Sun God would the stone harden and become difficult even to scratch.

I made a remark to Cuat, whose name means "snake," that I was sure we could carve out exactly that section of stone the great lord wanted, but my comment seemed only to frighten him. *Eyo!* Fool that I was, I forgot that Lord Janaab had had four men painted red yesterday and would have more condemned today if they displeased him.

"Are you sure you wish to help?" the headman asked. "You must be tired from your battle with the jaguar."

"Lord Janaab told me to help," I reminded him.

"Oh yes—yes, you're right. Only you must make the cut across the grain of the stone."

The cut against the pattern of the stone was the most difficult to make. If the stone were to be ruined by shattering, that was the most likely time it would happen. And Gray Dawn had cleverly tricked me into reminding him that I had been ordered by the Mayapán lord to procure the stone. The builder had not told me expressly to make the cut, but if the stone shattered, he would be displeased with me, which, to the headman, was better than the great lord taking his wrath out on him.

The tools used to cut out slabs of limestone are a flint chisel and a hammerstone. The flint chisel has a cutting edge and a blunt edge. We use the hammerstone, a hard rock attached to a club, to pound the blunt edge of the flint.

I discussed with the headman exactly how we would cut into the stone. Lord Janaab wanted a slab about the height and width of a man. Then we began the task, excising the shape and thickness of it from the surrounding stone. We first had to cut a trench around the stone, one wide enough for us to be able to kneel in while we worked.

Then we worked the hardest part, cutting under the stone until it was free and could be lifted off from where the gods had placed it. As we cleared under the piece, we used stone blocks to shore it up and keep it from cracking under its own weight.

We needed the entire day and part of the night—working by torchlight—to cut the stone free.

A crew of stone movers Lord Janaab had brought with him would haul it to Mayapán by laying it on hardwood logs. The workers would both push the stone from behind and pull it with ropes from the front.

As the slab rolled over the logs, the logs in the rear would be picked up and brought forward and reused until they were so worn, they had to be replaced.

If water needed to be crossed, the workers built a raft big enough to hold the stone without sinking, then floated it across.

Not just large stones were used. Some pieces were small enough for the workers to haul on wood sleds. Pieces even smaller would be packed to cities by carriers who worked for merchants. Artists inscribed sacred marks on the stones, and then the merchants sold them.

Even chips and scraps were used. These were burned in fires, and then the workers ground them into powders that, mixed with water and sand, were made into the mortar we used to cement the stone blocks with which we constructed our buildings and roads.

In the morning, the slab would begin its journey to Mayapán, the city of the king. There, workers would smooth its surface and cut it to the exact size Lord Janaab desired. Artists would then carve into it whatever inscription the lord had chosen before it was put into its resting place. All this work had to be done, of course, before the gods hardened the limestone.

My feet would follow the same road to the city that is the greatest of all in the land of my people. The stone would take five days to make the journey over logs, but our feet would carry us to the city by tomorrow.

The sickness that had killed my wife five years ago had also taken my parents. Why the demons, who spread these maladies, had spared me would forever in my mind remain a mystery. Whatever the cause of their demonic forbearance, I now had no reason to stay behind at the village—except my own fears of the unknown. Mayapán was not just a place to us villagers, but a fabled city where the king climbs to the top of a temple higher than the clouds and speaks to the gods.

A place where offending a great lord can get you painted red in the blink of an eye.

Eyo! The great lord was right: I felt more fearful contemplating what awaited me in the unknown than I had when wrestling the king of the One-World's beasts.

5

The city of the king was most of a day's walk. We set out at first light to cover as much ground as possible before the sun was high in the sky and the heat too oppressive.

Thirty of us were in Lord Janaab's party, including twenty guards, four of whom were painted red and disarmed. Having priests rip out your heart and drain your blood to feed the gods was considered a great honor, but the ones getting butchered often disagreed.

In the case of the crimson-daubed guards, Lord Janaab bound them like slaves in the caravans we so often saw marching along the roads. A long pole ran atop the men's right shoulders, their necks tightly tied to it. Men joined together with a stout pole lashed to their necks would not run fast or far.

I was uniformed in a cloak and carried a guard's sword. The other guards quickly informed me of the dangers on the road, and the great lord had sent a messenger up the road to noblemen whose territories we passed, ordering them to provide extra guards.

Although I had never ventured far from home, I knew something of the world beyond from the merchants and carriers who came to the village. Trouble was brewing throughout the king's domain and in the territories ruled by other kings.

The villagers traditionally raised their own crops, but the dearth of rain had driven many of them into brigandage. Now murderers and highwaymen haunted the roads. Chaac, our Rain God, had blessed us with few of his tears, causing crops to fail and many of our people to go hungry.

"They say that Chaac is angry at the king," a guard told me.

The king's most sacred duty was to fulfill the gods' wants, needs, and desires, the most critical of which would always be human blood. Blood gave the Sun God the necessary strength to quit his cave at dawn and cross the sky. Granting Chaac the moisture he required for his rain of tears, blood also fueled the Maize God's struggle to shove the corn stalks up from the ground.

Our people called it the blood covenant—we gave blood to the gods, and they yielded life's necessities.

"The king has not given the gods enough blood," the guard said.

When criminals', cowards', and other miscreants' blood failed to satisfy the gods, another source was available: the Flower Wars.

A Flower War was fought not for territory or riches, but for prisoners, each army fighting not to the death, but for hostages with whom the warriors could return to their land and sacrifice on their temple summits, their blood requiting the gods' indispensable gifts. These tame wars did not tip a region's balance of power or subject a king to mortal peril.

The blood pleased the gods, so it worked out well for all concerned.

Except for those who had their hearts ripped out on the sacrificial block.

6

En route to Mayapán, a messenger brought Lord Janaab a codex—a book of bound amyl paper.

I had seen a codex only once before, and I edged forward for a closer look. My mentor, Ajul—who was the village storyteller before he died and who encouraged my own storytelling—had a book and explained to me how paper was made and bound into a codex. Unlike others in our village, he was not born there but had traveled and lived in many places before he came to the village in the autumn of his years.

Fig tree bark produced the raw material for paper. Its inner layer was stripped off, then boiled in lime water. After it was softened, the material was pounded—first with flat stones and rolled over cylindrical ones—until it was thin and wide.

Flattened bark was spread out in layers, heated with warm stones, and worked until the paper was so strong and smooth that the scribes could write on both sides. After being trimmed, a large single sheet could be bound into a codex that would be about four hands square.

The codex-makers then painted both sides of each page with a thin plaster made from powdered limestone and water, after which they could draw the pictographs that composed our language.

When the paper was ready, the scribe drew whatever was desired upon it, whether it be the tales of the gods, the history of my people, or the accounts of a merchant. They used brushes made from animal hair and goose quills.

The word-pictures were painted on the paper with colored inks, black ink made from soot, reds and greens and yellow from dyes obtained from plants and insects.

The pages were tied to a wood frame and covered in animal skins. A merchant's account book would be covered with deerskin, while the skins of rare animals adorned the more precious volumes. The most prized of all codex-jackets was, of course, the sacred jaguar's hide.

Our writing was done with pictures, sometimes called *glyphs*, a single one of which could convey more meaning than the object itself. When placed alongside other glyphs, however, they could mean something diametrically different. A snake or a jaguar, a heart or a hand, when grouped together, could mean something utterly irrelevant to the images with which the glyph was aligned. The writing was read in the direction that the characters faced, and the scribes typically drew them facing right.

I was standing close enough to the great lord, when he unfolded the pages, to recognize the codex's images. It told how the Creator Gods made the first man out of maize dough.

I knew immediately that it was in error.

"Your Lordship—"

"Silence!"

The command came from Lord Janaab's captain of the guards, Six Sky.

"You never speak to His Lordship without being spoken to first."

The commander raised his whip to strike me and stopped when His Lordship told him not to beat me.

"What is it?" Lord Janaab demanded of me.

"I—I—" The words dribbled out of my mouth as Lord Janaab and the guard captain gazed at me.

"What is it?" the lord demanded again. "Why do you stare at my papers? This is the inscription that will go on the sacred stone I had your villagers provide."

"It is not accurate, my lord. It says the Creator Gods made the first men out of maize dough. The arms and legs were made of dough, but the flesh was made from the flesh of the maize itself."

"How do you know this?"

"Our village storyteller had traveled far and wide during his long life. He knew more tales than any two other keepers of our history. He read and taught me the sacred glyphs, and his readings were unfailingly correct."

Lord Janaab stared at the writing. "Yes, now that I think about it, you're right. And it is good that you tell me this. Misrepresenting a god's sacred acts could easily provoke divine retribution."

He gave me a long look. "We will pass many villages on our way to Mayapán. When we do, look at the buildings and tell me if you find fault in any of the sacred writings they have put on their temples and buildings."

7

After another hour's march, we took a rest stop. We were surprised when we stopped so soon, but also relieved, for it permitted us to find shade and get the glare of the Sun God off our heads for a bit.

Six Sky told me, "Lord Janaab commands your presence."

Our lord had spared the commander, because he was not present when his guards fled the jaguar.

The king's builder was seated under the shade of a tree. As I approached, he told me to sit down by him. He ordered his servant to give me a leaf containing slices of papaya and mango, then waved the servant away. As his aide approached, he waved him away also. Whatever the great lord wished to say to me, he did not want others to hear.

"The gods act in mysterious ways, do they not, Pakal?"

"Yes, my lord."

"Just look at the surprises you have brought me in so short a time."

"Surprises?"

"When you saved my life from the most savage beast in the One-World while my own guards ran in terror, I thought that you had been chosen by the gods because they approve of my work making monuments that shout their glories. No doubt the gods do approve of my work and saved me to continue it, but then you surprise me again by pointing out a mistake in the tribute to the Creator Gods."

"Yes, my lord."

I had no idea what he was getting to, but he was a man who could end my life with a wave of his hand, and I hoped that whatever other surprise I gave him did not displease him.

"Now I find that not only were you the village storyteller, but that you were taught many tales by the man who held that position before you. What was his name?"

"Ajul, my lord."

"Yes, Ajul, that is what I was told. Tell me, Pakal Jaguar, did this Ajul know many tales?"

"He was amazing. Those villagers who had traveled to other places, even to Mayapán, said that they had never heard anyone who knew so many tales or told them so well. The traveling storytellers who came to the village were never as good."

"What did Ajul do when other storytellers came to the village?"

"What did he do?" I thought for a moment. "He would stay in the forest until they were gone."

"Why did he do that?"

"He said he didn't want them to hear his stories and didn't want to hear theirs. He said his tales were true and pure, and listening to others might cause him to make mistakes."

"Ajul taught you stories?"

"Yes, my lord, but more than that. My parents died when I was young, and Ajul became like a father to me."

"What happened to your storyteller-father?"

"He died five years ago."

"Where is his body?"

"His body? My lord, I don't know where his body is."

"Then how do you know he died?"

"He—he went into the jungle. We found his bloodied cape."

"But you never found his body?"

"No, the headman said wild animals took it."

Lord Janaab was quiet for a moment. I found myself tense. I didn't understand why he asked questions about Ajul or why he was so curious about a simple village storyteller.

"Tell me, Pakal Jaguar, have you ever heard of Jeweled Skull?"

"Of course, my lord. Everyone has heard of the great storyteller."

"What do you know about him?"

"That he was the greatest storyteller who ever lived."

"He knew more stories than your Ajul?"

"I suppose so, my lord. They say that the goddess Ixchel herself taught Jeweled Skull all the tales of the One-World. It was our king's father, when he ruled Mayapán, who gave Jeweled Skull his name as a tribute to the knowledge stored in his head."

"Did you ever hear a story told by Jeweled Skull?"

My jaw dropped at the question. "Of course not, my lord. Jeweled Skull was taken by the gods before I was born."

"Taken by the gods . . ." Lord Janaab mulled over my remark. "Is that what Ajul told you? That Jeweled Skull was taken by the gods?"

"I—I don't remember where I heard those words. It's what we all know about the legend of Jeweled Skull. People say the gods took him so that he would tell stories to them."

"All right, Pakal Jaguar. Return to your companions."

I rose and started to walk away, when he spoke my name.

"Yes, my lord?"

"Have you ever heard of the Dark Rift?"

I blinked and tensed some more. My right knee started shaking.

"Of course, my lord. It's the road in the sky that leads to Xibalba, the Place of Fear."

"Is that the only Dark Rift you have heard of?"

I nodded, too scared to speak.

He dismissed me with a wave of his hand, and I almost ran to get away from him.

I had lied. The night before Ajul was killed by forest beasts, he had told me a story of the Dark Rift. In the morning, he claimed that the story was not true, that he had made it up under the influence of mescal, the nectar of the gods that steals people's minds when too much is drunk. And he made me take an oath never to speak of it to anyone.

I never had time to fear the jaguar I had fought with my bare hands, but as we got back on the road to Mayapán, the conversation with Lord Janaab stayed with me. I felt as if I were once again threatened by a jaguar—but this time the beast was behind me, breathing its hot hungry breath on the back of my bare neck.

En route, worries about having lied to Lord Janaab dogged me, but as hours passed and no retribution was delivered from either the great lord or the gods, I relaxed.

8

At midday we stopped, and Lord Janaab joined a nobleman for cool drinks and fruit served in the shade of the local lord's palace courtyard. It was easy to tell from the way the nobleman acted that Lord Janaab was of higher rank.

I stared in wide-eyed amazement at the palace. With their surrounding walls and interior courtyards, the building and grounds covered an area as large as the village next to it.

Six Sky scoffed when he saw my look of amazement.

"It's a rat's nest compared to the palaces of the king and great lords in Mayapán. Lord Janaab would not permit this oversized peasant's house to exist in the king's city."

"I've never seen anything like it."

"Then you had better prepare yourself, because you will see marvels in Mayapán."

I walked along the wall, reading the inscriptions—tales of heroes and kings, of wars won, prisoners sacrificed, blessings from the gods.

Just as Lord Janaab was having a story put on the stone slab, our tales had been written down in books, put on freestanding walls, and on the walls of buildings. We believed that tales that praised the gods would elicit favor from them. I had not gone fifty paces before I found an error in a tale. That the mistake concerned Chaac, the Rain God, suggested it could be a fatal one.

Rain was needed to grow crops, and Chaac provided it with his tears and by striking clouds with his lightning axe.

As with many of our gods, Chaac had multiple manifestations rather than only one, which is all we humans possess. Chaac had four representations of himself, one for each of the four cardinal directions.

While the men prepared for our march to the capital, I approached Lord Janaab and explained what I had seen on the noble-man's wall.

"As Your Lordship knows, a colored manifestation of Chaac is on each of the four cardinal points—white at the north, yellow to the south, east is red, and west is black."

"Yes, everyone knows that."

"Apparently not everyone, Your Lordship, because there is an inscription on the wall that has Chaac black to the east and red to the west."

I started to tell him it had probably gone unnoticed, because it was a very short inscription at a low spot on the wall, but he snapped: "Show me!"

Lord Janaab ordered the local nobleman to accompany us to the wall. The man came along, frightened and apologetic even before I showed His Lordship the faulty inscription.

"You have an inaccurate tribute to the Rain God," Lord Janaab raged at the nobleman.

"I'll have it removed immediately—"

"That's not good enough. You will return your palace, stone by stone by stone, to the earth and then burn everything that is not stone, including everything that was inside it."

"My entire palace? Great lord, please—"

"Do it, and hope the king himself does not decree that your fam-ily's blood nourish the God of Rain."

"I'll send slaves, fifty—"

"A hundred," Lord Janaab said, "and if that does not satisfy the king, your own blood will be required."

Lord Janaab stared at me after he sent the nobleman hurrying to gather slaves to paint red.

"Amazing. In one morning, a mere youth from a small village finds errors in tributes to the gods."

"Yes, my lord. My memory is good."

"Your recall is amazing and of far more value to me than your employment as a guard. The kingdom is in dire straits. Our crops will not feed our people despite the legions of sacrificial victims whom we have offered up. We keep feeding the gods blood, but we still lack rain. I fear our buildings are desecrated with blasphemous errata and that the gods are venting their rage. When we get to Mayapán, you will check all the inscriptions in the city."

"There must be thousands of them, my lord."

"Many thousands. It will take you months, perhaps even years, but it must be done. You will have my authority to command any inscriptions that are inaccurate destroyed."

"I—I don't know what to say. I have never been to a city, and I don't know if I could find them all."

"Of course you can. You fought a jaguar with your bare hands— though you will find beasts worse than those in the jungle when you bump heads with the citizens of Mayapán."

PART II

9

While Coop watched the Apachureros through the twin boulders' crevice, Reets studied the stand of pines, inside of which Hargrave and Jamesy were preparing their assault.

Finally, from behind the trees, Hargrave discreetly waved his Yucatán Lions baseball cap at them.

Twice.

She nudged Coop. "They're ready," Reets said.

"We walk up to those bozos," Coop said, "and say what?"

"We're looking for our friend?"

"And ask if they've seen him," Coop said.

"Your Spanish is better than mine," Reets said. "Hell, you even speak Nahautl, and Lord only knows what language those cholos are babbling."

"They sure don't look Spanish."

"They don't even look Indian," Reets said.

"If I don't understand them, I'll fake it."

"In the immortal words of Gary Gilmore, before he went in front of the firing squad: 'Let's do it.'"

Rechecking the loads, they coughed loudly to cover the sound of the racking slides. After throwing the ponchos back over their shoulder-slung weapons, they rounded their boulders, waving at the bandits, smiling brightly, gawking at them like lost tourists.

"Hey, amigos!" Coop shouted in Spanish, raising her hands. "You seen our compadre, Jack Phoenix?"

The bandits turned, leveling their AK-47s at them.

Just as Jack Phoenix emerged from the tunnel.

He had started to wave the dead snake dangling from his right fist, when, blinded by sunlight—from five straight hours in pitch-dark tunnels—he quickly lowered his head and shielded his eyes with his right forearm. Coop noticed that under his left arm he clutched a crimson container. For some bizarre reason, he continued to grip the serpent's head in his right fist.

Coop quickly understood that since Jack was surrounded by bandits, Jamesy and Hargrave could not fire their DU 000 buck into the group without killing their friend.

Coop also intuited that under his arm was the red ceramic oblong urn, and she knew instantly what it contained: the 2012 Codex—Quetzalcoatl's final prophecy—which Phoenix had e-mailed them about.

My God, Coop thought. *Jack, you're screwed this time. If Jamesy and Hargrave empty all that triple-aught buck into the mob outside the tunnel, they'll shred not only you but also the greatest archeological find of all time.*

That she could now envision Quetzalcoatl's 2012 Codex in the hands of the Apachureros disheartened her even further.

Slipping a hand under her poncho, she surreptitiously changed the PDW's selector from autofire to semi.

The Pach were so close to Phoenix, she'd have to cherry-pick her targets.

Out of the corner of her eye, she saw Reets do the same thing.

10

From a distance, Hargrave stared at Jack Phoenix crawling out of the tunnel. A bowie knife in his teeth, swinging a goddamn diamondback in his right fist, some kind of flat red container under his arm, Phoenix was covering his eyes with a forearm and painfully pulling himself to his feet.

He looked like hell. Decked out like themselves, in army surplus fatigues—the cargo pockets likewise bursting at the seams with gear—his dirty cut-off T-shirt bore the inscription BEER ISN'T JUST FOR BREAKFAST ANYMORE.

His left shoulder, however, was ballooning lividly.

Even Hargrave was shocked. *Looks like a malignant melon,* he shuddered.

Furthermore, the women were out from behind the boulders, irrevocably exposed, waltzing up to the bandit gang in plain view as if they were strolling into a church.

Dropping the shot-spreader and the fragmentation grenades, Hargrave mounted a flashbang grenade—a steel hexagonal tube with a perforated casing—on his shotgun's muzzle.

Jamesy, who had just eliminated the two sentries, was crawling back to the tree stand, his cut-off camouflage T-shirt covered with their blood. One glimpse of Phoenix and he, too, mounted a flash-bang grenade in his weapon's muzzle.

Oh, what the hell? Hargrave thought. *The flashbangs will at least distract those assholes.*

When the grenades were launched into houses, the blinding flash, deafening blast, and searing heat often ignited drapes and carpets. Flashbangs frequently incapacitated people for a full minute.

But they wouldn't kill Phoenix.

In fact, his vision might not even suffer the flash. Blinded by sunlight, he was still protecting his sensitive eyes with his forearm.

The women?

He hoped they'd remembered to set their weapons to semi.

Then he stopped worrying: He'd forgotten he was dealing with Coop.

Nodding to Jamesy, he counted softy: "One, two, three."

On *three*, they both fired their grenades the full fifty yards into the bunched-up bandits.

Only at the last second did Hargrave remember to shut his eyes.

He hoped Coop and Reets would think to do the same.

11

Even through clenched eyes and the forearm pressed up against them, Jack Phoenix sensed the flashbang's blinding glare and felt its scorching heat—heat, he thought briefly, like the opening of a blast furnace door.

He intuited its bang. This was amazing. Since shooting off a round in the tunnel and the snake attack, his hearing had dimmed, dwindled, and at last dissolved into nothingness until his world was now dead mute, soundless as the grave. Entombed in deadening deafness, he could not even hear or sense the blood-throb in his brain, which for the last hour had been his constant, nagging companion. He'd lived with that thundering throb nonstop since the diamondback sank its toxin-spitting fangs in his shoulder.

He'd worked enough dangerous digs in so many violence-torn Third World hellholes to have witnessed innumerable engines of military death, and he knew what flashbang grenades were. Overwhelming the retinas' photosensors, they locked the vision into a single freeze-frame, paralyzing their victims and their eyesight for up to a minute. If he was to flee, he had to forcibly lift his eyelids and run toward his rescuers, regardless of how excruciating the sunlight was.

Willing the reluctant orbs to open was not as hard or painful as building the Great Pyramid or digging the Panama Canal, but it was close. Nor did his vision readily return. Even though he was facing Reets and Coop, he could barely make them out. At first, he thought they were apparitions from hell. They strolled toward him with an almost hallucinatory grace, their PDWs—now out and up from under their ponchos—smoking and hammering. Their two male comrades—off to his side—ran toward him, bent at the waist with military shotguns under their arms, clearly afraid to fire buckshot into the bandit gang, still tightly congested around the tunnel entrance.

Stop the lollygagging, a still small voice whispered in his ear. *Time to run.*

But it was not to be.

His legs and arms wouldn't move, and his perceptions seemed surreal, as if he were frozen with catatonic dread in a bad dream. He felt as if he were backpedaling through time, returning to his twenties, teen years, grade school. Now he felt as if he were shackled to his childhood bed, with nightmare visions dancing around his room.

Then he was racing back even further, all the way into infancy. That was it. He felt infinitely infantile, locked immobile, irreducibly weak.

If he backpedaled any further, he knew he would vanish into the womb.

Into the void.

Is the venom causing me to hallucinate so? he wondered.

No, the little voice said in his head, *death is doing it, good buddy.*

So be it. Never thought it would come so soon, but then man does not know his time.

Who said that? Hamlet? Ecclesiastes?

Who cares?

You're dying, asshole.

Christ, Coop and Reets were still strolling toward him, calm as Sunday-go-to-meeting, their automatic weapons blazing, looking like a female *Fistful of Dollars*. Now the men were close enough that the spread of their buckshot pattern would stay compressed. Their guns were booming as well, as they worked their pump-slides as fast as they knew how, taking out two men to his far right, three more to his left.

Only five killer-bandits were left, but they were close enough to him that the men couldn't risk shotguns.

Which is where Coop came in.

Stepping in front of Reets, cutting off her friend, she raised her weapon shoulder-high and began dropping the blinded bandits around him with short, controlled semiautomatic bursts, which he still could not hear but whose muzzle flashes he could see.

Goddamn Coop. He laughed mirthlessly at the way she stepped in front of Reets, always protecting the younger sister. Reets forced her family to adopt Coop when the girl's moonshiner father had been murdered. Coop, the mother hen, covered her brood with her own body, shielding any incoming bandit fire. Reets, finally stepping around her sister, took out a fleeing bandit herself, but Coop was still doing the heavy work, the hard precision-shooting, firing that weapon like she and the PDW were born together, conceived together in the same uterus, her eyes unblinking over its iron sights, empty and expressionless as the Martian moons, cold and compassionless as her violent moonshiner youth.

For a while he blacked out. When he came to, he was curiously still on his feet, the urn still under his left arm, the diamondback dangling from his right fist; and even though he was still stone-deaf, he could tell the firing had ceased.

Of course it had stopped.

His friends had no one left to shoot at.

They'd killed them all.

Their enemies all lay dead in a gathering pool of blood.

Most them at Phoenix's own feet.

He was beyond light-headed now, feeling his very life leaving his body, as if his soul were being plucked from his expiring remains, like a white silk handkerchief from the sleeve of a diabolic magician-reaper, the lights in his eyes dimming, the earth itself drifting, disappearing, dying away.

He could feel himself dying with it.

Kill the body and the soul dies? he wondered absently.

Who knows?

Well, my friend, in seconds you will have a truly definitive answer.

You will solve the Eternal Enigma.

Will you have anyone to report your findings to?

I hope so. It'll be a hell of a find.

Thanks, Reets, Coop, you two guys over there, whoever you are.

Thanks for saving me from the Frito Bandito.

And for keeping my priceless codex from falling into the wrong hands.

I'd hate to see my death and my spectacular discovery go to waste.

Too bad you weren't in the tunnel to protect me from Quetzalcoatl's misbegotten scion, that goddamned diamondback.

I wonder if they serve beer in hell?

Somehow the thought of a cold one down there bucked him up.

12

"Bummer."

Rita Critchlow took her middle finger off Phoenix's jugular and stood. She and Cooper Jones were staring at the inert body of their friend.

"He's the closest friend we ever had," Coop said.

"Along with Monica Cardiff."

"We trusted him with *everything*."

"Now he's gone."

Yet even in death he was helping them. Coop knew; Reets knew it. Beside him lay the flat red ceramic urn containing, quite possibly, the greatest archeological discovery of all time. If the last codex was correct, Phoenix had unearthed the final Quetzalcoatl 2012 Codex—a find that would bring them fame and fortune of historic proportions . . . if they lived long enough to enjoy the fruits of his fatal labors.

Moreover, Reets was now starting to believe in the codex's bizarre mystique herself, half-convinced that the flat crimson urn contained something . . . something . . . something . . . *godlike*. . . . She seriously wondered whether the sacred screed would save humanity or prefigure its extinction.

But now Jamesy was coming toward them, shaking her free from her reverie. He was swinging a collapsible entrenching tool he'd found amid the bandits' gear. "I don't want those birds up there picking him clean," Jamesy said, glancing upward. "We'll bury him."

Raising her head, Reets saw two dozen vultures swirling in a funnel cloud and more zeroing in from all directions.

"This is mighty sudden country," Hargrave said, nodding.

"Only for the living," Jamesy said, starting to dig. "For Jack it's kind of slow."

"It's getting even quicker for us," Coop said, jogging toward them from across the cliff face. "We have a small army of Apachureros coming up the east slope. Seems this was just a scouting expedition."

"Maybe we should go back the way we came," Reets said.

"They'd have the high ground," Hargrave said. Glancing at the low summit to the northwest, he said: "Those high rocks look like our best defensive perimeter."

"Natural defilade," Reets said.

"We drag food, water, and ordnance up there—plus anything of use that we can scavenge from these Pach. Coop, you and Reets haul it all up to those boulders." He handed her their TriSquare TSX300 two-way radio. "Reets, you speak the best Spanish, and this thing has a twenty-mile range—more here, given this summit's elevation. Give the *federales* our GPS reading, and tell them we have an Apachurero army coming up on us. You have the map coordinates. There's a *federal* army base ten miles from here."

"We're up to our asses in automatic weapons," Reets said. "We took them off the Pach."

Hargrave was already grabbing shotguns and fragmentation grenades.

"The base isn't that far by chopper, and these frags hit like Gatlings," Hargrave said. "We have a chance."

"We can do this," Jamesy agreed. "Gravesy and I'll slow them down. On the two-way, Reets, you tell the *federales* about Jack's codex."

"Tell them how much it's worth," Coop said.

"I'll tell them it's their *mordida*," Reets said.

"They *sabe mordida* real good." Jamesy grinned.

"I'll tell them about your mama, too," Reets said.

Jamesy nodded. "If money doesn't move those mercenary bastards, nothing will."

Their packs filled with loaded magazines and grenades, the two men jogged toward the east slope.

13

"I hated leaving Jack's body for the buzzards," Reets said. Hunkering down behind boulders at the cliff's summit, she slid rounds into their empty magazines.

"We'll be joining him, those *federales* don't show."

"I told them we have a fortune in relics."

"That must have got their attention."

"You didn't tell me how many were in that Apachurero army."

"I stopped counting after a hundred."

Reets stared at her. "Jamesy and Graves against a hundred-plus?"

Coop started laughing.

"What's so funny?"

"You worried about Jamesy and Graves. I was feeling sorry for those goddamn Apachureros."

PART III

14

For miles approaching the city, the *sache*—an elevated road made of limestone and mortar—ran straight and true to the city gate.

Before we reached the gate, we passed endless fields of maize, beans, peppers, avocados, and other crops grown to support the thousands of people within who did not grow their own food.

The great wall surrounding the city looked impregnable. Ten to twelve feet thick, it was at least seven feet high. Made of large, irregular blocks and laid dry, it ran for over six miles around the city and had nine gates.

"Sentries guard every gate, day and night," Six Sky told me. "Hundreds of stairways and ladders allow men inside to mount the wall quickly. When the drums beat steady, day or night, every man in the city must come to the wall and be prepared to fight an invader.

"The city is vast," Six Sky said, "its walls stretching, it sometimes seems, forever. It takes a full hour to walk just from the south gate to the north gate. Our city has fifteen thousand people. You can walk twenty days in any direction and not find a larger one."

The number of people meant nothing to me, because I could not comprehend such a horde.

As soon as we passed through the gate, the king's city swallowed me like a frog snapping up a fly. My world had been one of villages with thatched-roof huts and cooking fires, a place where everyone knew one another and knew their place. I was unprepared for streets crowded by workers and masters and for buildings that rose taller than trees and pyramid temples that touched the sky.

The city closed tightly around me, squeezing me as we marched through, my heart in my throat as I gawked at the strange sights, sounds, and smells.

The people made way for Lord Janaab like parting seas. Still the crowds were so thick that as soon as he passed, the masses closed behind him, and I had to push myself through a crushing mob.

Inscriptions were everywhere—on the great walls that surrounded the city and on the walls of the palaces, residences, and temples. Most I knew; some were unfamiliar.

Lord Janaab was mistaken in his belief that in months or a few years I could examine all the tales—it would take a lifetime.

Six Sky explained the layout of the city as we walked.

"Once you understand how the city is formed, you will not get lost when performing your duties for our lord. The buildings nearest the city walls are the homes of merchants and workshops of merchants and craftsmen."

Any of the buildings could have housed all the living souls in my village of stoneworkers.

"The buildings are not only the living quarters for the owners, workers, and their families, but also the workshops where goods are made—for potters; toolsmiths; jewelers who construct ornaments out of gold, silver, jade, and lesser stones; rope- and cloth-makers who fabricate their wares out of maguey fiber and deerskin, creating sandals, cloaks, and codex covers."

The paper for the books themselves was made in the shop of the paper-maker.

"Fig tree skin makes the finest paper in the One-World," Six Sky said.

We passed pens where deer were raised for food.

"Everywhere else, deer must be killed, then brought to the markets and cook fires, but here in Mayapán, the king pens the deer up, raising and fattening them for his table and that of his lords."

Six Sky told me the city's riches were beyond comparison—its warriors the bravest and mightiest in the One-World—and I found no reason to disbelieve him. *Eyo!* He could have told me all the gods in the celestial heavens resided in the city, and I would have accepted his words.

A guard I knew, who had traveled extensively, gave me a look after Six Sky made the statement, but he quickly averted his eyes.

Passing through a marketplace, I was staggered by its size and the variety of its goods. Everything I had seen in my lifetime and on the road from the village to the king's city, as well as a thousand other products, was to be found there. One could buy a tortilla, a necklace for his loved one, or a lethally sharp obsidian dagger. Every kind of food, weapon, clothing, jewelry was available . . . for a price.

"Everything the Sun God passes over each day," Six Sky said, "can be found for sale in this city square. Three hundred paces long and two hundred paces wide, it is just one of many in the city."

As we continued north on the street, the houses grew larger, the temples and palaces higher, more spacious, and more complex.

Much of the construction was ongoing. A great deal of it consisted of resurfacing the old buildings because of the *katun*—a period that recurred about every twenty years, in which much renewal of temples and homes was made. This refurbishing was viewed as a rebirth, a new beginning in which old sins were forgotten.

Nearing the ceremonial center of the city, the beating heart of Mayapán rose above a wall higher than the outer city wall: the Temple of the Feathered Serpent, the mighty god my people call Kukulkán and the Aztecs to the north hail as Quetzalcoatl.

Finally, we passed through the gate to the ceremonial center, the realm of the king, high priests, highest-ranking nobles—and most important, the place where priests offer the gods their covenant of blood and the king speaks to the gods, imploring them for bountiful harvests and victory at war.

Many cenotes were scattered throughout the city, because the city's location was chosen for the presence of the underground reservoirs of water. The cenote with the biggest water supply was in the middle of the central plaza. Channels from the roof and streets in the surrounding area all fed rainwater into it.

Six Sky told me that the cenote was dedicated to Chaac, the Rain God, and that above the waterline inside, the walls had been elaborately inscribed with tributes to the gods—ones I needed to confirm were correct or Lord Janaab would have me painted red.

Fanning out from that cenote were the two largest structures in the city, the great pyramid temple and the palace of the king. Placed around them were temples of lesser gods and palaces of High Lords.

On the flat top of the Feathered Serpent's pyramid temple was a square stone structure, and atop that a teak sanctuary. The work of the priests was done inside the wooden temple, except for their bloody chore of obtaining sacrificial blood. That task was done on a slablike altar atop the temple steps so people massed below could see the heart being ripped out and the blood flowing down the temple steps.

The sanctuary at the top of the temple was also where the king went to speak to the gods. When he did so, no one, not even the high priest, was allowed near.

To the main temple's right was the observatory where the king's star-watchers studied the sky and reported their findings to him. The stars in the sky were gods, and they, not ourselves, determined what we did. Our very fate was written in those stars, and the astronomer who deciphers in those glittering orbs our destinies, our dreams, the meaning of our lives, that sage among sages the king exalted above all other men.

The observatory was a circular building with four entrances standing on a raised stone platform that was about twice the height of a grown man. Round-shaped structures were rare among my people.

"Everything was placed in the ceremonial center in a manner to please the gods," Six Sky said. "The main temple is positioned according to the four cardinal points of the One-World, as is the observatory in which star-watchers study the gods as they pass overhead each night."

Before we entered Lord Janaab's grand palace, which was second in size only to the palaces of the king and the War Lord, Six Sky asked me if I had heard the story behind the founding of Mayapán. For once there was something about the city that I did know.

"The god-king, Quetzalcoatl," I said, "built both Mayapán and Chichén Itzá after he left Tula in the north. They are similar in design, but the temples and buildings of Chichén Itzá are larger and grander."

"Say that to our lord, and he will flay you to the bone." Six Sky glanced around to make sure he wasn't overheard, then said, "But it's true. The buildings and temples of Chichén are grander, but Chichén is no longer a great city. It is now a vassal of our king, along with Uxmal, which is even older than either Chichén or Mayapán. But now both cities pay tribute to our king."

As a storyteller, I knew the tale of how a Mayapán king had gained hegemony over the larger and more powerful city of Chichén Itzá: A Chichén king stole the bride of the king of Mayapán during wedding festivities. Because of the insult, other cities aided the ruler of Mayapán in sacking Chichén Itzá.

"With so many problems facing the kingdom," Six Sky said, "and rumors that the gods no longer listen to the king, he has put a great emphasis on the *katun* refurbishing. Lord Janaab is in charge of the *katun* building projects, and now you are playing a role."

Six Sky gave me a sly grin. "Do not fail to heed this warning, you who broke a jaguar's neck. Our Lordship is now convinced that erroneous inscriptions have provoked the gods' wrath and created many of our problems. Find the ones that have erred. Make no errors yourself. And watch your back. There are many powerful people in the city who would like to see Lord Janaab's fall. He will tell the king about you and your task to correct the inscriptions. Lord Janaab's enemies would be pleased if you fail."

Six Sky saw the look on my face and laughed. "Lord Janaab's enemies would be so pleased that you failed, they would gladly assist you in that fiasco."

"I will not fail," I said.

"For sure, you won't fail more than once, because the temple priests will cut out your heart before you are given a second chance. Come, jaguar killer, let me show you to your grand quarters."

15

The room was small, no more than four paces wide and six long, with a large window that looked out at the center courtyard that the palace was built around. A sleeping hammock made of netted cords hung from ropes.

"You're lucky, country boy. It is the largest room given to single men, and only one other has one—and he is the head cook of the palace."

I already knew from talk during the trip that unmarried servants and guards lived in a common room, while married couples shared a room like mine, only larger.

I was alone in my room for only an hour when a servant came and escorted me to Lord Janaab's reception chamber, where he conducted the affairs of a High Lord. He sat in a thronelike chair in the high-ceilinged room while servants and visitors came before him.

When I arrived, he had everyone leave the room except four of his guards.

A guard brought a chair and sat it next to where I stood, ten feet in front of the High Lord.

"Sit," Lord Janaab commanded.

As soon as I sat, a guard put an obsidian blade to my throat. I flinched—but instantly froze. The cutting edge of the rock, spewed out by fire mountains, could cut halfway through my neck with little pressure.

"Your Lordship—"

"Don't talk, don't move, or your throat will be cut."

I sat perfectly still as my hands were tied to the arms of the chair and my feet to the legs.

"You lied to me when I asked you what you knew about the Dark Rift. Tell me what Ajul told you."

"He told me nothing, Your Lordship."

He nodded to a guard. "Introduce him to your friend."

The guard opened a wicker basket and lifted a snake from it that was tied to a length of wood. I recognized it—a poisonous serpent we call the jaguar snake because of its orange and black coloring. I saw a stoneworker die from the bite of one. The venom instantly paralyzed him, and his eyes opened wide in agony and shock until only the whites showed. His demise was excruciatingly painful, his death mask horrific to behold.

Keeping a grip behind the snake's head, the guard untied the serpent from the wood and turned to me, the snake wriggling in his grip.

The blade went back to my throat so my head could not move as they brought the creature up to my lips and pushed the tip of its face up against them.

"Untie the snake's jaws," Lord Janaab said.

I hadn't realized that a cord bound the snake's mouth, since the thongs bore the same coloring as the serpent. The restraint was unfastened, and the viper opened its jaws wide, its long fangs unfolding from the roof of its mouth.

The guard suddenly shoved the creature's head into my face. I leaned back, sweat dripping down the side of my face, the snake so close, I could smell its putrid breath. It smelled like a corpse moldering in a sarcophagus.

"Tell me what the storyteller told you about the Dark Rift," Lord Janaab said.

"Nothing," I gasped, "nothing."

"Untie him and leave," the great lord told his guards. "Take your pet with you."

When we were alone, I sat as if still paralyzed—my confrontation with the viperous fiend had unnerved me that much.

My heart was no longer in my throat, but I was wet from sweat, and my legs shook with a life of their own.

Lord Janaab gave me an appraising look. "You were either telling the truth or you are a lunatic who is indifferent to death. No man I suspected of lying has ever had the snake in his face and failed to confess his lie to me. Their reward for confessing is to have their heads severed quickly rather than to die slowly and agonizingly from snakebite."

He gave me another searching stare, as if he was still puzzled over something. "But still . . . you reacted oddly when I asked you about the Dark Rift."

"I'm sorry, my lord, but mention of the Dark Rift strikes fear in most people. Especially in these days, when the road to Xibalba seems crowded with so many."

"True, true. I'm glad you did not lie to me, because I can use your knowledge of the gods. Start tomorrow with my palace itself. Report any errors directly to me and no one else. The same goes for any other errors you find. You are to report them to me alone."

"Yes, my lord."

"After you finish the palace, observe the cenote in the ceremonial center. You will find its inscriptions are all exposed because the water level is low. Water is the nectar of life, and Chaac has shed few tears for us of late."

He dismissed me but spoke to me again before I left. I stopped and turned back.

"You've guessed by now Ajul's true identity."

I had guessed. And I didn't dare lie about it. "It doesn't seem possible," I said. "An old man who tells stories in a small village is actually the storyteller to the gods themselves."

"Had you known Jeweled Skull before he fell into disfavor with the king, you would have realized he knew many things. Hiding his identity would have taken little effort on his part. He was a great storyteller—he simply told you simple villagers a tale that you accepted."

That made sense to me.

"Forget that you know his name or that he was in your village. Never speak of it to anyone. There are those who would fry your feet over a hot fire to find out what you know about Jeweled Skull."

"Why? What could a storyteller know that would harm anyone?"

"Perhaps the gods told Jeweled Skull something that would affect the entire kingdom, and he fled the wrath of the king."

Lord Janaab laughed, but I had no inkling as to what he found humorous about a threat to the kingdom.

16

Lord Janaab was standing on his balcony when Six Sky approached and made a throaty sound to alert the lord to his presence.

"Come," Lord Janaab said. "I have a special assignment for you."

The High Lord gave his captain of guards a dark look. "Since your men failed me when the jaguar attacked, I've considered having you join them in the sacrificial line. They were your responsibility; their cowardice is yours. I have not made up my mind yet whether I will paint you red."

Six Sky trembled and dropped to his knees. "Your Lordship, I failed you, but it won't happen again."

"You're right, it won't happen again. I am giving you a special task, and you will not fail me. Without making it obvious, you are to keep an eye on Pakal Jaguar. You are not to let him believe that you are anything more than a friend and fellow member of my household. You are to report his activities directly to me and to no one else. Do you understand?"

"Yes, my lord. What is your suspicion of him?"

"Do not concern yourself with my motives. If he breathes, report it to me. However, any movement on his part other than his duty of checking inscriptions is to be reported to me immediately. To whom he talks, where he goes, anything beyond staring at walls."

"Yes, my lord."

"Don't let him know you are watching him. Act friendly toward him. I didn't have you in the room when I tested him with the snake, so he will not identify you with my suspicions."

"Did he confess his transgressions to the snake?"

"No, but that does not mean he was truthful. I'm sure he's lying." Lord Janaab scoffed at the confused look on Six Sky's face. "You assume that everyone who faces the snake will be so terrified, they will confess. Pakal faced a jaguar. The snake made him experience fear but did not break his courage."

17

I stood in my room and looked down at the courtyard below with strong emotions boiling inside, no longer feelings of fear, but of anger and rage. I could still smell the snake's stinking breath, still feel its cold face pressed against my own.

Lord Janaab had made a mistake, and he was a man who made few. He should never have tortured me. After the incident, I walked out of his chamber a different person. Fighting the jaguar had changed my life in one way. Staring into the eyes of the snake had changed me, too—had changed me on the inside. I had risked death for Lord Janaab, but he had betrayed my loyalty, my trust. True, he still commanded me and I obeyed, but only because he was my master.

I would never again face almost certain death for him as I had when I rode the jaguar's back.

He treated me as if I were an enemy. It's true, I had lied to the great lord and he was smart enough to suspect it. My only lie was honorable: I was sworn to Ajul not to reveal what he'd told me about the Dark Rift.

Ajul was the only father I had known, and I would have died rather than break my word to him. When he told tales, it was as if they came from the lips of a god.

Whatever trouble had forced him to flee the city was still there—as evidenced by the great lord's actions.

What had Six Sky said? Lord Janaab's enemies would willingly cut my heart out if I failed at my task of checking inscriptions.

After having a venomous viper shoved in my face, I realized that the quagmire I had stepped into was deeper than the writing on walls. And Lord Janaab had made it clear that he was my master, not my benefactor: He'd granted me a reprieve not out of gratitude for saving his life, but because he needed me to check the inscriptions.

I suspected that the great lord had uses for me other than checking the accuracy of the inscriptions. His purposes had something to do with the royal storyteller, the king's wrath, and the Dark Rift that led to the Underworld. Beyond that, I knew only I was utterly alone, ignorant, without friend or support, and fighting for my life.

Eyo!

18

The months passed with more speed than I remembered time passing at the village, but I was much busier, moving around city streets, down the stairwells into cenotes, going inside buildings to check inscriptions that I could not see from the outside. I quickly learned that those inscribed before Jeweled Skull left the city were accurate and that only the ones made since his departure contained errata.

Every day I encountered people who first stared at my facial scars, then at the claw hanging from the necklace around my neck. And quickly avoided me as if I had the plague.

I was a man who'd killed a jaguar with his bare hands.

That I'd broken its neck with a sturdy pole was ignored or forgotten.

That made me different from other people. As my fears that erupted when Lord Janaab told me I was leaving my village and going with him to Mayapán attested, people are afraid of what they don't understand.

Six Sky told me that tales of my feat had grown until people claimed I slipped off the wings of an eagle and dropped out of the sky and onto the jaguar's back—and they had been there to see it!

Eyo! I would have liked to see that myself.

Unfortunately, Six Sky was not pleased with my newfound fame or with the fact that I had achieved it because his own men had fled the jaguar. I had humiliated him before the High Lord, leaving him resentful and even jealous of me.

I suspected Lord Janaab had ordered him to watch me. He was not good at being sly, and too often I caught him hovering about or following me for no good reason I knew of . . . except to keep track of me for Lord Janaab.

Moving down a wall, I read the story of the Howler Monkey God. Howler monkeys screeched at dawn. No ordinary ape, the howler monkey was a patron-deity of scribes, sculptors, and musicians. The tale I was examining had this god writing a book and then carving a human head. A creation story, the book contained the people's birth sign, and the head represented their life force.

As I was carefully reviewing the glyphs for accuracy, I caught a movement out of the corner of my eye. At the other end of the long wall, a woman was bending over, writing on the wall.

I couldn't make out her features, because her head was covered with a scarf, but she appeared tall and slender.

For anyone to write on a wall except professional artists commissioned by the owner of the property was forbidden.

"Stop!" I yelled.

I started toward her at a quick pace. As I did, she appeared to quickly finish what she was writing and slipped around the corner.

By the time I reached the corner, she was out of sight.

Going back to where she had been writing, I stared in shock. It said, *Pakal—Royal Library—Blind—tell no one.*

Eyo! I went back to the corner and looked again, but she was gone.

I returned to the inscription, stood, and stared at it, unable to comprehend why the message was meant for me.

I saw Six Sky approaching. I took a cloth that I used occasionally for cleaning inscriptions and wiped away the writing she had done.

"What was that?" Six Sky asked, indicating the spot I had cleaned.

"A child with a piece of charcoal had defaced the tale of the Howler Monkey God. The god will be pleased that the scribbling has been wiped away."

Six Sky grunted. "We don't need any more angry gods. The price of maize and beans has risen, causing many to starve. The king needs to talk more to the gods, get them to listen to him. Have you heard about the rebellion?"

I shook my head.

"The people of a High Lord whose lands are on the western edge of our king's territory stormed the nobleman's palace and killed him because he sold their maize for a high profit and left them without enough to eat. The king has sent soldiers to gather up the rebels. The gods will get their fill of blood when they return with them."

I said nothing, but privately hoped that the people escaped. But where would they go? All but those in a city were tied to the land, growing food, giving a portion to their lord and eating the rest. When a peasant couldn't grow enough food to eat or a city worker no longer had a craft that paid for food, the only path in life was banditry. And a shortened life.

"There is news also that our king and the king of Cobá have agreed upon a Flower War."

The news excited me. I was still young enough that war intrigued me.

"Will you and I get to fight?" I asked.

He gave me a laugh full of anger. "Never. Do you think Lord Janaab would permit his pet hero to go into battle and show everyone that his killing of the jaguar was an accident?"

I was taken aback by the guard captain's insult. I knew he resented me, but his bitterness was surprising.

"You think you are too valuable to His Lordship to be sent off to war," he said.

I said nothing and simply stared.

Perhaps I was.

Why else would he be watching me, and why was I still alive?

19

The palace was a single large building surrounded by tall walls and replete with lush gardens inside the walls. It was not just the residence of the king, but also the heart of government, where all the kingdom's business was transacted. At any time of day, hundreds of people would throng the compound, ranging from servants to merchants and the lords of the land. At night the king held great feasts.

The Royal Library was part of the king's compound.

Lord Janaab went each day to the palace to meet with the king and give instructions to the king's servants whose duties were to ensure that the city's rebuilding went smoothly.

My scroll of authority did not get me past the gate guards—but one look at my claw scars and the jaguar talon festooning my neck and they stepped aside, letting me pass.

"The Jaguar Oracle," I heard one whisper, awed.

I flinched at the name. I had already heard it twice before from people on the street, one from a woman speaking to her child, another from a man who spoke the name loudly.

Word of the incidents at my village, where I had warned of an attack and then of a snake, had also spread around the town, and I had gained a reputation as a seer that I did not deserve.

I wondered if the stories of my feats had grown so tall that I could have gone straight to the king's chamber and cut off his head without being stopped.

Once inside the walls, I followed the crowded main corridor to a side hallway, which led to the king's library.

From talking to Lord Janaab's servant, who kept the accounting of the High Lord's income, I knew that the library was divided into two parts: The larger part stored the books, which recorded the possessions of the king, the taxes collected and owed, and all the other writings necessary for keeping track of the many functions of government.

My conversation with the great lord's accounts chief also solved part of the mystery of the cryptic message left on the wall: The Master of the Library was blind.

"In his youth, he was the best artist in Mayapán," the accounts chief told me.

"When did he go blind?" I asked.

"He was blinded before you were born. A War Lord who disliked a battle scene that the Master painted ordered his eyes burned out. The scene showed the War Lord behind advancing warriors instead of at the head."

"Was he behind his troops?" I asked.

The accounts chief's features turned arrogant and haughty. "None of us questions what a great lord does, the Master included," he said disdainfully.

The artist was blinded for offending a War Lord. Eyo! He was lucky he was not sacrificed. In fact, I was puzzled that he drew the scene in a way he had to know would offend the War Lord. I also felt that blinding the artist was crueler than putting him to death. To a painter, vision is everything, and the War Lord robbed the artist of what he most held dear.

"He was the king's favorite painter, so he was made Master of the Library."

The Master was in the smaller part of the library, which contained the codices that recorded the history of the king and royal ancestors, the history of the Maya people in general, and many tales of heroes and kings and gods such as those I once told at campfires and now entertained Lord Janaab's festival guests with.

More than once I'd wanted to go to the library and research an inscription that I questioned, but I had instead found the answer in older inscriptions, which I believed the Jeweled Skull had authenticated.

My authority to enter the library to check inscriptions was the scroll bearing Lord Janaab's mark. While Lord Janaab's own authority did not extend into the palace itself, I didn't think that the people running the library would counter a command from a High Lord, especially one who was second only to the War Lord in the king's favor.

The scribbled message on the wall had not left my thoughts since I saw it yesterday. Rather than rushing to the library immediately, and arousing Six Sky's suspicions by altering my routine, I kept on checking inscriptions for the rest of the day.

This morning I let Six Sky know I was returning to an inscription which I suspected had an error in it, but I wasn't certain. I needed to reflect upon it, do research, perhaps at the Royal Library.

He had little interest in my work but watched intently whenever I spoke to someone. After a man suddenly begged me to divine the fate of his sick child—believing that since I bore the jaguar name, I possessed powers of divination—Six Sky followed the man and no doubt interrogated him about our conversation.

Six Sky would have discovered that I told the man I was not a seer and that he should consult the priests at the temple.

Eyo! One does not want to go into competition with the priests, who get paid not only for telling the future, but also for cutting out the hearts of those that fall into their bloodstained hands.

The servant opened the door to the library and stared directly into my eyes, his own eyes barely touching upon my scars. He never bothered looking at my claw.

He wasn't blind—he obviously had been told to expect me. His nose and protruding teeth reminded me of a rat. He told me he was the assistant librarian.

"I wish to speak to the Master of the Library," I said. "I am on the business of the great lord Janaab."

I had Janaab's scroll, but the librarian never asked to see it.

"I will advise the Master of your request."

He left me wondering who had warned that I was coming. The woman who left the mysterious message? Or Six Sky because I mentioned the library to him?

No codices were in the entry room, but through an open doorway, I could see books laid out on tables.

Even though I had seen codices before, the sight of the books still stirred my emotions. Books were rare treasures, possessed only by royalty, nobles, and very rich merchants.

In a way, I lusted for the knowledge contained in the codices. It is true that I am a storyteller and that the gods have permitted me to accumulate in my head an incredible number of stories to be shared with others. But the library contained not just the tales of heroes and gods but the entire history of my people, perhaps even the history of the One-World, all the stories of the four previous times the world was destroyed by the whims of the gods, and the four times man and beast were re-created. The library represented illimitable learning, knowledge without end.

I was drooling over the prospect of someday reading all the books in the Royal Library when the assistant returned.

"The Master will see you."

20

I was led into an artist's studio. The seashells holding pigments were filled with dry paint; the brushes were stiff.

A blind man sat at a table with a book open in front of him. "Come to me," he said.

I stepped up to the table.

He gestured with his hand. "Please, I am too old and stiff to stand for long. The book you see in front of you I read with my fingers. Bend down so I can read your face."

I did as he requested, and his fingers felt my face.

"Ah, yes, the scars of the Jaguar Oracle."

"I am not a seer."

He shrugged and gave a chuckle. "You are what people believe you to be. Don't be quick to deny something about yourself that may help you someday. If I had been an oracle rather than a painter, I would not be using my hands for eyes now."

I offered him a short laugh. "I suspect that more oracles have found themselves in the sacrifice line for failing to please their lords than artists have."

"You are right. But remember this: A good oracle offers advice that is ambiguous enough to justify any outcome." He clapped his hands. "Chocolate for our guest!" he yelled.

He gestured at a chair. "Please, sit down. Tell me why you have honored this old man with your visit."

I took a seat. I was surprised that he asked me why I had come. I had expected that he would know of the message, that in fact he was the one who had commissioned it, though I could think of no reason why he would use such an indirect way of having me come to the library.

As the keeper of the kingdom's history, he could have found many reasons to summon me to the library—without having a woman risk the sacrifice line for defacing a sacred inscription.

"I have to research the Dark Rift Codex."

The words flew out of my mouth. I had no control over them. The Master of the Library sat perfectly still, his mouth a little agape, as if I had slapped him across the face.

I froze in my own chair, tempted to get up and run, but with no place to hide. Or anything to say. I was out of words and out of my mind, I thought.

A servant—bringing in cups of chocolate—filled the void. Under less trying circumstances, I would have relished the drink. I had never had an actual full cup of it, just a taste once when the head-man passed around a cup after a pleased stone merchant gave him some extra cacao beans for exceptional work.

The Master of the Library took a sip and licked his lips. He stared up at the ceiling, as if he were looking to the gods for guidance.

Finally, he asked, "What do you know about the Dark Rift Codex?"

I shook my head. "Nothing but the name. I have heard the name and am curious to read it."

"Why do you want to read it?"

"Why? Because I am a storyteller and have been given the task of ensuring that all the sacred writings in the city are correct. I want to read the codex to see if it contains tales that I am not familiar with."

He nodded. "Yes, I can see that you would. I was once a story-teller, besides being a painter who preserved them for all time. But it has been a long time since the king asked me to entertain him and his guests. Now I am merely the keeper of tales." He took another sip of the chocolate drink and then asked, "Have you found many errors in the sacred writings?"

"Some . . . the more recent the writings, the greater the prevalence of errors."

"Yes, yes, that makes sense."

"Because—"

I stopped because of the way he was moving his left thumb. He jerked it as if he wanted me to see something to his left. A doorway was to his left, and I got up and stepped quickly to it.

The rat-faced assistant who had let me in—and who had shown no surprise at the fact that the famous Jaguar Oracle had come to the library—was crouched down on his knees, leaning against the door, listening to our conversation.

At the sight of me, he let out a startled cry and got up and turned to run. As he did, I gave him a kick in the rear that sent him stumbling.

I closed the door and sat back down.

The Master of the Library was shaking with laughter he wasn't able to smother. "Very good," he said, "very good. I hope the kick at Koj was well placed."

"For a blind man, you see very well."

"True, like my fingers, my ears have also become eyes. But kicking an eavesdropping servant does not take away the danger of speaking of the unmentionable."

"Lord Janaab asked me about the Dark Rift. He wanted to know if Jeweled Skull told me about it."

"You knew Jeweled Skull?"

I told the old man about Ajul. I left out the conversation I had with Ajul about the Dark Rift.

"Did you also know Jeweled Skull?" I asked.

The question hung in the air like a dark cloud. Finally, the Master said, "Yes. When Jeweled Skull was the king's storyteller, not only did he approve all sacred writings on buildings, but he had many preserved in codices, as well. I was his chief artist. No books were approved until he had me review them to see that the scribes had done the finest job possible."

"Did he record the story of the Dark Rift?"

The Master shook his head. "You do not understand. The Dark Rift is a codex written long ago, further back than any of us can imagine. At first it was a tale passed down by generation after generation of storytellers, but long ago, in Tula, the golden city of the Toltecs, an astronomer-oracle put the legend into a codex for the god-king Quetzalcoatl."

"You have the codex in the library?"

"No. If it were here, those who fear its prophecy would have destroyed it long ago."

"Where is it?"

The Master shrugged. "Somewhere in the One-World. That is all I know."

"What does the codex say?"

He shook his forefinger at me. "That is a secret many want to know. There are those who believe they know, but have never actually seen the book. One man from Mayapán may actually know what it says, and he is said to be dead. The one you knew as Ajul and I as Jeweled Skull."

"What did Jeweled Skull know about the codex?"

"I don't know exactly what he knew, but whatever it was, he fled Mayapán rather than divulge the secret." He held up a hand to stop my onslaught of questions. "I was an artist, not Jeweled Skull's confidante. If he told anyone, it would have been her."

"Her?"

"The High Priestess of the Temple of Love."

His answer surprised me.

The Temple of Love was a pyramid about half the size of the main temple, dedicated to the Feathered Serpent. I had passed it many times but dared not go up the steps. The women in it were said to be the most beautiful women in all the land of my people. Selected while they were very young and still virgins, the women were not permitted to marry. Instead, they served as concubines for the rich and powerful.

The blind man chuckled again. "Who better to confide a secret to than the woman who soothes and pleasures you?"

21

Thoughts about the mysterious codex prepared for Quetzalcoatl stayed with me when I left the Royal Library. Quetzalcoatl, the Feathered Serpent, was first linked with the great city Teotihuacán, which had fallen nine hundred years ago. No one knew why Teotihuacán—once the largest and most powerful city in the One-World—was now a spectral city of gloomy ghosts.

More than a dozen times larger than Mayapán, much of the city still stands, including two great pyramids that reach all the way to the gods and dwarf all others in the One-World.

But it is a haunted shadow of its former self.

No one knows why its people fled and never returned, and few have ventured in this eerie place for fear that the angry gods who drove out more than two hundred thousand people would destroy them.

Even the city's name was lost in mists of time. Teotihuacán, the City of the Gods, was simply a name we bestowed on it centuries later.

Each year, the Aztec emperor, out of fear and respect, went to the city abandoned by all but ghosts and gods, accompanied by his great lords, to leave gifts for the gods and beg them not to destroy the cities of the Aztecs.

Even before Teotihuacán was shattered on the Wheel of Time, my people, the Maya, rose to turn the southern half of the One-World into a high culture with beautiful cities like Palenque, Uxmal, Tikal, and Copán. The cities had well-constructed temples and palaces, fine art, libraries of books, and powerful armies.

Eyo! But the gods tired of the petty squabbling of my ancestors and, about six hundred years ago, also broke the Land of the Maya on the Wheel of Time.

As with Teotihuacán in the north, the Maya cities were abandoned to the ravenous jungle surrounding them, the population decimated, arts and learning forgotten as the survivors fought the jungle to maintain enough room to grow food.

Yet each time the gods broke a civilization, they transferred their largesse to another, and after Teotihuacán, it was Tula.

Even the name of its god-king, Quetzalcoatl, was beautiful. Quetzals were the most stunning birds in the One-World, and their plumage was highly prized and reserved for royalty, nobles, and the wealthy merchants who could afford them. *Coatl* meant "snake." Put together, Quetzalcoatl was what the Aztecs called the Feathered Serpent in their Nahuatl tongue.

As I said earlier, we called the great Feathered Serpent god Kukulkán in our Mayan language.

Quetzalcoatl became the most powerful in the pantheon of gods of most cultures of the One-World.

After the fall of the great Maya civilization about six hundred years ago, Tula began its rise to dominance. Always an important city, it would not become preeminent in the One-World until the rise of a young prince who—after his father, the king, was murdered—had been wounded and driven out.

The prince went into the wilderness and lived with a pack of jaguars until his wounds healed. Then he returned to Tula with an army, conquering the city, and avenging the violence visited on his family.

The prince assumed the throne as god-king and took the name of the powerful deity and thereafter was called only Quetzalcoatl, the Feathered Serpent.

King Quetzalcoatl was not just a great warrior, but an artistic thinker who loved knowledge and great works of art.

His first task was as a conqueror, and he led Toltec armies against all, until every kingdom in the north either became his vassal or paid tribute to him.

The treasures he collected from the conquered went not into his private coffers, but was used to gather in Tula the finest artists and craftsmen of the One-World.

Thousands came and over the years turned the Toltec capital into the most beautiful city of the One-World, a city so wondrous that hundreds of years later, the legends about it and its god-king still made the kings of all the lands of the One-World drool with envy.

No city—not Tenochtitlán of the Aztecs, Teotihuacán of the Gods, or the great cities of my Maya—is thought of with the awe that golden Tula inspired now, five hundred years after it, too, was broken on the Wheel of Time by the gods.

Tula. The name rang in my head as I walked aimlessly, working off nervous energy.

To anyone in the One-World, the name was tantamount to a heavenly paradise. Learned men knew that there had actually been a Tula, and that it had been the capital of a great empire hundreds of years ago. But to most, the city was a fabled land of plenty, where ears of maize grew as big as men, and beans were the size of fists.

The Land of the Toltecs lay at the northern edge of the One-World, several days' walk from Tenochtitlán, the city of the Aztecs.

Our civilizations in the One-World rose to greatness and faded at the whim of the gods. Tula and its mighty Toltec empire followed that pattern but first attained an almost godlike grandeur, becoming the greatest citadel of science, architecture, mathematics, and art in our history. Transforming the great Toltec empire into a kind of earthly paradise, the land itself seemed to sing Tula's praises, producing beans, melons, and ears of maize of prodigious proportions. Its august emperor, the god-king Quetzalcoatl, ruled with bountiful beneficence, outlawing war, human sacrifice, and turning Tula into a peaceable kingdom and an earthly paradise.

But he had not anticipated the wrath of our priests.

Having robbed the priests of their power through his compassionate decrees, the god-king suffered their revenge. Rebelling, they whipped up the multitudes, sowing discord and violence. Even worse, Chaac withheld his rain of tears, and drought ravaged the One-World.

The land's bounty ceased.

To stop the insurrection, which was tearing Tula apart, Quetzalcoatl went into self-exile on a raft of reeds bound together with snakes, setting out into the eastern seas but promising one day to return and redeem the people who had betrayed him.

No king who ever existed in the four corners of the One-World has been more admired than Quetzalcoatl. A visionary master, he commissioned great works of art and architecture. He was a scholar who created the greatest library in the One-World and a mighty warrior who led armies of conquest.

Just as the gods break civilizations on a whim, so do they tire of kings and heroes. They broke Quetzalcoatl at the height of his power, forcing him to leave Tula to the petty nobles who would squabble endlessly until the gods crushed them, too.

The great god-king did not rise up to take his place as a star in the heavens. Instead, he came to the Land of the Maya with an army and quickly conquered the region that Mayapán now controlled.

He rebuilt Chichén Itzá, giving it a Toltec luster. And then he disappeared, leaving behind the mystery of the Dark Rift Codex.

From Ajul, I knew some of the legend.

Five hundred years ago, Quetzalcoatl commissioned scholars to amass all the knowledge of the One-World, the history and the legends, into codices that he stored in his vast library.

A Mayan astronomer-oracle, who was a favorite of his, and his assistant, a youth named Coyotl, who would one day rise to be a legendary astronomer-oracle himself, were given a special task: to compile all the information known about the rise and fall of the civilizations in the One-World.

Quetzalcoatl and his chosen astronomers knew not only that the gods destroyed civilizations upon whim, but that they also used the same method over and over—a heavenly blow that caused cities to be abandoned, their knowledge lost, societies producing barely enough food to subsist.

The knowledge of why this destruction occurred was compiled into a book called the Dark Rift.

Where the book was and what it said were now my problem.

22

I was at the gate of Lord Janaab's palace when a guard on duty told me the great lord commanded my presence. Tensing, I followed, wondering if I was about to be tested by the snake again.

I was left alone, facing Lord Janaab in his audience chamber. That was a good omen—at least he meant to permit me to speak before he had me tortured.

"Why did you go to the Royal Library?"

"To inquire about the Dark Rift Codex."

The truth spun off my tongue. It had to be the truth—I didn't know how much Koj the Assistant had heard.

"And why did you ask about the codex?"

"You gave me the task of checking all the sacred writings in the city. I know nothing about the Dark Rift. If I don't know what it says, or even what it might say, then I won't be able to correct any inscriptions about it."

"Have you found inscriptions you believe are from the codex?"

I shook my head. "No, my lord, though there are a few that I am having a difficult time placing and will have to speak again to the Master Librarian to see if they are correct. But I know that Jeweled Skull once performed the task I am doing, that of checking the inscriptions. He also advised the king and High Lords about which sacred writings we would inscribe on public buildings. He may have placed some part of—"

"Or some clue as to the codex's location or contents." Lord Janaab nodded and stroked his chin. "Very good, good. The Jeweled Skull would do something like that. He believed he communicated with the gods. I sometimes think he did and that he toyed with us mere mortals."

He thought for a moment and then asked, "What did the Master Librarian tell you about Jeweled Skull?"

"That he had been the artist for Jeweled Skull, the one who inscribed the codices that recorded the tales Jeweled Skull provided."

"Where does he think the codex is?"

"He told me he didn't know."

"He's a liar. He knows more than he says. He was not just an artist favored by the Jeweled Skull; he was the storyteller's best friend."

I had already surmised that the Master had a close relationship to Ajul.

"Tell me exactly what he told you about the Dark Rift."

"He said that Jeweled Skull was the only one who knew the book's true prophecy. Others thought they knew and wanted to destroy the book because they believed it was an evil omen. No one really knows."

Again, that was the absolute truth. I knew better than to lie to him. I had discovered early on that the great lord was not a fool nor could he be easily fooled. Before I mentioned the Dark Rift at the library, I should have confirmed that no one spied on me.

I held my breath while Lord Janaab stared at me with narrowed eyes, questioning my veracity.

"He told you nothing about how to find the codex?"

"He said to ask the High Priestess at the Temple of Love."

Lord Janaab slapped his hand on the top of his knee. "Ha! Good advice. The High Priestess had been the lover of Jeweled Skull. And if anyone knows all the secrets of Mayapán, it is she."

He got up and went to the window and stared out.

"I want you to find out everything you can about Jeweled Skull and where the codex is. You are to report only to me." He turned and met my eye. "Speak to anyone else about the matter, and you will wish I had only painted you red."

"Yes, my lord. I will scour the city for—"

"You will go to the High Priestess."

I caught my breath. "I would not be allowed—"

He waved away my objection. "I will arrange it. The High Priestess would not dare offend me by spurning my emissary." He raked me up and down with a stern stare. "Besides, she is a woman with a great hunger for love. And I'm told that besides the fat old nobles who pay well for her favors, she has strong young men dragged off the street for her pleasure."

"Yes, my lord."

He gave a laugh of dark humor. "Before you celebrate your luck, you should know something about her: When she tires of the young men, she sends them to the priests at the temple of the Feathered Serpent to be sacrificed."

His howling laughter followed me as I left his chamber.

23

After our evening meal, I lay in my hammock and through the small window slit watched the Moon God drift across the night sky.

I have seen love priestesses from a distance occasionally as they came out of the temple atop the pyramid—mysterious figures cloaked from head to toe in shapeless robes that revealed nothing of their shapely, supple bodies.

Eyo! Somehow, their covering made them even more desirable than the beautiful women I passed on the streets.

I had been lonely since my wife left to make her journey to a better place, and I had often thanked the gods that she would not suffer the terrors of Xibalba, the Place of Fear. Because she died carrying my child in her womb, neither she nor the unborn child would endure the Place of Fear.

My marriage was arranged when I was born. There were a few opportunities at the village for me to wed again, but something in me said to wait. Ajul had reinforced that instinct, Ajul being the name by which I still thought of him. I had to keep reminding myself that his true name was Jeweled Skull and that the name I knew him by was false.

He told me his feet had suffered from wanderlust, taking him along roads in all four cardinal directions: from the shores of the Great Western Waters to the sands of its eastern brother; from the dense jungles of the Maya peoples far to the south of Mayapán to the northern desert beyond Tenochtitlán, the city of the mighty Montezuma, emperor of all the Aztecs.

He had traveled many places, saw wonders of the One-World that the rest of us have only heard about—and that I have dreamt about.

Oracle that he was, Ajul had intimated that someday I would leave the village. Until Lord Janaab told me I was to become a member of his household in Mayapán, I had not given much thought to Ajul's remarks. I had always taken his vague references that I would someday leave the village and travel the One-World as simply another tale told by a master storyteller.

Was Ajul dead? I had never doubted it until Lord Janaab came into my life and told me that a simple village storyteller was a renowned master who told tales to the gods themselves.

Now I had to wonder. That Ajul could have wandered away from the village for any number of reasons and been killed raised no suspicions. People routinely perished from snakes, spiders, and bloodthirsty beasts. If one wandered a few feet into the jungle to get firewood, went out at night to relieve oneself, or slipped off one's hammock in the morning onto the dirt floor and stepped on something that had crawled into the hut during the night, something that carried the deadly poisons with which Xibalba's demons killed—any of these could spell death.

Ajul's body was never found—only his bloodied clothes. Again, a large animal could have dragged him off. Large male jaguars weighed over three hundred pounds and were longer than a man is tall. They were easily capable of dragging off a grown man.

Now that Ajul's life and a forbidden codex had brought danger into my life, it was time to rethink all he had said.

Did he realize that someday the king's men would come looking for him—and find instead a young storyteller with whom he might have shared his dangerous secret?

PART IV

24

Hargrave and Jamesy stared down at the bandits picking their way up the steep slope through the rocks and brush. Hunkered behind a cluster of big boulders, the two men had mounted a .30-caliber Browning machine gun between two contiguous rocks, and now they studied the approaching men over its sights.

"We can hold them here for a while," Hargrave said.

"Save four of the belts for the summit," Jamesy recommended.

"Save them all. Up there, the slope isn't nearly so steep, and it's over open ground. There's no cover and they'll come in a single push. We'll need every machine gun round."

Jamesy nodded and called Reets on their other TSX300 two-way: "Reets, come on down here and take back the machine gun. It'll be more useful up at the summit."

"We got two good 5.56 H and K assault rifles," Hargrave said. "Too bad we don't have scopes."

"Who needs them?" Jamesy said, staring over the machine gun's sights.

"Shoot straight as plumb lines," Hargrave agreed.

"Go for head shots. Four or five go down, and they'll think they're fish in a barrel."

"Indians in a shooting gallery."

"When they get within seventy-five yards, I'll start laying down frags."

The Apachureros, however, were on the move, and Hargrave wasn't listening anymore. He squeezed the trigger, and a bandit in a fake *federal* uniform fell backwards head over heels at full spread-eagle, a gaping, smoking hole between his eyes.

Jamesy, who was already mounting frag-grenades in his shotgun's muzzle, hadn't bothered to watch.

25

When Reets reached Jamesy and Hargrave, the Pach were hammering the boulders lining the top of the slope with rifle and machine gun rounds. Moving from boulder to boulder, her two friends were firing back, using every bit of available defilade. Sniping an Apachurero here, firing a gun-mounted frag-grenade there, they were too busy for conversation.

Head down, she picked up the tripod machine gun and ammo belts, then dogtrotted back up the summit's slope.

26

At the summit, Coop dug their fire trenches, all the while wondering what the *federales* would think when they choppered in and saw that bandit horde scrambling up the slope and over the rise, charging their trench at the summit.

Charging us like hydrophobic ants, Coop thought. *One round of Apachureros rifle-grenades, two machine gun fusillades, and that gaggle of morons'll chopper their* mordida*-thieving asses back to base just as fast as they know how.*

Their only hope was that *federal* greed would trump self-preservation.

Christ, Coop's back ached. Although she worked out religiously, nothing—not weight lifting, not long-distance running—had prepared her back muscles for shoveling a zigzagging trench through hard ground with a three-foot-long fold-out shovel.

Thanks to Reets' sciatica, it was up to Coop to do the heavy lifting. For the final assault on the fire trench, Reets mounted the big tripod Browning machine gun (BMG) in a hand-dug firing pit, behind a makeshift fortification of knapsacks—which she'd also taken off the dead bandits—now packed with dirt. Around the embrasure she'd also piled large rocks.

She'd now just finished loading the magazines and the M60 BMG's ammunition belts. After jogging up to the boulders fifty yards to their left, she cached the ammunition and assault rifles, which they'd taken off the Apachureros.

If Jamesy and Hargrave made it back in one piece, they'd fall back behind the first boulders and work their way to the trench, hammering the attacking Apachureros with rifle-launched fragmentation grenades and automatic weapons fire.

Anything to slow the Pach down, in case those *federales bastardos* were slow choppering in.

27

Hargrave angrily hurled his H&K G36 assault rifle on the ground. It could not have jammed at a worse time. The Apachureros had just ripped a twenty-foot section of jutting escarpments out of a long jagged ridge, opening up a breach, through which they now poured. For almost twenty minutes, the razor-edged barrier had stalled their assault—so much so that the two shooters picked them off at will whenever the bandits clumsily raised their heads above the impassable rocks.

But no more.

Now the Pach charged them uphill, unimpeded, and Hargrave had no assault weapon. Jamesy, for his part, was low on ammunition.

"Time to blow this pop stand," Gravesy said.

"Just as fast as we know how."

Gravesy nodded, and they broke for the slope's top. They had needed that second weapon and another half dozen clips to cover their retreat—especially with those Apachureros pounding up the slope as if all the legions in hell were at their backs.

Which seemed to be the case.

Gravesy had seen a dozen officers behind that mob of over a

hundred fake *federales*. They were armed with automatic weapons, while the regular troops had semiautomatics—perhaps because they lacked extra ammunition for more automatic weapons.

Or perhaps the officers feared the men would turn the machine guns on them.

Whatever the case, the officers continued to fire them from their hips, the bullets kicking dirt on the calves and thighs of the men before them.

They're flogging those men like slave drivers, Gravesy thought, *but with bullets instead of whips.*

At the top of the slope, the two men took off for the boulders— now a good two hundred yards distant. They had to reach them before the bandits behind them crested that rise. Otherwise they'd be open targets in plain sight.

We may not make it, Hargrave thought.

Glancing up at the boulders, however, he saw Coop now breaking out of their firing pit, where he'd ordered her to stay, and charging the rocky boulder-strewn defilade, forming their defensive perimeter. She held the M60 Browning machine gun low on her hip with the ammunition belt draped over her shoulders. Nor did she stop behind the massive boulders. Coop kept coming, diving behind a low incline in front of the boulders, digging an embrasure for the heavy gun, hunkering down.

Coop was covering their retreat.

He decided he would not lecture her on insubordination when they reached the fire trench.

Coming over the slope, the bandits charged them full-tilt, their shots ripping up the surrounding earth. He and Jamesy ran a randomly swerving S-pattern, but the shots were now increasingly close.

Coop, however, was also firing, the young woman raised by the outlaw moonshining father—who had trained her to hunt bear and wild boar—not even skulking behind her hand-dug embrasure but standing straight up, the machine gun on her hip, blazing at the bandits two hundred yards away.

Glancing over his shoulder, Hargrave was in awe.

Goddamn, he was thinking, *her moonshine-cookin' daddy raised his daughter right.*

The Browning M60's effective range was well over one thousand meters, and Coop was tearing them apart, reducing the Apachureros' barrage to near silence. Glancing over his shoulder, Hargrave saw the bandits drop down onto their stomachs. They were firing infrequent shots from the prone position, but the low angle was throwing off their aim. Coop was saving their lives.

Still, part of Hargrave was sorry she was there. They would miss all the rounds she was pouring onto the bandit horde when they made their last stand in the firing pit on the summit. Those assholes would swarm them en masse. At close range, the Browning would be their only salvation, and they would need every round they could get their hands on.

They reached the boulders, heaving with exhaustion. Coop was in front of them now, behind the ridge of dirt. Picking up two of the three 5.56 H&K assault rifles, which Coop had propped against the boulder for them, they covered her retreat back to the big rocks.

"Hardest two hundred meters I ever ran in my life," Jamesy said, still winded when she returned.

"More like four hundred, the way you guys swerved and zigzagged," Coop said.

But now the Apachureros were less than one hundred yards away, charging the boulders, the officers in the rear, their machine guns braced on their hips, the automatic fire flogging the backs of the men's legs with bullet-driven dirt.

Scared out of their wits, however, they'd failed to spread out and were still bunched together.

"Get that Browning back to the pit!" Hargrave shouted to Coop. "We'll need it more there."

He and Jamesy were already fixing fragmentation-grenades on the muzzles of their assault rifles.

28

Back at the firing pit, Cooper Jones waited for Reets to hook up the new cartridge belt. Staring over the gun's breech, she watched the bandit army jogging up the low open slope toward their makeshift redoubt, occasionally dropping to one knee to fire but for the most part not shooting all that much. Trapped in the open in plain view, there was no percentage in stopping to aim. Hargrave and Jamesy targeted those who did so and killed them for their efforts. The surviving bandits had to reach the dug-in shooters and overwhelm them with sheer numbers.

The bandit army was twice as big as Coop had surmised when they were still scrambling up the slope toward them. She now estimated well over two hundred bandit-soldiers charging them, and they did not show any signs of slowing down.

Behind the boulder cluster—a hundred or so yards to the front and off to their left—Hargrave and Jamesy were dropping Apachureros as fast as they could aim and shoot, mostly with head shots. Scared to death, some of them were starting to break. One man—after seeing comrades on both sides of him shot in the head almost simultaneously—turned to flee . . . only to be machine-gunned out of hand by one of the officers.

"Christ, they're shooting their own men," Reets said.

"I've seen them shoot wounded stragglers," Coop said.

"Anyone who falls back."

But now Coop'd slammed the breech shut. Pulling back the bolt and chambering the belt's first round, Coop leaned over the sights. Trying to conserve ammunition, she focused primarily on those clumped together, taking them out in entire groups with controlled bursts.

Still they kept coming.

Now the bandit horde was barely fifty yards from Jamesy's and Hargrave's position. While their two men fell back to the firing pit, Coop covered their retreat with the Browning, Reets with her 5.56 mm H&K assault rifle.

But there were too many.

They could never hold out.

PART V

29

While the sacred place of the priestesses was commonly called the Temple of Love, it was actually the Temple of Akna, the Goddess, of Love and Fertility. The mating of Akna and her priestesses with men who wore rich quetzal feathers was the central theme of the temple inscriptions. And the paintings described the purpose of the temple precisely—wealthy men went there to be entertained with music, fine food, nectar of the gods, and lovemaking.

The treatment conferred on privileged men at the temple paralleled that which warriors who had fallen in battle received after they joined the Sun God's honor guard. At night, when the Sun God had retreated into his cave on the other side of the western waters, the men in the honor guard were entertained by Akna's priestesses, with their every desire fulfilled.

Feasting, drinking, lovemaking—that was the life of a fallen warrior in the Celestial Heavens. And that was the life of the nobles and royalty who had the power of life and death over commoners like myself.

Eyo! To enjoy the tender ministrations of beautiful women and not even having to die for the privilege! I would have had to die in battle to gain the rights claimed by those few whom the gods had chosen to bless with the wealth and rank that made them dominant over others.

The priestesses were chosen young and spent a couple of years being trained by older women before they were permitted to entertain men.

I didn't know how old the High Priestess was. If she had been the lover of Jeweled Skull while in her teens, however, she would still be a woman of some maturity—at least into her late thirties or early forties.

I had checked inscriptions on the Temple of Love before and found them all to be not only accurate, but also the most exquisitely drawn and dazzlingly detailed sacred writings in the city. That Jeweled Skull had been the lover of the High Priestess would account for the exceptional beauty and detail of the legends about the goddess and her nymphs.

The next morning I went directly to the temple and around to the side, where an opening in a doorway allowed women wishing to conceive to leave gifts of food or jewelry for the goddess. The type of gift depended on their station in life.

I slipped a note inside stating simply that Pakal Jaguar wished to speak to the goddess. I was certain the High Priestess, reincarnation of the goddess Akna, would recognize the name. While my name was not shouted in the streets, the story of saving Lord Janaab from a jungle beast would have found its way to the temple, if not my reputation as a seer.

One source would have been the great lord himself—he went to the temple twice a week, apparently finding more passion and tender care in the arms of the priestesses than from his two wives and five concubines.

I hung around the door for a few minutes; then, feeling foolish that I had expected the door to swing open and a beautiful nymph to usher me in, I went about my task of checking inscriptions on walls and buildings.

Each morning, I walked past the door on my way to the part of the city I would check that day, returning to stroll by in the late afternoon before I returned to the palace and had my evening meal.

When I went in the afternoon on the third day, the door opened. A feminine figure, covered from head to toe by a robe, with only an opening for a pair of pretty eyes, opened the door and gestured me inside.

I entered a dark stairwell, which the wall torches barely illuminated.

The woman said nothing, but waited until I had entered and then went up the stone steps with me following. My guide obviously didn't intend to answer any of the many questions I had about where she was taking me. However, her exotic perfume—made from the flowers of the sacred Sac Nicté tree—compensated for her reticence.

Her perfume and hidden charms fed my imagination and my lust.

The love temples' legends describe the priestesses as the most beautiful women in the land, chosen at an early age. Just as artists and craftsmen have different talents, each, it is said, was taught a specialized skill with which to please men.

The priestesses used every part of the body in lovemaking—and every place on a man's body was tantalized and satiated.

The thought of what was hidden under the tentlike robe flowing up the steps in front of me stirred my juices. My rational mind knew that the priestesses were forbidden fruit to commoners, but the manly part of my body didn't get the message.

The cloaked priestess led me to a doorway guarded by two other priestesses—beautiful, delicate, sensuous young women—but the flint-tipped spears each held looked lethal.

Double doors opened as if by magic as we approached, and we entered a chamber with golden walls.

The living goddess was on the far side of the room, seated on a jade throne supported by stone jaguars facing opposite directions.

She wore the mask of Akna, the Earth Goddess, Mother of All

People. The image was frightening and grotesque, eerie and startling all at once, as all images of our gods were.

Her breasts were bare, with a sash of the finest material dyed
royal red. The sash was embedded with precious stones and fell
between her breasts. Her skirt was white, with strands of silver
woven through it. A heavy gold necklace held a life-sized jade phal-
lic symbol, which hung between her breasts.

The naked parts of her body were finely sculptured, her breasts
full and firm. I couldn't see her facial features, but nothing about her
vibrant body suggested her age.

I realized the chamber was not paint covered but gold plated,
with finely drawn glyphs showing every imaginable position for a
man and woman to mate.

Plants with sweet smells and brilliant flowers—none of which
would have grown in the golden room unless they were exposed to
the sun at times—filled the room both with an earthly ambience
and a heady scent that reminded me of the gods' own nectar.

I didn't know how I was supposed to greet the living goddess and
cursed myself for not asking Lord Janaab. She was also a powerful
entity in Mayapán and no doubt had the power of life and death
over a stoneworker turned oracle.

I also realized I should have brought a gift, but most of my worldly
possessions were on my back. They would be laughable compared to
the treasures bestowed upon her by the richest and most powerful
men in the land.

The woman who'd escorted me to the chamber bowed before the
High Priestess, and I did the same, hoping that was the proper way
to meet a living goddess.

"Leave us," she told the cloaked priestess.

"Come closer," she said as soon as the priestess left.

When I was within touching distance, she took my jaguar claw
between her fingers.

"A white jaguar," she mused, "the rarest of all the One-World's
sacred beasts. B'alam was looking after you that day in the jungle."

Her tone carried authority and the promise of something more provocative. Exotic sensuality glowed from her like the perfume worn by the priestess who had led me up the stairs and into the chamber.

"Yes, I was blessed by the Jaguar God's strength and mercy."

She gave a little laugh. "Pakal Jaguar, you were blessed that day with the luck of the gods. That must have been one sick, old cat, not to have thrown you off and ripped out your throat."

Coming from Six Sky, that description of my battle with the jaguar was insulting. The way she said it, though, rang true, spoken by a woman who knew more about the world than we mere mortals.

She took off her mask, and I gazed into mysterious pools of dark waters. She was not only ravishingly beautiful, but her dark eyes also registered depths below depths. A man could dive into those black, bottomless orbs and drown.

Her features, however, gave no clue as to her age. More than thirty? Less than fifty? I couldn't tell. She appeared ageless, as eternal as images carved from stone.

She offered me her hand. "Join me for a cup of chocolate."

She led me through the doors behind her throne.

30

We entered a small, comfortable sitting room with soft seats that one could sit or stretch out on. A low table was set with plates of food—not the beans, maize, and peppers that made up most of my meals, but fruits and nuts, some of which I had never seen before, and meats I recognized as turtle, venison, and turkey, which I'd rarely seen except on the High Lord's table.

Best of all, once we were seated, one of her cloaked servants brought us chocolate. Once again, I was partaking of the favorite drink of nobles who treated my kind little better than dogs.

Seeing my eyes trail the cloaked woman, who left after serving the drinks, she said, "Yes, the women under the cloaks are even more beautiful and sensuous than you can imagine."

"The gods could not have created a woman as beautiful as you."

A small smile told me my compliment amused her. "You want to know about Jeweled Skull," she said.

I shook my head. "Are there no secrets in Mayapán?"

"My priestesses can wrest secrets from the dead."

Eyo! I would fight another jaguar in exchange for their "gentle ministrations."

Her amused look said that she had read my salacious thoughts.

"Are men so easy to read?" I asked.

"When it comes to women. Both sexes have their needs, but women don't permit theirs to guide their actions. We would have fewer wars if men followed their hearts rather than their lust." She thought for a moment. "Jeweled Skull was different. He came here not just for the fleshly pleasures, but because I invited him. He told not just wondrous stories, his voice was magical. It could have tamed the wildest of the jungle beasts. I listened to him for hours. The gods spoke through his lips."

"Did you love him?"

I don't know why I asked the question. She was the High Priestess of the temple devoted to giving men pleasure—not just any man, but all whose rank and wealth gave them access to her and her priestesses.

"I respected and admired him above all others. Love is not an emotion I am entitled to possess."

"What did Jeweled Skull tell you about the Dark Rift?" I asked.

"The same as he told you: a mysterious reference to it but with little detail."

"Ah." I nodded. "That is exactly what he told me." How she knew was another mystery.

"Do you understand why he said so little?"

I shook my head. "Not really. Perhaps because he believed we might tell others?"

"More than that. Jeweled Skull loved me, and from what I have heard about your relationship with him and your abilities as a storyteller, I suspect he loved you as a son. He didn't tell us all he knew, because it would have brought danger into our lives. Just as it has now done for you."

I took a sip of chocolate to get my thoughts in order. The woman had amazing insight. Finally, I asked, "What sort of danger is there for me?"

She chuckled, not with humor. "Lord Janaab wants you to find the codex. Others want it, too. Because you had a close relationship with Jeweled Skull, they believe that he told you more than you are admitting. Lord Janaab apparently believes you when you deny knowing where it is. But there are others who would just as soon roast your feet over a fire to find out if you do know where it is."

"Do these, uh, feet roasters have names?"

She laughed again. "Go to the top of the Pyramid of the Feathered Serpent and look in every direction, and you will see the ones you need to fear. All the rich and powerful in Mayapán lust for the secret. Each and all would torture you hard to get it."

"They will waste their firewood—and my life. I don't know where it is. I thought it might have been at the library, but it wasn't."

"If the library contained the codex, the king would have had it destroyed long ago. And his father before him."

"But how can destroying the book cancel the prophecy? How can one alter the will of the gods?"

"Desperate men are not rational. Now tell me, young storyteller, how your villagers came to believe Jeweled Skull was dead."

I described the scene of bloodied clothes as I had for Lord Janaab.

"You told this to Lord Janaab?"

"Yes."

"And he told it to the king, which means the king's advisers were also told to spread the story. Lucky for you."

"In what way would the story of Jeweled Skull's death help me?"

She gave me a smile and a small head shake that told me I truly was still an innocent village boy.

"You must learn to be more deceptive and cunning, young storyteller. The seekers of the codex keep you alive in hopes that the one who can find the book will contact you."

Ajul will contact me? The idea stunned me.

"You had no thought of that?"

I shook my head. "No."

"But be assured it has occurred to others."

"Why would Jeweled Skull contact me? If he is, in fact, still alive."

"That is a question you must answer for yourself. The path—"

The double doors through which we had entered suddenly opened, and a young nobleman came into the room.

"What have we here? The High Priestess entertaining common dirt?"

The High Priestess rose from her chair, as I did my own.

The intruder was about my age and about my own size, with arms and legs almost as large as my own.

"Flint Shield! How dare you enter my quarters uninvited?"

The nobleman raised his eyebrows in mock astonishment. "I heard a commoner had sneaked into the temple, and I came here expecting to find him raping you."

"This is Pakal Jaguar. He is under the protection of both Lord Janaab and the king."

"Ah, yes, the one an eagle bore on its wings to slay a sacred white jaguar. But he doesn't look like a hero of lore. He appears to have the strong back and weak mind of his lowly class."

I kept my mouth shut and endured the insults, not daring to return the abuse to a nobleman, even in the face of arrogance and rudeness.

"Perhaps you had better watch your tongue, Flint Shield. Pakal killed a jaguar with his bare hands."

"I have been told that it was an old and sick jaguar, a toothless one. Is that true?" he asked me.

"You would have to ask Lord Janaab," I said. "I saw the beast only from the back, but I'm sure His Lordship can answer your question as to whether it was toothless, since it had His Lordship's arm in its mouth. And perhaps you should ask the king, also, whether his prized, rare white jaguar was too toothless to put up a fight."

The High Priestess let out a squeal of laughter. "You have just been backed into a corner, Flint Shield. What will the king say when he hears you called his white jaguar feeble?"

Flint Shield stepped up to me and slapped me across the face with the back of his left hand. His right hand gripped the hilt of his dagger. He grinned at me, hoping I would make a move.

The High Priestess stepped up to him. "You are a coward, not the man who will someday be the War Lord. Get out of here, now! Or I truly will inform the king you have insulted his prize jaguar and the hero who gave it to him."

Flint Shield first locked eyes with the High Priestess to show that he was not frightened of her threat. He turned back to me. "I did that because I could." He gave her a small bow and started to walk away, but stopped and turned back to me. "Perhaps next time I will kick you to death. Because I can."

The magic doors opened and closed behind him.

The High Priestess wiped blood off my lip with her finger. "I'm sorry that happened."

"Who is he?"

"Flint Shield is a captain of the king's guards. His father is the War Lord."

She didn't have to tell me who the War Lord was. The man chosen to lead Mayapán's armies in war, he was the most important High Lord in the land, second only to the king in power.

"I suspect I just met one of those men who would willingly roast my feet over an open flame," I said.

"An excellent guess. His father, the War Lord, competes with Lord Janaab for the king's favor. If you caused Janaab to lose favor with the king or other lords, the War Lord would not be disappointed. Or if he were the one who was able to obtain the codex. The War Lord is a cousin of the king, and some say he would like to be king."

I grinned sourly. "I should have stayed in my village. There I only had to worry about snakes that crawled."

"Flint Shield is not the only one of the king's nobles who has animosity toward you. That a commoner killed the most sacred and dangerous animal in the One-World did not settle well with the young noblemen who seek advantage for themselves."

"There is abundant blood on battlefields. Let them seek it there."

"Flint Shield is the best warrior in Mayapán. He captures the most warriors for sacrifice, which is why he believes we will select him to replace his father as War Lord when his father grows too old to lead the king's army. Unless his father doesn't do something to stop the rumors that he is more capable of speaking to the gods than the king. That his War Lord receives more acclaim than he cannot set well with the king."

"If Flint Shield is a warrior, he doesn't have to be envious of me. He can gain great fame in battle."

"Even so, the gods thirst for more blood, and there will be another war. He could never achieve in battle what you did the moment you jumped on that beast's back."

I didn't know what to say. The gods had set me on a path, and I could only watch my back and hope that when a fight came, the gods would favor me.

"I must get back to my duties," I said.

She shook her head. "I can't let you return to the streets carrying a bad impression of the temple with you. You have come to a place of pleasure. So you shall now have it."

31

The doors parted, and three young women stood perfectly still for a moment.

Naked.

All three were firm of flesh. The one in the center stood a foot forward of the other two. Reed slim, she had small, firm breasts, a flat stomach, and smooth thighs.

Most startling of all was that her private area was also bare.

Eyo! I have seen many naked women, young, mature, and old. While the women in some parts of our land go bare-breasted on all but the coolest days, most women cover their breasts—and the love nest between their legs, permitting only boys hiding in bushes to get a peek when they are bathing.

But I had never seen a woman whose love nest was bare. Only hers was naked. The other two had the expected hair.

Staring at her, I realized the priestess had not just shaved her private area, but from the way her skin shone, I could see that she lacked body hair also on her arms and legs.

I didn't know if the lack of hair was a feature given to her by the gods, perhaps by Love Goddess Akna, or if she had shaved her body hair. Whatever the cause, I experienced surprise and then more manly feelings.

The three women entered and two of them, smiling, took me by the arm. I hadn't noticed, but the High Priestess was gone, swallowed by the walls perhaps as I stared at the priestesses.

We left the chamber and went down a dark corridor and into another room. The priestess with the smooth-shaven body led the way.

We entered a room that had a small opening on the other side. After the two had removed my clothes, the tall priestess said, "You may enter the House of Stone Fire."

I should have known from the heat in the air that the opening led into a sweat hut. I had never seen one built as part of a building; the huts were usually built in the coned shape of a beehive in the open.

Inside, I sat on a bench by the heated rocks in the center and immediately began to sweat. The lead girl entered behind me and threw herbs on the stones.

As she started to leave, I asked, "What's your name?"

Her obsidian eyes met mine. "Sparrow," she said, "my name is Sparrow."

Sparrow reminded me of someone, but I couldn't put a name to the feeling. Not her features so much as her presence. Looking into her eyes, I also realized she was the guide who met me at the temple door.

She left, and I leaned back to let the heat do its work. Sweating was the purpose of the hot room, sweating that cleansed the body and soul, healed wounds and cured sickness.

When I had sweated out my sins and my discomfort, Sparrow gestured for me to leave. Out of the sweat house, she led me to a cool pool of water, a tropical pond somewhere in the upper reaches of the temple.

I waded into the pool, and the girls came in with me. Using soft cloths, they rubbed me down. My manhood was stiff and hard, and I had fought it long enough. I reached for Sparrow to give it some relief, but she slipped away.

"Not yet," she said.

We left the pool. I was dry by then and was invited to sit on a long bench.

"Close your eyes," Sparrow said. "Relax and feel the gift of the gods."

The three young women began to rub and caress my skin with soothing sensuous oil, their light fingers gently moving over my body, from the soles of my feet to the top of my head.

Sparrow was right about the gods. . . . I felt what a fallen warrior experienced when he went to the Celestial Heaven to be pampered by nymphs of the gods.

As I lay there naked, the women touched every place on my body with their caressing fingers and wet lips, then applied hot oil from my toes to the top of my head. At first my whole body trembled under their touch, but then Sparrow spoke softly in my ear, whispering not words but making sounds that flooded my body with warmth.

I stopped shaking as their warm, wet lips undulated on my own lips, and on my chest. Taking my member into her mouth, Sparrow massaged it with her tongue, her head gyrating and pumping.

I exploded so hard, I almost passed out.

I lay there a long moment, half-awake, half-asleep in a dream state. Lifting my head, Sparrow had me drink a potion. Again my soul soared, and I saw her naked flesh and beauty clearer than I had seen anything before.

I realized she alone was with me, that the other women had vanished, perhaps simply fading away, because I didn't see them leave.

There was only Sparrow. As I lay on my back, she mounted me. Women in my village would not have done this, because a man does not let a woman mount him. It was a man's privilege to ride the woman.

I was ready to shake her off, but she leaned down, her breasts pressing against my chest. Again she made the strange cooing sound in my ear that so inexplicably calmed my nerves.

Sitting upright, my hands on her breasts, she tightened the muscles around my male part as she levitated up and down with agonizing indolence, creating a hot wet sensation that no hand or mouth could have accomplished.

I exploded again when she gasped and groaned with the release of her own dammed-up desires.

Afterwards we lay together, Sparrow still atop me, my male part languishing in her garden. As power flowed back into my lower parts, I rose, with her still in me, her legs wrapped around my waist, my member impaling her, driving her unrelentingly until once more the grace of the gods obliterated us.

32

Before I left the Temple of Love, Sparrow and I shared a long, languid kiss, not a coming together of two people who had shared a moment of sexual pleasure, but that of lovers who had lost each other decades past and then rediscovered their secret selves.

Afterwards we sat together and were served cool juices, fresh fruits, meats and fish like those on the High Priestess' table. She asked me about my work, and I told her about my duty checking all the inscriptions in the city.

"Even the king's palace," I said, "not only the outside walls, but I have to enter all the public corridors of the palace and ensure that the inscriptions are accurate."

She was so fascinated with my work, and I felt so important describing it, I leaned closer and told her in a confidential tone that I had even more important duties.

"I am to find an ancient codex that holds great secrets," I told her.

Most of the time she said little, just cooing a bit as I boasted about my accomplishments.

When it was time to leave, I left reluctantly. I was connected to her in a way I could not explain.

As we parted, she leaned up to nibble my ear for a last time and whispered, "Trust no one."

Then she slipped away, leaving me at the top of the stairs that led back down to the street, where I was left with the reality of my unexalted position—that of Lord Janaab's faithful retainer.

Back to being envied by people with the power of life and death over me.

Trust no one.

The words stayed with me, echoing in my ears, floating in front of my eyes, roiling in my head.

What does she mean? Why did she say it?

She didn't have to tell me not to trust Lord Janaab—I was his servant; he was master; he could paint me red on a whim and would. He would keep me on only so long as I was useful to him. Or Flint Shield, who humiliated me, drew my blood, and declared himself my enemy. Or Six Sky, who spied on me.

Was the warning about the High Priestess?

Out on the street, I suddenly realized that my lips had been flapping nonstop when I boasted about my work to her. Even about the secret codex, a subject that was forbidden.

When she said trust no one . . . had she meant herself?

A warning that what went from my mouth to her ear would be reported to the High Priestess?

I thought about the feminine figure that had placed the message on the wall about the blind man at the library. It could have been her. But it also could have been most of the female population of Mayapán.

I had a feeling that I had not seen the last of Sparrow.

I wondered if I would ever get another invitation to the Temple of Love.

My talent as an oracle told me that I would see both the High Priestess and Sparrow again.

Or perhaps that was my male member's wishful thinking.

PART VI

PART

33

Coop was picking off Apachureros with her 7.62 when she first heard the chopper. The sight of it buoyed Coop's spirits . . . at first. An AH-1 Cobra "Huey," it was an ancient Vietnam War relic, swooping in behind them less than three hundred yards away.

Ah, what the hell, she thought. *It's not state of the art, but then most of the vehicles down here are antiques. Anyway, the only opposition is a demented bandit gang armed with semiautomatics. No problemo.*

Then she got a closer look. More than just old, this one had clearly been scraped up off some third world junk heap. Its Gatling-style multi-barrel machine gun mounts and M56 four-pack TOW (tube-launched, optically tracked, wire-guided) missile launchers were not only empty, but its fuselage was a crazy quilt of rusted-out, poorly welded scrap-metal patches, riddled with gaping bullet holes and ripped-apart seams, to boot.

On closer inspection, it did have some sort of tripod machine gun bolted to its cabin bulkhead, its muzzle pointing out the narrowly open hatch. Instead of strafing the Apachureros on the flank, however, the craft landed well behind their fire trench, the machine gun muzzle pointed directly at . . . *them.*

Boy, they do want *that codex,* Coop noted.

Jamesy was manning the Browning M60. Putting down the 7.62, she grabbed the shoulder pack containing the codex urn, and, pressing it to her chest, she slipped the straps over her shoulders. She took off her belt, shoved it through the straps, pulled it down across the middle of her back, and tightened it across her lower chest.

"What are you doing?" Reets shouted at Coop above the hammering of the machine guns.

"You three secure that chopper. Reets, you get there first. Tell them I have the codex strapped across my chest. If they turn that machine gun on any of us, they lose the loot."

"Shoot you, they shoot the money?" Jamesy yelled at her with an appreciative smile. "You think like me. I like it."

"I don't like it," Reets said.

"Have your guns out when you enter that chopper. Don't let them disarm you. They may kill us all once they get that their hands on the codex."

"I still don't like it," Reets said to Coop, unable to refute her logic.

Coop pulled Hargrave off the Browning and pushed him toward Reets, who repeated what she said. By then Coop was crouched behind the big gun. Keeping the codex below the rocks and dirt-filled sandbags, she hammered away at the bandit army.

Reluctantly, her three friends raced toward the chopper, H&K 7.62s in hand. The two men covered their retreat, picking off bandits with their assault rifles, while Reets raced on ahead, explaining that Coop would follow last with the codex strapped across her chest.

"Shoot us, shoot her, you lose the pesos!" she roared above the din of the rotor.

34

The sixty or seventy surviving Apachureros were now less than fifty yards away. *Time to haul ass*, Coop decided. Grabbing up the M60 and throwing its cartridge belt over her shoulders, she vaulted the trench's rear wall and ran toward the chopper, turning periodically to fire away at her pursuers, who were quickly closing the distance

She was forty yards from the chopper, then thirty, then twenty, then ten.

The bandit-soldiers were no longer shooting at her but pouring assault-weapons fire onto the chopper. Moreover, the last time she turned to cover her retreat, she saw two officers perhaps seventy-five yards away, mounting grenades on the muzzles of their weapons.

Shit, they were going to frag the chopper.

Throwing herself to the ground, Coop tried to take out the grenade-launchers in the back, but there were too many troops in front of them—as if they were using men for flack jackets.

The first gun-launched grenade went wide, detonating when it hit the ground forty feet from the Cobra's nose.

Ten seconds later, the second man fired a frag-grenade and scored—

a—

a—

a direct hit.

Glancing over her shoulder, Coop felt a surge of relief.

Her friends had not climbed aboard yet and seemed unhurt.

She guessed the chopper crew was dead.

Well, Hargrave was checked out on choppers—if the craft could still fly.

If not, we make our last stand there.

Turning, for the last time she ran to the craft. She could see Hargrave throwing the dead pilot out of his seat and flinging him across the craft's bulkhead. Jamesy dragged him and the rest of the dead crew out of the craft.

Now Coop was at the chopper. Shoving the big Browning up and through the chopper's hatch, she clambered onto the landing strut. Grabbing the side door, she swung inside the craft. Bullets sang past her ears, riddling the chopper's frame and its interior. Seating herself on the hatch's edge, feet dangling over the side, she grabbed the Browning off the bulkhead floor and swung it toward the charging bandits. They were now less than twenty yards away, and the big gun cut through them like a scythe.

They dropped to their bellies, attempting to return her fire from the prone position.

When Hargrave finally lifted off.

The Huey had not escaped the fragging unscathed. Its engine billowing black smoke, it lurched erratically. Hargrave was flying it toward the cliff's edge, was now over breaks of the Río Negro, the rapids of a black thunderous jungle river, which was narrowing precipitously toward a vertiginous series of waterfalls.

The chopper was shaking badly, swinging over, it seemed, all the abysses of heaven and earth.

Nor were they free of Apachurero gunfire.

Her legs hanging out the hatch, the bandits' assault rifles still had the range to hurt them, even knock out the rotor, which they seemed to be sighting in on.

But the Browning M60 had an even longer effective range.

Time to exploit that last, single advantage. Bracing the metal stock against the chopper's bottom bulkhead, she elevated the muzzle and sighted in on the bandits, lined up along the cliff's rim, pouring fire on them.

Again, the big gun cut through them like a machete.

Until some *hijo de puta* sharpshooter found his own range.

Four tremendously powerful rounds exploded through the top bulkhead—only inches from the rotor's rusted-out mount.

"A goddamn Barrett!" Jamesy shouted over the chopper's din.

Coop knew what that meant. A .50-caliber Barrett M81 sniper rifle, its effective range was upwards of three thousand meters, and it packed enough stopping power to take out tanks—even at that three thousand meters, which several Navy SEALS had done during Operation Desert Storm.

And the son of a bitch was sighted in.

Leaning out the hatchway, she spotted the marksman. He was crouched over the cliff, the big rifle not mounted on a bipod but handheld.

He's a strong son of a bitch, Coop thought. *I'll give him that.*

Well, two could play that game. She still had sixty or seventy rounds left. The chopper was pulling away, he seemed to be their last human threat, so she emptied the belt, the metal stock braced on the bottom bulkhead, the Browning's muzzle pointed almost straight up.

But not before he got off a final round.

She felt the jolt when his last .50-caliber round hammered the rotor casing like a cannonball out of hell.

The chopper bucked like a rabid bull busting up a squeeze chute.

That a microsecond later she saw the shooter tumble over the cliff face gave her no solace.

Coop was falling, too.

For a second or two, she seemed to descend in ultra-slow motion, so much so, she was able to extend her left arm and hook the landing strut with an elbow.

Pain shot through her shoulder like a hundred hornet stings.

Getting her right hand up to grip the strut made it hurt even worse.

Still, she did it.

"Coop, look up!" Jamesy was shouting, his voice dim, tinny, and distant in her ears.

She looked up, and he was dangling precariously, straddling the strut, one hand trying to anchor his body on a strut support, the other trying to take her hand.

Her shoulder felt dislocated, and she was blinded by pain.

Furthermore, the chopper was descending like a dropped rock, the rotor smoking like a volcano in hell. She saw no point in torturing her shoulder further if the chopper was about to crash.

Still, she couldn't disappoint her friend.

Clinging to the strut with her pain-racked elbow, she raised her right hand.

Jamesy had just grabbed the hand's lower half, when the elbow gave way.

She was dangling from one-half of a hand, the white-water rapids almost two hundred feet below her.

Then she felt the glove slip.

An quarter inch at a time.

Then there were no inches left.

She was falling, falling, falling—strangely peaceful, at one with her flight through the ether and the astral, through time and space.

Time enough to—

The codex! she realized with sickening dread. *The crash will destroy it.*

At the very last second, she remembered to pull up her legs and grip them under the knees with both hands.

She hit the rapids on her butt like an asteroid from outer space.

PART VII

35

War was on the tongue and minds of Lord Janaab's servants and workers during breakfast, and the talk followed me as I left for my duties along with others whose tasks took them outside the palace complex.

One thing had not changed from my days as a stoneworker—the workday still began when the Sun God left his cave on the other side of the eastern waters and started his journey across the sky to enter the cave from the western side.

All the lords and merchants had to send warriors to participate in the war, and Lord Janaab had sent half his household guard. Six Sky was angry that he had not been sent to command the great lord's contingent.

"It's a Flower War with Cobá," Six Sky confirmed the night before after the king's army had left the city under the command of the War Lord. "Great honor is bestowed upon warriors who take captives and bring them back for sacrifice."

Six Sky had captured an enemy warrior three years earlier. He pounded his chest with pride. "I was given his heart to eat after his blood was dedicated to the gods."

Being young and strong, ordinarily I would have been sent as part of the lord's contingent, but he held me back, telling me that my work was more important. And I knew why Six Sky had not been sent to join the army the War Lord marched out of the city with great pomp: Lord Janaab wanted him to stay and spy on me.

Almost a year ago, I had begun my task of walking the streets of the city and surveying the written tributes to the gods on the walls and monuments. The rule I had discovered in the beginning remained true—none of the inscriptions that dated back to the time of Jeweled Skull or beyond was inaccurate. All the mistakes were made when the great storyteller left to hide in a small village of stoneworkers.

Of my mentor, whom I still thought of as Ajul, I had heard no further word about and nothing in the inscriptions that illuminated the mystery of the Dark Rift, to which Lord Janaab had alluded.

Nor had anyone invited me again to partake in the pleasures of the Temple of Love. *Eyo!* I lusted for another time with Sparrow and the other nymphs.

When the High Priestess treated me like a noble, she spoiled me for life, I now feared.

No, I was not just jaded and pampered, but I had suffered a rude awakening as well. Having won Lord Janaab's confidence by killing a jaguar that would have eaten him, withstanding his torture and having suffered in silence Flint Shield's humiliation—when I felt I could have bested him man to man—nobility had lost its awe for me.

I no longer saw nobles as either invincible or all-knowing. Even the king had made a mistake, because I have no doubt that Ajul was right—the will of the gods cannot be broken by destroying a book.

The turn my mental attitude had taken over the months left me contemptuous of those better than me . . . and hungry for a woman who could offer her body only to those above me.

There was no solution to my predicament. In the One-World,

there were nobles and commoners. If I gave the slightest hint to Lord Janaab that—like starving peasants, who storm the palaces of their fat masters for food to feed their children—I had fallen from grace with my lowly status in life, he would paint me red without question.

36

I left the palace before first light, because I wanted to cross the city and check inscriptions before the Sun God brought forth the heat of day.

My task took me farther away from the ceremonial center each day, despite the fact that I had not checked all the inscriptions in the ceremonial center. I enjoyed venturing beyond the walls of the most privileged and out onto the streets, to the squares and market-places where people of all walks of life congregated.

I especially sought out travelers from beyond the domains of Mayapán. Merchants and vagabond storytellers from the distant cities of my people, chopped out of the jungles far to the south and those from the north—Aztecs, Mixtec, and other nations—congregated there.

The language of the Aztecs was Nahuatl. Ajul had taught me the tongue, so I could learn the tales of heroes and gods from the north. So many of them had a relationship to our own stories.

Mingling with the Aztecs in the marketplace, I sharpened my language skills. More than their language, however, I enjoyed hearing about their land. The Aztecs had a pride and arrogance that I had not seen from my own people.

From conversations I'd overheard between Lord Janaab and other Mayapán lords, I knew that the Aztecs were both admired and feared, even though our nobles also viewed them contemptuously. They considered their culture inferior to ours.

Inferior to ours? That was true, if the lords were considering the accomplishments of our ancestors, who built magnificent cities like Uxmal and Palenque. But those great cities were past their prime, having been ruled for hundreds of years not by builder-kings who expanded their territories by conquest and brought home the treasures to increase their cities' magnificence.

Instead of constructing bigger and grander temples and palaces, the kings in the Land of the Maya restricted themselves today with the twenty-year *katun* renewal projects: putting a shine on the greatness of the past rather than outdoing what our ancestors had done.

Our civilizational decay was evident in the legends of our peoples. The tales of mighty kings ended several hundred years ago after the god-king Quetzalcoatl came from Tula and rebuilt Chichén Itzá into the finest city in the region. After the time of the Feathered Serpent, a powerful king united Mayapán, Uxmal, and Chichén Itzá into a league.

From that time until today, few tales of heroes and kings worthy of being were placed on public display. The Aztecs followed a similar pattern—except they had not been a great and powerful nation for more than one or two hundred years.

That our warriors and leaders no longer inspired great tales of valor explained in part why the gods didn't favor us with the rain that we needed to grow our crops.

Because of the attention, which the talon strung around my neck and my scarred face drew, I had begun hiding the claw necklace under my clothes and covering the marks with paint. That way I could do my work without constantly getting curious glances, and I could talk to people in the marketplace and streets without the same reaction.

Several times I had stood anonymously in a crowd and heard

storytellers relating tales of my fight with the white jaguar, my magical powers growing with each telling.

Yesterday I had been stunned to find the story painted upon the wall of a small temple outside the ceremonial center. I didn't bother marking the inscription as inaccurate, even though it related that I had leaped onto the jaguar's back from the wings of an eagle.

Who was I to doubt my greatness? *Eyo!* How many heroic acts of lore grew with the telling?

Besides feeding my ego, mythologizing my deed served another purpose: Nobles jealous of the public recognition I received might hesitate to harm me because the people would be angered.

Eyo! That train of thought was wrong. The greater my legend grew, rather than just earning awe and respect, that legend would make me a target for nobles like Flint Shield. He could well enhance his own reputation by cutting off my head and hanging it on a city gate.

The High Priestess said Flint Shield wanted to be War Lord when his father was too old to command the army. Reason enough to kill a simple young stoneworker who lacked rank or privilege.

What did Flint Shield say about kicking me to death? He would do it . . . because he could?

37

It wasn't full sunrise, and the large gate leading out of the ceremonial center would remain closed until dawn. Still, I could get the guards to let me pass through a half door, which was barely large enough for an individual to enter and exit but too small for armies to utilize en masse.

Deep in thought, I had almost reached the entrance when it hit me—*the gate was open*. Nor were any guards present on the walkway above.

Normally guards were on that walk, spaced easily within shouting distance, day and night.

A guard was lying on the ground near the gate, his spear beside him, an arrow in his chest. And another one had fallen not far away. I couldn't see the arrow, but it was obvious that he would have one, too.

And then I saw them coming—a host of warriors coming up the street, running straight for the open gate.

The ceremonial center was under surprise attack.

"Invaders, invaders, the gate is open!" I shouted at the top of my lungs.

A large upright drum, which stood near the gate, was used to welcome ambassadors and other dignitaries from other kingdoms. I ran for it and grabbed a wooden club. Hammering it several times, I repeated my yell.

I saw ceremonial center guards coming from both directions on the wall and more running from nearby barracks, but none would get to the gate in time to close it before the invaders reached it.

The city drums briefly boomed three times a day, signaling the beginning of work, lunch break, and the end of the workday, but when the beat was steady and protracted, it indicated an invasion alarm.

The drums would then bring all the king's soldiers out of their barracks, but if the enemy's plan was to take the ceremonial center—without securing the city—they had only one purpose in mind: to kill the king.

As soon as the drums started, war cries—designed to terrify us—exploded.

Eyo! Why were we being invaded? The war was with Cobá, and it was a Flower War, the clash of two armies on a battlefield that would last only hours and the "victor" was simply the one that took the most prisoners. Slaying enemy soldiers wasn't the purpose—the staged war was fought solely to get prisoners for sacrifice. No cities were invaded; it was done at a rural location agreed upon beforehand.

I got to the gate and began to close it. It was meant to be moved shut by three men, but I was able to start it closing. I pushed it not just with the strength I had developed pushing great blocks of stone, but also with power ignited by panic, the same source of strength that allowed me to break the neck of a great jungle beast.

City guards came off the wall and down the steps as I pushed, but it was too late to keep out the invaders who were closest to the gate. Three of them came through at a run. I crouched down next to the door as the warriors engaged guards in combat. The bulk of the invading horde was still running for the gates.

A city guard with a spear attacked an enemy warrior who was finishing off another guard that was on the ground. The enemy warrior, who wore the quetzal feathers of a nobleman, turned and lashed out with his obsidian sword, catching the man charging with a club across the chest.

The Mayapán guard staggered back, dropping the spear as he fell.

I launched myself at the nobleman, sending the club flying at him as I did.

He raised his shield, blocking the club, but I'd thrown him off balance.

Without breaking my stride, I grabbed the spear from the fallen guard off the ground. As the enemy warrior raised his sword to lash out at me, I swung the spear at him like a club, hitting his sword, blocking him from swinging it at me. Stepping in with the spear in my two hands spaced apart, I bashed the warrior with one end of it, again using the spear as a club.

The blow caught the man on the forehead and sent him reeling.

Before he could recover, I kicked his knee, and he went down. Grabbing his sword arm by the wrist, I twisted the blade from his grip.

He snarled up at me, blood running down his forehead and over his eyes.

I kneed him in the face and heard his nose cartilage pop.

One of the invaders inside was pulling the brace back, and the horde was about to breach the gate.

I raced for the gate.

For a blurry moment I saw nothing but the blood I drew with the nobleman's fine sword, as we drove back the invaders, falling backwards on each other as the jaguar-killer in me swung the obsidian-bladed weapon with frenzied bloodlust, angry and panicking.

Six Sky was suddenly beside me.

"The gate," I said.

Now more of our own guards from the palaces in the ceremonial center joined us, driving the attacking warriors back until the gate could be closed.

"They're finished," Six Sky told me, both of us breathless.

"For how long?" I gasped. "They've breached the city walls."

"No, it was a sneak attack. I saw them from the walls, not an army, perhaps no more than a couple hundred warriors. Guards from throughout the city will fall upon them as they try to get out."

After the gate was closed, a group of twenty warriors wearing the uniforms of the royal guard joined those of us at the gate. A muscular man about my own age—who strutted up wearing the quetzal feathers of a nobleman as if he had just saved the king and city, and was about to be named War Lord—led them.

I had an impulse to ask Flint Shield why he hadn't "strutted" up to us moments earlier when there was fighting to be done.

I heard movement behind me and turned as the warrior whose nose I had broken was rising with a dagger in hand.

Still filled with the excitement of the battle, I swung the sword, catching him on the side of his neck, lopping off his head.

"Fool!"

The insult came from Flint Shield.

"You never give a prisoner a killing blow. Now you have no enemy to sacrifice, no heart to devour. The king will have your ears for your stupidity."

"My lord," Six Sky said, "Pakal Jaguar saved the battle. He fought alone here at the gate until—"

"Silence. You," he said to Six Sky, "join the others on the wall. They may try to come over it."

Flint Shield went over to the head and nudged it with his foot to make it roll over so he could see the face.

"The king's brother. The king will not be happy that a commoner killed his brother. He will have you painted red for it. You should have left the killing for a nobleman."

"There were none present. They were hiding with the women."

Six Sky was walking away when I made the statement, and I heard him gasp aloud.

Flint Shield stared at me, taken aback. He looked as if I had slapped him in the face, which I had—at least, with words.

"Take him!" he shouted to his guards.

"Stop!" The command came from Lord Janaab. "What are you doing?" he demanded of Flint Shield.

"This man killed the king's brother and insulted me. He will be sacrificed for his sins."

"He will not be sacrificed."

"The king—"

"I was with the king and watched the fight with him from his balcony. He knew his brother was going to attempt to kill him—it was just a matter of when. You are a hero, Pakal B'alam, once again you killed a jaguar." Lord Janaab indicated the head: "Prince Jaguar Paw."

"He insulted me," Flint Shield said.

Lord Janaab stepped up to me. "Give me the sword."

I gave him the sword. He stared at it for a moment, twisting it to see the double edge. I wondered if he was going to use it on me.

"Take him back to my palace," Lord Janaab told Six Sky. He turned to Flint Shield. "I will question him and decide his punishment."

Flint Shield said nothing, but I could see from the look on his face that the matter was not settled.

38

An hour later I was called to Lord Janaab's reception room.

"The attempt to kill the king has completely failed," he said. "All the participants are either dead or captured."

"Why did Prince Jaguar Paw try to usurp his brother's throne? Over the discontent due to the lack of rain?"

"The failure of crops and hunger are an excuse for stealing the throne. The prince was motivated by a lust for power. That unhealthy desire cost him his life. Now his entire family, wives and children, will be sacrificed along with all his slaves and palace staff. Unfortunately, the king's brother is not the only one who desires the throne."

From what the High Priestess told me, the War Lord was somewhere on the list of potential usurpers.

Lord Janaab paused and gave me a look that told me he was not entirely happy with me.

"You were a fool twice. Once for killing the prisoner and secondly for insulting a nobleman. If the king had not seen your fight to get the gate closed, not even I could have saved you from Flint Shield's wrath. Do you know who he is?"

"Yes. I saw him at the Temple of Love when I went there to talk to the High Priestess."

"You would find him there often—he's the lover of the High Priestess, as is his father."

"I had suspected that and found it interesting that he is probably half her age."

I didn't think that even Flint Shield would have intruded into the living goddess' quarters unless he knew it was his privilege.

"She chooses her lovers among the most powerful. Flint Shield hopes to someday follow in his father's footsteps as War Lord. His father's absence from the city with most of the army, leading them to battle with Cobá, gave the prince the opportunity to attack."

"Why didn't Flint Shield follow the army into battle with Cobá?"

"He is considered the best warrior in Mayapán and was deliberately kept back at the palace rather than sent to the Flower War. From lips loosened by torture, the king suspected that his own brother would attempt to steal his head and his kingdom. He kept Flint Shield with a contingent of soldiers at the palace in case his suspicions proved true. If it were not for you, Flint Shield would have had the honor of being the hero of the day."

I didn't know what to say, so I kept my silence, but Lord Janaab, perceptive as a hawk, anticipated my words.

"Speak. Tell me what you fear to speak."

"Perhaps it is my own false impression, but when Flint Shield and his men were coming toward me at that moment just before the gate was shut, I had the impression that he was going to attack me."

"He may have thought you were one of Prince Jaguar Paw's men."

"He knows who I am. The High Priestess told him when we were at the temple together."

"Because he recognized who you are, doesn't mean that he realized what side you were on."

"It wasn't just that." I hesitated again.

Lord Janaab's features grew grave, and his lips pressed together as he stared at me. I had the feeling that I had raised an issue he didn't want to hear, because it involved problems he would rather not deal with. "Speak," he said.

I spit the words out. "My impression is that his intent was to open the gate, not keep it closed."

"You're telling me that Flint Shield went to the gate to make sure it remained open to permit the rebels in?"

"Perhaps Flint Shield wished to ensure that he will indeed be War Lord. It also took members of the palace guard considerable time to make it to the gate after the alarm was sounded. Guards from farther away were already there when Flint Shield reached the gate. Something else happened, too. After I turned to face Flint Shield, the warrior on the ground, Prince Jaguar Paw, drew his dagger and was going to stab me in the back. Flint Shield had to have seen the man. Flint Shield's obvious intention was to let the man knife me and then use his men to force open—"

Lord Janaab hit me across the face with the back of his hand. The blow caught me completely by surprise, and I staggered backwards.

He picked up a wood staff. "Down on your knees."

I knelt down, and he lashed out at me, beating my head and shoulders until I was prone on the floor and bleeding.

"Get up," he said.

I rose, my whole body shaking. Blood flowed down the side of my face from an open gash across my head. I wiped at blood on my face and tasted it in my mouth.

"You are a commoner, but you speak and act as if you were a lord of the land. You have no right to judge the actions of those above you. You can report what you see, but only I will judge the actions."

He tossed aside the bloodied staff.

"You were right in not expressing your suspicions to Flint Shield. You erred enough in implying that he had acted cowardly."

He gave me a long look.

"The beating was to teach you not only never to repeat to anyone what you told me, but never to even think of such things about a High Lord. The War Lord commands more status than even I, who am favored by the king. If a word of this accusation passed out of this room, you would cause problems for me, and not even the king would stop the War Lord from having you flayed before the priests cut out your heart.

"Most of all, you must remember your place. Common people tell stories of your slaying of the jaguar as if you were a man-god, but the nobles know that you slew the beast because your years of hard labor gave you powerful muscles. Many nobles are angry at me for making you a member of my household. They have asked me to send you back to the village of stoneworkers because you have embarrassed them."

Lord Janaab paced for a moment, pursing his lips. "Regardless of your impressions, which do not count, something unusual did happen this morning. The drums you beat warned us of the attack, yet the battle for the ceremonial center gate was all but over by the time Flint Shield and his men got there. I don't know if the king noticed it. But I will make sure he realizes it."

He gave me another look, nodding, but it was a stare that went through me as if I were just part of the furniture. "The War Lord suggested that Flint Shield remain back at the palace. He recommended his son stay, because of the uprisings and food riots that have been occurring. He wasn't aware that the king had come to suspect Prince Jaguar Paw of plotting against him, and it all would have worked out perfectly for the intruders if you had not left the palace early and saw the gate open. Most of the army is en route to the Flower War with Cobá."

He expected no comment from me, and I had none. My head still rang from his beating. Lord Janaab had no more gratitude toward me than if I had been a dog that had thrown itself at the jaguar. Perhaps less—his pet dog would guide him through Xibalba after he dies.

He gave me a dark look. "There are ways that this matter of Flint

Shield can be dealt with, but none to which you are privy. No word of this leaves the room," he warned me again.

I nodded.

"You'd best leave the city for a while. Right now Flint Shield's rage is that of an angry fire mountain god. If your suspicions are true, you won't live long, anyway. A blade will find its way to your back to silence your tongue." Lord Janaab shrugged. "That may happen anyway. Your insult to Flint Shield will have to be avenged. That means you will not live to a ripe old age."

He spoke with the same emotion as he would have if his household majordomo had told him the price of maize had risen.

He paced some more. "There is a task for you to do. There is a man I want you to speak to in Tulúm."

My eyes and mind lit up. Tulúm was a city on the seacoast. An important city, it was a place to see and learn about—before Flint Shield exacted the revenge Lord Janaab was so certain he would.

"The man in Tulúm is a slave who tells a strange story of living in a tribe of people, which was lighter skinned than we are and worships mightier gods than ours. I am told that his skin is indeed lighter than ours and that he and his light-skinned companions washed ashore after their boat sank in a storm.

"Moreover, he boasts that warriors from his tribe will someday come with boats big as palaces and spears that travel a hundred times farther than our own."

"He's a madman!" I said.

"Without a doubt, and his insane ravings seem to flow as quickly as water into a cenote."

"What is it you wish me to speak to the man about?"

"The king has great curiosity about him. He makes claims that his powerful gods will vanquish our puny ones."

"Eyo! And he hasn't been painted red!"

"Most of his companions were, but he was spared because the headman of the village, who found him, believed gods were speaking through his lips."

People who said crazy things and acted oddly were believed to be possessed by the gods and exempt from sacrifice.

"The king wonders if the gods of the man's tribe are causing our crops to fail."

"The king believes the stranger's gods are more powerful than ours?"

"Of course not!" His expression went dark again, and he looked to the staff he had beaten me with. For a moment, I thought he was going to pick it up and hit me again.

He got control of himself and spoke in a calm, flat voice. "Pakal Jaguar, those lips of yours that flap like a flag on a windy day. They are a threat not just to yourself but also to me. Servants cannot say such things."

"Yes, my lord," I said with humility I didn't feel but did not dare not show.

"The king wonders whether the man's gods have loosened some demons in our region. That is all. Go to Tulúm and speak to the light-skinned slave. Six Sky will go with you."

I started to leave and turned back as Lord Janaab spoke.

"If you had not left the palace earlier than usual this morning, you would not have found the gate open and called out the alarm. The news of your gift of prophecy again will spread like wildfire."

"I found the gate only because I wanted to get ahead of the day's heat."

"Perhaps," Lord Janaab mused. "But it has happened before, so heed this warning: If you have the gift of prophecy, look to your own future, because the admiration you get from some will be a blade from another. Bear this in mind—Jeweled Skull was also said to have the gift. And where he is now?"

Dead or in hiding was the answer that stayed with me as I left the High Lord's chamber.

39

Because the king of Tulúm paid tribute to Cobá, which was engaged in a Flower War with Mayapán, we traveled as merchants from Uxmal.

We had six porters with trade goods as a cover for our journey. For merchandise, we selected crudely carved, inexpensive wooden images of Chaac because the carvings would not tempt thieves.

"The king of Tulúm each year sends Cobá slaves for sacrifice, dried fish, and cacao beans," Six Sky explained. "He would not dare seize Mayapán merchants during normal times, but the Flower War makes it permissible. Besides, we have more to fear from bands of thieves than we do from kings."

We left before dawn, quickening our stride to put as much distance between ourselves and any possible assassins Flint Shield might have sent to dog our trail. Tulúm was a five-day walk with porters, and we wanted to make it in four.

Only Six Sky and I bore weapons—daggers and short obsidian swords. The porters were hired from groups that hung out in the marketplace and knew nothing of our mission.

I knew little about the mission myself. Talk to a madman about which demons the gods might have unleashed upon the land?

Still, I was content to leave the city, visit new lands, and get away from the treachery of the royal court.

Exiting the city was more complicated than I had thought. Because the incident at the ceremonial center gate had enlarged my reputation, I was unable to walk the streets anonymously.

I felt sorry for the people who viewed me as a hero and a prophet. Times were desperate, and people were growing more frightened as food supplies dwindled. Farmers accused of hoarding maize to feed their families were executed, and the city-dwellers routinely rioted as the price of food went up in direct proportion to the lack of it.

People needed a savior in times of trouble, and in each retelling of my adventures, they magnified my feats many times over. As my legend grew, people came to believe I was touched—even chosen— by the gods.

I carefully covered my facial claw marks with makeup and hid my claw necklace. I awoke Six Sky in the wee hours and told him we were leaving now rather than waiting for dawn.

"Why?" he asked.

"Because His Lordship commands it," I lied.

That was enough to stop any questions, even though it wasn't exactly true. Lord Janaab had not instructed me on how to proceed other than to tell no one my purpose.

Six Sky was not privy to either the reason for the sudden trip to Tulúm or the fear that Flint Shield would avenge himself on me, but I knew he suspected why we were leaving the city under cover of darkness: I had offended the nobleman.

When Six Sky started to leave by the main door to the High Lord's palace, I stopped him because assassins would expect me to leave that way.

"We're using the back door," I said.

To his annoyed "Why?" I gave the same response—the High Lord commands it—and received the same blind obedience.

What a life the nobles led, surrounded by servants whose tended to their every whim.

"It's not safe going through the city at night," Six Sky complained. "Hungry people would murder us for a few beans."

"I'm more worried about the ones who kill for pleasure," I said under my breath.

Under ordinary circumstances, as commander of the High Lord's guards, Six Sky could have kicked me like a dog any time he felt the urge, and while he had been my constant companion since leaving the village, he was not a person in whom I could confide.

I had made no other friends. The people in the High Lord's household treated me with a mixture of awe and fear, while others sought my ruin, even my life. Not having friends made me lonely and sometimes frustrated because I could not share my thoughts. When Six Sky talked about punishing hungry people who were rioting, I wanted to point out to him that no lords would be found among those crying for food to feed their families.

Even the servants suffered from the food shortages. After Lord Janaab's lavish feasts for the city's rich and powerful, the servants previously could eat all the leftover food. Now, however, the staff's food was rationed . . . even though the guests at the feasts still gorged themselves.

Out on the dark streets, we moved quickly, and again I surprised Six Sky with another diversion.

"We are not going out the west gate of the ceremonial center and the city," I told him.

"What? The porters are meeting us at the city's west gate."

"We're not using those porters. I hired another set, ones waiting for us at the south gate."

He stared at me, his jaw hanging. He started to say something, but I turned my back on him and walked in the direction of the south gate. He grumbled under his breath but followed me.

My plan was simple: Get out of the city without being seen. Out on the open road and set as fast a pace as possible in the hope of outdistancing pursuers if I was indeed being followed.

As we passed under the torchlight of a guard's station, I saw that Six Sky's features were locked in anger. I decided the dog had been kicked enough for one morning.

"Lord Janaab has told me that there are people in our city who would like to see me dead. We're leaving the city in a way that will prevent me getting a knife in my back."

I don't know what I said that struck him as funny, but he howled behind me with laughter. Perhaps he found the notion of people wanting to murder me not so much humorous as pleasurable.

As we went by the Temple of Love, I looked to the building atop it, knowing I would not see anyone up there while it was still dark, yet having yearnings I couldn't control.

Before night fell yesterday, I sneaked out of the palace and walked around the temple, hoping to see the tall, slender figure of Sparrow among the priestesses who came out atop the temple for air or on errands. They were always fully clothed, but she would have stood out as taller than most of the others.

One of the prostitutes available almost anywhere in the city could easily have sated my lust, but I couldn't bring myself to lie in the arms of a stranger.

Even worse, knowing from personal experience that the priestesses often teamed up to give a man pleasure, I tormented myself by imagining Sparrow joining the High Priestess to make love with Flint Shield.

Eyo! . . . Obviously I deserved all the beatings Lord Janaab gave me and then some. Why else would I allow myself to be jealous of a slave girl making love to a High Lord? I was no doubt more demented than the stranger in Tulúm who talked about boats as big as palaces.

40

We met our merchandise carriers at the rendezvous grounds for porters outside the south gate of the city, and I immediately set a quick pace, telling the porters that their wages would be doubled if they were able to maintain the pace I set.

Six Sky exposed his curiosity as to why I was being sent to Tulúm again by fishing for information. He asked if I would be inspecting the inscriptions in the coastal city.

I merely grunted an evasive reply rather than tell him that I had been warned by the High Lord not to disclose the reason to him. Besides, I felt no need to give him any answer.

Eyo! I am merely a lowly stoneworker turned hero. Who am I to decide whether to tell a lie or not?

We were two hours out of the city when disaster struck: Six Sky twisted his ankle and fell. When he got up, he began hobbling.

I didn't know what to do. All my maneuvers to get out of the city and to Tulúm safely were being jeopardized.

"I'm sorry, Pakal Jaguar. You should go on without me."

I couldn't. And I cursed myself for my stupidity. The main route to Tulúm took us toward Cobá. To avoid the war zone, we had to turn off. I had not chosen porters who regularly made the

Mayapán-to-Tulúm run, but simply picked porters who appeared best able to maintain the fast pace I wanted.

I felt no loyalty to Six Sky. For a certainty, I felt none that would make me risk my life for him. I would have left him to hobble behind us, but only he knew the route we must take.

"Let's get moving," I told him.

I made a decision that at the next village we came to, I would hire porters to carry him on a litter. They would not be able to carry him as fast as I wished to move, but it would be faster than the lame pace he maintained.

Later that afternoon, a few minutes' walk from a camp where merchants gathered for mutual protection for the night, Six Sky halted us, telling me he had to relieve himself.

I was tempted to tell him that he could piss as he limped, but went ahead and told the porters to drop their loads and rest.

After Six Sky disappeared into the bushes, I paced, pondering the questions I would pose to the madman in Tulúm, when five men approaching us from the rear caught my attention.

They were dressed as porters but had no packs. Had they been at rest, that would be expected, but these men were coming down the road toward us at a quick pace. A group of porters on the road without packs was unlikely. Few porters dropped off a load without picking up another.

The second thing that caught my eye was that the lead man had a sheathed short sword and the others had spears. None had shields, because more than anything else, shields would have identified them as warriors.

I looked to my porters to tell them to get in position to fight, but they were already hurrying away, on the run down the road to the large encampment area. Each of them carried a stick to fight off thieves and wild animals, but they had had the same reaction to the oncoming men that I had: The advancing men were warriors, out for a kill.

"Six Sky!" I yelled. "Under attack!"

My companion was nowhere in sight.

I didn't dare run for fear I'd get a spear in my back. With four spears cast, at least one was likely to find its way between my shoulder blades.

The commander would be the one with the sword, and he was outpacing the others, eager to get the credit for my death.

I drew my obsidian short sword, but immediately switched it to my left hand and drew out a small wood handle with a stone tied to it. It was a hammerstone, a tool I had spent half my life using to pound a chisel. During breaks from works and rare time off, the men of the village would compete at throwing the stone tools.

I waited until the charging man was nearly to me before I let it go. He saw me getting into position to throw. He held up both arms, forearms forward, and I realized that under his clothes he had hard wood braces strapped to his forearms that would act like a shield to stop or ward off a blow.

I let the hammerstone go with all my might when he was almost atop me, not aiming for his head but for his knee. It hit his knee, pulverizing it, I'm sure. He screamed, and I sidestepped as he fell forward.

I sidestepped again, dodging a spear cast, and caught the spear thrower with a slash across his chest as he came in with a dagger.

Three more came at me. I knew it was hopeless without Six Sky, but as I engaged the front man, an arrow suddenly hit the chest of the man behind him. Then the third man let out a scream as another arrow found his throat.

The spearman I struggled with saw something behind me I didn't see and tried to break loose and run, and my sword blade caught him on his right side where his neck met his shoulder, biting deep into his flesh.

I swirled around to see who had joined the fight on my side and saw two archers: a very short, broad man, almost dwarflike, and a slender figure I took to be a woman, disappearing into the jungle.

I yelled to them, but they kept going.

The leader of the group was on the ground, screaming with pain from his broken knee. I started for him when Six Sky suddenly appeared and put his own spear into the man's back.

We stood looking at each other; the man on the ground between us had stopped his screaming to take the time to die. The spearman who had caught an arrow in his chest was dying a little slower, but much more painfully, foaming at the mouth.

"I'm sorry, I was too far away when I heard your shout," Six Sky said.

"I'm sorry, too. I was about to find out from him," I gestured at the man on the ground, "who sent him."

"No one sends these people. They're bandits."

"They're no more bandits than we are. Look at the quality of his sword."

Six Sky picked up the sword. It was a better weapon than his own.

"They're warriors. Flint Shield obviously found out I would be on the road to Tulúm. Your twisted ankle permitted them to catch up with us."

Six Sky dropped to his knees. "Forgive me, Pakal Jaguar. It is my fault. If I had watched my step—"

"It proved convenient for you to relieve yourself at the very time I was to be attacked."

Six Sky suddenly lurched up at me with the sword he had picked up from the fallen attack leader. I was expecting the movement, but he moved faster than I thought he would, and the edge of the blade grazed my abdomen.

My own blade came around and sliced off Six Sky's sword hand at the wrist. The stump sprayed blood on me as he waved it wildly as if he still gripped a sword.

He stopped waving the hand and stared stupidly, puzzled, at the bloody stump where his hand had been. He reached for the blade still in the severed hand with his left hand, and I chopped off his left hand at the wrist.

He stared up at me, his mouth agape, both hands gone.

"How much did Flint Shield pay you to lead me into a trap?" I asked.

He shook his head. "For pleasure," he said. He pitched over and fell flat on the ground, facedown.

I understood what he meant. He was not present when the guards under his command ran from the jaguar attacking Lord Janaab, but the cowardliness of his men had doomed him. He knew it would be sooner than later when the High Lord replaced him as commander of the guards and offered his blood to the priests.

I gathered clothes to change into because mine were bloodied, though my own wound was little more than a scratch. I selected the best of weapons before I dragged the bodies into the bushes and hid the other weapons.

Now I offered his blood and the blood of the others to Chaac, asking him to send rain in return for the generous blood flowing in the clearing.

I also offered blood to thank Kukulkán, the mighty Feathered Serpent, for letting me win the battle . . . and pleaded with him to permit me to win the fights to come.

41

I walked away from the scene of carnage, slipping into the jungle to hide and sleep rather than joining the rest area for porters ahead, where I would have to answer their many questions.

I had many unanswered questions myself. Not who or why I was attacked, but the identity of the two archers who came to my rescue.

Removing the arrow from one of the dead spearmen, I carefully cleaned off the bloodied tip before I examined it. From the ugly way the man had died, I was certain the tip had contained a poison.

Not many archers used a deadly poison on their arrows, though the method was well known. Using a poisoned tip made it easier to kill a man or animal because merely a graze would kill. But the poisonous tips also posed a danger to the archer himself and to others around him who might be pricked by accident.

Assassins frequently relied on poisoned arrows.

If the men sent to attack me had had poisoned weapons, I wouldn't have been surprised, but that the two who came to my aid used them as professional killers would, I found dismaying.

The woman for certain I had seen before—she was about the same size of the cloaked woman who left me the library message on the city wall, though I had not seen her face either time.

The man with his strange build would have stood out anywhere, so I doubted I had crossed his path before. He was fortunate that he was simply short and not a dwarf. Few dwarfs survive to become mature adults. Their features are so similar to that of many of our gods, they are sought after by the temples for sacrifice.

What their motives were for helping me, how they knew I would be attacked, and why they kept their presence and identities a secret was known only by the gods.

42

In the morning, I set out on the road, at a faster pace than before. My carriers were gone, probably on their way back to Mayapán. They would carry a tale of the attack, as would other travelers who found the bodies because of the stench.

I gave a message to a Mayapán-bound merchant to carry to Lord Janaab. My report to the High Lord of the attempt to murder me said little: We were attacked by Mayapán warriors, I survived, Six Sky did not.

I said nothing about Six Sky's treachery for a good reason. I was certain that it was Flint Shield who sent the attackers and enlisted Six Sky to leave me alone when the ambush would be executed. Six Sky had neither the resources nor the guile to arrange an ambush by five well-armed warriors.

If I revealed the guard commander's treachery, the assumption would be that he was responsible for the attack, leaving my enemy free to arrange another attack. I also didn't dare name the War Lord's son as being behind the attempt to kill me. But at least now, Flint Shield might hesitate to send more killers after me because my message made it clear that I was not attacked by roving bandits, but warriors from my own city.

As my only known enemy, he would be suspected of the attempt to murder me. In good times, killing me would cause him no more trouble than if he had stepped on an insect. Openly murdering the Jaguar Oracle in these bad times was not a good idea, which was why he attempted an attack far from the city.

The attack removed any doubts in my mind that Flint Sky had been rushing the ceremonial center gate to keep it open rather than to stop the attack. He didn't go through an elaborate scheme to have me murdered when I was under the protection of both a High Lord and the king just to allay his anger over my affront. Silencing me was an even better reason.

I now knew more about a powerful enemy in Mayapán and a false friend who led me into an ambush. But the revelations had come at the price of more mystery as I continued to ponder the identity of the two who had come to my rescue with poisonous arrows.

They could not have happened upon the attack and decided to throw themselves into it. The woman had to be the same one who left me the message on the wall. Besides, no one in their right mind would have stepped in to assist a single man against well-armed attackers. Had it been a random act of rescue, they would have stayed to accept my thanks and a reward.

It was no coincidence. The two had repelled the attack expertly, as if they had expected it and had been waiting for it to happen.

Waiting for it to happen.

How could they know that Lord Janaab would send me to Tulúm? Or what Flint Shield planned? Perhaps even Six Sky's treachery?

With so many complications, another thought nagged at me.

Was Flint Shield's only motive for harming me the insult that I gave him at the city gate and his fear of my exposing his treachery? Taking offense at a commoner's remark was the privilege of nobles, having them put to death was also a right they could usually exercise with impunity, but Flint Shield had been offended by me before the gate incident.

Thinking back about his actions at the temple, I was certain he had burst into the High Priestess' private chamber because he knew I was there. He had seemed a little out of breath. A man who was as strong and in as good a physical shape as he was would not have gotten out of breath simply by going up the temple steps. It would have taken more effort than that.

Had Flint Shield become angry when he went to the temple and found a commoner in the High Priestess' chamber?

Or had he been told I had entered the temple and rushed over there to confront me?

I now realized he had gone there because I had entered. The proof had been obvious, but I had ignored it: I went to the temple in the afternoon. Nobles did not go to the temple until dark, after the workday. His reason for being there that early had to be that he was told I was there.

Who told him was also apparent: Six Sky had been following me.

That meant there was a connection between Six Sky and the War Lord's son before the incident at the gate.

I mulled that one over. It wasn't probable that Flint Shield and Six Sky had a connection before my slaying of the jaguar humiliated Six Sky and made young warriors of noble descent jealous. Or was there a possible connection? Both Lord Janaab and the War Lord competed for the king's ear. Had Six Sky been in the War Lord's secret employment even before he fell out of favor when his men ran from the jaguar attack?

Regardless of whether Lord Janaab's own guard commander came to be in Flint Shield's camp before or after he fell from favor, something else about Six Sky became apparent: He also had arrived at the gate late during the invasion.

The night before I left for the gate, I had casually let Six Sky know that I would be leaving the palace earlier than usual. I deliberately did that because I knew he followed me each day, and I didn't want him to report to Lord Janaab that I had sneaked out.

Eyo! My life had become complicated since I left the task of a simple stoneworker and became a hero.

PART VIII

43

Dr. Monica Cardiff studied the men as they filed into the conference room and seated themselves at the big oblong mahogany table. President Edward Raab strolled in, wearing a custom-tailored black Brioni suit, the kind made famous by Pierce Brosnan in his James Bond films. With his craggy good looks, easy manner, and ingratiating smile, he was the most popular American president in years, and one of her best students when he was an undergrad at Berkeley in her Catastrophic Studies Program.

The man following the president in the military uniform with four gold stars blazoning his shoulders was General Richard Hagberg. His nickname was Hurricane Hagberg, and the general did move, gesture, talk, and shout like a force of nature. With a stocky, heavy-shouldered build, he had a nose like a badly busted knuckle and a grin like a tiger's smile. At first Cardiff had dismissed him as a fascist bastard and a demented moron, but then when Rita "Reets" Critchlow had been kidnapped by Apachureros in an attempt to steal the first of Quetzalcoatl's prophetic codices, General Hagberg was the one who'd ordered the special ops team into Chiapas to rescue her—in violation of international law and jeopardizing his own career.

Rita was as good a friend as Cardiff would ever have, and Cardiff realized immediately she would owe the son of a bitch forever.

Not that she found his belligerent manner and loud language any less off-putting.

Dr. Cardiff thought of Bradford Chase, a big bear of a man, who almost never smiled, as General Hagberg with brains. Former Director of the CIA's Directorate of Covert Operations, Chase was the man who had organized and run the black ops team that went into Chiapas, wiped out an entire cadre of Apachureros—the most powerful drug cartel in Central America—and saved Reets. He'd personally mounted that illegal operation to save her friend. Cardiff suspected she wouldn't like his politics any more than she liked General Hagberg's.

But now she owed him, too.

Monica Cardiff did not like owing people.

She rose and placed briefing papers on the table in front of the three men. The president's Chief of Staff had warned her she had only fifteen minutes and that she was to stick to her report—nothing else, nothing extraneous. Nor did they seem any too eager to be here. Talking softly to themselves, they were clearly preoccupied with other business.

Nodding at her, they muttered their brusque, inane greetings and sat down.

Ignoring her briefing papers, they then took out the Defense Department memos from the previous meeting, placed them over her stack, and began perusing them.

Not a good sign.

The Chief of Staff had warned her to stick to "global threats," but she could not restrain herself. "What's happened to Coop and Reets?"

They had disappeared in the wilds of Mexico three months before with a small army of Apachureros hot on their trail. They had not been heard from since, and they all feared they'd been kidnapped or killed.

"If we had something, Cards, you know we'd tell you," President Raab said.

The other two men lowered their heads and buried their faces in their Defense Department reports.

"We have to find them," Dr. Cardiff said, "for the work if nothing else. The codices they sent us clearly state that we will suffer the same disasters that obliterated the Toltecs—the greatest of all the pre-Columbian cultures—one thousand years ago. They are not only on their way to discovering the nature of that threat, they believe they'll find corroborating evidence that those cataclysms are almost upon us."

The other men, utterly entranced in their Pentagon briefing papers, treated her as if she didn't exist. Only President Raab looked her in the eye. "Cards, I told you before that you would discuss them with me in private only, not at meetings."

"Because we have a rat here, informing on them to the Mexican Mafia?"

"Monica."

Christ, the president is calling me by my first name, not Dr. Cardiff or even Cards, the nickname Reets and Coop gave me.

A very bad sign.

"That's what they said when they broke communications with us and went into hiding down there."

The president continued his mute stare. The others sank their faces even deeper into the briefing papers.

"How else could the Apachureros have known where our people would be every step of the way and where to ambush them?" Dr. Cardiff pressed on. "We were the only people who knew their itinerary and plans."

"We can't help them if they're in hiding," General Hagberg said, not even looking up from his papers, blatantly ignoring her accusation.

"They had to do it—to protect themselves from *us*. From someone *in this room*."

There. I said it.

"General Hagberg, Brad," President Raab said, "please read Dr. Cardiff's notes. They are only four pages. When I saw them, I felt them important enough to warrant an instant meeting. Read."

Now the president lowered his eyes, too, reading her report a second time.

Well, at least they were reading them.

What the hell, she turned her own eyes to her report . . . even though she'd only read it maybe twenty times already.

She had nothing else to do till they were done.

44

"A press-pulse extinction?" President Raab asked Dr. Cardiff, putting down her briefing paper and looking up at her.

"Our studies of the advanced vertebrate extinctions indicate that environmental pressure—*press* for short—had degraded the soon-to-be extinguished species so thoroughly that when the catastrophic strike, or pulse, occurred, those species were already in grave peril, if not half-dead. The extinguished species could not recover from the blow, which then annihilated countless species root-and-branch."

"There weren't any environmental pressures that knocked off the dinosaurs," General Hagberg said. "An asteroid did them in. We all know that. It hit off the Yucatán coast, the dinosaurs died, end of story."

"The K-T rock—short for *Cretaceous-Tertiary*—was only the coup de grace," Dr. Cardiff said, "the bullet in the head after the execution. Continentwide tectonic rift explosions— which included megavolcanoes erupting seriatim across their entire world—had plagued them since their inception for well over a hundred eighty million years. Cracking the continents apart and driving them halfway across the newly formed oceans, these endless volcanic detonations saturated the atmosphere with planet-killing pollutants and greenhouse gases, playing incomprehensible havoc with their climate.

"When the Bering Strait land bridge formed," President Raab said, "their crisscrossing migrations spread dinosaur plague throughout Asia, Europe, and the Americas."

"In other words," Bradford Chase said, "the dinosaurs were in an extremely weakened condition when the asteroid struck."

"We aren't facing anything like the dinosaurs faced," General Hagberg said. "Sure, it's a little warmer, but for the most part, it's media hype."

"Media hype?" Dr. Cardiff asked, a derisive smile forming on her lips.

"In fact, I think it's over," General Hagberg said. "Antarctica's glaciers are growing, if you haven't heard."

"*That* is an example of media hype," Dr. Cardiff said. "The most recent, most definitive South Pole study proves that Western Antarctica's glacial melt will single-handedly elevate global sea levels over one meter by the century's end, inundating countless oceanfront metropolises. That estimate does not factor in the deliquescence of the Greenland Ice Sheet."

It was General Hagberg's turn to give her a supercilious sneer.

"General Hagberg," President Raab said irritably, "we could still be facing the asteroid's pulse of extinction. Reets and Coop fear we could be facing the same thing, and Quetzalcoatl seems to predict that the fireball that incinerated Tula would return to raze our world."

"I still don't see the 'press' you talked about, Dr. Cardiff," General Hagberg responded. "I don't see that we're in a weakened state that renders us vulnerable to extinction."

"But we are, and we're growing weaker at a record rate. In fact, we are undergoing the fastest mass extinction in evolutionary history."

General Hagberg stared at her, incredulous.

"In the largest survey on record," Dr. Cardiff said, "seventy percent of the world's top biologists confirm that *Homo sapiens* is experiencing an extinction event of unprecedented rapidity. Previous mass exterminations required thousands, even millions of years to wreak their devastations. The Late Devonian Extinction, which destroyed seventy percent of all planetary species lasted fifteen to twenty million years. The Ordovician–Silurian Extinction, which was the second-largest event in evolutionary history, lasted ten million years. During the last half century, ninety percent of all large fishes have vanished, and one-third of all amphibians and one-quarter of all land mammals face eradication during the next thirty years, ninety percent of the lion population having already died off. *Homo sapiens* will have terminated one-half of the planet's species by the century's end.

"Those freshwater, marine, and terrestrial species not threatened are susceptible to climate change and will soon be in jeopardy, specifically thirty percent of the currently nonthreatened birds, fifty-one percent of nonthreatened corals, and forty-one percent of nonthreatened amphibians."

"And you think these codices will help us stop that destruction?" the president asked.

"The environmental pressures, which undermined the magnificent Toltec civilization, are identical to those ravaging our own, particularly that of drought. The first codex also alluded to hyperviolent events that shattered the Toltecs' world forever, and the codex suggested those catastrophes would return during our time with a vengeance. We need to know what they were and will be."

"Dr. Cardiff," Bradford Chase said, "the Toltecs were a nonindustrial society. How could they have produced enough greenhouse gases to affect their climate?"

"A supervolcanic detonation in the Pacific Ring of Fire did it for them, flooding the atmosphere with greenhouse gases, which eventually led to massive global warming. The droughts, which that climate shift produced, wiped out the Toltecs' water sources."

"Maybe in India or the Mideast," General Hagberg said, "but the U.S. is getting by just fine."

"Really?" Dr. Cardiff's sneer scintillated. "Water destruction is not only a global pandemic, it is raging through the United States."

"Look at page three of her report," President Raab said. "United States' water shortages combined with other environmental pressures are setting us up for the extinction's pulse."

General Hagberg and Brad Chase returned to her report, the section in which Dr. Cardiff described America's water crisis:

Lake Lanier, Atlanta's major water source, has almost run dry. Only unexpectedly heavy rains and a federal order—banning Atlanta from tapping into the lake for its water—saved Lanier from totally drying up. All of which leaves Atlanta desperate for a new water source. While Georgia fights the federal order in court and insists on its right to deplete Lanier, Florida and Alabama are battling Atlanta in court and attempting to save the lake.

Over thirty cities are currently suing each other over water rights.

Not that the rest of the South is any better at water conservation. Floridians have dried up countless lakes through uncontrolled groundwater pumping. South Carolinian courts have stopped that state's industrial firms from releasing wastewater into rivers plagued by low water levels. In Tennessee, one city went dry and had to truck water in from Alabama.

Nor is the North immune to water shortages. Water levels in Lake Superior, which encompasses more square miles than any of the other Great Lakes, is now too low to accommodate fully laden commercial ships, forcing them to transport partial loads, driving up costs and overhead.

"Exploding populations exacerbate the problem," President Raab said.

A yearly influx of 100,000 new residents is turning Atlanta's water shortage into a catastrophic crisis. In the last seventeen years, California's population has increased by over seven million people, not counting undocumented, unreported residents. During the next 40 years, the U.S. population will grow by over 120 million people—or one new resident every eleven seconds.

America's water shortage reduces many of the alternative energies, particularly biofuels, to absurdity. To grow enough corn to produce one gallon of ethanol requires 2,500 gallons of water. Nor is the rerouting of rivers through dams, aqueducts, and irrigation a reliable solution. The U.S. is down to 60 undammed rivers, and well-pumping is drying up our aquifers.

"No wonder we're reduced to such radical schemes as hauling Alaskan icebergs down our coasts," President Raab said, "diverting and pumping out Canada's rivers, piping water out of those Great Lakes that are still viable, desalinating seawater, recycling sewage, charging—even taxing—people for the water they consume, rationing water consumption.

"Read," President Raab said.

Hagberg, Chase, and the president returned to the briefing paper.

Drought-accelerated dust storms have blanketed the Rockies with dark, heat-absorbing dirt, melting the ice- and snow-covered slopes a full month ahead of schedule, depleting late-summer water supplies. Many of these dust storms come from hundreds of miles away. Dozens of them envelop the semiarid sections of Arizona, New Mexico, Utah, and the Colorado high plains, more than doubling the typical quantities of dust in those regions. Colorado, which is federally mandated to supply New Mexican cities— including Santa Fe and Albuquerque—with almost 40 million gallons of water per annum, may have to renege on that obligation.

Just as many renewable biofuels deplete U.S. water reserves, the opening of federal lands for alternative energy programs, such as solar collectors, wind turbines, and geothermal generators, along with thousands of miles of transmission lines across these water-starved regions, are exacerbating future dust storms.

Global warming is causing plants to blossom early. Insufficient water kills them, the rotted vegetation exposing the dehydrated soil, generating dust. Wind-whipped dust storms then suffocate the fragile ecosystems, destroying more plants, which hold the soil together, liberating more dust.

Moreover, as drought grows, our use of that water will become more inefficient. Irrigation squanders prodigious quantities of water, most of it drying up or seeping away unused. Farmers in the Texas high plains are already depleting U.S. aquifers, pumping groundwater faster than precipitation can replace it. Farmers in the region are draining 12 billion cubic meters of water out of the Ogallala Aquifer, which, stretching from Texas to South Dakota, is the biggest in North America, annually. So far they've pumped over twenty Colorado Rivers' worth of H_2O.

An arid waste, the Los Angeles basin can barely sustain a million citizens with its indigenous water sources. Stretching from Mexico to Santa Barbara—the L.A. megalopolis is already home to almost 30 million people and is growing by over 2 million per annum. Within ten years, it will swell to over 41 million . . . even as its meager water sources shrivel.

California's population during the next decade will expand from 50 million to over 75 million. Like the L.A. megalopolis, the state's farmers, fruit growers, factories, and cities are also watching their water supplies run dry.

"Still think the U.S. has no drought problems, General?" Bradford Chase asked.

"Not so bad as the rest of the world," the general grumbled, returning to the briefing paper.

"You're right about that one," Dr. Cardiff said. "As much as forty percent of the world's population is dependent on the Himalayas' glacially fed rivers, and they are disappearing at record rates. When they go, Pakistan will turn into irretrievable desert, even as India and China face mass famines of an indescribable order."

"It is only prudent to assume that wars of mass destruction will be a direct consequence of such water shortages," Bradford Chase said.

"So many of our military-diplomatic threats emanate from the Mideast," President Raab said. "What kind of water threats do we face there? Could you remind us again?"

"We will discuss the Mideast at the next meeting," Dr. Cardiff said. "Very briefly, however, Turkey's damming up of the Tigris and Euphrates rivers is diverting water supplies that Iraq and Syria desperately need. They openly proclaim they will sell Manavgat River water through the region."

"We don't have oil, fine," General Hagberg said. "We'll take your water."

"And sell it back to you," Bradford Chase said.

"Central Asia's Aral Sea—the fourth-largest inland sea on earth—is now a bone-dry desert, itself and its environs a toxic, arid waste," Dr. Cardiff said. "Dwindling water supplies will in all likelihood force Yemen to evacuate its capital, Sana'a. If so, drought will have eradicated the planet's first capital city."

"In other words, the Mideast is going to hell in a handbasket?" President Raab asked.

"I'm saving the worst for the next meeting," Dr. Cardiff said.

"I notice you didn't cover Australia," Bradford Chase said, "which has been consumed by wildfires."

"I left it out because it's so remote that it wasn't a national security concern, but Australia, too, is burning up. Water supplies for its major cities are down fifty percent, even as temperatures soar. Drought now threatens sheep, cattle, dairy, and cotton production as well as electrical power. To accommodate its shrinking water supplies, Australia will have to cut its population from twenty-one million to ten million.

"Its drought-induced water shortages have irretrievably devastated over half the country, including Victoria and the entire

Murray-Darling basin, turning Perth into a prospective ghost metropolis—the first of its kind in world history."

"You described the death of Asia's major rivers," General Hagberg said. "Anything beyond that?"

"Asia's central problem is part of a global pattern. Worldwide, water tables are plummeting from China to India to Pakistan to Iran throughout Africa to Mexico and the United States. Compounded by global warming, pandemic drought, desertification, record heat waves, and exploding populations, wasteful irrigation, and the massive overdrafting of global groundwater, the inexorable planetwide water shortage is reaching apocalyptic proportions.

"Over a billion people have little or no access to clean drinking water. Almost three billion people lack sufficient H_2O for sanitation. Only twenty percent of the world's population has access to clean water, while fifty percent have insufficient water to meet basic sanitation needs. Sewage contamination of their drinking water and the diarrhea-related diseases those conditions create soon turn their communities into virtual petri dishes—breeding grounds for disease and death."

"Meanwhile," President Raab said, "demand for clean water outstrips the planet's ability to produce it."

"And global warming gets worse annually," Dr. Cardiff said, "even though it should be the other way around. The arctic is getting less and less sunlight—due to the earth's wobbling axis—yet it is getting hotter. Arctic ice melt has elevated some oceanic regions as much as two feet this last year, and the frigid ice water has cooled, weakened, and slowed the warmwater Gulf Stream. Yet in the more than one hundred twenty years since scientists first began recording global oceanic temperatures, the seas are still the hottest on record."

"September water temperatures off the Maine coast recently reached the high seventies," General Hagberg grudgingly acknowledged. "I was there. I was stunned."

"What do you conclude?" President Raab asked Dr. Cardiff.

"*Homo sapiens* have access to less than .08 percent of the world's

H_2O, but during the next twenty years, we will require forty percent more. In ten years, the world's farmers will require almost twenty percent more water than is available if they are to feed the world."

"Anything else?" Bradford Chase asked.

"We still haven't gotten into the coming supervolcano crisis," Dr. Cardiff said, "or the real global warming threat."

"You mean more stuff about drought?" General Hagberg asked.

"No, about the seven trillion tons of methane in the seas," Dr. Cardiff said. "I believe global warming will soon liberate that greenhouse gas into our atmosphere."

"And what do you want to do with it first?" General Hagberg asked. "Convert that methane into some kind of alternative energy?"

"No, those emissions have forty-five times the greenhouse gas power of CO_2, and frankly, I fear all that methane will soon convert our world—not the other way around."

"Convert our world into what?" the general asked.

"I think it will turn Mother Earth into Planet Venus," Dr. Cardiff said. "But I will cover that scenario in my next briefing paper."

Suddenly, the president's beeper went off.

"Sorry," President Raab said. "My Chief of Staff knows not to interrupt me unless it is urgent. I have to take this call." He clicked on his BlackBerry. "Ed Raab here." The president listened a long moment, his face grave. "Yes . . . Yes . . . Yes . . ." He abruptly hung up. "Dr. Cardiff," President Raab said, "the Mexican police reported that they located your two former students in southern Chiapas. A small army of Apachureros bandits were assaulting them, and they called for and were attempting to escape in a *federal* helicopter. One of the women was spotted hanging from a landing strut, from which she fell over a hundred fifty feet into a white-water cataract leading to a chain of three precipitous waterfalls. She is presumed dead. The chopper was hit by a rocket grenade. In flames and billowing black smoke, it was last seen limping off over a remote section of rain forest. The *federales* are attempting to locate another chopper to mount a search, but it doesn't look promising. It might take another day or two to borrow one and haul it in from the nearest military base. I'm sorry, Monica. I know how much those girls mean to you."

Dr. Cardiff said nothing. After picking the papers and notes up from the conference table, she put them back in her attaché case. She got up from the table and left the room without looking back or saying good-bye.

She needed a drink.

45

Monica Cardiff finished her rocks glass of Hennessy brandy and stared into the television screen of her Georgetown apartment. As she watched Los Angeles blaze, she tried to take her mind off the almost certain demise of Reets, Cooper Jones, and their two friends. Staring absently at the burning city, she reached again for the heavy beveled glass and poured herself another two inches of Hennessy. She'd never liked L.A. much—in part because she'd been forced to live there for two long months while consulting on a global-warming disaster documentary based on one of her books. She'd found both the people and the film industry money-crazed, sex-obsessed, work-averse, and cerebrally superficial.

Still, she had not wanted L.A. to die like *this*.

Christ, the wildfires were now roaring down from the Mulholland Hills into the outskirts of Beverly Hills. The same was happening throughout much of the city. Hot torrential winds were sweeping the brushfires in the scrub hills surrounding Los Angeles down into the L.A. basin.

No, this was much more than the death of L.A. Cardiff feared she witnessed not simply a city in flames but the earth itself ablaze.

Back in the 1920s, Los Angelenos had turned their hot, dry,

earthquake-prone city into an ostensible oasis by siphoning water away from other regions and states. With this purloined water, they transformed their desert basin into a vast urban sprawl composed of millions of prefab, shake-and-bake houses and thin-walled buildings.

These flimsy wooden structures were now bursting into flames before Dr. Cardiff's eyes like the kindling they were.

A city of firewood, Dr. Cardiff thought, *with air so dirty, you could almost write your name on it.*

The transformation of the region into a major metropolitan city in just a few decades may have been the largest building project in American history—and one of the most ill planned. No one took into consideration that the metro basin and its millions of flammable homes abutted dry hills choked with brush and stunted scrub oak. This parched chaparral grew so dense that people and large animals could not penetrate it, and those hills were plagued with wildfires driven furiously by scorching Santa Ana winds.

To the twenty million people crammed into the Los Angeles basin, the Santa Anas were synonymous with terrifying fires. Started by firebugs, careless people, lightning storms, or all of the above, the searing, gale-force gusts off the Mojave Desert fanned and spread the conflagrations. These tempestuous fires then generated their own burning winds, turning brush fires into firestorms, red-hot hurricanes with greater killing power than the nuclear superfires that destroyed Hiroshima.

The current fire had begun in the desiccated scrub brush north of the Glendale hills and quickly moved toward downtown L.A., destroying tens of thousands of homes and threatening the business and government high-rises in the heart of city.

"The worst urban fire in history," the news media was calling it, but Dr. Cardiff saw it more as the Revenge of Planet Earth, whose climate *Homo sapiens* and her country in particular had sent careening downhill toward global meltdown. The evidence was all around them—shrinking ice caps, shriveling glaciers, towering tsumanis, and preternaturally powerful hurricanes—the whole apocalypse fueled by rising ocean temperatures.

My world is sinking into a sea of fire.

"The Age of the Mega-Fires" had started in 1988, with the Yellowstone forest fire. Burning through the park with unparalleled fury, it inaugurated a relentless cycle of catastrophic wildfires, each year's conflagrations worse than the last, culminating in the twenty-first century's Great Amazon Rain Forest firestorms, which threatened to alter forever the world's oxygen–carbon dioxide balance and whose greenhouse gas emissions, Cardiff believed, were burning a hole in Antarctica's ozone shield.

My God, Dr. Cardiff silently moaned, staring at her TV set, *the whole world is burning. And Reets, Coop, the boys? Where are you? Where are you?*

The whole world, Cardiff thought, *is sinking into a sea of fire, as brilliantly lit as a Viking funeral.*

PART IX

46

Flint Shield's assassins had failed to kill me, and I doubted he had a backup plan. Still I kept an eye peeled—one behind me for those who would put a dagger in my back and one in front, hoping to glimpse the two archers with the poisoned arrows.

Rather than travel alone and leave myself vulnerable to attack— either by bandits or those temple bounty hunters who kidnapped the innocent for priests lusting after blood—I hired on to shoulder loads for a merchant, replacing a porter who had gone lame.

I did not want be spotted as a warrior, and the job gave me cover— a reason to be out on the road—so I concealed my sword and dagger. I would not stand out.

Those who traversed the One-World's roads knew there were many reasons for a man to be on them. Rather than make an enemy by asking personal questions, people minded their own business and kept their own counsel.

Before I went far, I stopped and gave a personal sacrifice of blood from a nick on my leg to Xaman Ek, the God of Travelers, asking him to permit me a safe journey.

The merchant was from Tixchel, a port city on the Great Eastern

Waters. Tulúm also sat on the coast of the Great Eastern Waters, but in a different region from Tixchel.

Travelers could ask about geography, the prevalence of bandits, and other nonpersonal subjects, and my thirst for knowledge drove me to ask the merchant many questions about the great waters.

He could have transported his goods to Tulúm by water. Merchant seamen plied the coast all along the great waters—both east and west—the man from Tixhchel explained. Our region protruded out far into the water, however, and sea transport required a far longer route. Most merchants employed caravans of porters, which they viewed as both shorter and safer.

"When the Gods of Wind and Sea battle each other, they whip up the waters, often capsizing boats, consigning both men and merchandise to the eternal sea."

Fishermen also fell victim to the wrathful sea, as the gods clashed and frolicked with each other, stirring up vertiginous waves. Even though Chac Uayab Xoc, the Fish God, blessed their catches, he also ate them—when they fell into the sea and drowned.

Because of the dangers, the merchant said he used boats to transport his goods only for short distances.

"Coastal vessels range from small canoes to longboats, some as many as forty paces in length," he told me. They required years of labor—from felling the giant trees to hollowing out the compartments for rowers and goods.

I had never seen anything but the small canoes, which we used on our few rivers and lakes. I could have told him all that was about to change. I was on my way to speak to a light-skinned madman, who boasted that his people's seafaring vessels were the size of palaces.

The merchant was a learned man, who knew much not only about goods, but also about the people he encountered during his many travels.

Ajul had traveled widely and told me much about the One-

World. Like Ajul, the merchant's feet had also taken him to many places, and I plied him with questions about what he had seen.

When I speak of the One-World, I, of course, am referring to all the known world—from the Aztecs, Mixtec, Toltecs, and others to the north to the various Maya kingdoms in the south, running all the way down to Copán.

While we of the Mayapán League spoke the same language as those Maya in Palenque, Tikal, and Copán, we felt no special solidarity and were often at war with the other Mayan cities.

The Mayapán League itself, which included Uxmal and Chichén Itzá, was not unified as it had been during the time of our grandfathers. Instead, the cities were now allies in name only, with each waiting for the other to show a fatal weakness that would permit them to be attacked and conquered.

There was always talk that the Aztecs, who had subjugated most of the northern regions, would invade us. Although that had not happened, the emperor of Tenochtitlán had gained sway over the Mixtec, and now the influence of the Aztecs had grown stronger among the Maya.

Ajul said the Aztecs had not invaded, because the vast distance between the regions, and the jungle terrain, which they would have to traverse—except on the *sacbe* roads linking major cities (and they were easily sabotaged and of limited utility)—made mounting and maintaining an army so far from home unfeasible.

Also, the differences in language made it difficult to govern so large a mass of people, and the climate was inhospitable to the northerners—ours being much hotter, wetter, and swampier than in the north.

Ajul had told me other cities, such as Palenque and Uxmal, were better built and more beautiful than Mayapán, and I asked the merchant what he knew about the work of our ancestors.

"Cities like Mayapán do not compare to the great cities built by our people hundreds of years ago," he said. "Not even the great

Aztec city of Tenochtitlán compares to the greatness of Palenque and Copán."

I wanted to ask the man if he had ever encountered stories of the Dark Rift Codex in his travels, but had the wisdom to remain silent.

47

Tulúm was small compared to Mayapán but had a picturesque location that must have pleased the gods. Situated on a stony sea cliff elevated high above the countryside, its rocky ridge made Mayapán's temples and palaces seem—to approaching sailors and other travelers—even taller and more magnificent than they actually were.

The land side of the city was protected by a thick wall—taller than two men standing one atop the other's shoulders. The side facing the sea had the soaring cliffs as a natural barrier.

But grander than the city, more spectacular than any sight my eyes had set upon, were the Great Eastern Waters. Turquoise green, they were as endless as the Celestial Heavens and, I was told, as deep as the Dark Rift itself.

I had envisioned the sea to be like dark, cold cenote water or the muddy waters of a river, but the great waters were colorful and warm, as if the Sun God had specially blessed them . . . perhaps because his cave was located at their far end.

When I commented about how well protected the city seemed, the merchant told me that Tulúm was an important trading center.

"The jungles to the south of here are difficult to penetrate, so it is easier to transport goods by water. Trading canoes from up and down the coast bring goods here that are in turn transported to inland cities. A fire is kept burning atop the main temple. Its smoke directs canoes in the daytime, and at night its flames guide them through the sea rocks to a beach where they can safely spend the night on the sand."

The city's location was determined not only by the sea cliff, which offered protection on one side, but also by an unusually large cenote, which provided drinking water to the city. It had not occurred to me that the endless seawaters could not quench thirst.

"The gods made the great waters bitter so they would not have to share them with people," the merchant told me.

He also told me why Tulúm was so well defended.

"Mayapán did not build those high, thick walls to protect the salt and cacao beans brought to it. Sea vessels bring obsidian from Ixtepeque, a fire mountain far south of here. Ocean vessels transport the knives of the gods far safer and quicker than caravans do."

I parted company with the knowledgeable merchant and set out to find the master of the light-skinned slave.

I believed I was on a fool's errand—coming all this way to speak to a madman. Getting out of Mayapán, however—and out on my own for the first time in my life—had a strange affect on me. My entire life had been spent in tight proximity with others. Life in the stoneworkers' village had involved the same routine, day after day, for almost all my life: sleeping in a hut with others, eating, working under the supervision of the headman, and sleeping again, without any break in the monotonous activities except a few feast days in which we stood around and talked for a few hours instead of working.

Life at the palace had been different in the way I slept and ate, but I still did exactly what I was told. Traveling on the road to Tulúm, however, was different. I'd escaped a master's commands. For the first time I was free to think about what I would do with my life.

The freedom gave me a chance to think about myself and the world around me. I realized the life I wanted to live was that of a traveler—the sort of life Ajul had once enjoyed, experiencing the peoples and the cultures of the One-World.

That impulse had propelled me on my quest to meet the madman.

Perhaps afterwards, I could become an itinerant storyteller, wandering from village to village and the marketplaces of cities, earning my tortillas spinning the tales of heroes, kings, and gods.

A peaceful life of travel and adventure.

Until Lord Janaab caught up with me and had the skin flayed from my stomach, back, and loins and then turned me over to the priests.

48

While most exchanges were barter transactions, jade and cacoa were used to buy merchandise or services outright. Lord Janaab had given me cacoa beans and small pieces of jade with which to purchase provisions and to bribe those he wished me to question. Both were small and universally prized, with jade being the most valuable and the easiest to conceal and carry.

Finding the slave and his master was not difficult—everyone in Tulúm appeared to know of the light-skinned man. Perhaps even more than my own reputation in Mayapán, his light skin made him easy to spot and raised many questions about who—or what—he was.

When it became known I was from Mayapán, people asked me about the Jaguar Oracle, wanting to know whether he could fly on the wings of eagles and divine all things past, present, and future.

I assured them that he was indeed a master of eagles and prophecies. *Eyo!* I wish I could have sold my services as a seer to these people.

The slave-master was a salt merchant with sheds near the beach, where bags of his wares were stacked and stored after coastal boats off-loaded them. A thin man with pinched, close-set eyes and a rawhide whip looped to his wrist, he fixed me with a narrow, menacing look.

"Why do you wish to speak to my slave?" he asked.

"I'm a traveling storyteller," I said, "and have heard that the man claims to come from a strange land far from here. He will have sagas of his own people, which I would incorporate into my own repertoire of tales."

Casting myself as a harmless storyteller dispelled the man's suspicions. Also the lie had the semblance of truth to it, at least the part about my being a storyteller.

"He has learned to speak our language," the slave owner said, "but he will say words in his own language that we cannot understand. Because he might use them to beseech his own gods for deliverance or wreak retribution on his captors, I have forbidden him to utter words from his language. His name is Jeronimo, but it's not a name that can be written in our Mayan tongue." The man gave a harsh laugh. "He told me that his gods are mighty and vindictive and will someday destroy us. I said that if I heard him say that again, I would donate his flayed, sobbing carcass to the temple priests for sacrifice. I've seen him cut, and his blood is the same color as our own. The priests are eager for it anyway. They are convinced his blood is white."

An extra piece of jade convinced the slave owner that the man could utter a few words from his native tongue.

"There are others like him?"

"Only one other is alive, another man. But unlike this man, the other one has accepted our gods and married the daughter of a powerful headman. He's said to be a good warrior, too."

"What happened to the others?"

"There was a boatload of them, Jeronomo claims. They abandoned a larger boat—one that was sinking—for a smaller one, about a dozen or so, including a couple women. Many died at sea from hunger and thirst before the boat sank near land. He and some others washed up on shore. Most died from their sicknesses or were eaten by villagers who were curious as to the color and taste of their meat."

I sat in the shade of palm trees and waited to meet the madman. The image of men surviving the savage sea, however—only to wash up on an alien shore where cannibals devoured them—haunted me.

49

The meeting took place in a grove of palms near the huts where the master's trade goods were being loaded and unloaded. There, the slave kept a tally. His skin color was disconcertingly light. On rare occasions in the One-World, a baby was born with skin as white as teeth and whose eyes had a pinkish cast to them. As with dwarfs, the temple priests sacrificed the babies as special offerings to the gods.

The man named Jeronimo was not so pale as white babies, but his skin—now heavily tanned—was only a few shades lighter than mine. His owner told me that beneath the slave's loincloth, he was much, much lighter.

He was taller than I was, and I was tall for a Maya. While some men grew to greater heights than either of us, I personally had never seen anyone so tall and thin and bony. He was so gaunt, his ribs could be counted, and he had the face of a skull.

The slave master said that the man's ordeal at sea had starved and sweated the meat off the survivors who made it to shore with Jernonimo, and they had to be fattened up before they were eaten.

Seated in the palm shade, we each drank milk out of a holed coconut. I told him that if he did not answer my questions directly and honestly, I would tell his master he was the devil.

"He will have you flayed whole, then sell you to the temple priests," I said. "Do you understand what I am saying?"

I saw contempt in his eyes. "My master tells me that all the time. Still you and your fellow cannibals have not eaten me nor have your heathen priests ripped out my heart and drained my blood. I find that miraculous. I think I'll live awhile longer."

I had never witnessed such ludicrous lunacy. "Tell me about your own gods."

"There is only one god, the mighty Jehovah. We don't worship a menagerie of idiotic idols who devour their subjects like jungle animals."

"Watch your tongue, or you'll anger our gods."

"If they had the power, they would have killed me years ago."

"They have the power, and you should fear their wrath."

"I piss on your gods from a great height—like they were ants."

I gaped, speechless, petrified with terror. I had never heard such blasphemy. No one ever dared say anything like that. To even think such a foul thought would ensure the divine vengeance of our notoriously vindictive deities. "You are mad!"

He laughed hoarsely. "I know. If my endless journey on the sea had not driven me insane—the sun broiling and parching even my insides, turning them dry as salt—watching your barbaric brothers and savage sisters eat my friends alive would have completed the job."

"We are not *savages*," I hissed.

He gestured at the activity on the dock. "Look at those workers. They seem civilized. Yet they worship demented demons to whom they slaughter the innocent and in whose name they cannibalize their fellow man."

"We eat human meat only during special occasions—the flesh of our enemies after battle. The hearts of the best opposing warriors enhance our own strength and courage when eaten."

He scoffed again. "My friends, whom your compatriots devoured, were not warriors on a battlefield."

I shrugged. "Perhaps the villagers were hungry."

He leaned closer and said, "Your people are going through hard times. Your crops are failing, and your people starve. Better watch yourself on the way back to Mayapán. Your roads are awash with cannibals. You might yet end up in a pot or roasting over an open fire like a chunk of venison."

My rage was rising, and I could barely contain it. If in blind fury I killed the madman, however, I'd have to requite his master for the loss—a sum I did not possess. The master would therefore demand and receive me in the man's place.

"What is your full name?" I asked, taking a deep breath.

"Jeronimo de Aguilar. In my language, it means 'Jeronimo from Aguilar.'"

"This Aguilar, it is a place? Like Tulúm?"

"Yes, only larger."

"Where is it?"

"In an even bigger place called Spain, which lies on the other side of what you call the Great Eastern Waters."

"You are lying. There is nothing on the other side of the waters except the cave where the Sun God rests each night."

"There is no cave, and the sun is not a god. It is a ball of fire that circles the world each day. This place you call the One-World is only a tiny part of a much, much bigger world. If you got on one of our boats, you would see they are not the kinds of toys you people hollow out of trees—"

"—but are the size of a palace?" I taunted the madman.

"Bigger. The size of your puny mountains."

"Where would that boat take me?"

"If you sailed east to Spain, or west to China, you would come to lands a hundred times larger than the One-World. Because you don't have boats large enough to cross oceans, you believe that you are alone in the world. You are not alone. You and your cousins to the north who call themselves Aztecs are just a tiny part of a big world."

His ravings were the nonsense of a broken mind, but I let him ramble on so I could report them to Lord Janaab. Also he used a word from his language, *ship,* that he said meant the "giant canoes." I could tell he was struggling to translate his meaning and descriptions from his own language into ours. While I did not understand everything he said, I got the gist of it. Recalling the great lord's remark that the madman boasted of weapons that made our sharpest swords and spears puny in comparison, I asked him about the arms his warriors carried.

"Our ships have great weapons that can knock down not just your city walls, but the very cities themselves." He pointed at Tulúm above the sea wall. "Our ships can lie out beyond the range of your spears and arrows and fire weapons that would destroy all of Tulúm."

"Does your army fight with these boats alone?"

"No, most fighting takes place on land, and the ships are used to transport armies to the place where battles will be fought."

"How are your warriors themselves equipped?"

"Our warriors have armor far superior to those quilted cotton vests your fighters wear. It is a material that your spears and arrows cannot penetrate."

"What is this material?"

"It's a hard metal that comes from the ground, harder than your silver and gold."

"As hard as flint?"

"Harder—without brittleness and infinitely more resilient than flint. Imagine warriors encased in the limestone you use to make buildings. That's what our 'steel' armor is like."

"It would be so heavy, they wouldn't be able to move."

"Not the way we make the armor."

"What other weapons do you have besides this stone armor?"

"You shoot arrows. Our people have weapons that shoot a small object." He picked up a pebble. "Something like this, but made out of murderous metal."

I scoffed. "Throwing pebbles is for children."

"The pebbles our weapons fire can kill a man two thousand paces away. At close range, a single pebble shot out of what we call a *musket* can kill three men standing back to back."

I burst out laughing. "You are a storyteller like me."

"My stories are true."

"So are mine. Our gods have destroyed the world four times with weapons more powerful than you have described."

"Your gods do not exist. They are the creations of ignorant people who are unable to understand the world around them."

I leaned closer and spoke harshly. "You blaspheme more freely than temple priests spill blood. Because of your madness, the gods have not punished you, but if you keep it up, you will be painted red."

"I'm not afraid of your priests. I manage trade for a rich man who believes I bring him luck and profit. He won't turn me over to your priests until I am too old or sick to enrich him. And I do not fear these imagined creatures you call gods. There is no god of rain, of maize, of the sun, the moon, or anything else. There is one god, the mighty Jehovah, whose son, Jesus, gave his life for all of us." He leaned closer, almost spitting words at me. "He will rain fire and brimstone upon your infidel civilization because you are not believers."

"Did your god send you here?" I asked, probing to see if he would admit that his god sent him as a demon in our midst.

"I serve God in my heart, but I am not fully ordained into the priesthood, so I still serve King Carlos with my body."

"Your king sent you to spy on us," I said.

"We are conquerors, not spies. We were en route to an island, Santo Domingo, when our ship went aground near Jamaica."

"Where are these places you speak of?"

"Islands"—he gestured vaguely out at the Great Eastern Waters—"out there, too far for you to reach without a large boat with provisions."

"Why have I not heard of these places?"

"Because you're ignorant."

I held my temper, but my patience was wearing thin.

He may have sensed my mounting fury, because he tempered his words. "To be honest with you, we have not known about you for that long either. I washed up in your One-World in 1511. Nineteen years before, in 1492, Captain Cristobal Colón discovered these territories for Queen Isabella, who has since ascended into heaven, God rest her soul."

Female rulers were not unknown in the One-World, but what amazed me was that the man seemed to be claiming that the One-World belonged to her.

"Nineteen of us took to a small boat, one not much bigger than your coastal canoes. It drifted for more than two weeks before washing up on a beach on a large island down the coast from Tulúm. Only eleven of us survived the sea, and all my companions except one were devoured by your demented friends."

"What happened to your companion who survived?"

"He became a traitor to God and king. He accepted your idolatrous religion, married the daughter of a chief, and acts as if he were a son of this primitive land."

"You speak as though your warrior Colón conquered us for your now dead queen. If such an event had happened in the One-World, I would know about it."

"What Colón discovered were the islands in this sea we call the Caribbean. We have already gained dominance over those islands and the Caribs, who live there. Our people are still exploring, moving west. They will be here soon."

"Your gods are sending armies to conquer us?"

"I told you, we serve God with our hearts, and our king with our sword. My brethren will conquer you in the name of God but with weapons forged by men, not divine fire. Once you have been conquered, your pagan worship will cease, and we will raze your temples and altars."

"Why are you so certain that your warriors are superior to ours?"

"Because your weapons are so pathetically primitive."

I showed him my sword. "I could cut off your head right now. Would your god stop me?"

"God permits all people to exercise free will. He will not stop you from decapitating me, but after you die, He will burn you eternally in the fires of hell for your sins."

"Our swords have obsidian edges; our spears and arrows have tips of flint. Your big boats cannot come onto land to battle us. Before our warriors meet your warriors on the battlefield, we will ask our gods for their intervention. We will then destroy you."

"Do you know what a deer is?"

"Of course."

"Imagine an animal many times larger and more powerful than a deer, an animal with hooves that would kill you if they struck you. We call these beasts *horses*."

I repeated the word and asked if his warriors would turn these giant deer upon us.

"Encased in steel armor and bearing weapons that can kill at two thousand paces, our men will come mounted on these great beasts. No weapons known to you can stop them. They will ride over your armies, killing all that don't run like scared rabbits."

"You're mad!"

He stopped and locked eyes with me. "Why am I mad? Because I tell you there is a different world across the ocean than you know about? Because I tell you there are weapons superior to yours? Am I mad? Or are you simply ignorant?"

"You are mad."

He leaned forward and stared me in the eye. "A man makes a big mistake when he thinks he's seen everything."

I took a deep breath to control my blazing rage.

He sneered at me. "Our God is mighty, our armies invincible."

"Tell me the truth. Is this mighty god you speak of bringing destruction to the One-World? Stopping the rain so our crops wither?"

His eyes glittered with priestly fire. "The truth? The truth is that

God is punishing you for your pagan acts. Cannibalism and human sacrifice are mortal sins. He will destroy your land and scourge it from the face of the earth unless you repent and allow him into your hearts."

"When will your god come to destroy us?"

"God acts through his servants. I am one of them. Someday soon, there will be many thousands like me coming from across the sea in the great ships. Nothing in this land of yours, not your pagan gods or your primitive weapons, will be able to stop them. When your warriors are dead, your cities will be burned to rid the world of your filthy—"

I hit him. My hand flew up by itself, and I hit him across the face.

I walked away, leaving him kneeling in the palms and mumbling what I took to be a prayer to his god, Jehovah.

50

As I walked the beach, a sense of dread and impending doom chased me like a rabid dog snapping at my heels. Dark thoughts placed in my head by the strange man who called himself a "Spaniard" taunted me.

I went back to the heart of the city, knowing that I had not struck him in anger.

But in fear.

His crazed words and the mad, passionate conviction with which he spoke them frightened and panicked me. He was a lunatic. No sane man would have even imagined the strange things he spoke of. Still, he described these things with a certitude I could not deny.

And I had already encountered places and people beyond my comprehension.

A man makes a big mistake when he thinks he's seen everything, the maniac had said.

I was shaken by those words.

I could not truly disprove his statements, because I had not seen everything he had. Given my ignorant upbringing, I understood better than most. In hard truth, none of us knew the world from which he came—not our king, not our priests.

Destruction of the One-World had happened four times in the past. What he had described was another destruction of the One-World, this time by conquest.

His demented diatribes haunted me. Why? It hit me all at once: *He is intelligent.*

Jeronimo was not a raving derelict wandering the streets, begging for handouts, and taunted by children. He had mastered our language in a remarkably short time and adapted to our lifestyle. Defying our priests and refusing to accept our gods, he had still avoided the sacrificial altar and held a high position as the head accountant to a rich merchant, a task that involved dealing with many people about valuable goods.

He had also not been irrational in any way except when he talked about the land of his people. When he spoke about the treatment he and his companions received when they were washed ashore, he had been angry, but his anger was justified.

An intelligent, rational madman who spoke of the end of the One-World in a short time? An invasion of invincible warriors on giant deer, brought to our shores in canoes the size of palaces and capable of destroying cities with weapons that shot huge objects? Was that what I was to report to Lord Janaab?

On a dark, morbid, overcast day, I left Tulúm.

Still no life-giving rain fell.

51

I attached myself to a merchant with a hundred salt-porters, but their slow pace frayed my nerves. I found myself getting ahead of them even though leaving them was dangerous. Starving villagers everywhere were taking up the bandit trade.

My dark mood deepened when I heard shocking news from travelers: Cobá had won the Flower War with Mayapán when it captured the War Lord of Mayapán.

Eyo! Such a disaster had never happened before in a Flower War. Small armies of each kingdom marched onto the field, but the wars were fought not as a bloody clash between them but as scrimmages in which a few dozen on each side battled at a time. There was even a festival atmosphere, in which bets were made on whom would be a victor.

The War Lord, once a powerful warrior, had been taken prisoner, while leading a force. Cobá's king was to sacrifice him, and the warrior who captured him would eat his raw, beating heart atop the sacrificial temple.

To have a war lord fall in battle was a great defeat, almost as disastrous as the fall of the king himself.

Added to Mayapán's drought and failing crops, the Cobá victory confirmed the people's fear that the gods had spurned our kingdom and were deaf to our king's implorations.

This was no small matter. Each day, the king went to the top of the main temple and asked the gods for favors. A king whom the gods failed to favor with rain, sunshine, prosperity, and peace would lose the respect of the people.

The plots to depose him would soon proliferate.

I had no feelings for the War Lord. To me, the news meant that Flint Shield had problems other than myself to deal with—the humiliation was so vast, the king might very well order the War Lord's entire family and slaves painted red, including the warrior son.

While the War Lord's disgrace might help me fend off his son, it had another possible effect, which I would hate to see happen: utter chaos.

As a storyteller, I knew well the history of kingdoms that lose their head. Most often, the throne passed from one usurper to the next, each looting the kingdom's treasures, until a neighboring king spotted the weaknesses and invaded.

If history remained true, Mayapán would soon face chaos, which would bode ill for any of us who relied on the city for our sustenance and shelter.

Eyo! If Lord Janaab fell out of favor because the king was removed, the victor would customarily paint his family and chief aides red, then sell the rest of his servants into slavery.

I would be sold in a heartbeat.

I had outpaced the salt caravan when an arrow striking a tree a few feet from me shook me out of my meditations.

My hand went to my sword, but spotting the archer, I left the blade in its deerskin sheath.

The short, powerful stump of a man who looked like an oversized dwarf and the tall slender woman who shot arrows with murderous accuracy were on a hillock ahead of me.

The man had fired the arrow to get my attention. The man

pointed down to something at his feet, and the two of them turned, then disappeared into the brush.

I pulled the arrow out of the tree and carefully shoved the point in and out of the dirt until the green poisonous tinge disappeared. I tucked it away as a token to remind me that the archers were not figments of my imagination.

I paused at the spot where the man had pointed.

The glyph of Huehuecoyotl, Old Coyote, had been drawn in chalk on the flat side of a rock. The God of Storytelling.

Ajul had called me Old Coyote when I went to live with him and he discovered my ability to remember tales.

They had let me know that they were in contact with Ajul.

I had already made that connection, and I had a question: Did Ajul give them the information about me voluntarily—or under torture?

52

Approaching Mayapán, I saw smoke rise from the fires at every temple. The fires were fed during times of sacrifice to alert the gods that a blood feast was under way. This time it was grim evidence that the king was wreaking vengeance on those who had plotted against him. From the king's point of view, no doubt, those conspirators included rebels who had stormed the corn storage sheds for food after the corn prices had soared.

On entering the Mayapán marketplace, I asked a merchant I knew about the War Lord's family—especially his son, the celebrated young warrior, Flint Shield.

The merchant provided fine Cholula dishes and bowls to the richest homes in the city and always seemed to hear everything, not from the men running Mayapán but from their wives.

"The War Lord's son has fled the city," the merchant told me. He looked around and then spoke to me in a whisper. "They say that the War Lord's own guards were bribed to fall back and expose him during the battle."

"So he could be captured and sacrificed?" I asked.

"Killed, preferably," the merchant said. "The king found out there was another plot brewing. The War Lord planned to march the army back to Mayapán and take the throne as soon as the Flower War was over."

At the palace of the High Lord, the majordomo related more rumors while I waited for Lord Janaab to summon me to his reception chamber.

"The king suspected Flint Shield had betrayed him, and in fact, Flint Shield had allowed the king's brother to enter the ceremonial center with the warriors. Under torture, one of Flint Shield's warriors revealed the plot and implicated the War Lord's son. The priests, however, argued that the gods had punished the War Lord for his schemes against the king by having him lose his life and his reputation."

When I met with the High Lord, his sole interest was in the foreigner.

"What did the light-skinned man in Tulúm tell you?"

I chose my words carefully, uncertain what effect the man's ravings would have on the great lord. I didn't want him to punish me for the man's insane harangues.

"He says that the One-World is only a small part of an infinitely larger world."

He listened in grim silence as I laid out a reasonable rendition of what the man had said to me, easing in more of the "Spaniard's" boasts about the might of their weapons as the great lord seemed to accept the tale.

When I finished, I could see he was reacting as I had. He was disturbed, not outraged.

"Tell me your opinion of the man. Is he as completely mad as he sounds?"

I hesitated again, giving thought to what words I would choose. I started by explaining that the man gave no outward sign of madness. "To the contrary, he runs the salt merchant's business efficiently and has earned the man's complete trust."

"But how could such things be true?" Lord Janaab asked, not really expecting a response from me.

"Perhaps they are true only to him," I said. "This other world he speaks of may be just in his own mind."

He disappeared deep into thought for a while, looking past me, through me, then posed the question I feared he would ask: "Tell me, Jaguar Oracle, you who are said to have the gift of prophecy, what is your conclusion from talking to this foreigner?"

Eyo! He'd posed a dangerous question. Truth-telling is a precarious profession. A great lord could punish the prognosticator for being wrong or for speaking unpleasant truths.

"Tell me what you really believe," Lord Janaab said.

In other words, he would punish me severely if he thought I lied. With no way to dodge the truth, I gave it to him. "At first I took him to be a storyteller like myself. The stories I tell about the machinations of the gods are themselves fantastic. So are the weapons the gods had used to destroy the One-World in the past. Strange things are happening, though. There is not enough food to feed all the mouths. Sickness plagues the land. Not only are ordinary people hungry and discontent, even the king's nobles have been inflicted with a dark side." I raised my eyebrows. "I heard shocking stories in the marketplace as I passed through. About—"

He waved away my attempt to share with him the allegation about the king having arranged the death of the War Lord. "What is your conclusion about what the foreigner said about his gods?"

"The man was adamant that his people have only one god—"

"What? One god only?"

"One god and not a god of war."

"His god is impotent?"

I shook my head. "No, he says his god is all powerful. And that in the name of that god, an army of conquest, such as I described, will attack us."

"And the demons that plague us?"

"He denied our ills are due to demons."

"Do you believe this?"

"I believe our own demons vex us, causing the discontent, food shortages, and other problems we face." I leaned forward to give him what I foresaw as the future. "We have weakened ourselves so catastrophically that if a foreign army came, as he claims one will, we will not be able to fend it off."

He chewed on his lower lip for a moment and then said, "The Dark Rift Codex is at the heart of Mayapán's darkness. It prophesies our demise, and that prophecy must be rewritten." He gave me a long hard look. "I will speak to the king. I believe you are the chosen one to find it."

53

I was back in Mayapán only a few hours when I stepped out on the street to watch and listen to people. I wanted to reacquaint myself with the city, because I felt different about it than when I had left for Tulúm.

When I first entered the city, I'd just left a village of rustic stone-cutters and was in awe. But now I was more cynical. I saw instead a cauldron seething with plots and intrigues, murder and chaos, the people hungry, in panic, afraid.

I didn't know whether I had changed or whether the city had. Perhaps the simmering turmoil had always been there, and the city's sights and sounds, excess and extravagance had blinded me to the sordid reality underneath. Whatever the case, I felt as if I were seeing it with new eyes. I now realized how fragile peace and order were.

Deep in thought, I didn't realize that my feet had taken me to the entrance to the Temple of Love. A cloaked feminine figure in the doorway gestured for me to follow, bringing me back to reality. I knew from her shape that my guide wasn't Sparrow.

"Is Sparrow here?" I asked as I fell in behind the woman leading me up the narrow stairway.

She didn't answer.

We passed through the doors and entered the throne room where I had met the High Priestess and continued into her inner chamber. My guide whispered something to the High Priestess and left.

The High Priestess waited for me, reclining on a couch. She was not dressed in her ceremonial clothes, but simply, her breasts bare, a sheer skirt offering little covering below the waist.

"Join me," she said.

I sat on the couch.

"You asked about Sparrow. She's gone."

"Gone where?"

The High Priestess shrugged. "Ran away to become a nobleman's concubine. It happens once in a while, when one of my girls falls in love with a man she has entertained." She leaned closer and whispered: "Sometimes a man pays the temple, so we won't complain to the king."

I didn't believe her—or perhaps I just didn't want to believe her. What did I know about Sparrow? I lay with her once. She may have fallen in love with a wealthy merchant or nobleman, or the man may simply have purchased her. From what the High Priestess intimated, her flock of priestesses had a price.

Drawing me to her, she kissed me. "Don't worry, I will take special care of you myself."

I stared into her eyes and saw what I had pondered and puzzled over earlier but which was now clear to me. "You're Sparrow's mother," I said.

She reacted as if I had slapped her, jerking back, her eyes going wide. Leaning back, locking eyes with me, she no longer had the features of the seductive and mysterious love goddess, but those of a jungle cat.

I forced myself not to look away.

Shutting her eyes, she took a deep breath. Taking my hand, she placed it on her breasts. When I cupped their warm flesh, they became instantly aroused. "You are as everyone says of you on the streets, Pakal Jaguar. You truly have the gift of second sight."

I shook my head. "It's your eyes. When I looked into your eyes, I saw Sparrow."

She took my hand and pushed it up her skirt and into the warm flower between her legs. "You know, of course," she whispered, "that priestesses of the temple are not permitted to bear children."

I knew that, but after hearing how the women were sold to wealthy men, it was evident that everything about the temple had a price.

"A long time ago," she said, almost dreamily, as she thought back over the years, "I was a young priestess and had taken a powerful nobleman as a lover. I could have left the temple and lived as his concubine, but I wanted to succeed the High Priestess. I had become her favorite, her lover, and she promised that I would claim her position."

She stroked my cheek with her fingers. "That was why I was permitted to have the child. Because she loved me, she did not send me to the temple priests. And the child was permitted to live because the father was wealthy enough to buy its life."

"Where is Sparrow?" I asked.

"When I told you she was gone, I spoke the truth. Unlike the other girls here, who spend most of their lives within the temple, she has been outside enough to know the ways of the world."

"Where'd she go?"

"I don't know. Don't think about her. Sparrow is not for you. I have other girls who will please you more."

Her hand went around my head, and she pulled me to her succulent lips. "I can please you more than any of them."

My lips moved from hers, down her neck and to her breasts, tasting each one in turn.

She pulled my face back to hers and kissed me again, the sheer power of her sensuality firing my body. She placed a cup to my lips. "Drink," she said, "and you will walk with the gods."

I gulped down the liquid and tossed the cup aside as she pulled off her skirt.

I started to remove my shirt, but my fingers felt numb and unco-ordinated, unable to fully grasp the material.

My vision blurred over, and my ears roared.

I said something, and even I realized that the words had come out in a jumble.

A dark figure approached.

Flint Shield grinned at me.

I knew he was there, knew he was my enemy, but my arms and legs were as impotent as my tongue. I couldn't rise to strike him. I could only stare as he spoke words to the High Priestess I under-stood but could not react to.

"You better not have given him too much. He has to answer my questions."

"I gave him enough to make him malleable—nothing more."

She grabbed Flint Shield's arm. "You said you will not kill him."

"I say many things." He laughed and pushed her aside. Then he stood in front of me. "Remember how I said I would hurt you one day simply because I could? Well, that day has come."

He kicked me in the face.

PART X

54

In Cooper Jones' dream, General Richard "Hurricane" Hagberg—whom she'd come to dismiss as a demented psychopath—was water-boarding her. As he stuffed the soaking-wet rag deeper down her throat and into her nose, then inundated them with H_2O, his partner in crime, Bradford Chase—brutally bludgeoned her with a blackjack. The whole while, the two men grinned and guffawed, laughing as merrily as Hamlet's gravediggers. . . .

. . . *Those sick sadists didn't fool around. Before dumping her into the tub and filling it with blood-chilling ice water, they had hammered a pair of iPod buds into her eardrums. Ripping through her skull case, the two maniacs had buried the twin listening devices smack in the center of her temporal lobes. Pumping up the volume on Wagner's "Flight of the Valkyries" to the blasting point, they thundered that End Time anthem into Coop's neurons and synapses at warp-speed, exploding the gray matter out of her skull and up through the stratosphere. The remains of her cerebral cortex were even now, Coop believed, circling the globe in a high geosynchronous orbit. The cacophonous Wagner, combined with anoxia and water inhalation, made for a hell of a crescendo—a thermonuclear Götterdämmerung, fulminating fire, brimstone, apocalypse, Armageddon.*

Her skull, chest, groin, legs, toes throbbed from the blackjack beating. Her brain and lungs blazed from water inhalation and oxygen depriva- tion. Her entire corpus was ballooning into one spectacularly livid bruise.

At last, that deranged degenerate of a general lifted her head out of the frigid, ice-packed liquid.

Opening her blinking eyes, she vomited out enough aqua to sink the USS *Nimitz*, looked around at the big steel tub and the chamber of horrors in which those cackling cretins tormented her, and—and—

Christ, I'm not in a tub at all!

She was soaring through snowmelt-swollen white-water rapids.

Her ears detonated now—not with Wagnerian thunder but with the deafening din of an approaching waterfall, the river propelling her so swiftly, she could not even hide beneath its surface and pass out. It rocketed her toward that abyss as if she were an inflatable flotation device, not a barely conscious, water-puking, pain-racked thing.

She was less than a hundred feet from its edge and catching ran- dom glimpses of her imminent doom. She was hurtling toward three consecutive falls, each at least ten stories high. Reaching the brink, she instinctively pulled her legs up into a fetal position and strug- gled to conjure visions of the mother she never knew.

All that came to her was an image of her redneck daddy with a sweeping gunfighter's mustache, wearing a black slouch hat and a matching frock coat, raising a jug of moonshine to his lips, the butt- stock of his trusty 8-gauge pump braced on his hip.

And then she flashed to Reets.

Good-bye, Reets.

Legs up tight, hands locked under her knees, she dropped toward the bottom of the first waterfall, her butt pointed down.

At the last second, she realized her legs were also protecting the codex and its urn, still in her knapsack, which was somehow mirac- ulously strapped to her chest.

She grabbed her legs even tighter.

Vanishing into the mist below, she hit that foam-filled cauldron like a hell-bent death star rocketing toward the earth from beyond time and space.

Again, the darkness closed.

55

Once more, the dream.

In this one, Cooper Jones soared. Arms tight at her sides, she slipped the surly bonds of earth. Skydiving through the clouds with godlike grandeur, she screamed at the top of her lungs: "Free at last, thank God, I'm free at last."

Liberated from earth and from care, she frolicked with twin bald eagles, which continually circled her in ever-tightening spirals. The male wheeled near her now—almost close enough for her to touch—his white glistening nape, arched beak, blazing raptor's eyes, and eight-foot wing span gorgeous as any angel's. Coop focused fanatically on him and his mate, on the heavens and the clouds, on anything in the sky that kept her mind off the world below. She knew the eagles and the clouds to be her natural soul mates, her true home and habitat. She ignored at all costs contemplating the benighted land below.

There, dragons lurked.

Still, she could not avoid fleeting glimpses of Planet Earth rising up to meet her. The river, in fact, grew horrifically huge with each passing glance.

Still, her brother and sister eagles—not wishing her to return—shrieked in her ear: "Don't pull the rip cord. Stay with us forever in the clouds and the sun."

Somewhere, however, deep in her brain, she knew that was madness. She had to open the chute. Even as every nerve in her body howled, "No!" she reached for the cord, yanked it, and—and—

And—

Nothing happened.

Except that the river was now shockingly immense. In fact, it seemed to double its size almost by the second. Her landing zone, she could now see, was going to be a tremendous pine tree, its long, heavily needled boughs thick as a man's arm.

Oh Christ, this is going to hurt.

Crashing through its massive limbs—breaking at least fifty of them on the way down—she felt as if her entire body had been run through a hammer mill.

She landed next to the stump on a soft bed of green deadfall like a bloody bag of rocks. Rolling over onto her back, she—she—

She—

She was on her back under a tree, but she saw no broken boughs, and instead of a soft bed of pine needles and dead limbs, she was sprawled supine on a rock-strewn, gravel-packed stream bank, vomiting river water out of her nose and mouth.

Ah hell, she hadn't soared with eagles at all but had been swept over cataracts and falls like a busted-up spar.

Lifting her head, she attempted to survey her surroundings, glancing first at her feet.

She was sorry she had.

Instead of ten toes, she stared into the vertically spiked pupils of an amber-eyed jaguar—the biggest one she'd ever heard of, let alone seen. From hind flanks to tip of nose, the tom stood four feet tall and over six feet long, his switching snakelike tail adding three more feet to his imposing length. Jaguars are rare, but this one had few peers—it was a sacred white beast, so pale that even its claws were pearl white.

The jaguar's favorite killing method was to shatter the skulls of its victims with a single bite, its jaws powerful enough to crack turtle shells—one of the cat's favorite snacks.

Even so, Cooper Jones did not find his gaze intimidating. Instead his eyes seemed . . . curious.

In fact, Cooper Jones found his eyes strangely . . . relaxing.

The cat seemed to feel the same way. Sidling up alongside her, he dropped belly-down on Coop's right—between her and the pine—purring, paws folded beneath his chest, his eyes still locked on hers.

Ah, what the hell? Coop thought grimly. *In the destructive element immerse.*

Rolling over onto her back, she stared up at the pine boughs above her and prepared to meditate on the meaning of life.

Instead she was now staring at something far more ominous than thick heavy branches. Ten feet above her, *Eunectes murinus*—the dreaded anaconda—was coiled around the trunk on twenty or so stout limbs. Olive green, its gargantuan twenty-five-foot body was overlaid with black blotches striped yellow-orange on each side. Compared to its body—which was at least ten inches in diameter— its surprisingly narrow head featured high-set eyes that bore into her own with an almost surreal fixity of purpose.

Still, the gaze was not disconcerting. Bright shimmering yellow, the anaconda's upwardly pointed pupils studied her without malice or menace. If anything, the big snake seemed pleased at her pres- ence. The eyes almost seemed to ask if she needed help.

Weirder still, a bald eagle perched next to him on a broad limb, the biggest, fiercest-looking bird she'd ever seen.

Yet even his eyes were nonthreatening, almost . . . kind.

Nonetheless, she wondered if she should break for the river. That was probably not a good idea, since jaguars and anacondas were both superb swimmers, the latter capable of shooting through streams like aquatic lightning bolts. If either animal got hungry, she'd be theirs for the asking in the drink.

In any event, the jaguar—whose purr motor now hummed and thrummed like a finely tuned racing engine—clearly did not want her to leave.

Still, she glanced at the river—only a few feet to her left—just in case her situation took a turn for the worse, and she needed a hasty exit.

She was again sorry she had turned her head.

Slithering toward her out of the water was a sixteen-foot green-ish brown crocodile with a spectacularly long tail and narrow jaws, its exposed fangs glaring grotesquely in the afternoon sun.

Oh Christ, Coop, you're in for it now.

Crocodiles were snakes—fast in warm weather, and right now even dripping wet, it was hotter on that riverbank than the hinges of hell. In the water, the croc could also rocket toward her like a high-tech torpedo locking on to a sub. Moreover, the croc's bite was preternaturally powerful—six times stronger than that of a great white shark—all of which meant the river was out of the question.

He trundled halfway up the riverbank, dropped his snout six inches from her pain-racked ribs, then lowered his belly into the shallow shorewater. He observed her with casual insouciance, his stare empty as void, meaningless as the Martian moons.

But not . . . not . . . not . . . *unfriendly.*

What is it with these sissy killers, anyway? She wondered, *Whatever happened to "nature, red in tooth and claw"?*

A jaguar lying on her right, a croc on her left, an anaconda and an eagle overhead—they acted more like brothers-through-blood, as if they were totemic protectors, her secret sharers, her spirit guides.

Who were they?

What was going on?

What did they want?

Let the jaguar lie down with the lamb? Let the child sleep under the anaconda's tree? Let the woman soar with the ravenous raptor and kick back with the bloodthirsty croc? she thought, grimly parodying Isaiah's verses on the "peaceable kingdom."

Exhausted, surrounded by Mexico's most lethal killers, she realized she had no place else to go. Miraculously unharmed, the codex urn was still in its knapsack, so lying on her back, she tried to focus her eyes on the tree trunk. There was no getting away from the ferocious foursome above her and at her sides. The croc even blocked her egress to the river.

She was about to throw her head back and ask the heavens: *Why me?*

—when she heard the baying of the hounds and the shouting of the men.

She knew in her soul who they were: *The infamous Apachureros—the "Breakers of Bones."* Mexico's most feared narco-killers were back on her trail, this time tracking her scent with bloodhounds.

Time to haul ass, Coop said. *No rest for the wicked, little girl.*

Pulling herself to her feet, she painfully headed up the riverbank. Around the next bend she spotted a small creek, which branched sharply to the right. Frightened of the howling dogs on her back trail, she jogged toward the tiny tributary.

Reaching it, she immediately waded into its center. Heading upstream, she was determined to stay on the random rocks dotting the shallow brook like stepping stones. She hoped and prayed she would not leave tracks and that the water would cover her scent and that it would throw off the dogs.

Glancing over her shoulder, she noted to her amazement that the croc and the anaconda were following her up the stream with the jaguar wading right behind them.

Again, she threw back her head to once again ask the eternal question: *Why me?*

—when to her dismay, she saw the bald eagle circling overhead.

Are these beasts planning to eat me after all?

Apparently not.

The croc and the anaconda shot past her on their way upcreek.

Then the jaguar raced past her.

Then the eagle rocketed out of sight.
They were taking off like bats out of hell.
Or rats deserting a sinking ship.
What the hell is going on?

PART XI

56

Two of Flint Shield's warriors dragged me by the feet to the temple's inner sanctum. At first I felt nothing but the sheer helplessness that the High Priestess's nectar had induced. It wasn't until my head banged along the steps that I first experienced pain.

Pain is good.

I needed something to snap me out of the mind-numbing, strength-robbing drug the High Priestess had plied me with. Pain told me I was alive. Maybe it even intimated I could fight back. But my arms and legs still felt numb, disembodied.

I heard the High Priestess arguing with Flint Shield, then crying out with pain. He hit her and told her to shut up.

"He knows where the codex is. I'll be gone from your temple as soon as he tells me what he knows."

Why the High Priestess thought Flint Shield would only question me and then let me go was puzzling. Did she think he would leave me alive to sound the alarm that he was still in the city?

In the middle of the room was a fire encircled by rocks. I smelled the smoke, felt the heat. Then I heard a muffled agonizing moan and smelled burning flesh.

Turning my head, I saw the source of the moans and of the stink.

The Master of the Library was lying on the floor not far from me, his mouth gagged. The smell came from his feet. They were roasting in the fire.

"What has he told you?" Flint Shield asked the man tending the fire.

"Nothing. He says he doesn't know where the codex is; he just keeps saying Jeweled Skull knows."

"Did you ask him about this fool?" He kicked me to leave no doubt whom he meant.

"He said he doesn't believe Pakal Jaguar knows where the codex is located."

"Pull his feet out—he won't be feeling any pain in them by now. I'll put our oracle's feet to the flames, and if the librarian is still alive after I'm through, their heads will go into the fire next—to make sure they've told me everything."

I took deep breaths and begged Kukulkán to give me back my mind and strength. I began to imagine that I was back in the village of stonecutters, where I was the strongest man in the village with powerful muscles that could lift a stone slab that no two other men could raise.

My fellow workers would stand back and chant until I lifted the piece that we needed, and then would break into cheers and laughter.

Once a year on a festival day, there would be a contest of strength, and I had won it from the time I was eighteen years old.

I lifted the heaviest pieces only by reaching deep down into myself and asking the gods for assistance.

That was what I needed now—a helping hand from the gods, fueling my weakened arms and legs.

Flint Shield let out a yell of surprise. "Are you insane? You almost cut me!"

"You promised not to kill him," the High Priestess said, waving an obsidian dagger. "He's protected by the gods."

"Get out of here, you stupid old woman." Ripping the dagger out of her fist, he began to drag her out of the room. "Put his feet in the fire!" he yelled back to the man who tended the fire.

The man reached down and grabbed both my feet. I jerked my right foot out of his grasp, cocked it back, and slammed it into his chest. He flew backwards into the fire himself.

I rose dizzily to my feet, the room swirling around me, but my strength returning. The two men who had dragged me into the room were grappling with me, and I threw one against a wall. The rage, which burned in me now, fueled my strength. I grabbed the second man by the throat and lifted him off his feet. Stepping forward, I rammed his head into the wall. When I heard his skull crack, I let him go, and he slid down the wall, leaving a bloody streak all the way to the floor.

The door, through which Flint Shield had dragged the High Priestess, flew open, and he stepped in, a bloody blade in his hand. I grabbed a dagger dropped on the floor by the man I'd battered and went for the War Lord's son. He stepped back through the door, slamming it. I heard a bar drop into place on the other side as I threw myself against it, but the door held.

Still in a rage, I slammed into it again and again until I broke through and found myself in another almost bare room. The High Priestess was on the floor in a gathering pool of blood, her throat cut.

As I reentered the room, which Flint Shield had converted into a torture chamber, the man who had tended the fire rushed me. I kicked him in the stomach and smashed him across the head with my elbow. He went down, and I dragged him to the fire and pushed his face into the hot ashes, leaving him screaming and convulsively jerking on the floor.

The blind old man was breathing shallowly as I knelt beside him. "It's me, Pakal Jaguar."

He grabbed my arm with a shaky hand. "I told them nothing."

"It's all right," I said.

He spoke again, so low, I had to bend down with my ear almost to his lips to hear him. "Tell Jeweled Skull that his old friend told them nothing."

"I will tell him," I said.

His mind slipped away, and he talked to someone, maybe Jeweled Skull, about artwork in some long-forgotten codex. His mind was gone, and there was nothing of life left in him save suffering.

I gently cradled the old man in my arms for a moment. "I'll buy you a yellow dog," I told him, "to guide you through Xibalba."

I slipped my arm around his neck and squeezed until all life was gone from him.

Flint Shield's fire-tender was still moaning. I stamped on the back of his neck until he stopped squirming.

The man whose skull I had cracked was dead, but the third man was still alive. He was getting up, and I battered him back down.

"Tell me where Flint Shield hides," I said.

He tried to fight back, and I pounded his head on the floor for a moment and asked the question again.

"A different place each night," he said.

"That's an unfortunate answer for you," I said. "You might have lived if you had helped me find him."

I cut his throat and went looking for Sparrow.

I went through the innards of the temple, kicking doors open, shouting at terrified priestesses.

"Where's Sparrow?" I demanded over and over.

I received nothing but fearful replies that they did not know.

"The High Priestess," one of the priestesses asked, "is she all right?"

"She died bravely," I said, "protecting my life. How long has Sparrow been gone?"

"For days."

"Was she taken by a man?"

"No, she left on her own. The High Priestess let her come and go, while none of the rest of us could. I don't know why."

The reason was that Sparrow was her daughter, but I said nothing.

And I didn't believe the High Priestess when she said that Sparrow had left with a man.

I got out of the temple as news of the trouble within was spreading.

57

The captain of the king's guard was waiting for me at the entrance to the great lord's palace.

"The king commands your presence," he said.

"May I tell Lord Janaab?"

"He is already with the king."

Before my journey to Tulúm, I had twice entertained guests at a royal feast with stories. My impression of the king was that he was a short, sullenly ill-tempered man, but perhaps with his own brothers and nobles wanting his throne, he didn't have much to be cheerful about.

I waited in the great hall with two guards while the guards' captain went to find Lord Janaab. As had been my habit, my face was colored to hide my claw scars, and the claw necklace was tucked inside my shirt. I was glad I didn't attract attention because much of the conversation buzzing about the room concerned the events at the temple. Everyone wondered what had happened.

My master came and took me to a quiet corner where we would not be overheard.

"Quickly, tell me what happened at the Temple of Love."

"Flint Shield set a trap for me. He planned to torture me to get the location of the codex."

I told him everything. He dismissed the death of the librarian as insignificant. When I told him that the High Priestess had first entrapped but then attempted to save me, he cut me short.

"She was finished anyway. She knew it. She had been plotting with the War Lord and his son, using her body and those of her priestesses to get information for them and to persuade potential allies to betray the king. The king would have accused her of crimes and had her painted red."

An official pulled Lord Janaab aside. He still had not told me why we were meeting at the royal palace. Was I to be punished for not killing or capturing Flint Shield?

After a whispered conversation, the great lord returned to me. "We are meeting with the king privately rather than in his public reception room. When we enter, I will bow, but you will kneel and look to the floor. Do not look up until he commands you. Do not speak unless he indicates he wishes you to say something. Do you understand?"

"Yes, my lord."

I doubted that he would speak to me in private to learn the details of the fight I had with Flint Shield. That, too, Lord Janaab could explain. My instincts told me the discussion was going to be about the Dark Rift Codex.

Eyo! I had nearly been murdered twice over; others had been killed in my presence, and still I knew little about the legendary book. But how was I to explain that to the king?

With plots to kill and dethrone him swirling around him like flies around droppings, he would frown on the fact the indispensable Dark Rift Codex was still lost.

Escorted by the captain of the guards, we passed through the great reception public hall, a room many times larger than Lord Janaab's own reception area. The guard captain led us through a series of hallways that were easily barred. The route was puzzling until I realized that it was designed to slow down attackers who rushed from the public area to the king's inner chambers.

We entered an opulently decorated chamber where the king sat on a jaguar throne. Unlike the stone throne on which the High Priestess sat, this one was made entirely from pieces of jade.

It had to be one of many thrones he had. The value of each must have been worth more than this poor, stupid villager had imagined all the treasures of the One-World to be worth.

It also occurred to me that he could buy maize for all the hungry in his kingdom for the value of just one of his thrones.

On the wall behind him was also something rare and prized: the hide of a white jaguar.

Lord Janaab bowed, and I dropped to my knees.

"Stand up, Pakal Jaguar."

I rose and looked up at the king. Beside him stood a thin, hatchet-faced adviser.

I had seen the man going from the royal palace to the observatory. He was the king's stargazer, an astronomer who divined the Star God's will.

The astronomer stared at me intently, like a buzzard eyeing a piece of bloody meat.

"Tell me what you know about the Dark Rift Codex," the king said. "Speak of everything you have heard. Leave out nothing. Do you understand?"

I understood. I started at the beginning, carefully repeating every conversation I had had with Lord Janaab, certain that the king was already aware of them.

When I was done, he confirmed it.

"You disappoint me. Everything you have told me, I have already heard. I believe you know more, but you withhold it from me. You don't want me to harbor such opinions."

He was telling me that if he didn't like my response, he would have me put to the question in his torture chamber.

"I know nothing more about the book."

"Jeweled Skull treated you as his son and heir to his storytelling, yet you deny that he told you about the most important legend that ever existed? Is this what you want me to believe?"

I didn't dare share with him what Jeweled Skull had told me, not after lying to Lord Janaab.

"It is true," I said.

"What do you say, Lord Janaab? Does he speak the truth?"

"He was put to the question and never faltered," my master said.

Ha! What else could he say? That his servant was a lying bastard he couldn't get the truth from?

The king looked at me for a long moment. "They say you are an oracle, Pakal Jaguar. If you are one, can you tell me how a war with Cobá would fare if I warred against them?"

The astronomer at his side visibly flinched at the question, and I realized I was having another snake shoved in my face.

The king was planning a real war, not just a Flower War, to avenge the humiliation suffered by the War Lord being captured and sacrificed. It was a smart move because the war would distract people from the problems the kingdom faced and distract his enemies from their plots against him.

Short of a complete debacle, it was a good political move.

But I said nothing of these thoughts. "I am not an oracle, my king, despite what I have heard about myself on the streets. I do not speak to the gods or know their wishes or how they would react to the things we do."

"Then how do you explain what is said about you?"

I didn't dare volunteer that people in his kingdom were so desperate, they called me a soothsayer because they sought someone who could tell them what the future held. "I am observant. I see things because I look."

"Tell me about something you see in this room. Not a thing that is obvious."

"The white jaguar, my king."

"What about the white jaguar?"

"It's not the one I killed."

"How do you know that?"

"Because it has all its claws. And the one I killed is missing this one." I pulled the necklace out from my shirt.

He nodded with approval, and the astronomer bent down and whispered in his ear. The king called Lord Janaab to him, and the whispering continued.

I was still tense as I awaited whatever decisions or machinations were being discussed. Was I to be rewarded or punished? Allowed to live or tortured unto death?

The whispering ended, and the king spoke. "The Dark Rift is a book of fates, but it is a very special one. We all know that books of fate are consulted by soothsayers to divine what the gods have determined to be the destiny of a person. The Dark Rift Codex does not foretell the destiny of a person, but of the One-World itself."

I was shocked, and I'm sure that it showed on my face. "How can that be?"

"It can be because that's what the gods have ordained. Story-teller, you know that the gods have broken the One-World on the Wheel of Time four times in the past. The secret contained in the Dark Rift tells what will happen to the One-World in the future."

I didn't dare ask him why he was so desperate to know. Perhaps he thought that if he knew what would happen and when, he could convince the gods to change their minds. Or if the roof was going to collapse, he could move out from under it.

Regardless of his motives, knowledge was power.

"You are going to get the codex for me."

58

Lord Janaab explained more about the task given me as we walked back to his palace. "No one knows how old the Dark Rift is," he told me. "As with all our history, it was at one point recorded in a book. Whether that happened once or many times, we don't know. What we do know is that the great god-king of Tula, Quetzalcoatl, set out to gather at Tula all the knowledge of One-World.

"Tula was conquered and destroyed by the Aztecs after the Feathered Serpent left in disgrace and came to our land to build a new empire with Chichén Itzá at its core."

"Had the codex been kept in the royal library at Tula," I said, "it would have been destroyed or taken by the Aztecs."

"The legend is that before the city fell to the Aztecs, the codex was hidden by a scholar."

"That's a story I have never heard."

"Few people have heard it, even storytellers, because even the existence of the codex has been hidden by members of a secret society over the ages. That knowledge is passed down from generation to generation by members of the society to a few they choose."

He stopped, and his eyes searched my features as if searching for lies and deception.

"Jeweled Skull is a member of the group. You are the person he chose to pass the secret on to."

59

In the palace we sat in the shade in the courtyard, where servants served cool fruit drinks and stared at me, wondering why I was once again getting special treatment.

The last time the great lord granted me such privileges, he had shoved a snake in my face.

This time a secret society was sending me on a mission that I did not understand but which I was sure boded ill.

I wanted to explain that I was just a simple village stoneworker—that the existence of a codex going back to the time of nameless ancestors whose own existence has been wiped away by the winds over the eons was beyond my comprehension.

Proclaiming innocence would only persuade him I was lying.

"Why do you believe I have been chosen?" I asked. "Is it because you believe that Ajul—Jeweled Skull—is a member and that I lived with him for part of my life? I can assure you he never told me about a society or the location of the Dark Rift Codex."

"Jeweled Skull was a member. The discovery that he knew where the codex was hidden and refused to tell the king is what sent him into hiding in your village."

"He told you that he knew where it's hidden?"

"The members of the society are fanatics who reveal nothing, not even under torture. But what they won't say when put to the question with fire, they often tell when under the influence of a beautiful woman and a potion that robs them of their senses."

Eyo! I understood. The High Priestess had been Ajul's lover. She had gotten him to reveal something by giving him the elixir that robbed men of their senses. The potion did not take all my senses, but he had a smaller body than I, and perhaps it affected him more.

The great lord read my mind. "Yes, just as she was going to loosen your tongue with her wiles and drink, she had done the same to Jeweled Skull. You are fortunate that Flint Shield was in too much of a hurry to wait for her to gently extract from you what he wanted to know. He could have waited until her chicanery worked and then cut your throat when she was finished."

"In the end, she saved me."

He shrugged off her deed. "He most likely coerced her assistance. She was not a stupid woman. She knew Flint Shield was finished and that her complicity would come to light. If she could learn the whereabouts of the codex, she probably figured she could leverage the book for leniency.

"She was not the High Priestess when she drew information from Jeweled Skull, but she was ambitious. He fell in love with her, and she used her lust for power and position to draw enough out of him to confirm the king's suspicions that Jeweled Skull knew where the codex was hidden."

"What did Jeweled Skull actually reveal to the High Priestess?" I asked. "Not the location of the codex. They still do not know where it is hidden."

"As soon as he recovered his senses, he vanished. But the king never gave up trying to find him. For years there was no word of him; then someone would recognize him. The king sent me, but he would leave before our warriors arrived."

"That's why he left my village? He realized that someone had sighted him?"

"Yes. A merchant saw him and boasted when he returned to Mayapán that he had seen Jeweled Skull. I don't know all the details—my father was still High Lord, and I was not an adviser to the king back then. I have been told that the king sent someone to your village who had known Jeweled Skull to see if it was truly him. The man reported the death, and the king realized Jeweled Skull had simply moved on again."

He paused and eyed me again narrowly. "No one reported that he had in essence adopted a son. Had your relationship with him been known back then, you would have been put to the question."

"And then painted red?" I asked, knowing the answer.

"There wouldn't have been enough of you left to drain blood from." He leaned forward and locked eyes with me. "Remember that. And don't think that when you leave Mayapán you will be free to vanish as Jeweled Skull did. We will hunt you down, and before we're through, you will beg us to kill you."

I sipped juice and kept my eyes averted. I didn't want to raise his already suspicious attitude about my loyalty and inspire him to give me a beating to ensure my continued obedience.

"The blind librarian? Was he also a member of the cabal guarding the secret of the Dark Rift?"

He shook his head. "No. He may have known it existed, but he was not part of it. Little information was obtained from him when he was put to the question years ago, not even when he was told he would be blinded."

I didn't realize that was how he had lost his sight. The picture he drew of a war lord must have been the excuse he told others.

"Tomorrow you will leave for Tenochtitlán."

"What?" That surprised me. "I'm being sent to the Aztec capital?"

"The secret to where the codex is hidden is there."

"In the emperor's library?" It was a guess on my part.

"The Aztecs still have everything they stole that bears the mark of Tula on it, because they treasure it. After they conquered the city, those who could even took Toltec wives for the prestige and to infuse Toltec blood into their children."

"They admired the Toltec?"

"Like a starved, beaten dog watching its master eat raw meat, the Aztecs stared at the Toltec capital blinded by their lust for the treasures and the knowledge within the city walls. And the Toltec kings after Quetzalcoatl handled the barbarian horde badly. Instead of keeping them outside their walls as the Toltecs dissolved into internal fighting over the throne, they invited the hungry dog in, hiring Aztecs as mercenaries to fight their internal disputes and foreign wars.

"The Toltec leaders who succeeded Quetzalcoatl were fools who grew fat and lazy. Worse, they became enthralled with their own cleverness. To rely upon the Aztecs to fight their battles—to literally invite hungry beasts into your home to watch you gorge yourself— was the height of stupidity and went against everything that the Feathered Serpent had stood for. While he was king, the Aztecs were kept at bay, like the rabid dogs they were."

The picture Lord Janaab painted for me about the Aztecs was a new one to me. I knew little about them not just because I was Mayan, but also because they did not appear to have the great number of legends we had. I said that to him, and he explained why.

"When the Aztecs conquered Tula, they were still wandering tribes of half-naked barbarians with dirt between their toes. They had no great cities, no great temples, no architecture of note, no art in terms of books or inscriptions that were significant. They were a people without high culture, but with something even more important—they were militant. They fought like people who had nothing to lose because that was their state.

"When Tula burned, they took everything they could as loot. Unfortunately, they were ignorant savages, and at the time, books were less valuable than sandals. They burned books to cook their newfound supplies of food, which is why the answer to your question as to whether the codex found its way from the royal library at Tula to the one in the Aztec capital of Tenochtitlán is no."

I found his statement that they burned the great library at Tula astonishing. "Are you certain that they didn't burn the codex when they destroyed the rest of the library?"

"The legend, which Jeweled Skull knew well and freely related, was that the codex was hidden before the city fell to the Aztecs."

"Did he say where it was hidden?"

"No. And I'm not sure he knows. To make it more difficult for anyone to discover the hiding place, not all the members of the society know the exact location of the book. Membership in the society is passed down, and the secret is passed to a chosen one."

"Then how am I to find the book?"

"We don't know where the book is, but we do know who can tell you. Have you ever heard of Huemac the Hermit?"

"I've heard the name." I didn't mention that Ajul cited him one night during a drunken talk about the Dark Rift. "An oracle of some sort."

"Yes. He's said to be Toltec. And no one knows how old he is. Some say he worked in the royal library at Tula when Quetzalcoatl was king."

He laughed at my look of surprise.

"That would make him over five hundred years old," I said. "Can he really be that old?"

He shrugged. "We don't know or care how old he is. Like the soaring eagle you were supposed to have jumped down from onto the jaguar's back, the deeds of heroes grow in the telling. What is important is that we are sure he knows where the codex is."

"Is that what Jeweled Skull told the High Priestess?"

"It's what we know not from the members of the society but from their messages. The members are willing to die under torture to keep from exposing their secret, but over the years, communications sent by ordinary messengers have been intercepted. One directed to the Hermit was intercepted recently."

"Why don't you just get the information from him?"

I didn't elaborate by pointing out that torture and mind-breaking potions had been used in the past.

"He is in Aztec territory, under the protection of the emperor Montezuma. The emperor respects and even fears the old man. He believes the Hermit walks and talks with the gods. Montezuma would go to war if he found out we have considered cutting even a toenail off his pet."

Which meant, of course, that torturing the information out of the old man had been considered but rejected as too risky.

"Do the Aztecs think he knows where the codex is?"

"No. If they did, they would have it and let the world know it is theirs. We just learned about the Hermit's involvement recently."

"Wouldn't it be the best course to work with the Aztecs?" I asked. "Certainly they must be interested in discovering the codex themselves."

"The Aztecs are not our friends. They are no one's friend. Worse, they can't be trusted. I told you, when we had a high, flowering civilization, they were barbaric savages, and they still have the blood of savages in them. They don't think like we do. They will shake your hand one moment and cut your throat the next if it is to their advantage."

In other words, they would keep the Dark Rift Codex for themselves—exactly what our king planned to do.

Eyo! I didn't volunteer that observation, either.

"Besides, the Hermit is said to be old and fragile and ready for the journey through Mictlan, the Aztec underworld. He wouldn't survive torture long enough for us to draw an answer from him."

"I can't get to him if he's in the emperor's palace—"

"He lives in a cave, and the location is kept secret. Amazingly, when the emperor wishes to consult him, he goes to the cave rather than disturbing the old man."

Lord Janaab shook his head and rolled his eyes after he told me that. "Can you imagine that?" he asked. "The emperor of the most powerful nation in the One-World, who receives tribute from other kings, leaves his palace and goes to the cave of a recluse begging advice like a mendicant."

I couldn't imagine it, but it made my estimation of the Hermit's powers of divination soar.

"How will I find the man?" I asked.

"There are ways of finding out once you get to Tenochtitlán. Emperor Montezuma never leaves the palace unless it is in a great procession. That would be true about his visits to the Hermit, too. You will have enough jade with you to buy the information."

He gave me a sharp look. "Pakal Jaguar. The king has given you a task of supreme importance. The One-World's survival depends on finding the Dark Rift Codex. You must not fail."

"I won't," I assured him, without the slightest confidence that I would be able to back up my promise.

"No, you won't fail. You won't fail, because you have never failed yet, not when wrestling the most powerful beast in the One-World or when ambushed on the road or when you defeated Flint Shield and stymied his attempt to torture information from you. Somehow, you even managed to survive the potion the High Priestess has used so successfully upon others."

"Thank you, great lord. My only wish is to serve you and the king," I lied. "If the codex still exists, I will find it."

"It does; that is a certainty. And understand this: If you find the codex and bring it back to me, you will find your rewards are more than you can imagine. The vast estates of the War Lord are being given to those who served the king best. You will get a large estate with many slaves and a noble title for your reward."

"What if I am not able to find the codex?" I asked.

"You will find the codex."

Eyo! In other words, I would be skinned alive if I didn't bring back what they desired.

"I have a question, great lord."

"Speak."

"If this Hermit is the chosen protector of the codex and will not divulge its location even under torture, how am I to get the information from him? Surely not by bribery—he would not take a king's treasures for it."

"He will tell you when you ask."

Was it that easy? Why would an ancient old cave dweller who after all these years had concealed the secrets of the ages take one look at me and give them up?

I was skeptical.

"Why . . ." I shook my head. "Why would he tell me?"

"Because you are the chosen."

60

I bought a yellow dog and had it killed to be buried with the Master of the Library. I hoped that the blindness that hindered him in this world would help him in the dark underworld of the stone houses of Xibalba.

As I prepared my own journey, which would take me through much of the One-World, I received bad news.

Twice.

The quickest route to the Aztec north was to travel by foot to the eastern waters, where I could hire a series of boats for the journey up the coast to the land of the Tlaxcala. At that point, travel reverted to going up and over the coastal mountains to the Valley of Mexico.

Lord Janaab decided against the route for two reasons: During this time of the year, the Sea Gods fomented ferocious storms, and the Tlaxcala and the Aztecs were often engaged in Flower Wars. I could end up a conscripted soldier or even a sacrificial captive.

"Each side needs warriors to be captured, and they sometimes press travelers into battles to get them."

Instead, I would be making the journey by land, heading toward Palenque in the beginning.

"You will make the first part of the journey traveling in a large group that includes a Mayapán princess, a daughter of the king, who is being taken to Palenque to be wed to a prince of the ruling family," the High Lord told me.

A caravan of porters would move too slowly to suit my anxious feet. A royal procession would go at a snail's pace, but it would provide needed protection, the High Lord told me, until I reached regions controlled by the Aztecs.

"The roads are dangerous," Lord Janaab said. "The worst part is between here and Palenque, where villagers who are not able to grow enough food to feed themselves have become bandits and even cannibals. After Palenque, you will travel with a caravan of porters until you reach the land of the Mixtec. It will not be safe to travel in a small group until the Mixtec region. They are under the control of the Aztec emperor, whose legions maintain order."

They were not taking these precautions to ensure that I was protected but to ensure that my mission did not fail.

The second half of the bad news was that the Assistant Librarian, Koj, who had spied on me when I visited the blind librarian, was to journey with me—along with a captain of the king's palace guards and three warriors who would be disguised as porters.

Lord Janaab casually mentioned that the librarian would come along to see that I was not given a false book as the codex.

Why would the librarian recognize an ancient text he had never seen? I didn't dare ask the great lord. The reason the man was being sent was obvious—he was to spy on me.

The presence of the guards added another dimension, a more sinister one—I was not to be trusted. A handful of royal guards would offer little protection against a band of hungry Mayan bandits or Aztec warriors protecting Huemac the Hermit.

The king did not trust me with the Dark Rift Codex.

Lord Janaab had never trusted me. Even when I roamed the city checking inscriptions, he'd spied on me. My connection to Ajul, in his eyes, made me suspect.

Eyo! I could have told Lord Janaab that his suspicions about my loyalty were not groundless paranoia but heightened awareness. My fidelity to the great lord had lasted about as long as his gratitude to me for saving his life.

I didn't know what I would do if I had the codex in my hand. Return to Mayapán and give it to the great lord for the king? Collect the incredible reward that I was being told would be mine if I succeeded?

Leave it in its centuries-old hiding place?

The High Lord's mistrust and the presence of the librarian and the guards made me wonder if their instructions were to cut my throat as soon as I had the codex in my hands.

The more I thought about it, the more convinced I became that the librarian and the guards would view me as a liability.

I had learned in my progress from ignorant stoneworker to a royal agent that even loyal agents were intrinsically expendable and that those in power would kill them on a whim for no reason at all.

And never think twice about it.

Ajul had served Mayapán well, but when he refused to do their bidding about the codex, he'd fled for his life.

I had to wonder how many common people could be fed from the storehouses of maize and beans that were being hoarded for the royals and nobles.

61

I had one last question for Lord Janaab before I joined the procession of the princess. "The sacred white jaguar. I thought the king had only the one that attacked you."

"The one you saw belonged to the War Lord. The king had always been envious that his liege had one and he didn't. But the king also believed that the white jaguar I gave him provided more power than the one the War Lord had. The War Lord's died of old age. Mine died in battle."

"And now he has both," I said.

From hearing Lord Janaab's description of how the king got the hide of the jaguar I killed, it was apparent that the High Lord had taken all the credit for providing the skin to the king.

62

I left Mayapán with fifty warriors and a hundred servants and porters to carry the possessions of the princess and see to her needs.

I saw to my own needs when the guard captain told me that one of his men would carry my weapons.

In other words, I would travel weaponless.

"Lord Janaab's orders," he said. "He doesn't want you to tire on the long trip."

Or flee, I thought.

The High Lord had gone to the royal palace that morning to consult with the king about a plot by nobles in the western region to break off and ally themselves with Cobá.

"Lord Janaab gave me different instructions," I said. That was true, though none of the instructions related to my weapons.

The guard captain hesitated.

"Do you doubt my word?" I gripped my sword.

"Of course not, Pakal Jaguar."

I carried my weapons with me when we left the city.

Koj greeted me with a false smile of feigned friendship moments before we set out, reminding me once again of the rat he was when I had given him a kick at the Royal Library.

"I am honored to serve you, Pakal Jaguar," the rodent dissembled.

"I can't tell you how much it means to me to know that you will be at my back," I lied.

The princess rode on a litter carried by slaves. And there was a litter for me.

"For your comfort," Koj said.

"So I don't tire," I added, not pointing out that I was stronger and in better physical condition than even the best of the warriors in the procession.

Eyo! They wanted to strip me of weapons and imprison me in a litter so I couldn't run.

"But I spend my days walking and will not find the journey ahead a trying one. Why don't you take the litter?" I asked the pudgy rat.

He was only too happy to ride in the litter in my stead.

Did they think I was going to flee the moment the city walls were at my back?

Where was I to run?

63

The city had organized a great Mayapán parade celebrating the marriage of the princess to the leader of a neighboring principality. The union was supposed to reinforce peace and harmony in the region, but I saw little cheer or enthusiasm on the people's faces as we marched through the city to the west gate—no sense that prosperity was just around the corner.

To avoid offending the king, nobles and wealthy merchants ordered their slaves and servants onto the streets. Even so, they could not fabricate the festive atmosphere the parade would have generated in better times.

"People are too frightened of the future to be full of cheer," I confided to the rat as I walked alongside his litter.

As to the bride, I'd seen prettier faces on beached carp, but I kept that critique to myself.

When the great lord told me that Koj would be my companion on the journey, the mention of the library assistant's name had made me wonder how much he had to do with the Master Librarian being kidnapped and tortured. He was in a good position to betray his master and had already proved willing to do so when I visited.

I decided that regardless of how the search for the codex turned out, Koj would not return to Mayapán. Hearing him talk like a fawning parasite of a courtier strengthened my resolve to avenge the death of the gentle old blind man.

"Palenque is not the great power it once was," Koj said. "But the king wishes to cement a close relationship with the city so his dynasty will spread further over the One-World."

My interpretation of the king's motives was that he wanted a place to hide when Mayapán went to hell.

Koj also showed off his knowledge, telling me that I bore the same name as the great king of Palenque during its days as a mighty empire, Pakal B'alam, which translated to "Pakal Jaguar."

I slipped away, walking alone, thinking about how so much had changed since I came to Mayapán. Things were even different on the roads. Porters transported goods on their backs, supported by tumplines across their chest for heavy loads, and forehead for lighter ones. A healthy porter could carry half his own body weight, but I noticed that the porters were skinnier than before, even though their loads were every bit as heavy.

The variety of goods had not changed—caravans of porters carried honey, maize, beans, peppers, woven cotton cloth, and cacao beans from the territories controlled by Mayapán. From the coastal kingdoms came dried fish, seashells, and salt. And from much farther south came jade and obsidian.

It all flowed along the roadways, but as times became leaner, the honesty level of merchants was strained. I heard more stories of dishonest methods than ever before. I already knew that the universal method of buying and selling when bartering could not be done was by payment in jade or cacao beans. But now I heard stories of how traders defrauded customers by scooping out the powder used to make chocolate drinks and filling the empty shells with dirt.

"Never accept cacao beans as payment without biting some to make sure they are real," a merchant told me.

Slaves were always present in cities and on the road, but their numbers were now staggering. Whole families, whose village life had been devastated, had been sold into slavery. The legions of slave children were everywhere, because their parents were too poor to feed them. The caravan slaves—as opposed to war prisoners—could not be mistaken for anything other than slaves. Their hair was cut down to the scalp, their bodies painted black with white stripes.

As Koj boasted about his soft life in the palace, I thought about how families starved while leftovers from the feasts of the king and lords were thrown to dogs.

I was angry enough to drag the rat-faced assistant librarian from the litter and kick him to death.

An impulse I controlled, though it was getting more difficult to resist the temptation.

When I was forced to sit near Koj during a roadside break, I complained about the slow progress. "We're crawling along at a snail's pace because the princess' baggage is weighing down the porters." I didn't add that she should leave her possessions along the side of the road for poor people. "The constant stops are even more time-consuming than the onerous loads. We have to stop all along the way so villagers can admire her, and our soldiers can take food and goods from them." *All of which should go to feed their families*, I muttered under my breath.

"We will make many stops along the way," the haughty rodent said, "so the public can hail the princess and her marriage as eternal salvation."

I was a little slow, but I finally got it. The marriage of the princess to a minor prince in Palenque was supposed to make up for the failed crops, pandemic famine, and pervasive lawlessness.

Very clever.

"Perhaps you might suggest to the princess that we travel faster and lighter. I constantly hear from merchants not only about peasants gathering together as bands of highwaymen, but that Cobá and other states are on the march."

I was too conscious of keeping my head on my shoulders to repeat what one merchant told me: Mayapán's neighbors sensed its weakness and were snapping at it like a band of wolves circling a wounded animal. At some point, they would stop snapping and begin ripping with sharp teeth.

The rat scoffed at my concerns. "We have nothing to worry about. We have fifty warriors protecting us."

Fifty warriors.

A mighty army to a librarian.

The captain of the royal guard heard the librarian's statement. He raised his eyebrows and walked away, shaking his head.

I could not resist the urge to put the bastard in his place. "The War Lord had five thousand warriors. And the enemy ate him."

Eyo! I went too far. Koj's jaw dropped, and his eyes bulged. I thought the poor rat was going to faint at my blasphemy.

64

We were two days out of Mayapán, still moving at a sluggard's pace so the princess could feast at every village we passed—she was a big woman—and take food out of the mouths of starving people.

During one of these stops, however, I spotted the poison-arrow archers who had protected me on my journey to Tulúm.

As the long, slow column trudged along, I saw the slender feminine figure and her short, powerful companion atop a ridge.

They had not shown themselves to amuse but to arrange for a meeting.

A private meeting.

The assistant librarian was sound asleep in his litter, and the captain of the guards was entertaining one of the princess' handmaidens with his exploits in wars, which were probably nothing more than skirmishes.

I made a pretense that I was going into the bushes to relieve myself.

The hillock they awaited me on was a steep climb and one I took at a good speed, hoping to keep my visit short enough to avoid suspicion.

Frankly, I did not think the guards capable of such vigilance.

I now got a good look at the two archers. A scarf shielded the woman's face, but I had already divined her features. The man was not a dwarf, as I said before, but was so broad and short that he left that impression from a distance.

Because I knew the woman's height, I could judge his size from afar, and I knew that he was much shorter than I, the top of his head would come only to my chin, but he was also considerably broader, so massive that he reminded me of the stout bottom of a large tree trunk.

As with the woman, his weapon of choice was a bow and arrow, which I already knew, but even at a distance, I saw the end of a long battleaxe poking up, which was strapped to his back.

I imagined that a large number of enemies would fall if he waded into a battle, swinging the axe with the power of his massive frame after taking down the enemy with his arrows.

As I got closer, I saw he was mostly torso, with long thick arms, huge hands, and short legs like trunks. He had a broad, ugly face, with fat lips and a flat nose three fingers wide, reminding me of the glyphs I'd seen of the great Olmec heads, statues of heads as tall as buildings built by a now vanished civilization that left behind nothing but figures in stone and mystery.

What first struck me was that the gods had smiled upon him or he would long ago have been painted red. Some people had features that made them especially desirable to the sacrificial priests. These holy men believed the Water God especially favored wavy hair, because it reflected the water's ripples. Dwarfs had a short, stumpy stature, as had many gods.

Even though he was not an actual dwarf, mighty priests would have lusted after his blood.

The mystery woman contrasted him. Tall and slender, she had first reminded me of an antelope. She seemed ready to vault a wall when I saw her without the robe, in which she was now cloaked head to foot.

Underneath the loose-fitting garment would be the bow and the lethal dartlike arrows she and her companion in arms fired with murderous precision. While men openly carried weapons, if she was armed with anything more than a small dagger, that blade would draw attention.

Only a small area around her eyes was exposed, but those eyes were the same ones I had seen on the High Priestess and the same ones I had seen on Sparrow.

I knew that behind the disguise stood a beauty with firm, lithe muscles, who surpassed all the priestesses of the Temple of Love.

A woman I loved.

Standing together, Axe and Sparrow—one short and massive, the other narrow and thin—reminded me of a massive war club with an obsidian blade.

As I approached, Sparrow gave up the disguise and pulled the hood back to expose her head.

"Do you have names? Besides the one I know you by," I asked, referring to Sparrow.

"Sparrow and Axe are good enough."

Staring at her, knowing I had been deceived, even manipulated, anger rose in me—but I controlled it. There were things I needed to know.

"Why have you, who protect me, become shadows?"

"We are not protecting you," she said. "Our duty is to the Dark Rift Codex. If it becomes necessary to kill you to protect it, we shall do that."

"Are you part of the secret society sworn to protect the codex?"

"Just thank the gods that we are keeping you alive."

Arrogant, I thought. Not the tender, loving, and seductive Sparrow I had lain with, but a strong-willed woman who was determined at the onset to get across to me that she was in charge.

Apparently, Axe did not have a tongue or was reluctant to use it, because he stood stoically and said nothing. Even standing, he appeared menacing.

"Since you know everything, you must know why I am on my way to find the codex."

"You have been sent to fetch it for the king, and you will be rewarded with wealth and position if you act like his dog and bring it back to him clenched in your teeth."

"Ah . . . I see you don't trust me."

"Why should we?"

"And why should I trust you? The last time we met, you were using your body to try to get information from me. When that didn't work, your mother used hers, along with some torture."

She tried to keep her features stiff and formal, but I could see that my accusation struck home. "I am not like my mother. I was not even raised by her."

"I know. You were raised by your father. Where is Jeweled Skull? Hiding in a small village somewhere, filling another youth's mind with tales of gods and heroes?" I challenged her with a narrow look. "Are you going to deny that you're the daughter of Ajul?"

"I am not answerable to you for anything. I am here to take charge of you and lead you to Tenochtitlán. And to make sure when the codex is found, it will not be turned over to the king."

I laughed. "Take charge of me? A wisp of a girl? And this tree stump who is no doubt strong but appears to have a weak mind? Has someone told you that I need you for a master?"

"You have little chance of making it to the land of the Aztecs and even less of retrieving the codex."

"Why?"

"Because you don't know the ways of the world. You are still a villager in heart and mind. You have fallen into one trap after another. We saved you from one; my mother died saving you from another." She held up a hand to stop my protest. "I know, she drugged you because she was afraid of Flint Shield, but the point is that your vision of the world is too small. You need guidance."

"Where is Ajul?" I asked again.

"Jeweled Skull passed beyond the sorrows of this world and has now passed his duty to protect the Dark Rift on to me and Axe."

"Tell me about the society that protects the codex."

"You will be told that when you earn our trust."

"And what will you do to earn my trust?"

"We saved your life."

"Saved my life and directed me to the Master of the Library. But I am still waiting to hear a reason for this effort on my part. I know that there must be some purpose in your acts. You want me to go to Tenochtitlán, you want me to find the codex or you wouldn't have appointed yourselves as my protectors. But what is your purpose?"

"We are protecting the codex. That is enough for you to know."

"If I am also to protect the codex, I should be told everything about it and the society."

"You will be told when it is necessary."

Maybe that was enough for her to give, but I had not decided that was enough for me. The codex was more than a book of fates; to some it was a king's treasure, perhaps even a magic amulet that would give the bearer great powers.

I needed proof from them that they were, in fact, members of the secret society and that their only motive was to protect the secret—evidence besides her bare statement that I was a naïve villager who needed to be told what to do.

Sparrow knew a great deal about my current movements. Her mother was dead. She claimed her father was dead. Who was the source of her information?

"We must go," Sparrow said.

"I have to return to the princess' procession. Soon they'll know I'm gone and start a search for me. I'll catch up with you later."

That was a polite way of telling her I wasn't joining them. But I also wasn't planning on returning to the snail's-pace procession where others wanted to control me, either.

"Travel with them, and you will be killed."

"We have fifty warriors. It would take a large band."

"There are many people. Unhinged by hunger, they do more than rob and kill defenseless travelers. They roast them over an open fire and devour them."

She led me to the edge of the hillside, where a good view could be had of the area for a long distance. "Your friends are about to learn these harsh truths the hard way," she said. "Do you see?"

Her remark required no answer. The princess' procession was walking into an ambush. Below, around a bend that the procession would soon reach, was a large group. They appeared to be a shabby band, a ragtag army of what were, no doubt, farmers and servants before the gods' divine drought wiped out the crops and drove them to steal, murder, and feast on human flesh.

The weapons I could see were almost all clubs—hardwood limbs or, like Axe's weapon, a rock tied at the end of a piece of wood.

They would do battle with trained warriors, but they were a small army, numbering in the hundreds.

After spending days with the warriors protecting the princess, my opinion was that other than the four from the palace guard, the rest were past their prime, the sort used to guard the city walls rather than go into the field and do hand-to-hand battle.

"The warriors will run when they see the horde rushing them, screaming for their blood."

Eyo! She spoke my own thoughts. The procession was doomed.

"I should warn them." Even as I said it, I knew it was hopeless. They were too far from me and too close to the ambush to be warned.

"It's too late, but even if you did, you would only accomplish the deaths of more starving peasants fighting to get fed, because the royal warriors will be slightly better prepared to do battle. In this famine-ridden land, a fat rich caravan of lords and ladies has little hope of surviving. Moreover, not all the bandits are farmers with clubs—some are roaming bands of warriors, mercenaries, and trained killers.

"When Flint Shield and his brothers fled the city to avoid the king's red paint and the sacrificial altar, the War Lord's guards feared that the king would color them crimson as well. Also, the War Lord had the largest private army in the kingdom, second to only the king's itself. They are now well-armed, well-trained robbers, capable of challenging anything but a sizable army."

Sparrow pointed to a bundle on the ground where we had been standing. "Those are your new clothes."

"I have clothes."

"Your clothes will draw every killer and brigand between here and the Eastern Waters. These clothes are the same peasant's attire that you wore when you were a stonecutter."

She was right, but I chafed hearing it from her.

"Hide your sharp weapons underneath your clothing," she said, "but carry a stout staff so that others will know you are not harmless. We will move quickly, trying to link up with porters as much as possible. There is some protection in numbers."

"Where are we going?

"To the place you want to go—the city of the great Montezuma, emperor of all the Aztecs, and to Huemac the Hermit, to whom even he bows."

"What will I find there?"

"Answers."

"What do I do with the codex after I find it?"

"We know what must be done. You will be told at the proper time."

I grinned at her. "As far as I'm concerned, this is the right time."

"You must trust us."

"Why?" I held up my hand to stop her reply. "I know you've saved my life, but only to gain some advantage for yourselves. I just can't figure out what that advantage is or why you seek it."

Angered by my remarks, she got into my face. "We have no time for these endless questions and doubts. You have no other choice but to do as I tell you. Return to Mayapán, and the king will give you to the temple priests. Go on by yourself, and you will die before you reach the land of the Aztecs."

"If I am the chosen—"

"You are not the chosen!"

That took me by surprise, but I was sure she said it to belittle me so I would obey. "If I am not, who is?"

"Questions, questions, questions. We leave now."

I looked down to the right, over the edge of the hill's vertiginously steep slope. "What's that?"

Axe stepped over to look down past the edge, and I gave him a body block. It was like hitting a tree, but he lost his balance and teetered on the ledge. A hard shove, and he was tumbling head over heels downslope.

I turned, pulling out my dagger, and held it at Sparrow's throat, my other hand grabbing her wrist as she tried to pull her own dagger out from beneath her robe.

"You don't know what you're doing," she said.

"I don't know what *you're* doing. Did you lie when you said Ajul is dead? Tell me, and I won't cut your throat."

"You won't cut my throat."

"Why won't I?"

"Because you're too soft. Besides, you don't have all the answers you need." She stared at me with a gaze that revealed nothing. Her eyes were unfathomable in their blackness, enigmatic pools of darkness and death.

"You're right," I said. "So join your friend."

I shoved her off the edge.

I grabbed the bundle of clothes they wanted me to put on and hurried down the other side of the hill, avoiding both the battle that would soon erupt below and the path Sparrow and Axe would have to take to climb back up and get their packs.

I moved as fast I could to get through the forest and onto the road ahead of where a starving horde would soon fall upon the princess' greedy, gluttonous caravan.

Throwing them over the ledge gave me perhaps an hour's head start. But even though Sparrow was fast on her feet, I could outpace them because the tree trunk had short legs.

Keeping up a fast pace, I could reach the Aztec capital of Tenochtitlán ahead of Flint Shield—if he and his brigands were on the road searching for me.

I had too many enemies and too many unanswered questions to trust anyone—even people who had reason to protect me.

65

I heard the battle taking place on the road behind me as I cut across the country to get far ahead of it.

In my mind's eye, I saw the guard captain's face—he would have killed me the moment I got my hand on the Dark Rift Codex. Then I flashed to Koj, the rat—he would have grabbed the codex from my dead hand and taken it back to Mayapán for the proffered reward . . . after slipping a knife into the captain's back.

Generally I wished no one harm, but I was pleased that the gods had killed them before they cut my throat or I slit theirs.

As for the princess and her contingent, after the starving villages confiscated their food, the brigands would most likely dress them out, quarter them like deer, broil the choicest cuts over a cook-fire, and feed them to the village children.

Before I hit the road, I put on the beggar's cloak and found a solid limb to use as a walking staff and club. I then joined up with the porter caravan.

I could not travel as quickly as I wished, because I could not stray from the group's protection. Porter caravans were not only well armed, but the merchants who employed them paid regular protection money to the highwaymen, who did not want to lose that regular stipend. Still, they moved slowly, burdened by their trade goods.

How much the land had changed in such a short period of time was amazing, but it took only one bad crop to create pervasive hunger and mass desperation. We had had four bad years already, and now we had no crops at all due to pandemic drought.

I studied my back-trail for Sparrow and Axe yet always kept up with the flow of porters. Falling behind was not a viable option. Over a short distance, Sparrow was capable of catching us, but over the longer haul, the tree stump's short legs would give us the edge.

Carrying no food was no problem if you had money. Despite the food shortages, periodically along the road women sold fruit, tortillas, beans, and peppers, with sometimes even a piece of meat. Food was in short supply overall, but the women sold the items at a premium that permitted them to buy more food with which to feed ravenous families. But the women were smart enough to stay hidden in the bushes and not come out until they saw they were dealing with merchants and not thieves.

An even steadier supply for me was paying merchants for the privilege of eating what they fed their porters, but not all merchants had food to spare even at a price.

I tagged along with a merchant hauling honey. The merchants traveling in the opposite direction apprised me of the road conditions ahead and the prevalence of bandits. Their predictions proved so accurate that I became too trusting in their assessments. I frequently hurried ahead, gambling that I would outpace Sparrow and the stump and catch up to the next caravan.

Spending the night at a rendezvous clearing where hundreds of porters were camped out, I bought dinner from a merchant and then sat around a campfire with others and listened to a storyteller speak of the Hero Twins and their battles with the Lords of the Underworld.

I gave the storyteller two cacao beans after he was done and received a look of surprise that he got a reward from a beggar. The claw marks on my face were covered with the dye I used, but I still hurried away, worried he might see through my disguise and realize that I was the most famous storyteller in the land.

No traveling was done at night, because it was too dangerous. Not only were hungry two-legged animals out hunting after the fall of night, but four-legged ones were on the prowl, too.

The next day I increased my pace, putting one caravan after another behind me, buying food, and spending the night.

The bandits seemed to have miraculously vanished, and each day I became more confident. Increasing my speed, I left one caravan behind and hurried forward to find the next one, even though I had to sometimes traverse miles alone to join it.

I had left behind a cloth merchant and set out on my own to get to the next caravan ahead when a pretty young girl, no more than fourteen, slipped out of the bushes with a basket of fruit. It was the middle of the day, and I was famished.

A pleasant girl, she gave a nice smile as I waved to let her know I would buy her wares.

When I was fifty feet away, a man suddenly rushed out of the bushes and grabbed her. She screamed as he grabbed her hair and pulled her into the bushes.

I broke into a run as he pulled her into the foliage. They disappeared from sight around a fat tree, and I went around the tree after them, suddenly finding myself in a clearing.

The man stopped on the other side of the open space, and releasing the girl's hair, he turned to face me.

One look at the girl's face, not the man's, and I knew I had walked into a trap. The little bitch smirked.

They came at me from all sides—poor villagers by their dress, all armed with clubs, not charging, but slowly closing in from all sides.

I got a good grip on my staff, and twisting back and forth, I tried to watch my front and back at the same time, ready to smash the first one who came close.

The girl stared at something above my head.

I looked just in time to see the blunt end of a club coming at my head from someone in a tree.

A volcanic eruption exploded in my head. Lights flashed everywhere—all the colors of a blindingly bright rainbow, and I was falling, falling, falling into the underworld's deepest, darkest pit of hell.

When I hit hell, the lights went out.

66

I awoke to the smell of fresh meat broiling on red-hot embers.

My sight was blurred, my ears rang, and my head felt as if it were in the jaws of the jaguar I had once wrestled, but my sense of smell was still good and the cooking meat that my nose detected was a feast fit for a nobleman or rich merchant.

The scent of good food roasting on a fire had a warm, friendly feel to it.

I slowly opened my eyes

The first thing I realized was that I was in a cage. An animal cage, the sort of thing in which you might keep animals like deer and dogs while you were fattening them up for the supper fire.

Then I noticed my hands and feet were tied.

Despite the ropes, I could sit, but sitting up caused a shot of pain to my head that felt like it had been whacked again.

There was no room to stand in the cage, but when I got my balance, I was able to kneel. That was about it.

At last the ringing in my ears subsided, and I was instantly sorry it had. I heard the sounds of villagers laughing, drinking mezcal, and toasting the feast to come. One of them was even offering up our blood to the gods, thanking and praising them for their bountiful gifts.

I wondered if they needed a storyteller.

I got a whiff of something else and realized it was not only the godly nectar that elevated their spirits but also the smoke from a plant. Snaring their souls and robbing them of their senses and inhibitions, the evil herb was notorious for transporting the smokers them into ethereal worlds and surreal realms.

I twisted around to get a better look at my captors. They were, in fact, gathered around a fire. It was still daylight, but they were getting an early start on their evening meal.

It took a little squinting, but I made out what was roasting over the fire.

A human leg.

I checked my own legs and found I still had two attached.

Eyo! Sparrow was wrong. I was not a naïve villager, but a country bumpkin who needed a keeper when I ventured into the world.

She had misjudged me, giving me too much credit for having even the common sense of a simple villager. I had not even the intelligence or wisdom level of the fourteen-year-old girl who lured me into the forest to "save" her from an attacker.

The people—who inhaled the dream-smoke, hammered down mezcal, and would now dine on my limbs, loins, and balls—were simple villagers, the kind of people who, as I did once, worked hard and enjoyed the companionship of their neighbors around the cooking fire at night.

Only protracted famine had forced these people into cannibalism.

The comment made by the light-skinned foreigner called Jeronimo flashed in my head. What had he asked me? Something about how I would feel if I washed up on a beach, watched as savages devoured my companions, and knew almost beyond a doubt I would be next.

Mine was the only cage, and I knelt in it alone. There was no one else around.

I am next.

67

During the night, after the villagers had their fill of their fellow man, their mezcal, and dream-smoke, they fell asleep. Exhausted, I tried to get free of my bond, failed, and finally fell into a troubled sleep of my own.

Before dawn I got another smell, this one striking more terror in me.

Fire.

I smelled smoke and heard the crackling of the flames. At first I thought the eager cannibals had started an unusually early cooking fire to roast some tasty morsels, perhaps my meaty buttock or a succulent thigh.

I quickly realized it was a forest fire. In seconds, the foliage, which had had the moisture sucked out of it by years of drought, ignited like kindling and spread as if the gods were blowing it.

The flames ate hungrily through the dry brush, spreading at a speed I didn't think possible.

The people got up and ran in mindless panic as the flames roared, not bothering to free me.

As they ran, I shouted at them. "Open this pen! The gods will punish you! I'm Pakal Oracle!"

The ignorant bastards had probably never heard of me.

They left me to burn alive.

I squirmed around until I was in a position to kick at the gate, and I let loose with every ounce of strength I had. After repeated kicks, the door broke off its frame.

The opening ran along the cage floor but was surprisingly tiny. In time, I would worm my way through it, the now open doorway, and the pen, but by then I would have suffocated from the smoke, which was already blinding and gagging, or be cooked alive by the flames.

With superhuman effort, holding my breath to prevent smoke-asphyxiation, I worked my way through the crawl hole. I was two-thirds of the way out. I was going to make it.

No such luck.

Suddenly, a dark figure came toward me—the man who had pretended to drag the girl into the bushes. He had a sword in hand, and from the look on his face, I didn't think he was there to cut me loose.

I'm sure he had come to cut off a succulent piece before the forest fire burned me to a crisp.

I recognized the sword. Someone had taken it off me after I had been knocked unconscious.

The man suddenly jerked back, a look of surprise on his face . . . and an arrow in his throat.

A small dartlike shaft that I knew would have a poisoned tip.

Sparrow was there, sending arrows into the clouds of smoke that were so thick, I couldn't see what she was shooting at.

She grabbed the sword off the ground, where the cannibal had dropped it, and sliced my ropes.

She gave me a look of contempt as I got up. "You are too stupid to live," she said. "Now stay behind me."

Stay behind a woman.

Coming from a man, it would have been an insult that could be answered only in blood.

But I was all out of manly pride.

She had created a forest fire that drove my captors away, saving me because she believed I was too stupid to take care of myself.

What could I say?

Maybe she was right about me.

Maybe I was too stupid to live.

68

"Women are treacherous," I complained, back on the road with Sparrow. "Not only the High Priestess, but also the village girl who enticed me with food—then attempted to roast me for the evening meal."

That a woman had saved me from that fate was a reality I angrily and irrationally ignored.

That she ignored my tantrum only heightened my rage at having to be saved by a woman half my size.

"Where is the tree stump?" I asked.

"Axe moves slow, but steadily. He will catch up with us," she said, giving me a look of amused contempt. "I realized you would try to outpace us because he could not move so fast, so I set out alone."

Daylight had broken. Behind us fire still raged, sending up black, billowing smoke, some of which I was still coughing up.

The moment we reached the road, we had fallen in with a line of porters carrying rubber from the land of the Rubber People near the Eastern Waters.

I was back into my beggar's robe, my sword hidden beneath it. The cannibals had taken my sandals, and I would be barefooted until I could buy another pair at the next village.

"How did you find me?" I asked.

"It wasn't difficult. When I was alone, I saw the innocent-looking young girl all by herself with the basket of fruit. When the man charged out of the bushes to grab her, I put an arrow through his heart. I then 'persuaded' the girl to tell me where they had taken you . . . before I sent her to Xibalba."

"How did you know they would have taken me? Do the gods speak to you? Do you read minds?"

Shaking her head as if she still found me amusing, she tapped my chest where my heart would be.

A small tear and a stain that was difficult to see because the material was so dark, but when I looked where she tapped, I saw the blood-stained hole.

When she shot the man who charged out the bushes in the heart, he had been wearing my robe.

"Woman, you keep up your act of superiority, and I will beat you as if you were a disobedient wife."

She gave me a long sideways look from the corners of her eyes. "I save your life—I can't even count how many times—and how do you thank me? With threats of physical violence."

"My gratitude is sincere," I said truthfully. "You are an amazing woman. But you rescue me for your own ends, not mine—and I know your ends will harm, even kill me."

We walked for a moment, and then I added, "You are right about me. I am not so wise to the ways of the world as you are. The people in my village wore only one face. Now I see people with many faces, some forced on them by circumstances. If you had not come along, I would have ended up as meat for villagers who were not unlike the ones with whom I spent most of my life."

"These people do not eat the flesh of others except out of simple starvation—horrific as that may be," she said.

"Our priests say that eating the heart of a strong enemy enhances one's own strength."

"Perhaps you should ask the man whose heart they rip out."

I grabbed her arm and stopped, pulling her around to face me. "Why are you baiting me?"

She stared at me with derisive disdain.

"We can't travel and work together unless we are honest and open with each other," I said.

She looked away, as if she was struggling with my ultimatum. "I am Jeweled Skull's daughter," she finally said, meeting my eyes. "You are the son, whom he didn't father but loved. A legendary storyteller, he was the keeper of the secret surrounding the Dark Rift Codex, but he did not share all of the secret with either of us."

"You know more than I."

"Only because when I was fourteen, my mother summoned me to the Temple of Love and trained me. I learned more about the Dark Rift from my mother and men who came to the temple than I did from my father. I don't believe even Jeweled Skull knew where the Dark Rift was hidden. But I believe the Hermit knows."

"How did Jeweled Skull die?"

"He was living in a coastal village. I am told he had waded into the water to cool himself and one of the Sea Gods' beasts dragged him to his doom."

"You weren't there?"

"No, I was at the temple, but I hadn't seen him for years."

"You said I wasn't the chosen. Who is?"

She shrugged. "I don't know. The chosen will be named by the Hermit. He is the chosen now. That I know from Jeweled Skull."

"How were you permitted to become an archer? And your companion, Axe? Who is he?"

"I was raised by a friend of my father's, a man who had once been War Lord of Mayapán. Axe had been one of his guards and was assigned to protect me. I convinced Axe to teach me how to shoot arrows." As we walked, she asked, "Is that all your questions?"

"No. Do you know where Huemac the Hermit is?"

"No."

"Lord Janaab told me that it shouldn't be difficult to find out in

Tenochtitlán, because the emperor visited him each year and that the emperor didn't go anywhere unless there was a great procession."

"He may be right. But even when we reach the land of the Aztecs, we must be careful. Those in Mayapán who desire the secret have a long reach."

"Their reach must be shorter now," I said, referring to what I imagined to be the massacre of much of the princess' procession.

She gave me a look that told me I was once again being naïve.

"What is it?" I asked. "The king has sent more spies to follow me?"

"Not the king. His henchmen are probably dead or fled into the forests and then back to Mayapán to be painted red after the attack. Lord Janaab."

"Lord Janaab works for the king," I said.

"Lord Janaab works for the king—and for himself."

I thought about that as we walked along. The great lord had competed with the War Lord for the king's ear. Now the War Lord was gone. That meant Janaab had risen in power and prestige.

Risen in power and prestige as the king's own power waned.

"Lord Janaab seeks the throne himself," I said. "He wants the codex because he believes it will help him gain the kingdom."

She nodded. "The king is unpopular because people believe the gods no longer listen to him. Janaab is no fool. If the king falls, he also will fall, and it's likely that the king will lose his head and his throne soon."

I shot a glance to our rear. "So you believe that Lord Janaab has also set out spies on our path."

"He won't be behind you, making it obvious that you have a shadow. I believe he is far ahead of us, sent by Janaab days before you left Mayapán. It's not necessary to follow you—he knows where you are going. Once we reach Tenochtitlán, he will already be there."

"Who is he?" I asked.

"Flint Shield, of course."

I grappled with that for a moment. "Flint Shield may be after me, but certainly not for—"

I cut my reply short because I realized that once again I was not thinking the situation through. She knew something via her mother.

Or more likely through bed talk with Flint Shield himself.

"Flint Shield and Lord Janaab," I said. "That is what you are saying."

"A natural mating of snakes," she said. "Flint Shield had lost everything and was on the road to ruin."

"And Lord Janaab needed someone who had nothing to lose and was not loyal to the king."

I thought about the snake-kiss Lord Janaab had made me endure to torture information from me after I had saved his life.

"My master has set a rabid dog on my heels," I told her.

69

That evening, Sparrow washed the smell of cannibals off me in a secluded pond. Afterwards, she came to me and, standing in the pond, her legs around me, we came together as one.

At the temple, titillation had fired our lovemaking. Now we came together again, but while the connection was still intense, it was more than just physical.

Now I knew for certain that I loved Sparrow, and despite her hard edge, I believed she loved me.

Later, as we sat in the grass, I admired her lithe body and told her I loved her.

"Tell me that you love me," I begged.

She looked away a moment before answering. "I'll tell you if we live to see the codex."

70

Drawing close to the Valley of Mexico, we passed an endless caravan of goods and slaves escorted by a large contingent of Aztec warriors. Everyone on the road quickly made way for it.

At the head of the caravan was an Aztec prince, a nephew to the emperor Montezuma. He rode in an enormous litter carried by ten slaves.

His clothes were made of the finest cloth threaded with gold and silver, much of it exquisitely embroidered. His quetzal feathers were longer, taller, and brighter than those which the Mayapán king wore.

The prince personified all the strength and richness of the One-World's most powerful kingdom.

Sparrow gave me a nudge as we hurried by the slowly moving procession. "Don't gawk like a hick. They'll paint us black. They have no respect for anyone but fellow Aztecs."

She was referring to the fact that slaves were painted black with white stripes so they would be easy to spot.

When we left the chaos of the Mayan lands behind and passed through the Mixtec region, where the Aztecs kept order, we changed from beggars' clothes to those of a merchant and his wife.

"The punishment for thievery in Aztec territories is so swift and harsh, the crime isn't common," she said, "nor is begging. They force roving beggars into slavery."

We both kept up a disguise in a sense—dye covered my scars, and Sparrow obscured her pretty features with painted-on facial tattoos, which came off with hard scrubbing.

The caravan's size and splendor dazzled me. "I've never seen a caravan this large, opulent, and so rich in goods and slaves," I said to Sparrow. "And it's protected by an army. It's as if an entire kingdom were loaded onto the backs of porters, who were then ordered to move it somewhere else."

All the porter caravans that I had ever seen carried the merchandise of a single merchant, whether it be pottery, religious icons, jewelry, salt, or a thousand other things.

Eyo! This caravan was a treasure trove of different things—bundles of bright feathers, sacks of cacao beans, woven cloth of many colors, animal skins, pottery, and reams of paper. However, the most valuable of all these trade goods we transported was mortal flesh. Overseers divided their cargo—often consisting of hundreds of slaves—into groups of a dozen each with collars around their necks attached to a long pole to keep them from running off.

I already knew from talk at camps along the way that the Aztecs had more slaves than any other kingdom because they needed them to work the gold and silver mines to the north as well as their fire mountains, from which they obtained their obsidian.

The healthiest of the slaves would be sent to work in the mines, the oldest and frailest to the holy temples' sacrificial altars. The work was backbreaking, the conditions so lethal that the rate of attrition verged on 100 percent.

Consignment to the mines was a de facto death sentence.

Still, our lust for the precious metals was so strong that production was everything, safety conditions nothing. Hence, the demand for replacement slaves was continuous and unending.

"Their warriors are different from ours," I told Sparrow as a company of soldiers marched by.

I had never seen common warriors dressed for battle as these Aztec soldiers were. Their quilted armor—which consisted of cotton quilting sewn over maguey or wood—equaled or surpassed that which our lesser nobles wore. Their spears, swords, daggers, clubs all had obsidian edges—thicker, better obsidian than the weapons of our own warriors, which were more often than not flint.

Commanders of the legion were easy to spot—dressed in uniforms mimicking jaguars.

"Those are the Jaguar Knights," Sparrow said of them, "under the command of Montezuma himself. There is also an order of Eagle Knights. Only the finest warriors attain such a privileged and exalted status."

"And the richest," I said. "Each knight has only the finest, most expensive obsidian blades."

"The Aztecs control the obsidian trade," Sparrow said, "so warriors can more easily obtain it than in our land. Moreover, the Aztecs limit obsidian's availability, so little of it ends up in the hands of the subservient cities, which pay them tribute."

Control of obsidian explained a lot about their success as conquerors. The nation that controlled obsidian could fit its weapons with blades and points far superior to flint and wood.

"By hoarding obsidian, they limit their enemies to second-rate weapons," I noted.

"And undercut their killing power."

But more than weapons, the Aztecs possessed superior bearing. Arrogant contempt for all outsiders was manifest not only among the Aztec military but also in their merchants and overseers.

And nobody but nobody met their disdainful stares.

The price for insubordination was the slave-labor mines or the priest's sacrificial knife.

"We have not yet entered Montezuma's actual domain," Sparrow said, "but you already see how even foreigners clear a path for the Aztecs."

More impressive than the scurrying feet were the looks on the faces of those getting out of the way. I saw furtive, sideways glances of hate and fear on the faces of those who cowered before these Aztec interlopers.

"They grovel like dogs who fear the whip," I said.

"And well they should," Sparrow said, "even in their own territories. Those who do not humble themselves, the Aztecs punish hard. Aztecs will rape the wives and daughters of men who convey even a hint of disrespect . . . *in front of those husbands and fathers.* Afterwards, they hand the men over to the priests for sacrifice, then seize his property and enslave the man's raped women. What the Aztecs don't rape and steal, they destroy, pissing on it like dogs."

She gestured back at the long caravan that our faster pace had left behind.

"The immensity of this caravan demonstrates how the Aztec emperor rules the northern half of the One-World. Every year, the emperor sends a list of goods that he wants delivered back to Tenochtitlán. A long list. In each conquered city, an Aztec ambassador gathers the treasure each year that the emperor demands."

"What if the tribute isn't paid?"

"Any city that fails to pay will quickly come to grief with Montezuma. They will learn that the gates of Xibalba have opened and Montezuma has unleashed all of hell's hordes on them. The emperor has legions of Jaguar and Eagle Knights standing by in Tenochtitlán, which are ready to march against any city that balks at prostrating themselves to him. When they attack a recalcitrant city, it is without mercy. The city is plundered, all the nobles and rich are murdered, much of the population is forced into slavery."

"Are we any different?" I asked. "If the king or Lord Janaab controlled the obsidian in our land, would they act differently from these Aztecs?"

"Yes, they are different from us. Our Mayan rulers are no less greedy or ambitious, but they are not destroyers of culture. When our Maya people were building temples that reached the stars, these now mighty Aztecs were naked barbarians who wrestled vultures for carrion. They had no knowledge of or respect for art or architecture, mathematics or science then, and they have none now."

Sparrow said the Aztecs called themselves the Mexica, but others knew them as the Dog People.

"Angry gods drove them down from the north and into the Valley of Mexico. Those same deities then turned the area into an eternal desert of dust and wind. They came not as a proud nation of people, but as nomadic savages."

Lord Janaab had already explained to me that before they reached the lush valley, the Aztecs came into contact with the great Tollan civilization and its capital at Tula. I already knew some of what she told me from Lord Janaab, but I listened to learn more.

"Tula was a golden civilization, a land of milk and honey to these savages. They had never seen anything like the city the god-king Quetzalcoatl had turned into the most magnificent city in the One-World."

Tula became an obsession with them, something they desired in the same way men lust after women and riches. It took decades, but ultimately after the god-king left the city, they were able to over-run it.

They not only destroyed Tula itself but also stole its culture.

"They had no books or drawings, no great cities, temples, or palaces. Wearers of animal skins, not quetzal feathers, they were barbarians who could neither read nor write. So they took every-thing they could from Tula, even its gods and its legends, rewriting their own history so that they were a proud people rather than Dog People with dirt between their toes."

Lord Janaab had told me what came next: They made up a fraud-ulent history, claiming they came from a paradise called Aztlán, which is why many today call them Aztecs.

When they entered the Valley of Mexico, at first they were hired as mercenaries by the existing kingdoms because they soldiered well in war, but their manners were so brutish, their hearts so murderous and thieving, their neighbors warred against them, forcing the Aztec savages to seek refuge on two swampy islets on Lake Texcoco.

"There, piling up dirt and plants in the lake's middle, they constructed an island on which they would then build their city. Serving as a moat, the lake offered protection from invaders. The Aztecs also built causeways, which they spanned with bridges, under which their canoes navigated. They always erected bridges, however, which they could take down in the event of an invasion.

"When they were strong enough, they allied themselves with other city-states and began to conquer the surrounding territories. They warred with unparalleled savagery and with no sense of honor. They would ally themselves with one city against another, and after they won that war, they turned on the ally and conquered them as well.

"They waged campaigns of unprecedented butchery and terror—campaigns so horrific, many cities capitulated and paid tribute rather than mount a defense."

Sparrow shook her head. "How these people who once grubbed for worms could so subjugate so many kingdoms so quickly is puzzling."

"They were lean, hungry, and fought against armies whose leaders had grown fat and lazy," I said. "The same thing happens in the jungle. It's the hungry beast that is always the most dangerous."

"They are now fat, however, and no longer hunger after food—only treasure and power. That insatiable appetite, however, could prove to be their undoing. The fear they provoke unites their enemies against a common foe—themselves."

"From the looks of the Aztec warriors and their obsidian weapons," I said, "the enemies had better come prepared for a fight."

"All they need is the right leader to rally them."

"You said they have a monopoly on the best weapons."

"True, the empire they built has an obsidian heart," Sparrow said. "The blades given to us by the fire gods cut deep, but it is easily shattered when struck from the right direction. They have humiliated too many nations, raped and robbed and murdered too many times. Someday the ghosts of those whom they have devastated and defiled will come after them with a thirst for blood-vengeance."

"When that happens, we will all be in jeopardy," I said.

"What do you mean?"

"The Aztecs control most of the northern half of the One-World, we Maya the southern territory. Our own society is weak from drought, decadence, and war. What will happen to the One-World when the only healthy part of it is ripped asunder by bloody conflict?"

I asked the question because the words of the man who said he was of the tribe called Spanish haunted me.

If we destroyed our own power to resist by warring against each other, who would fight the gods on giant deer when they came?

I saw a group of men speaking to travelers ahead and pulled Sparrow off to the side of the road, where women were selling water.

"What is it?" she asked.

"Trouble."

71

"Keep moving," I told her.

We had reversed direction and headed back the way we had come.

"What did you see?" she asked as we hurried.

"Some of Lord Janaab's men up ahead watching as people go by. I recognized one of them, and I think he saw me."

She shot a look back, and so did I.

The six men I had seen had come onto the road. They followed us in a hurried pace, but tried not to draw the attention of the people in the busy market area that paralleled the road.

"They'll hesitate grabbing you because we're in Aztec territory. The Aztecs do not take kindly to highwaymen, killers, and kidnappers."

Still, they were closing in.

"The man I spotted had been sitting in the shade behind the others," I told her. "Months ago, he attended a feast at Lord Janaab's. The High Lord had had me display the claw marks on my face to them as if I were a prized animal from a hunt. He's the son of our king's ambassador to the emperor Montezuma."

Someone behind us shouted in Mayan, "That's him!"

The signal was made to three men coming out of a marketplace stall ahead of us carrying food.

The others were coming up fast behind us. It was time to make a break, but there was a solid wall of merchant stalls on both sides of the road and the men were closing in front and rear.

From our pursuers behind came a shout of "Thief!"

The bastards were covering their kidnapping of me with the accusation.

Horns blew and a commotion broke out on the crowded street as people shouted and moved to clear the road.

We flowed with the people massing to the side as the procession of the Aztec prince we passed earlier came down the street, warriors in front blowing horns.

The men trying to reach us got off the street, too, for the moment unable to reach us.

The street grew silent, no one even whispering as they awaited in awe and fear the passing of a member of the imperial family.

Sparrow suddenly poured water from our catfish bladder onto a cloth as the prince's litter came into view. "Hold still," she said. She began wiping the coloring I had over the scars on my face.

"What are you doing?" I asked.

"Shhh."

As the prince's litter approached, she took a step into the street and yelled, pointing at me, *The Jaguar Oracle! The Jaquar Oracle!*

I stood perfectly still for a moment, frozen in place. Then I looked to my left and saw the Aztec prince staring at me from his litter.

The prince said something. I didn't hear his words, but the effect was stunning. The warriors stopped in place.

"The Jaguar Oracle!" Sparrow yelled again, pointing at me.

The guards suddenly rushed me. The last thing I saw before being grabbed was Sparrow slipping into the crowd.

72

Guards brought me before the prince with my hands tied behind me. The street had been cleared of people by a cohort of his guards.

He was a man about forty, soft from good living, but with hard eyes filled with Aztec arrogance.

He examined the claw marks on my face closely and then gave me a look filled with more dangerous contempt than Lord Janaab could have projected in my worst nightmare. "Your name?" he said.

"Pakal Jaguar."

His head jogged up and down several times. "I have heard this name, Pakal Jaguar. News that he earned that name by killing a white jaguar with his bare hands. His ability to foretell the future has reached us in the north." He gave me a hard stare. "But you are not this legendary storyteller and seer. He sits next to the King of Mayapán. Advising him on all matters, he also is older than my father."

The description was a mixture of Ajul, me, and pure fantasy, but telling an Aztec prince he was wrong was not a viable option.

"Can you tell me what I plan for your future?" he asked, wiggling his little finger, a signal that brought burly warriors next to me, indicating that he had little faith I could do it.

I pulled the jaguar claw necklace from its hiding place under my shirt.

He stared at it for a moment, then reached down and jerked the necklace off my neck.

He examined it, rubbing the white furry part between his fingers, and then looked at me with wide eyes.

Had it been an ordinary claw, he would not have been impressed, but the white claw was so rare and sacred, he could not doubt my word.

73

Huitzilíhuitl, Prince Hummingbird Feather, was a learned man, a scholar who spoke many of the One-World's languages. As a collector of tribute, he'd also traveled the length and breadth of the One-World. His intellect and learning intimidated me. Sitting on a throne of teak and mahogany ornately inlaid with silver, jewels, and gold, he gave off an aura of omnipotence and omniscience, which seemed to say, *Nothing escapes me. Lie to me at your peril.*

Still, my dissembling had begun when I first knelt before him and he began his cross-examination. I had no other options.

"What are you doing this far north?" he'd asked.

"The King of Mayapán," I answered, "has sent me to visit the sacred places of the northern peoples, where I am to ask their powerful gods for guidance concerning the terrible problems afflicting us."

Sparrow had concocted that response when we first set out on the road.

"There have been strange occurrences that trouble the Lord and Forever Almighty as well," the prince had told me in Mayan, lapsing occasionally into Nahuatl, which I could follow and was on the verge of mastering.

I recognized the title as that of the emperor.

"Can I be of service?" I asked.

He waved off my question. "That is not for me to speak of. Any words of that matter must come from the emperor himself, and by the way, he has heard of your visionary gifts, Pakal Jaguar, and has expressed interest."

"Anything I can do, my lord," I said, lowering my vision even farther.

He stared at my scars. "You really killed a jaguar with your bare hands? Amazing. The emperor has several of the sacred beasts in his palace zoo. They are so big and powerful, one cannot imagine a mere human being slaying one without a spear."

"I didn't slay it by myself. The Feathered Serpent gave me the strength."

"Yes, only with the help of a god could it be done. But that shows you are a favorite of the gods. Anyway, the emperor has spoken of you. Had you not been a liege of your king, he would have invited you into his court."

In other words, had they come up with a way to steal me from Mayapán, the Aztecs would have done it.

Not that I felt any safer here with the prince. Chaos did not disrupt his streets, but only because Montezuma crushed his opposition more ruthlessly than any monarch in the One-World's history.

He would crush me with even greater ferocity if I didn't meet his every expectation.

74

I had not seen Sparrow since she disappeared into the crowds when I was taken captive. Nor had the ambassador's son or his henchmen shown their faces. I hoped that the ambassador's son didn't pursue her and that she would know to head for Tenochtitlán, which was our destination.

The prince had broken off from the long caravan and was proceeding ahead—with me in a litter behind him—at all speed to the Aztec capital.

Even in the prince's company, I was sure my Mayapán enemies were preparing a trap for me. Lord Janaab and the king would learn via fleet-footed couriers that the princess' procession was attacked and that we were not among the survivors.

Lord Janaab would not rest until he had me or my remains.

His agents knew that.

My Mayapán enemies would still be waiting for me. The king or my master would have sent a messenger north with instructions long before before I left Mayapán, telling the ambassador in Tenochtitlán to be on the lookout and seize me when I arrived.

That realization provided answers to other questions that had haunted me.

I had not been trusted from the beginning by Lord Janaab.

From the day he realized my connection to Ajul and the codex, he must have planned on sending me north. He had also set up a scheme to have someone accompany me and others front and back.

It smacked of the attention to detail and lack of trust that my master had about everything and everybody he dealt with.

The feast—in which my face was paraded in front of the ambassador's son—had not been a moment of Lord Janaab showing off his trophy, but a means for the man to recognize me when the time came.

Eyo! He was like a spider, spinning webs, catching everyone in them who he could use to further his ambitions.

Now I was on my way to meet the ruler of the mightiest kingdom in the One-World.

Keeping my eye out as the litter carried me toward the great city, I hoped to catch sight of Sparrow signaling me that she was all right.

I desperately wanted her safe and at my side again. I wondered what mischief I might get myself into when I was asked to demonstrate my "gift" of divination to the emperor.

PART XII

75

Night was falling, and the stream—which Coop still waded and slogged through—flowed down from the high hills surrounding the big river. Crouching and panting behind one of the big rocks lining the uphill riverbank, Coop could hear the trackers with vivid clarity, the baying of the hounds louder and more hysterical.

From upstream and around the next high bend, Coop also heard a devastating din that unfortunately sounded like another . . . another . . . another . . .

Please, God, not another . . .

WATERFALL.

Then in the quickly gathering gloom, she looked down and saw blood billowing in the water and dappling the stepping stones behind her.

Her whole body ached so violently from four long falls and from banging off the white-water rocks that she did not even notice her open wound.

Everything hurt too much for one painful spot to draw her attention.

Day was dying, the dark around her deepening, but she finally found where she bled. Under her right arm, the shirt was soaked with blood. She'd busted the topmost rib under her armpit, and it was exposed, protruding through the skin.

God no, they would now be tracking her blood-spoor—which explained the hysterical howling of the hounds downstream—and worse, because of her exhaustion and physical injuries, they were gaining her.

When they caught up with her, the busted rib would only be an appetizer.

By my rough estimates, they'll be up to me in less than fifteen minutes.

She needed a place to hide.

If she left the riverbank, they'd follow her bloody, water-dripping trail.

She needed to hide in the river.

But where?

Rounding the next uphill bend, she saw her last and only hope— a huge towering pine overhanging another—another—

Another—

Another goddamn, no-shit, 120-foot-high waterfall.

No-o-o-o-o-o-o-o!

The thick wet mist rising up from the falls combined with the dark dense clouds, the blackening night, and the thick matrix of branches would offer her almost impenetrable cover.

Suddenly, the sky turned black and with a tremendous thunder crack—which was brilliantly illuminated by sheet lightning—seemed to split the heavens in two. A nanosec later, rain hammered her in layered slabs. She knew the tree was her only hope for survival, but still she doubted she could reach that overhanging bow, then make her way to the top.

She was hurting that bad.

But she had to.

If she didn't, the Apachureros would catch her and earn their notorious name—the Breakers of Bones.

And even worse, they would plunder Jack Phoenix's codex—the

greatest archeological find of her or anybody's career —arguably the greatest find in five hundred years.

Arguably in all of history.

The codex, which Monica Cardiff now believed might solve not only the riddle of Quetzalcoatl's—the god-king's—life but the secret of the coming 2012 apocalypse as well.

Dr. Cardiff would learn nothing if Quetzalcoatl's 2012 Codex fell into the hands of the drug bandits dogging her trail.

She stared upstream at the overhanging bow.

Where did that strange beast-trio vanish to?

Who were they, anyway?

She'd taken some bad blows to the head.

Were they an hallucination?

She slowly, painfully, haltingly headed upstream toward the massive pine, precariously bent over the cataract, which roared like Götterdämmerung into the 120-foot waterfall.

God, she hated waterfalls.

76

Cooper Jones crouched near the dense top of the tall pine. Its thick branches and the blinding rainstorm provided her with dense cover but not much comfort. In her whole life, she'd never been so tired, rain-soaked, and sore. . . .

. . . The only reachable bough had been a good nine feet above her and jutted out over the cataract. The knapsack now strapped to her back, she positioned herself as closely as possible to the limb, then leaped out over the abyss, grabbing the wet limb first with her left hand, then her right, gravity swinging her out over the white-water rapids sixty feet below. Hanging there between heaven and earth, watching the cataract below as it thundered over the 120-foot falls, she flashed to Odin's description of his own ordeal at the World Tree, where the Norse god had hanged himself for six days and nights. Staring at the ancient runes—smoking on the cliff face across from him—Odin had hoped to divine their secret meaning. He later described his self-immolation:

> Long I swung from the windswept tree
> For six long days and nights.
> Offering in the end only this:
> Odin to Odin, myself to myself.

Coop also recalled the terrible truth that the fiery stones had told to the warrior-deity:

The gods, too, were mortal.

The gods would die.

Odin would die.

Coop sometimes wondered what Odin felt when the runes had spoken. Had he at last known despair? No, she decided, only rage—which she felt now—rage that God, Fate, Karma, Nature, call it what you will, would force people to such murderous extremes.

"Goddamn it to hell," she muttered, staring at the overhead limb.

She then executed the hardest pull-up of her life and launched herself belly-up over it. Flinging a leg over the bough, she straddled it and grabbed the one above her. Pulling herself to her feet, she stood on the limb and worked her way one limb at a time into the big pine's dense crown of branches, needles, and cones.

She knew her side was leaking blood and that the pounding rain made coagulation impossible. She could only hope the same rain would wash away any blood that had splattered onto the ground beneath her.

Oh well, if those bastardos Apachureros wanted to chase her up that tree, they'd have their work cut out for them. . . .

77

Sitting on an upper bough next to the trunk, Cooper Jones grabbed an overhead branch with her right hand and attempted to stanch the bleeding below the armpit with her other arm. However, the pain from protruding bone made that almost impossible, and when Coop removed pressure from the open wound, it dripped blood into the thick mesh of branches below.

She also had to worry about the Apachureros at the big pine's base. She could hear them over the din of the cataract and the falls. One man argued that they should send someone up the tree to look for her. The climb was difficult, and it seemed unlikely she'd be up there. Moreover, none of them wanted to clamber up over the abyss and swing out onto the wet slippery tree limb, and others argued that chasing her would be a waste of time.

The lowest limb, which did not overhang the stream, was nearly twenty feet off the ground. They knew that Coop never could have reached it and did not believe she would have attempted the limb overhanging the cataract.

Abandoning the tree, the bandits followed the stream running along the cliff face. Their flashlights illuminating the dark driving rain, they searched the cliff face for signs of Coop.

When a droplet of blood leaked through the dense mesh of needles and limbs and splattered a rock below, a straggling dog caught the scent and howled.

Coop was stunned by how many rounds they fired into the treetop. It shook the tree like a hurricane of lead.

Don't they understand they could destroy the codex?

Apparently they didn't know or care.

That she was unhurt she considered a miracle.

After softening her up, however, they did attempt to negotiate: "Hey, *chiquita*, we ain't gonna hurt you. Come on down with the stuff, no?"

Yeah, right, she thought glumly.

Knowing now they had her treed, they determined to send someone up to flush her out. Removing their belts, they looped them together into a crude rope and formed a human ladder. The bandit at the pyramid's summit then looped the belt-rope over the limb and began pulling himself up the trunk.

Through the sheet lightning's blaze, she saw the man work his way up the tree.

Aw shit, he's coming up.

She reviewed her weaponry. By the grace of the gods, she still had a Beretta strapped inside the combat fatigues to her thigh and a KA-BAR combat knife sheathed to her calf.

Not much against a dozen Apachureros.

They were raising their weapons again—apparently hoping to soften her up for her tree-climbing visitor—when in the sheet lightning's blaze she saw the croc explode out of the stream. The shooters' eyes were focused on the treetop, and the croc, snake-fast, blindsided them. Knocking bandits off their feet with its massive tail, it dispatched them with its gigantic jaws, quick as the flashing lightning. Thunderbolts boomed and blazed again, and through the branches, she glimpsed the croc snapping off heads, legs, and arms with almost incomprehensible fury.

Nor was the croc alone. The big white jaguar—brilliantly lit up by the storm's pyrotechnics—detonated out from behind a clump of boulders and took out a shooter who was sighting in on the killer croc. Hitting him laterally, it knocked him off his feet and crushed his skull with its massive jaws.

Chain lightning streaked across the sky. In its dazzling light, Coop saw the eagle swoop. Raking men with its beak, claws and flogging them with its wings, it screamed at them as if all the banshees in hell were inside it, fighting to get out.

The bandits—in blind panic—fired chaotically into the dark. The lightning forked, and she saw three of them drop, shot by their own comrades.

Then all was still, and when the lightning flared again, she saw they were all dead.

Her animal friends had killed them all.

All save the sole survivor assiduously working his way up the tree, a knife and a semiautomatic pistol strapped to his hip. "Hey, gringa," he said, "I know you up there, and them animals can't get me, not way up here. They no follow me up no tree."

He had some stones, Coop had to give him that. He wasn't bothered at all that those animals had just killed all his friends. He was going to be trouble.

"I hear you got some stuff with you, no? Well, fewer amigos for me—I mean for you and me—to share? It all ours now, thanks to them loco animals. Man, I never seen nothing like that. We wait in the tree for them to leave, and I split everything with you. Then I look after you, protect you, be your amigo. See, I ain't a bad guy."

All the while he talked, he continued to climb the tree, hand over hand, limb over limb.

Then she could see him.

God, he was ugly—black teeth, black eyes, black hair, a black heart.

"Come on, gringa, we friends, no? I no hurt you. Give me the relic, and I go. You then go wherever you want. You just no go with the stuff."

"What about our split?" Coop asked, smiling.

"I get my stuff, you get your life. That's a fair split, no?"

"Can I trust you?"

"Do I look like a man who would lie to you?"

Coop did not dignify his question with an answer. Instead she slipped the .32-caliber Beretta out of her shoulder holster. It was a purse gun with limited stopping power, making her only hope a head shot. But she could barely see him through the intersecting branches. Even worse, she did not know if her pistol would fire. The rapids had slammed Coop, her gun, and her KA-BAR against rocks and logs, then hurled them over three consecutive waterfalls. That she had any weapons at all was a miracle.

Still, the pistol was her best chance.

Her only chance.

She had to let him get up close.

He stopped a dozen feet beneath her limb. Obscured by branches and cones, he braced his gun arm on a limb and leveled his pistol at her. "I know you ain't got no weapons—not after going over them falls."

Coop could see his gun clearly now—a no-shit .45 semiautomatic. He was studying her over its sights, the interposing branches and the gun offering him a surprising amount of cover. Still, she had to go for the shot. She turned around and surreptitiously slipped the pistol and knife into her waistband.

"I'm coming down," she said.

"Toss me the bag on your back."

"It's fragile. I'll come down and give it to you."

"I have you covered, bebé, every inch of the way."

She had to turn her back to him to descend. She didn't like turning her back, but she figured he'd think twice about shooting into the knapsack. He also would not want to shoot her and then watch her tumble into the cataract.

She climbed down the branches, and when she turned around,

he was face-to-grinning-face with her, pulling the .45 out of his cross-draw nylon holster.

With her eardrums blown out by the rapids and falls, she hadn't heard him sneak up the tree.

"Keep hell hot for me," he said, his grin now ugly.

Still, Coop had her .32 Beretta out and shoved it into his belly.

Only to hear a sickening *click!* as the hammer dry-snapped on a dead, waterlogged cartridge.

He had the cocked .45 under her chin before she could reach for her KA-BAR.

"Say *buenas noches, chiquita,*" he said.

There was no time for an adios, however. The big anaconda—exploding out of the pitch-black night—clamped its fanged jaws onto the bandit's gun arm. His gunshot hit the trunk, but by then Coop had hurled her KA-BAR between his eyes at point-blank range.

The throw's forward momentum, however, pulled her off her perch. Falling into the bandit full-force, Coop was shocked to feel his arms embrace her in a death grip, even as her blade—buried to the hilt between his eyes—pushed against her cheek.

Then she, the bandit, and the anaconda were plummeting through the branches, the man and the snake breaking them off in front of her. She tried desperately to throw him off, but his arms'' rictus-grip constrained her like hoops of steel even as the man and the snake snapped off the branches before her, which she tried to grab but failed to reach.

Limb after limb after limb, they shattered, and then they were free of the boughs, needles, and cones.

They were falling through space.

Even so, the lightning storm continued unceasingly, illuminating the white-water hell sixty feet below.

Trapped in his death lock, Coop, the dead man, and the massive snake hit the rapids like a megaton of bricks.

Yet again, the bandit and the snake cushioned Coop's fall.

Well, she thought grimly, *at least this time you didn't get knocked out.*

Then she heard the thunder of the falls, and she wished she were unconscious.

Locked in the man's unbreakable death grip, the big snake still affixed to his upper right arm, the three of them rocketed toward the 120-foot falls, its din now ear detonating.

Four waterfalls in one day.

God, no.

The rapids swept Coop and her two friends over the brink and into the mist rising up from the thundering water below.

They vanished into the mist and the frigid foam, then crashed into the water beneath it.

Again with the bandit and the snake under her.

Again, they cushioned her landing, and this time the concussion broke Coop free of the man's deadly embrace.

The cataract continued downstream and took her with it.

She wished for a moment that the codex urn were still strapped to her chest, so she could cling to it.

But then her thoughts went onto other things.

She was now . . . sinking.

Swim! she thought frantically.

But her arms and legs would not move.

Brutal, battering, freezing water and terminal exhaustion paralyzed her.

Coop was going into shock.

And going under.

Please, God, Coop prayed to the god she'd never believed existed, *don't let me lose the Quetzalcoatl prophecy. Kill me if you must, but, please, let the codex live.*

Then she knew no more.

PART XIII

TENOCHTITLÁN
THE CITY OF THE MIGHTY MONTEZUMA

We were amazed and said that it was like the enchant-
ments they tell of in the legend of Amadis, on
account of the great towers and temples and buildings
rising from the water, and all built of masonry. And
some of our soldiers even asked whether the things
we saw were not a dream.

— Bernal Diaz del Castillo, a captain of Cortés,
upon seeing Tenochtitlán for the first time,
A.D. 1519

78

I got my first glimpse of the Aztec capital coming down a mountain and into the valley the Aztecs called Anahuac, the Land Between the Waters, and which the rest of the One-World called the Valley of Mexico.

Tenochtitlán glittered under the noonday sun like a polished gem in a valley lake the size of a vast sea. The whole city seemed to erupt from the waters—temples high enough to reach the gods and lofty buildings, all brightly colored—greens and yellows, reds and blues. From a distance, it looked as if a rainbow had fallen from the sky and settled upon the city.

The valley itself was a dark, dramatic framework for the brilliant city. Ringed by mountains, many of which boasted the smoking summits from which the gods occasionally blew fire, while others were snowcapped. The tallest and most stunning of them, I learned from the guard officer assigned to walk beside my litter, were Smoky Mountain and his lady, White Woman. Both were abodes of the gods.

The first time I saw Mayapán, I thought no city could be bigger or more magnificent, but now I realized that Mayapán was a fly and Tenochtitlán an eagle—a rich, powerful, and arrogant bird of prey that carried back to its nest the treasures of its neighbors.

Sitting on the lake, it was two miles from land, with four paved roads, each ten paces wide, extended out to it. The causeways were packed with people entering and leaving the city.

The roads over water were interrupted by bridges that allowed canoes and other traffic to pass freely.

"The bridges can be pulled away to defend the city," the guard officer told me, confirming what Sparrow had said earlier, "though no king would be foolish enough to attack us."

Canals threaded through the city like a spiderweb so that all sections of the city could be visited either on foot or by canoe.

Countless canoes, like swarms of water bugs, came and went, delivering food and raw trade goods to the city and returning filled with manufactured goods to their towns and villages.

Sparrow had told me that Tenochtitlán was perhaps ten times bigger than Mayapán. With nearly two hundred thousand people, it was the largest city in the entire One-World.

I could not fathom such a number, nor could I imagine why the emperor of such an empire would fear anyone or anything. The gods must listen to him even when he whispered.

The air in the valley was not uncomfortable, but was cooler than the Land of the Maya. It was a place where one wore pants and a top, not just a loincloth.

I had never thought much about changes in weather before; though it gets hotter and wetter some months in my own land, it is always warm.

"Eternal spring," the guard officer called it, with the temperature getting cooler as one went north and warmer going south.

Traveling north, for the first time I saw wide rivers, broad lakes, and tall mountains with snow.

Cenotes were not used, because there was plentiful water in lakes and rivers.

The causeways were crowded with people entering and leaving the city, from farmer families carrying in crops and goods made in

the city out, to armies of porters loaded with goods—and tribute—
from the four corners of the One-World.

As we entered, a herald blowing a horn warned the people on
the causeway that a royal prince was coming. As on other crowded
roads, everyone made way.

I should have felt a bit giddy—riding in a slave-carried litter
behind the prince—but each step took me closer to the most powerful person in the entire One-World, who would no doubt discern
that I was little more than an ignorant stoneworker.

As I was carried in the litter, I had time to think and wonder
about the strange paths my feet have taken me since I fought the
sacred beast. I also thought about the people of my village and wondered how they fared in this time of troubles in our land. Of course,
they had heard stories about the "Jaguar Oracle."

I chuckled to myself at the thought that the villagers were hearing tales that I sat beside the king and was spoon-fed the food of
royals.

What did my friend Cuat and the others think now, when as a
boy I competed against them in contests of who could spit and piss
the farthest?

Eyo! What would they think when they heard that at the sight
of me and hearing my lying tongue, the Aztec emperor painted me
red and sent me to the temple priests to have the skin flayed off me
while I was still alive?

Coming off the causeway, we went down wide streets and through
squares and marketplaces the likes of which I had never seen.

The guard officer boasted that at the north side of Tenochtitlán
was the great marketplace of Tlatelolco, which could have swallowed the entire city of Mayapán.

A marketplace bigger than Mayapán was too much for me to
grasp, but remembering Sparrow's accusation that I still had the
mentality of a villager, I tried to look wise and thoughtful rather
than gawk.

Which was hard.

I'd never imagined—let alone seen—such an incredible array of foods and goods in the marketplaces, which I now passed, divided into sections so that the gold workers were grouped in one, the silver shops in another section, precious stones in a third . . . feathers, mantles, embroidered goods, cloth weaving, makers of shoes and sandals, the skins of jaguars, other jungle beasts, otter, snakes, and deer; meat of chickens and ducks and birds; young dogs, venison, and fish; honey, timbers, firewood, even slaves in their own market. . . .

Eyo! Everything under the sun, and everything bigger and richer than what we had in Mayapán.

Yet for a people famous for their power and ferocity, I saw also in their capital city a people dedicated to indulgence and privilege, perhaps more interested in decadent affluence and enjoying the spoils of war than in winning the wars themselves.

Observing the Aztecs' vast wealth, I could not help but wonder whether the fruits of the Aztec conquests did not contain in them the seeds of that empire's own destruction.

79

We entered the ceremonial center, with its stone palaces, pyramids, and temples. The most spectacular monument I saw was the 150-foot-high pyramid with a large temple atop honoring Huitzílopochtli, the God of War.

As we entered the emperor's palace, I had a difficult time not ogling its grounds. Even the guard could not resist commenting on the prodigious pomp and elaborate luxury of the emperor's abode. The size alone was incomprehensible, seeming to go on forever, more than eight hundred paces on each side.

"It's a city in and of itself," the guard officer told me as I stretched my legs after getting off the litter. The prince had gone into the palace to confer with his uncle, leaving me in the hands of guards.

"The House of Birds has every kind of avian variety found in the One-World," he said.

The same was true for the House of Animals. I could hear the rasping roar of jaguars and the less powerful scream of pumas, the chatter of monkeys, and the shriek of birds.

"In the House of Javelins there is a great storeroom of shields, bows and arrows, swords and lances—enough to equip an army with the finest weapons. There are even shields that can be rolled up for easy carrying."

The House of Books was in two parts, as was the library in Mayapán, but the size of each part dwarfed our entire building. One part was filled with the thousands of books of records needed to run the empire, from keeping track of taxes paid by nobles to tribute paid by other kings. The other books were of the One-World's history and legends, including whatever wasn't eaten by the Fire God when Tula was sacked.

The House of Food was a great storehouse for the palace alone.

"Three hundred different types of food are prepared each day for the emperor," he told me. "The palace has enough food, weapons, and treasure to survive—prosper, in fact—for years, even if the rest of the city starved to death."

"Does he have a great feast for his nobles each day?" I asked, wondering why there would be so many dishes.

"The three hundred dishes are prepared just for him, so no matter what he might ask for, it would be there to satisfy him."

Even as my own people are forced into cannibalism, I thought gloomily.

But I did not point that out to him.

The man was telling me that before the emperor ate, four beautiful women brought water for his hands, and—

And then we were interrupted by a nobleman sent by Prince Hummingbird Feather. "The emperor commands your presence."

FIRE FROM THE SKY

Aztec *Codex Telleriano-Remensis* reported at around a date that translates to the early 1500s, the Aztecs observed fire from the sky shaped like a flaming pyramid.

Montezuma, the last Aztec emperor, asked Nezahualpilli, the ruler of neighboring Texcoco, the meaning of the fire in the sky.

Nezahualpilli, who was admired for his support of the arts and sciences, and had gathered astronomers, engineers, architects, and artists to his royal court, gave his fellow monarch an incredibly accurate assessment of the meaning of the phenomenon:

It was an ill omen, he told Montezuma. Terrible calamities were about to befall the land, disasters that would destroy their world.

Within a few years, both rulers were dead and the Aztec and Maya worlds had been swept away.

80

The nobleman who fetched me gave me instructions on how to present myself to the most powerful man in the One-World.

"As you walk toward the emperor, at the proper moment I will tap you on the back. You will drop down and lie flat with your nose on the floor until you are commanded to get up. Do you understand?"

I understood.

"You must never speak to the emperor unless he speaks directly to you first. That happens rarely. He speaks to a prince royal, who speaks to me, and I speak to you. Do you understand?"

I understood that I was even more insignificant in the Aztec world than I was in my own.

Ever since Prince Hummingbird Feather had told me I was going to the palace to meet the emperor, I wondered what he'd say. I feared he'd recognize me instantly as the fraud I really was, intuiting that I was here to pillage, not seek divine guidance for my king.

I could have used Sparrow's infinite wisdom.

I was taken into a great reception hall, easily capable of seating a thousand people. The main room alone was the size of a small palace, yet it held fewer than a dozen people.

Montezuma was on an elevated throne, his back at the great hall's far end.

The throne room of my Mayapán king paled in size and richness next to the emperor's surroundings.

Montezuma's clothes were burdened with imperial regalia, and his head supported a hat that was twice the height of a man. I could not imagine how he stood and walked away from his throne at the day's end. I'm not sure I could have lifted him up from the seated position without extra assistance.

Sparrow had told me that two royal princes held him up by the arms when he walked in public because his clothes and hat were so cumbersome. I didn't doubt it. Among other things, I did not know how else he could have kept his balance.

I knew that the emperor was forty years old, about the same age as my king. He was taller than most men, though not so tall as I. His hair fell to just over his ears, and I was surprised to note he wore a short, meticulously trimmed black beard, which most of our men can't grow and regard with disdain.

Unlike my king, he did not lock his features in a perpetual frown. He even looked capable of smiling and laughing—assuming matters of state were not at stake.

Of course, he had much to smile about.

Even so, he was irate. As we entered his throne room, he was berating the Tlaxcalan ambassador. Tlaxcala was not in the Valley of Mexico, but down along the mountain slopes abutting the Great Eastern Waters, and although Aztecs had not conquered it, the Tlaxcala still paid tribute to the emperor, who also forced them to participate in his eternal Flower Wars. Lord Janaab had told me that Tlaxcala engaged with the greatest reluctance in these conflicts. Their sole purpose was to supply the Aztec priests with an endless river of sacrificial victims, which primarily comprised Flower War soldiers captured in battle, and Tlaxcala felt that they did not have soldiers to waste in such spectacles.

The emperor, for his part, objected to Tlaxcala's parsimony, meaning they contributed too little treasure and too few prisoners.

Mostly, however, I sensed the emperor was incensed with Tlaxcala's annual quota of sacrificial captives.

The emperor wanted more.

He was so furious, he would not let the ambassador stand while dressing him down.

As with most of the northern region, the Tlaxcala also spoke Nahuatl. From what I gathered from the whispered conversation between the two nobles who escorted me into the great hall, the emperor was angry about the amount of tribute the Tlaxcala had sent.

I hoped that the emperor vented all his anger on the ambassador before I was called before him.

The ambassador left, and Aztecs nobles escorted me forward, one on each side. My cheap wood-soled sandals clattered noisily on the floor. A tap on my back, and I dropped to the floor. Another tap, and I rose.

"You may look at the emperor, but do not speak," the nobleman said. "Answer only to me."

During the conversation, the emperor never addressed me directly nor I him. A royal prince instead repeated the monarch's words to me and my own back.

"Why did your king send you to our land?" was the first question.

The answer had to satisfy the emperor's interest in my alleged prophetic gifts and also seem credible.

"Misfortune and many calamities afflict the land of my people. Because the gods have not been generous to our farmers, there has been widespread hunger—even thievery."

"I am told it is much worse than what you describe. Starvation is widespread because the lack of rain is killing your crops. Order has broken down throughout your land. Tell me what you anticipate for your kingdom."

"The king will fall."

That caused a stir in the room, and if it did not come to pass, I was doomed—either here or in Mayapán. But it popped into my head, and I believed it would happen, based on what I knew. Still, I had blurted the prediction without thinking.

The emperor made a gesture with his hand. "How will the king fall?" he asked.

The noble spoke to me in an awed tone. "The Lord and Forever Almighty has spoken directly to you."

The emperor was addressing *me*? I was in shock but had to respond.

I could have said that my master lusted for the king's throne, but I could not sound as if I'd inferred his death from events. I had to imply I'd divined the king's removal from office.

"I do not know the details, Lord and Forever Almighty. The gods act in mysterious ways, sometimes killing people, even kings, on a whim."

"When will your king lose his throne?"

I shook my head. "I don't know. The gods have not revealed that to me."

"Then you are not aware that your king has already fallen?"

My surprise made my prediction seem authentically prophetic.

"How did it happen?" I stammered.

"We received word only an hour ago from one of our spies in Mayapán, who brought us the news via the sea route. Having been in Prince Hummingbird Feather's custody for three days, you could not have known what happened." He looked at me respectfully. "So you do have the gift of prophecy."

"No, it—it was a guess."

The nobleman next to me noticeably stiffened. After all, I had contradicted the emperor. Still, my denial seemed to please Montezuma.

"Those with the true gift are the last to admit it. As to your question, he made one of his brothers War Lord. The brother repaid him with treachery, killing him and seizing the throne."

There was disapproval in the emperor's tone. Regicide was probably not a popular act to any monarch.

"Tell me more, Jaguar Oracle, about why your king sent you to my land."

"The king believed that the gods were not listening to his pleas for my people. He had gathered all the wisdom of the Maya to answer the question and learned nothing. He sent me here to ask Huemac the Hermit why chaos has gripped his kingdom."

Mentioning the Hermit was risky, but I hoped a partial truth would add credence to my story. I left out the part about how I was sent to steal the codex and return it to Mayapán to be destroyed.

His features grew grave, and he appeared to mull over my statement. He was quiet for a long time, long enough that I felt my life slipping away. Just as he had wiggled his finger to tell his attendants he would speak directly to me, a second finger wiggle could terminate my earthly existence.

"We live in strange times," he finally said. "The gods are frequently capricious, smashing kings and empires for no apparent reason at all. To the gods, we are little more than ants and flies. They kill us for their sport." He stared down at me, frowning. "Do you foretell the future in your dreams?"

"No."

"I don't either, but I have had strange dreams which seem to foreshadow even stranger events. We, too, have suffered a long drought because the Rain God has been stingy with his tears, but we are still able to feed our people.

"Other things have happened that my stargazers cannot explain. For the first time while I have occupied this throne, a temple burned. A bad omen indeed, an affront to the gods, tantamount to spitting in the face. A fire then was seen in the sky, blazing as if the sky itself was aflame.

"Soon after the sky fire was seen, the ghost of a woman rose from her grave, casting off the stones covering it, sending them flying into the air. She came to me while I slept and told me that invaders had come to subjugate our land and that divine deer would transport them on their backs and—"

I gasped, and he stopped and stared wide-eyed at me.

"What is it? What did you see?" he demanded.

I took a deep breath and tried to stop the shaking in my knee. "Warriors on deer," I said. "Another told me of his vision of them. A man I considered to be mad."

Montezuma appeared to have trouble controlling his own emotions. "Yes," he said, almost in a whisper, "a madman would be the source. Someone whose mind has been destroyed so the gods can speak through it."

The room was quiet again as the emperor's eyes grew vague, remote. He seemed to be looking inward, perhaps remembering his nightmares.

"Each year I go to Teotihuacán," he said, "the City of Gods, to give offerings to the gods and to speak to Huemac the Hermit." He stared down at me as if I was about to challenge his words. "I am told he was a young man five hundred years ago when he walked with the god-king Quetzalcoatl in the sacred city of Tula.

"Now for three years, Huemac has not spoken. Not to me, not to anyone—only to the gods, with whom he converses in private in a dream state. During his three years of silence, drought has killed our crops, desiccating them on the stems. Strange events have also occurred.

"I, emperor of all the Aztecs, have gone to his cave and asked for his guidance, and he stares at me, mute. I have sent emissaries, but he will not grant them an audience. I could have him cut into ten thousand pieces, and if he were an ordinary man . . ."

Montezuma left the threat hanging. It needed no elaboration.

"You will go there," the emperor said, "to the cave of the Hermit. He will speak to the Jaguar Oracle of the Maya. He will reveal to you the plan of the gods for our future. And what I must do to ensure our prosperity. There is said to be a book of fates in which the plans of the gods are laid out. You will find that book. You will bring me that codex."

It was not a request or even a command. It was a statement of fact—I would go, get the book, and return. And what if Huemac the Hermit spit in my eye instead of revealing the machinations of the gods or where the book was hidden?

If I failed, I would receive no more mercy from the Aztec emperor than I would from my late king.

I would also be well "protected" on my journey to the City of the Gods.

And on my return.

Escape would not be an option.

81

"You are truly honored," a guard captain told me after I was brought to the room where I would spend the night. "We will bring an *auianime* to pleasure you along with good food and drink."

An *auianime* was a woman assigned to entertain warriors who fought well. Not a prostitute, but more akin to the erotic women of the love temple. I was honored as well as titillated.

After I had sweated body and soul in a House of Stone Fire, I washed the perspiration off in a cool pool.

Despite being placed in a palace room, I had a guard at the door, who brought me food. For all the luxurious palace living, I was still a prisoner.

The food was as good as Lord Janaab himself feasted upon: turtle, fresh fish, and pheasant, with vegetables I had never seen before. I was even given a chocolate drink with peppers and a small jug of Aztec nectar—not the three hundred dishes the emperor enjoyed, but the finest meal I had ever eaten. Yet I still felt like a fly caught in a spiderweb rather than an honored guest.

Spiderwebs had been everywhere I stepped since I left my village, enveloping me even tighter when I tried to pull loose. This one was perhaps the tightest, because I was in a foreign land and in the hands of the mightiest monarch in the One-World.

I gave little thought to the fate of my king, but wondered how my fellow stoneworkers fared in the chaos. And what I would face when I returned—if I lived long enough to return.

I was relaxing on a bed of straw on the floor when the guard officer opened my door. He gave me a wide grin and ushered in my companion for the night.

I gaped, but Sparrow kept a straight face.

"Enjoy," he said, shutting the door behind him as he left.

We stared at each other for a long moment. Then I wiggled my finger as I'd seen the emperor do and told her, "Come over here, and show me how an Aztec woman makes love."

82

"Fine food, good drink, a beautiful woman—what could make life better?" I asked Sparrow as she lay naked in my arms.

"Surviving long enough to see the Sun God journey across the sky one more day?"

I could not argue the point.

She had paced ahead of Prince Hummingbird Feather's procession on the road and arrived in Tenochtitlán in time to make contacts at the Temple of Love. She told me Axe had arrived just hours earlier and found her by hanging around the temple, their agreed plan.

After bribing the woman from the Temple of Love who'd been selected to entertain me, she sent the priestess off to be with her own secret lover, while she came to me. So far, making love was the limit of our intrigues and plans.

Getting up, she dressed and gave me a smile. "Time to leave," she said.

"I wish I were a bird, so I could fly out of here and join you."

"You'll wish you had wings if the vine doesn't hold."

I blinked. "What vine?"

She went to the small window that overlooked a street and indicated something outside. "That one."

I stuck my head out the window. My room was on the third floor, the top floor. Vines from a dirt bed rose all along the wall. The vines looked strong enough to hold a woman. But I was a solidly built man.

"It's a long ways down," I said.

"You'll be halfway down if it breaks."

"You don't know that."

She shrugged. "If you are too much of a woman to try, I'll leave by the door and go to the City of the Gods without you."

Eyo! I was tempted to have her leave through the window, head-first. The woman had a unique ability to stir my blood both when I was on my back and on my feet.

"How do you know I'm being sent to Teotihuacán? Did you have a spy in the emperor's own chamber?"

She shook her head at my obvious ignorance. "How long do you think it took for the news to get from the emperor's lips to the women at the Temple of Love?"

I was slowly realizing that my biggest fault was in failing to fathom not royal intrigues but those of the women around me.

She took a piece of charcoal and wrote in Nahuatl on the wall, CALLED BY THE GODS.

"What's that for?" I asked.

"Confusion. The emperor is very superstitious. He will debate for at least several hours whether he should have you hunted down."

I took another look at the vine and the street below. "What about the guards?" I asked, not seeing any.

"The city is the least protected, most impregnable in the One-World. No sane king would attack it, and if they did, Montezuma's advance sentries and partisans would warn him far in advance. More-over, the invading army would have to come across the causeways, bridges, and the lake-moats. Montezuma considers the city so impreg-nable that its only regular security is the causeway guards, whose main function is to collect taxes on the goods that merchants bring in and out of the city."

"What happens when I'm missed?"

I already knew what would happen if I were caught.

"We have a plan. No more talk. I'll go down first. If the vines hold me, they'll hold you."

Untrue, but pulling her toward me, I stole a kiss. Then I stepped aside so she could slip out the window. "I love you," I said.

She stroked my claw marks with her fingers. "I love you, too—even if you are ugly."

She had the courage to jest—I hope it was a jest—even while facing danger. I couldn't do less or she would again tell me I was a woman.

The vine did hold her. Gritting my teeth, I looked back at the door and wondered if I should fight the guards in the hall rather than risk falling three stories to the street below.

Sitting on the window, I slipped one leg over and leaned out. Grabbing a thick heavy vine with one hand, I clutched the ledge with the other, then eased myself down so my weight would not test the vines all at once.

I let go of the ledge, and grabbed on to a vine with both hands.

It began ripping loose from the wall.

I got another handhold on another vine, but it, too, began pulling away from the wall.

With nothing under my feet but thin air, I went down, pulling the two vines with me. Hitting the bottom, I fell backwards on my rear.

"Hurry!" Sparrow snapped, already moving fast down the street.

I ran to catch up with her.

"You probably woke half the palace when you ripped that vine out," she scolded.

When I ripped the vine out? As if I had had a choice?

Why me? I asked the gods.

What had I done to deserve the wrath of kings and of this woman?

83

We slowed our pace to avoid attracting attention. The few people on the streets were porters with late-night deliveries, brothel patrons, and the men selling Aztec beer called pulque.

"How are we going to get across a causeway if they're guarded?" I asked her.

"We're leaving by boat. Axe is waiting with rowers who will take us to the end of the lake in the direction of the City of the Gods."

"Can the boatmen be trusted?"

"Yes. They're smugglers."

A captain of the guard, who commanded the company of soldiers, had told me on my journey to Teotihuacán that the city was a two-day march from Tenochtitlán.

They didn't know in which direction I would flee, but because the plan to send warriors to Teotihuacán was already in place, they would probably look for me there.

Sparrow and I could travel faster than the warriors, and with the half-day head start, she thought we might end up a full day ahead of the pursuit.

Or look back and find them on our heels. Montezuma ran an

empire, and he might very well send his fastest warriors after us. He'd have them at his disposal.

I explained to Sparrow that regardless of how the pursuit unfolded, Axe's short legs would jeopardize us.

"He will follow us again at his own pace and meet up with us at the City of the Gods," she said.

84

Before we reached the boat, Sparrow rubbed dye on my face and warned me not to speak Mayan.

"They think we're lovers fleeing a jealous husband. If they found out the king wanted you, they would increase their price or simply sell you to the emperor."

Axe came out of a dark place as we approached the edge of the lake where the boat was waiting.

He gave me no greeting, and I offered none to him. I wasn't sure he even had a tongue with which to speak.

"Prepare to pull your weapons," Sparrow told us.

I saw no one threatening but pushed open my shirt and slipped my hand onto the hilt of my sword.

Three rowers were in the boat, and a fourth man, whom I took to be the head smuggler, was standing on the shoreline as we hurried up to board.

The head smuggler gave us a sly grin and held out his hand. "More money, or you can swim away from your jealous husband."

"Kill them!" Sparrow snapped to Axe and me.

"No!" The smuggler backed up, splashing in the water as Axe and I drew weapons. "Come aboard, friends."

Axe waded in to get a firm grip on the boat, and I gave Sparrow a look of bemusement as I followed.

"How did you know they would try to cheat us?"

"They're men, aren't they?"

PART XIV

TEOTIHUACÁN
THE CITY OF THE GODS

85

Late in the afternoon, when we were less than an hour from the abandoned city, we paid women to fill our water bag from their earthenware pot. We bought food from them, and Sparrow asked the women if they ever went to Teotihuacán. The response was a firm no.

"The ghosts there will steal your soul," one told us.

We took the food to a high spot that gave us a view both of the road to our rear and the ghost city before us.

We could see a great distance down the road that we had traveled. No pursuit was in sight, but other roads to the City of the Gods—on which they could be traveling—probably existed.

Axe was not in sight either.

We had kept a fast pace, saving our energy for our feet, and had hardly spoken since leaving the smugglers' boat.

We sat and looked at the city in the distance.

"The Aztecs call it the City of the Gods now," she said. "At an earlier time, however, it was called the City Where Men Become Gods. The Pyramid of the Sun was so high that the people standing on it felt they had their heads in the heavens."

The city appeared more frighteningly mysterious and far more mystical than what I had imagined.

The temples, pyramids, and palaces in all the cities I had entered were garishly colored in blues and greens, yellows and reds. Even the city walls were painted.

The paint on Teotihuacán's structures had long since faded away, exposing the gray stone underneath, giving the city a vast funereal graveyard presence.

I'd never experienced anything like the two pyramids. Sparrow told me that we would have to stack the pyramid at Mayapán atop the one at the Aztec capital to equal the height of the ghost city's Pyramid of the Sun.

Now, however, we were looking at the Pyramid of the Moon.

"The Pyramid of the Moon"—she pointed at the tall structure at the end of the city—"appears to be about the same height as the Pyramid of the Sun, but it's not. It looks that way because it's on higher ground. No pyramids in the One-World come close to the height of these giant sentinels."

I knew legends about the City of the Gods and had told tales about it around the supper fire.

Once the center of the greatest empire that ever existed in the One-World, its influence extended north and south, including all the territories that today were held by the Aztecs and the Maya kingdoms. No other empire had managed to spread its influence as far.

Teotihuacán was successful at gaining hegemony over the entire One-World because of two things: obsidian and tortillas.

Obsidian weapons cut deep. A good sword of hardwood embedded with a thick obsidian blade could cut through shields and quilted armor. Just as control of the obsidian deposits in the northern region contributed to Aztec success, Teotihuacán controlled the main sources of obsidian found in both the northern and southern regions.

From Ajul I learned about tortillas, the second reason that Teotihuacán was able to demand tribute from far-flung kingdoms.

An army could march only as far as its food supply would permit.

And the main food supply of the One-World was maize, supplemented by small amounts of meat and vegetables such as beans and peppers.

None of the foods were portable, especially maize, which required cooking even after it was harvested and stripped off the cob.

Tortillas could be made in large batches at one time and could last for days. Easily transported, they greatly extended the range that a large army could march.

Sharp blades and tortillas were the main source of the success of the City of the Gods, but they did not explain the many mysteries about the city that made it a frightening place of ghosts feared even by kings and emperors.

Who were the people who had lived here? Were they Nahuatl, like the Aztecs and the Toltec, or some other breed of mankind?

What did they call themselves? The people in my land called themselves Maya, and I can name all the other significant peoples of the One-World. But here was a great city, the center of a powerful empire, and no one knew even their name.

Who were their gods? There is a large temple dedicated to Quetzalcoatl, the Feathered Serpent, the fierce world-creator and -destroyer, but little is known about other gods in their pantheon.

Why was the city abandoned? *Eyo!* A city larger than the Aztec capital, one with as many as 250,000 inhabitants, abandoned by its people, who simply left their homes and magnificent palaces and soaring temples? Abandoned to crumble under the weight of time?

They build the highest pyramids in the One-World—most notably the Pyramid of the Sun. Even with a modest temple on top, it would soar over 250 feet high, and the Pyramid of the Moon was only slightly lower.

Why would a mighty people build these mighty structures—lofty enough to touch the heavens, vain enough to embrace the gods— and then abandon them?

Ajul believed that the very height of the pyramids offended the gods, permitting ordinary mortals to grace their domain and that the gods sent down a terrible scourge to punish the intruders and drive the people from the city.

Whatever catastrophe drove them away, it had continued to frighten people through the ages because it still lay abandoned. No other people were willing to take over the ghost town, despite its incredible pyramids and the many other stone edifices still standing.

Fearing it in their souls, the Aztecs and other kingdoms before them never attempted to occupy this most magnificent of our cities with their own people. As Sparrow and I entered the city, I wondered what gods or demons lurked in Teotihuacán that were so horrific, people fled their palaces, homes, and factories and no king dared claim it as his own.

PART XV

86

In Cooper Jones' dream, she sat on a riverbank with the late Jack Phoenix. The sun was down, and the stars and moon—if there were stars and moon in this very murky afterlife—were hidden by black clouds. Jack held her hand in silence. They were still dressed in combat fatigues, cut-off T-shirts, and boots—Jack's olive green T-shirt bearing the inscription BEER ISN'T JUST FOR BREAKFAST ANYMORE.

His other hand still clutched the diamondback, which had miraculously returned to life, but which now seemed to be a friendly serpent. Jack and the Quetzalcoatl viper meanwhile coexisted in harmonious concord.

She felt strangely serene, far more at peace than she'd ever been in life. She finally broke the silence. "Where are we, Jack?"

"In hell, hot stuff. You didn't know?"

"I don't see any devils and pitchforks."

"Nor will you, Coop."

"Then what is hell like?"

"A very dull dinner party."

Coop treated Jack to her up-from-the-gut, roll-out-the-barrel, shake-'em-till-they-rattle-the-rafters belly laugh.

"Bet I can liven it up!" she roared.

"I purely believe you could."

"How long before sunrise?"

"What sunrise? I said 'very dull dinner party,' not an al fresco champagne brunch."

"What about Bloody Marys?"

Jack shook his head.

Cooper studied his BEER ISN'T JUST FOR BREAKFAST ANYMORE T-shirt. "Cerveza?" Coop asked.

He dragged a rope bag up from the river, filled with chilled Dos Equis bottles. Taking two out, he removed a key ring from his pocket. He popped the caps with the key ring's brass opener and shook some red-and-white pills out of the plastic bag. He handed her a Dos Equis bottle and extended a palmful of capsules. "Take two of these," Jack said.

"What are they for?" Coop asked.

"What ails you."

"Which is?"

"A premature case of death."

Coop shrugged and looked around.

"You don't want to live?" Jack asked, amused.

"I kind of like it here."

"But it's not your time."

"You should have told that to God."

"When?"

"When he dropped me over those falls."

"I asked him what he wanted."

"And?"

"He didn't answer."

"Sounds like we don't have much say in the matter."

"We always have a say. We always have choices."

"What are my options?" Coop asked

"You have men to kill, codices to crack, bullfighters to bed. You have to look after Reets, Graves, Jamesy, Cards. You have to break hearts around the world. This isn't your time."

"I'm at peace here, Jack, with you. I don't think I was ever at peace before. I don't want to leave."

"*This is one choice you don't get to make.*"

"*But why should I go back if I'm at peace?*"

"*Reets needs you.*"

Reets.

Yes, always Reets.

"*She's in trouble, Coop—Reets, Cards, Graves, Jamesy, the entire US of A, the whole goddamn planet—everyone is.*"

"*But what about me? Don't I get anything out of this?*"

"*You get 'promises to keep.'*"

"*What about happiness, joy, fun?*"

"*Those items are long out of stock.*"

"*I get nothing?*"

"*You get the satisfaction of a job well done.*"

"*Fuck satisfaction.*"

"*Then you get to save Reets.*"

There it was: He played the trump.

The one hand Coop could never call, let alone raise.

"*And how do you plan on resusitating this dead woman?*" Coop asked, thumping her chest.

He held his hand out again. "*Take these two pills, and call me in the morning.*"

Coop stared at the two capsules a long hard minute. Then she stared blankly at Jack and the Dos Equis bottle.

Reets.

Yes, always Reets.

She took two pills and washed them down with the beer.

She chugged the rest of the bottle; and when Jack handed her another, she chugged that one, too, then another, then another.

Cooper Jones did not stop till she was sucking air.

. . . Not until clouds broke, and the sky scintillated with a billion-trillion stars, which, converging, merged, blurred, then exploded into a blindingly bright, iridescently beautiful fireball.

The earth opened up, and the blazing maw of the molten-iron core gaped.

"If you stare into the abyss," Jack whispered, "the abyss will stare into you."

She stared into it and saw its black obsidian eye glare back.

"Say hi to Quetzalcoatl," Jack whispered again.

She felt his godlike pull, and she was falling, falling, falling.

Until she hit hell, that is, and the jaws of the pit clamped shut.

Eternity closed.

And the rest was silence.

87

When Coop came to, she lay by a wall inside a thatched Mayan hut. A fire burned in the middle of the dirt floor, smoke billowing up through the roof's smoke-hole. Everything reeked of aromatic herbs and woodsmoke. Drenched in sweat, her throat hot and parched, she desperately needed fluid.

A skinny, aged, deplorably wrinkled crone with a face brown as a burnt hide and a thin white frock made of woven maguey fiber appeared over her, apparition-like. Her thin gray hair was flung back over her shoulders, and she held a brown ceramic cup of some sort of pungent, steaming herbal brew. Thirsty as she was, Coop stared at the cup with misgivings and shook her head.

Suddenly Jack Phoenix hovered over her as well. The temperature in the sweat lodge must have topped 130 degrees, and his olive green BEER ISN'T JUST FOR BREAKFAST ANYMORE T-shirt was soaked through.

"Good choice, Coop," he said. "You don't want any more of her tea. It's spiked with mescaline, peyote, guarana—God knows what else. She's pounded enough of it down you to hallucinate a regiment of rhinoceri. Any more, and you'd be out for another week."

"Cerveza," Coop whispered weakly.

"Good girl."

As if by magic, Phoenix produced a bottle of Dos Equis and popped the cap with his brass key ring opener. He held it to Coop's mouth. It felt cool and soothing, and she drank a third of a bottle.

"That's my girl."

"Where—?" Cooper Jones wanted to ask where she was but lacked the vocal strength.

"You got rescued by the same Mayan men who found me, then were also brought back to life by the female shaman here who saved me. She pumped us both full of the herbs and hallucinogens. You were dead a lot longer than I was and were out of your mind way, way longer. But you sweated it out like I did, here in this sweat lodge."

Coop's eyes were now starting to focus. She saw that Jack had skinned and cured the diamondback and now wore the skin as a belt, the head and tail hanging from the buckle.

Averting her eyes, she shook her head wearily.

"When they found you on the riverbank, basically dead, you had four defenders, you know?"

Coop stared at him, silent.

"A white jaguar, an eagle, an anaconda, and a crocodile surrounded you. The old lady here thinks they were protecting you."

Once more, Coop looked away. *The animals weren't a dream.*

"She saved me, because some Mayan hunters found me with the diamondback in my fist. They thought the snake was a sacred omen and brought me back to her lodge. She spent four full days fasting and chanting and making medicine in this sweat lodge. It was pure torture for her, but she did it because she thought the diamondback was my spirit-guide. She needed those ten days to bring you back from the grave, and the ordeal in the sweat lodge practically killed her—toward the end, she had to stand up and go outside to a tree. She had some men stick a stake sideways through her trapezius muscles and string her up from a low-hanging limb. She did a no-shit Mandan sun dance, chanting and swinging there a full twelve hours—sunup to sundown—her eyes locked unblinking on the sun the whole time. That is no lie. Where she learned that retarded rit-ual, I have no idea, but she did it, and she brought you back from death. She did it because of your friends—the cat, the snake, the bird. Who says the ancient Maya didn't know their shit?"

Coop motioned for more Dos Equis, and Jack poured the rest of the bottle down her dehydrated throat in four long swallows.

"Where . . . is . . . the . . . codex?" Coop asked weakly, haltingly.

"That's my girl," Jack said, smiling. "I knew the first complete sentence out of your mouth would be about the codex."

He rose, walked outside, and returned within thirty seconds.

He placed her knapsack beside her. "The codex urn is inside, unopened, bone dry, not a drop of H_2O leaked inside. Those Mayan bastards knew how to make and vacuum-seal watertight vessels—you have to give them that. I decided not to open it until you were well enough to begin decoding it."

He took the oblong crimson urn out of the pack, the Feathered Serpent's image blazoned in black along its flat side.

"Relax, Coop. You done good. Your codex is safe."

For a long moment, Coop studied the image of the legendary Mayan god, Quetzalcoatl—the Feathered Serpent.

It was uncracked, unharmed.

The codex *was* safe.

Slowly, quietly, Cooper Jones began to cry.

PART XVI

88

We walked up the main concourse to the dark gray Temple of the Feathered Serpent. The temple was in ruins, but the menacing images of the god-beast were still there, snarling.

Many of our main gods had physical human attributes, but Quetzalcoatl was a beast with the snout and fangs of a snake, the feathers of a giant bird.

We lived in a dangerous world, subject to the vicious whims of capricious gods. The one with the most frightening appearance, however, was this great serpent beast. Terrifying to behold, his powers awesome even to imagine, he was a benevolent/malevolent god—both the creator and the demonic destroyer of worlds.

Sparrow knew from the Temple of Love women in Tenochtitlán that the Hermit lived in a cave under the ruins of the Feathered Serpent's temple. It was located near the Pyramid of the Sun, on the main concourse.

We found no evidence that anyone resided in or around the ruins except for an old woman with shaggy hair, wrinkled skin, and strange, unfocused eyes. She was tending to a cook-fire, yet one look at us and she slipped away, silent as a wraith, ignoring Sparrow's gentle greeting.

And was gone.

Images of snarling beasts flanked the temple's main staircase. To the staircase's right, we found the cave's darkly ominous opening from which neither sound nor light emerged.

"I hope he has not passed into Xibalba," I whispered to Sparrow.

"He wouldn't do that, and let the secret die with him."

"Maybe he already has."

Standing at the entrance, she called his name and repeated it when no one responded.

With one hand on my sword hilt, I pushed by her. Cool and surprisingly dry, the air was redolent with the smell of burnt-sap torches. Where the cave turned a dozen feet in, I detected a faint glow.

Stepping slowly, I called his name. Again, there was no response, but I approached the glow and rounded the turn, and then I saw Huemac the Hermit in the dim light of a single torch.

As old as the earth was my first impression, and immediately I understood why even the Aztec emperor spoke of him as a man who had walked with distant ancestors.

He lay in a single blanket on a bed of straw, wearing only a loincloth despite the cave's coolness.

His long white hair—pale as any albino's—hung below his shoulders. His dry, leathery skin—so tight against his frame that I could count every bone—had the color of the temple's own gray stone. In fact, he looked like the stone effigy of a dying god.

His eyes were so milky, I could not make out his pupils in the dim torchlight.

Sparrow approached and knelt before him. His eyes did not seem to take her in. "I am Sparrow, the daughter of Jeweled Skull, a keeper of the secret."

He made no response.

"This is Pakal, the Jaguar Oracle, whom Jeweled Skull treated and taught is if he were a son."

His eyes finally fell on me as well, but they were empty of expression, unreadable as the grave. He gestured toward me with a frail hand. "Come closer." His voice was as old and arid as his leathery skin.

I moved closer.

Reaching out, he felt my face. He ran his fingers over the claw marks, and they trembled against my skin. "The sacred talon," he said.

I pulled the claw out from under my shirt and guided his hand to it. When his eyes failed to move toward it, I knew he was blind.

Taking the claw necklace in his wizened fist, he pulled my head closer. My body was rigid, but my soul trembled. This ancient, enigmatic man—in whom the gods vouchsafed their eternal wisdom—was about to whisper in my ear.

"Why am I not the chosen?" Sparrow interrupted angrily. "I am the daughter of a keeper. I have the right to bear the secret . . . by blood."

The old man lay back on his bed of straw and answered Sparrow's plea in a hoarse whisper that tore at my heart. "Because—calling your name—the gods will soon demand that blood."

Xibalba awaited those whose name was called by the gods.

Whispering the secret of the codex in my ear, he then lay back on his straw bed. With a small sigh, his body settled.

Having designated a new Protector of the Dark Rift Codex, the old man abandoned the sorrows of this earthly existence and succumbed.

The mortal vessel of the all-knowing gods was gone.

And I was chosen to take his place.

89

We left the cave of Huemac the Hermit with dark clouds in the sky and darker storms in our hearts. We were both in shock at the old man's words. Heading for a nearby hill, we had to learn if Axe was approaching or if Aztecs were in sight. We made the walk in silence. I did not know what to say to Sparrow about the old man's prediction.

Ironically, Huemac's rejection of her as the Codex Protector seemed to hurt her more than his belief that her days were numbered. However, his last words—that she would die—devastated me completely . . . so much so, I was mad at the old man.

I loved Sparrow, the gods be damned.

"It's not true," I told her. "He cannot divine the future any more than you or I can."

"But he did know," she said stoically. "So did Jeweled Skull. That's why Jeweled Skull prepared you to become the Bearer of the Secret and why he commanded me to help you."

"You're not going to die," I told her savagely. "Not until you have lived a full life with me."

"Whatever the case," she said, more irate than fearful, "we still have a mission to complete. What did Huemac tell you? Where is the codex?"

"In Tula."

"Tula? The legend is that it was taken from the city for safekeeping during the Aztec invasion."

"I don't know. Huemac didn't explain. He said to go there and move the codex to another place. In the One-World, we have too many kings seeking the book, and ultimately they will unearth it because it is identified with Tula."

She thought for a moment. "Jeweled Skull told me that the person who helped create the codex and safeguarded it was a young stargazer named Coyotl. To keep secret the hiding place he chose after he left Tula, he spread word that the codex was in many places, adopting a trick used by Huehuecoyotl, the trickster who appears as a coyote. Perhaps the biggest trick of all was that he actually left the codex where everyone thought it would be."

We spotted Axe approaching on the road. Leaving the hillock, we went down to meet him and head for Tula.

"We will need Axe when we get to Tula," I told her, "and help from others—villagers, if we can find them. We have to move something heavy to get the codex."

My question about whether Axe ever spoke was answered when he and Sparrow conferred. He used his hands to speak to her, not his tongue.

I had seen people who couldn't speak make gestures that most others understood, but Sparrow and Axe had their own language. Axe spoke with his hands but he could hear what she said.

He had bad news for us.

"We have to hurry," Sparrow said. "A hundred warriors from Tenochtitlán are not far behind us, and Axe has spotted another group, too. He's not sure who they are, but ten or twelve men who don't march in the open like the royal guardsmen."

"Flint Shield," I said.

Axe grunted and nodded.

I didn't need Sparrow to translate his conclusions, too.

"We have more to fear from Flint Shield's band than from the hundred Aztecs," I said. "Montezuma's warriors will find the old man has begun his journey to Mictlan, their Place of Fear. They may spread out in different directions to hunt for us or return to Tenochtitlán for instructions. Either way, they won't know we are headed for Tula. But Flint Shield may have learned a great deal about the codex from the High Priestess."

"He did," Sparrow said. "He will guess we're heading for Tula once he knows the Hermit is dead, if for no other reason than it's the place most connected with the codex."

Tula was a full day's walk. If we set a good pace and walked part of the night, we would be there in the morning. We were well appointed with weapons, but would have to purchase shields along the way.

We set a quick pace, once again leaving Axe behind to follow.

"Why is Axe unable to speak?" I asked as we walked.

"His tongue was cut out when he was young for disobeying his master. He wasn't sacrificed, because he was exceptionally strong and the master used him for a bodyguard."

"May the master falter during his journey through Xibalba and may ravening beasts rend him to his soul," I offered.

"The master fell in battle and will spend an eternity in a heavenly paradise with beautiful women, good food and drink, and with comrades-in-arms." She met my eye. "There is no justice in the One-World. The gods decide our fates, and sometimes they play with us as if they enjoyed our suffering. Why else would evil people prosper?"

I couldn't explain the gods but knew that when it came to Sparrow, I would not assist in her annihilation.

Huemac had told her she did not have long to live.

He whispered to me that I was to kill her and anyone else who helped me retrieve the codex.

PART XVII

COYOTL THE STARGAZER

As we crested a high hill, the sea of maize and other foods was laid out before us. But it was not the richness of the supply of food or the two rivers that met and flowed among it that caught my eye, but the sight of Tula.

In the distance, it glittered and sparkled like the reflection of the midday sun off a pool of pure water. Its sloping pyramidal temples with their heaven-piercing summits soared high above the city's white walls.

I shivered with excitement, with anticipation and fright . . . it would swat away an Aztec raiding party like smashing a mosquito. I could not even imagine the city falling to an army of all the Clans of Azteca.

—*Gary Jennings' Apocalypse 2012*

90

Like the cannibals of culture the Aztecs were, they had chewed Tula to pieces, broken its bones for marrow, then hauled off the gnawed, gnarled skeleton, using its shattered fragments as building blocks for their own cities.

The brilliant city and civilization that the Toltecs had built was gone. Before us were the bare bones of a city from which all the flesh and marrow had been taken.

Tula, the golden city, had been the custodian of the One-World's most glorious art and of Tula's own irreplaceable historical codices. An unrivaled repository of knowledge, Tula's legendary library contained uncountable codices, which innumerable scholars had collected over the millennia. Now, thanks to the Aztec barbarians, nothing remained in that inexhaustible fund of wisdom to pass on to future generations.

"My father told me that the nomadic Aztecs shivered half-naked around their campfires in the windy, parched deserts to the north," Sparrow said, "and stared at warm, green Tula with lust for the city's golden life. The savages dreamed of maize ears that grew as tall as men and fountains that effervesced clear, bubbling water that was pure as the gods' own ambrosia."

She told me that the Toltecs stunned the Aztecs by transporting water to their cities in clay pipes and aqueducts and by bathing in it. Later, they would model their own city's water supply—along with their temples and palaces—after what they saw in Tula.

Hundreds of years after they destroyed the city, status-seeking Aztecs still "traced" their bloodlines to the Toltecs.

"If there was such a bloodline," Sparrow said, "it came from rape, not marriage."

The Tollans god-king, Quetzalcoatl, had collected books, artworks, and historical writings throughout the One-World, sending his legions to gather them as tribute and blooding any city that refused his demands.

Among the "treasures" he brought to Tula were the codices used to create the one that we had come seeking—the secret of the ages that Mayan astronomers in Palenque, Tikal, and other great Maya centers had preserved, along with the knowledge of the Olmec, Mixtec, and other nations in the One-World. Quetzalcoatl had ordered all the End Time codices brought to Tula and their contents combined into several codices. Into these august tomes he had interfused his own apocalyptic revelations. The primitive Aztec barbarians—ignorant and incapable of appreciating the codices' importance—would have used those invaluable books as cook-fire fodder.

What direction Tula and its empire would have taken—had Quetzalcoatl not left his city in the throes of civil war and gone to the land of the Maya to rebuild its cities in the Toltec image—is left for kings and philosophers to argue.

"The Aztecs sought to destroy all historical records, because those writings would have demonstrated that while the Toltec feasted on venison, the Aztec dogs had subsisted on grubs and worms," Sparrow said. "What wasn't stolen or razed during the Aztec conquests, they later seized when they enslaved the survivors. One of the few things that they had not destroyed was the Temple of Warriors, because they feared angering the War God."

The stone warriors were more than twice as tall as I was. They stood atop the temple—silent sentinels standing guard over dead memories of ancient glory.

Perhaps as punishment for the Toltecs' sins—in permitting their wondrous city to fall under the brutal bludgeons of a barbaric horde—the gods had scorched the once lush valley, blistering the land, trees, and grass until it was baked yellow brown.

To save time, I sent Sparrow and Axe to the village below to hire workers for the labor necessary to unseal the cache that had entombed the final codex for hundreds upon hundreds of generations. I went up to the ruins by myself, to the few stone mounds where a city of sixty thousand people had once stood.

The Thundering Paw, Huemac the Hermit had whispered to me. *Look under it.*

Thundering Paws were sacred stone statues of a man reclining on his back, with his elbows on the ground, head and shoulders raised up, and his feet pulled back. The posture provided a surface on top, in which a bowl or other vessel could be placed. The hearts ripped out of sacrificial victims by temple priests went into those vessels.

The statues' sacrificial function was no doubt the reason the Aztecs and other plunderers had left them alone. Thundering Paws played an integral role in the sacred blood covenant. Removing them from the city would have offended the gods.

The statues were easy to spot, because they were located near the main temple, where most of the sacrifices probably took place.

Unfortunately, when the Hermit said to look under a Thundering Paw statue, he did not inform me I had to select a statue that would be surrounded by nineteen other Thundering Paw monuments. My chances of picking and turning over the right effigy were slim.

Moreover, the stone statues were not just heavy, over time the bottom edges of the statues became affixed to the stone beneath. Moving them would be a backbreaking, time-consuming job. If we had to move twenty statues before we found the right one, we would still be tipping up statues when Montezuma himself arrived at the head of an army.

I examined each one, looking for some clue that a passageway might lie beneath it.

I found nothing.

As I looked them over, I detected another dilemma.

I didn't know the size and nature of the final codices' hiding place. A small area just big enough to put the final codex? Or a large one, perhaps even containing other books?

I had assumed that moving the statute would immediately reveal a hiding place for the final codex. But stones—even cemented brick—might block the entrance to the cache.

Jeweled Skull had told Sparrow that the attack on the city had come as a surprise to the occupants and that the walls had been breached quickly.

The circumstances would have left Coyotl little time to hide the final codex.

I sat in the shade and thought about what the stargazer named Coyotl, who hid the final codex, was thinking as he searched for a cache with barbarians flooding the city.

The ruins were in the city's ceremonial center, near the royal palace, pyramids, and temples. Located behind a second set of walls, it would have been the last place in the city to fall to the invaders, along with the royal palace itself.

The god-king would have kept the final codex in the royal library or the house of the stargazer. And it was unlikely that a Thundering Paw would be found in those areas. Tula's Thundering Paws were located where the statues were commonly found in other cities—near the temple where sacrifices were conducted. The bloody deeds were done atop pyramids—to let the gods see the blood flow—and the hearts were later brought to Thundering Paws' sacrificial vessels.

That Coyotl would hide the codex beneath a statue that was out in the open area while a battle raged in the city streets and perhaps in the center itself made no sense.

I wondered if the gods had possessed Huemac the Hermit's mind, and he was mumbling dreams and not facts.

Moving back to a higher spot, I tried to visualize how the ceremonial center had been laid out. I saw something that puzzled me: The Thundering Paws faced east to catch the rays of the rising sun—all except one, and it looked to the north.

The north was where Mictlantecuhtli, the lord of Mictlan, presided over the Aztec netherworld. As with Xibalba, Mictlan was where the unhonored dead went to face violent demons.

I was certain the Dark Rift Codex was beneath the statue facing hell. But why would Coyotl hide the codex there?

Coyotl didn't hide the codex in Tula.

The legend was true. He had taken it with him and had hidden it somewhere else, perhaps in Chichén Itzá, the city his king had rebuilt in Toltec fashion. Over the centuries, however, the Keepers of the Secret had brought the codex back to Tula's sacred ground and hid it, choosing to place it beneath a Thundering Paw. Perhaps Huemac himself had done so, changing where the book was hidden when a previous hiding place was jeopardized.

Sparrow and Axe were coming back up the hill with a group of villagers. Since the local people would balk at moving a Thundering Paw, even at touching it, I could play on their fears. By telling them that the statue faced the wrong way, I could convince them that the statue was visiting the wrath of the gods on their village.

I stared at the statue with foreboding. Not because I identified the statue with sacrificial death and the codex beneath it foretold the One-World's death, but because Huemac had predicted the death of the woman I loved.

91

The villagers were apprehensive about even approaching the statue. Sparrow was smart enough to have bought a hammerstone and chisel from them, but when I started chipping away at the monument's base, the villagers fled in fright.

"I will tell them their fear is an affront to the gods," Sparrow said, starting to run after them.

"It's all right," I said, grabbing her arm. "Axe and I will be able to move it."

When I had broken the cement bond ringing its base, Axe and I put our backs into it. My prodigiously powerful comrade made the difference, and we moved it far enough to expose the base.

I stared at the stone beneath it with dismay.

"There's nothing here."

Sparrow got down and cleaned the base. "It must be beneath the flooring."

"No, it's not there. If a hole had been made in the stone, you would still see it even after it was resealed. I was wrong. It's not under the statue."

"What if it's not under it," she asked, "but in it?"

"It's not hollow."

But even as I said it, I realized it didn't have to be completely hollow. A book would not occupy a big space.

"We'll turn it over," I told Axe.

Eyo! If the villagers saw us flipping the sacred statue, they would come back armed with stones and clubs.

We pushed the statue until we'd jammed it up against a small ridge, and it wouldn't go any farther. Undismayed, Axe put his shoulder against it, tipping it up over the ridge. When it rose to a hand's breadth, I slipped a stone under it.

Squatting down, we shoved our hands underneath it. I had done this movement a thousand times, while lifting large chunks of limestone, and the Thundering Paw was composed of the same material.

Toppling it over with an earthshaking *thud*, I was sure the crash carried all the way to Montezuma's palace. I shot a glance to the villagers. They had stopped their retreat and were turned around, staring at us in fright and shock.

I didn't see a hole in its bottom, but I did find a small groove, which had been carefully cemented over. With the chisel and hammerstone, I chipped at the concealed cut until I was able to prise out the chunk of stone. My heart was pumping with excitement. I was now sure it was there, under the stone plug concealing the final codex, the One-World's Book of Fate. After chiseling around its edges, I pried and pulled it out. An object covered in heavy cloth lay underneath it. I removed it with fear and trembling.

I looked up at Sparrow, but she wasn't watching me. She was staring at something in the distance.

I got to my feet, thinking the villagers were returning, armed with rocks and clubs.

But it wasn't them.

Flint Shield was coming.

92

Axe was wrong. There were more warriors in Flint Shield's band than he had estimated—fifteen, including Flint Shield—all armed with spears, swords, shields, and quilted body armor worn over chest-protectors of hard shafts lashed tightly together.

Flint Shield was festooned with the feathers of a Maya war lord. His men weren't hungry farmers fighting for food but professional warriors. The markings on their shields identified them as members of the royal guard.

There were fifteen of them, we were three. They outnumbered us five to one.

I had a sword. Sparrow had her bow, arrows, and a dagger. Axe had a bow, arrows, and the hammerstone we had used earlier. We had shields, purchased en route to Tula, but they did not compare to those of the approaching warriors.

As they advanced, seven of the warriors broke off in a unit and began to circle around us. Flint Shield and seven others approached us head on.

The eight in front of us slowed their pace so that the others could position themselves on our rear flank.

We had the high ground, which was an advantage against the warriors in front. But the moment we engaged them, the attackers to our rear would impale our backs with spears.

The stoical expressions on the faces of my two companions told the story.

It was hopeless.

Fifteen were too many.

Sparrow's and Axe's arrows had a longer range than the spears, but the hard thick shields and body armor would provide the warriors with considerable protection.

"Stand back to back," Sparrow said to Axe. "We'll shoot for their legs."

The true purpose of the poisoned tips came home to me—it gave an advantage over regular arrows when fighting a warrior with a shield. Even grazing opponents in places that the shield could not cover would kill them.

Protecting each other's backs and shooting for their legs would take down some of them, but there were still too many. Splitting their force up had doomed us. When one of us went down, the backs of the other two would be exposed.

"No!" I said. "We kill Flint Shield, and the others will run."

Was it true? If they were forced conscripts—who wanted only to survive and had no personal or professional interest in killing us—they might.

Whatever the case, killing Flint Shield was our only hope.

And it allowed us to utilize our sole advantage. We'd use our commanding height to kill him before the other men could position themselves on our rear flank.

Kill the head of the pack, and the others will run?

Flint Shield had a reputation as the finest warrior in Mayapán. I was stronger but not as battle trained and combat hardened as he. If we had to kill him as well as the seven other warriors besides him, the men to our rear would have time to spear us in the back.

We charged—not with war cries but with the twang of bows as Sparrow and Axe each let an arrow fly. One found its mark, and a warrior went down screaming, clutching his leg.

Flint Shield's other men formed a wedge, with him in the center of the V.

Before we engaged in close combat, Sparrow suddenly grabbed my arm to hold me back.

Axe flew past me, his hammerstone-like battle club held high. He struck down the lead warrior in the pack as spears coming at him from both sides jabbed into him. He bellowed animal noises as he swung wildly, spears in his sides.

Crazed confusion erupted around me as I ran headlong into the group, wildly swinging my sword, insane with rage. The screams ringing out around me merged with my own into a single, deafening, protracted roar. My vision turned bloodred, then a blazing crimson, then blindingly, agonizingly bright—until the whole world burst into flame. One of Flint Shield's warriors slashed my shoulder to the bone even as I hacked his sword arm off at the elbow, our combined wounds flooding my face with frothy gore.

Suddenly, Flint Shield's yellow and green headdress thrust itself in front of me, and I swung frantically at it.

One of the men, who'd flanked us, hit me in the back of the head, and I pitched forward onto my knees. When I lifted my head, I was staring into Flint Shield's malevolent grin. Howling like a rampaging beast gone mad with feral suffering, he lifted his sword high above my face and brought it down on me with both hands as hard as he knew how.

Sparrow threw herself in between us, her neck and shoulder intercepting his blade, her blood inundating me. Erupting in mindless rage, I threw myself at him. Twisting his sword arm, I heard him scream as I ripped it out of its shoulder socket.

As I tore off his headdress, he tried to stab me with his dagger, but my forearm parried his, blocking the thrust. Lifting him off his feet by the throat, I crushed his windpipe. Screaming in rage, I slammed him to the ground. Rolling him over, I climbed onto his back. Jerking his head backwards, I broke his neck as I had once broken the neck of a sacred beast.

Turning him over, I spat in his face.

Getting up, soaked in blood, I turned to face the seven warriors who were now joining the battle.

My sword was gone, and I faced them unarmed. Weaponless, I was no longer a man but a jungle animal. I let out a roar and started for them, but they fled, every one of them, running down the hill in terror.

I stood a long moment, drenched in death.

Kneeling, I picked up Sparrow and took her in my arms, saying nothing. Clutching her to me, I sobbed.

She had traded her life for mine.

The Hermit had been right.

The gods had called her name.

Then I heard Flint Shield moan.

I leaned down and looked deep into his eyes. "I'm going to cut out your heart and eat it . . . because I can," I told him.

I cut open Flint Shield's chest, grasped his heart with my hand, and squeezed hard as I pulled it out of his chest.

PART XVIII

93

Dr. Monica Cardiff sat at the big conference table across from President Edward Raab, General Richard Hagberg, and Bradford Chase, former Director of the CIA's Directorate of Covert Operations. Her friend and former student, President Raab, stared at her attentively. The other two men looked terminally bored.

She had once told Rita Critchlow: "If those two cretins can't shoot it or bomb it, they'll piss on it like dogs."

At this moment, that was exactly how she felt about them.

Handing out her eyes-only, ultra-classified briefing paper, she began her presentation:

"We recently took our scientific data—including our databases, projected global catastrophes, past apocalyptic predictions, and estimated prognoses—then fed them into the new supercomputer at NASA. Running them through their recently developed, cutting-edge software program, we were able to evaluate the planet's most probable disaster scenarios and those scenarios' estimated outcomes. In this case, the Probable Catastrophic Scenario and End-Game Program (PCSEG) spat back some surprising results.

"We were a little facetious when we included analyses of past apocalyptic predictions. I personally felt that the odds of some ancient prophet—through chance, genius, or some preternatural predilection—might have anticipated our current crisis were remote. Still, I saw no harm in adding them to the mix. We factored in threat data on all kinds of disasters, including seismic, supervolcanic, global warming, nuclear terrorist catastrophes, and comet-asteroid bombardments.

"We never imagined that PCSEG would validate any of these threats, but who knows? There was always a chance. We threw them in as a lark as much as anything.

"PCSEG's most likely end-time scenario and probable outcome prognoses prefigured in shocking detail the prophecies of Revelation."

"You're kidding," President Raab said.

"Revelation tells us that at the world's end, four apocalyptic horsemen will scourge humanity from the face of the earth. The first, the White Horseman, is often described as Pestilence. Dressed in red, Horseman Number Two is War. The third, the Black Horseman, is Famine. Horseman Number Four, the Pale Equestrian, will unleash hell's horrors on mortal flesh.

"Revelation 16:2 and 16:11 depict the depredations of Rider Number One, the White Horseman of Pestilence. He covers the followers of the Antichrist—who are worshippers of Mammon and Money, not God—with 'grievous sores.'"

"And you think we're all about to be plastered with these lesions," General Hagberg asked, his face incredulous, "because of some demented prophet's babblings?"

"No, but global warming is destroying glaciers throughout the planet—that is an established fact—and many of the world's most important, glacially fed rivers are drying up even as we speak. Many of the huge Himalayan glaciers feed such rivers as the Yangtze, Yellow, Mekong, Salween, Indus, Brahmaputra, and Ganges rivers, and they are shrinking at unprecedented rates. Over two-point-five billion people are dependent on these diminishing waterways and their vanishing drainage basins. Over five hundred million people rely on the Ganges River alone, and by some estimates, these rivers and basins supply as much as forty percent of the world's population with food, water, and electricity. When we factor in the farmers, whom these rivers support and who feed many hundreds of millions of people who live beyond these river basins, the numbers of people sustained by these waters is almost incalculable; and these people are watching those glacially dependent waterways die.

"South America is also watching its water supplies vanish. The rivers of Bolivia and those in the Amazon basin, in particular, depend almost exclusively on the Andean glaciers for their water, and those waterways are disappearing with stunning speed. The death of the Chacaltaya and other Andean glaciers already threaten the existence of La Paz and El Alto."

"And the disappearance of those glaciers will spread plague?" General Hagberg asked, confused.

"Look at your briefing paper, starting with paragraph number three," Dr. Cardiff said.

The three men looked at her paper and read:

The deaths of those rivers and the consequent water shortages will inflate the already sky-high water prices in these threatened regions, forcing nations and individuals to restrict their H_2O usage to cooking, drinking, and agricultural projects. The dearth of H_2O will devastate sewage-treatment facilities as well as public and personal sanitation. Global warming will then have effectively closed the food–feces circle, proliferating diarrhetic diseases and inciting the sorts of plagues so graphically depicted in Revelation.

Global warming also encourages the spread of disease-bearing insects into regions whose climates had not previously supported them, and the lack of proper sanitation will aggravate those illnesses as well. The spread of mosquitoes carrying malaria, yellow fever, and West Nile virus are only three obvious examples of the White Horseman's lethal labors.

General Hagberg raised his head to disagree. "Those diseases," he said, "are disastrous to the people afflicted with them, but they hardly constitute apocalyptic, end-of-the-world plagues."

"That could change," Dr. Cardiff said. "Look at paragraph number four."

The men lowered their eyes and read.

In the developing world—most notably in China—farmers raise pigs and poultry in close proximity. Those two species are uniquely susceptible to human influenza viruses, and when those viruses repeatedly circulate through people, pigs, and poultry, the viruses sometimes mutate into influenza pandemics. Global warming and the water shortages it provokes will stimulate the spread of those plagues.

We are just beginning to understand the significance of avian DNA in influenza viruses. For instance, we now know that most of the DNA in the 1918 Spanish influenza—the most fatally contagious influenza virus of all time—was avian. That plague killed far more people than World War I. The developing world's countless pig/poultry farms are incubators for influenza. Without the domestication of pigs and poultry, these influenza viruses could never have achieved their pervasive virulence.

Eventually, those farms will breed a virus to rival the Spanish influenza of 1918, which killed as many as 50 million people worldwide, and humanity will be no more equipped to combat it today than in 1918. In all probability, *Homo sapiens* will die in far greater numbers than they did 100 years ago, because today's world is so intensely and incessantly interconnected. A plague such as the 1918 Spanish influenza will burn through the species far faster, far more furiously than it did in 1918. The lack of water for proper sanitation will also fan the flames of that pandemic.

Nor are our pig/poultry farms breeding only superinfluenza viruses. In the United States, 84 percent of all antibiotics are being pumped into the animals we eat—North Carolina's farm animals ingest more antibiotics than America's entire human population—and these drugs are creating and spreading other superbugs as well. Microbes exchange genes in these prodigious pig and poultry pens, so the microbes that survive tend to be resistant to antibiotics. The use of animal antibiotics is thus breeding a superlethal generation of superbugs.

The most infamous of the superbugs is of course MRSA—a variety of the staph virus—which kills almost 20,000 people in the U.S. each year. Now, however, ESBL E. coli, Acinetobacter and KPC Klebsiella are challenging its pathological preeminence. Unleashing a widespread wave of superstrong ultravirulent, increasingly lethal diseases, these new megaviruses will be utterly resistant to antibiotics, and their spread will prove intrinsically unstoppable.

Congress and the White House avoid the issue like the superbug plague it is and do nothing to stop the overuse of these plague-proliferating antibiotics—the sole purpose of which is to produce cheaper meat and generate more revenue for the farmers. Hence, the tide of unnecessary superbug deaths rises at a shocking rate. We could soon be facing global pandemics of lethally untreatable, inherently invulnerable supervirus diseases, created by pig/poultry farms worldwide.

Now it was Brad's turn to raise his head and question her findings. "So global warming inflicts the White Horseman of Pestilence on *Homo sapiens*," Bradford Chase said. "You need war, famine, asteroid strikes—all kinds of disasters to wipe out a species as tough as *Homo sapiens*."

"I describe those scourges on page five," Dr. Cardiff said.

The men turned to page five and lowered their eyes.

The Red Horseman of War and the Black Horseman of Famine will soon make their presence felt. As global warming accelerates global drought, nations will increasingly threaten each other over shared rivers and lakes, which, to their horror, are already shrinking dramatically. In Revelation 9:13–18, a global war kills off one-third of humankind, and nothing will drive *Homo sapiens* to apocalyptic violence faster than thirst and famine.

Revelation 16:4–7 describes the world's rivers turning to blood, and Revelation 16:12 describes the Euphrates—the greatest agricultural river of that region and of that time—drying up. As we shall see, there is ample evidence that the Euphrates may well vanish, and those rivers could turn bloody before they die, particularly when their shrinkage generates wars of survival— the bloodiest kind of war there is—among those nations sustained by them.

The Red Horseman of War will wreak his most horrific havoc when the world's major mountain glaciers melt away. Global warming will then have destroyed many of the rivers supplying the world's most productive croplands and largest cities, including, as we have mentioned, the Yangtze, Yellow, Mekong, Salween, Indus, Brahmaputra, and Ganges rivers.

Africa's eternal curse has always been aridity, not swampy rain forest. Production of one ton of grain requires 1,000 tons of water. African farmers need 88 percent of all their available water to raise their crops. Africa's water shortages are already passing the point of no return, and UN studies predict during the next fifteen years water disputes will provide the casus belli for most of Africa's wars. Already Egypt, which is watching the Nile dry up before its eyes, is threatening Ethiopia and Sudan militarily over their diversions of that river for irrigation and electrical power production. Moreover, the massive Ruwenzori mountain glaciers, which run along the border between Uganda and the Democratic Republic of the Congo, have lost 50 percent of their mass in 50 years. Known as "the Mountains of the Moon," the Ruwenzori glaciers are the Nile's highest and most important water source. When the Mountains of the Moon vanish, their deaths could well be the Nile's coup de grâce. Some experts estimate that the Ruwenzori glaciers could disappear within 30 years.

During the next 40 years, the populations of those three nations will more than double, drought conditions will worsen, and the Nile might very well run dry before reaching the Red Sea.

Other African countries that are at odds over their individual access to shared lakes and rivers include the Congo Republic, Angola, Zambia, Zimbabwe, Botswana, and Mozambique—all of which are battling one another over rights to the Zambezi, Okavango, and Cuito river basins. Mali, Guinea, and Nigeria are inextricably bound to the Niger River, and Ghana relies on the Volta River for most of its electrical power. Both rivers are disappearing.

Fifty years ago, Africa's Lake Chad covered more territory than Israel. Now that once-massive body of water has shrunk by over 90 percent, and scientists predict that within two decades, global warming, which will accelerate overuse of water in that region, could easily eradicate the lake. The 30 million people who rely on Chad's waters for their very existence would be forced out of their homes.

Nor is the nightmare restricted to the nation of Chad. Nigeria, Niger, and Cameroon border Lake Chad, and four other countries—Sudan, Libya, Algeria, and the Central African Republic—share its hydrological basin. That region, which already faces chronic food shortages, will face irreversible famine. Sanitation facilities and personal hygiene will, of necessity, deteriorate, and infectious diseases will become pandemic. Children, who are especially vulnerable to diarrhea-related illnesses, will be the first victims.

Regional water shortages are already bankrupting farmers and livestock herders, both of whom are watching their crops and grasslands dry up at record rates. With the cost of feed soaring, farmers and herders in that region are already contesting

408 · GARY JENNINGS

croplands and pastures. Fishermen around Lake Chad have watched their catches fall off by more than 60 percent."

General Hagberg looked up to disagree. "Wars in Africa are as old as the species, and while ruinous for those involved, they hardly constitute a global apocalypse."

"They will in India, Pakistan, and China," President Raab said. "Continue with the paper."

Armed conflicts will plague billions of people in China, India, and Pakistan, who will be forever devastated by the destruction of the Himalayas' glacially fed rivers. India's mountain glaciers are the Indus River's major suppliers of H_2O, and the destruction of that river system will turn all of Pakistan into irretrievable desert. When India and Pakistan run dry, the likelihood of another Pakistan–India War will increase. This time, however, the stakes will be apocalyptic—so much so that a conflict could easily go nuclear.

Turkey's damming up of the Tigris and Euphrates rivers is diverting water away from Iraq and Syria, which they desperately need. The Turks brazenly proclaim that they will sell that dammed-up riverwater throughout the region. They almost seem to say: "You have all the oil? Fine. We'll take your water and sell it back to you."

Central Asia's Aral Sea—the fourth-largest inland sea on earth—is now a toxic bone-dry waste.

"I didn't include the methane cannon in this paper, since we discussed it before," Dr. Cardiff said. "We should add, however, that when global warming raises the ocean temperatures beyond the methane-release tipping point, it will liberate the seven trillion tons of methane gas in those waters, and Revelation 16:3 describes the seas turning to blood. A greenhouse gas of apocalyptic proportions, methane has forty-five times the global-warming power of CO_2.

Even now, methane plumes are bubbling up out of the arctic seabed north of the Scandinavian countries in the West Spitsbergen region as well as throughout Siberia and Alaska. In the arctic, atmospheric methane concentrations are already three times higher than the world average. Unleashed in sufficient quantities, those methane exhalations will effectively transform the planet into one gigantic hot box."

"You said before," Bradford Chase pointed out, "that this methane cannon could turn Mother Earth into Planet Venus, destroying most of the living species on land, in the sea, and in the air."

"Exactly so," Dr. Cardiff said.

The men continued with their reading. Dr. Cardiff was pleased to see that Revelation had piqued their interest.

Revelation adds many other catastrophes to the more abstract categories of pestilence, famine, and war. Seismic events, including earthquakes and volcanic eruptions, loom large in Revelation's end-time prophecy, and they have posed a serious apocalyptic threat both in the past and in the present. Revelation 16:18–21 describes an earthquake in Judea "such as had not occurred since men came to be on the earth. . . . And the great city [of Babylon] split into three parts, and the cities of the nations fell." Revelation 6:12 describes with the opening of the Seventh Seal a terrible earthquake and the sky turning black. Afterwards, in Revelation 8:1–5, an angel fills a censer with holy fire and hurls it at the earth, inflicting earthquakes, thunder, and lightning.

Seismic disasters threaten a number of countries today, including Israel and Palestine. Situated on the Alpide Fault Belt, Israel and Palestine are increasingly menaced by massive tectonic plate collisions, specifically those of the northbound Arabian and Indian Plates, which are colliding with the Eurasian Plates along Israel's Dead Sea rift. That rift created the Beqaa Valley, which runs through the Jordan River and flows into the Dead

Sea. At the southern tip of Sinai, the Dead Sea Rift meets the Red Sea Rift, then crashes into the East African Rift and the Aden Ridge in the Afar Depression. This trio of rifts is sometimes called the Afar Triple Junction, and it makes that region singularly vulnerable to seismic destruction. Satellite photos of this region delineate these fault lines with frightening clarity, and recently that rift inflicted 500 tremors on Israel in one three-month period. Israel and Palestine face potential seismic ruin just as they suffered massive quake disasters in 749 B.C., 362 B.C., 31 B.C., A.D. 363, A.D. 1033, A.D. 1202, 1837, and 1927.

A recent 5.3-magnitude earthquake ripped a hole in the Temple Mount Plaza near the Dome of the Rock, and many experts now fear that quake was only a precursor to far greater seismic destruction. The Jordan Valley Fault is especially dangerous, generating 7-magnitude-plus earthquakes every 1,000 years, the last one along this fault having occurred in 1033. Earthquakes now threaten Jerusalem—Israel's most populous city—among other urban centers. Some scientists believe these colliding rifts, in the near future, could kill as many as 500,000 people in Israel alone, a country of only 7.5 million people.

Next to the Pacific Ring of Fire, the Alpide Belt is the second most seismic region on earth with 17 percent of the world's largest earthquakes and 5 percent to 6 percent of all earthquakes globally. Its tectonic plate collisions are so powerful that many seismologists believe its southern African Rift—which is riven by 30 active volcanoes and enormous geothermal violence, all of which drives the northbound Arabian plate relentlessly into the Eurasian plate—could split Africa into two landmasses within a few million years.

"Okay, we're getting earthquakes in the Mideast, like Revelation said," Bradford Chase groaned, looking up from the briefing paper. "That's hardly the end of the world."

"Those seismic events trigger supervolcano explosions," Dr.

Cardiff said, "which have exterminated more species historically than any other extinguishing pulse, including comet or asteroid strikes. Look at page six."

Seismic events also trigger supervolcano eruptions, which have extinguished more past species than any other "extinction pulse"—including asteroid and comet strikes—and today supervolcanoes threaten the United States, Italy, and Asia.

The potential devastation of these supervolcanic events cannot be overstated. One supervolcano almost exterminated all of *Homo sapiens*, and another one obliterated every major civilization worldwide. The first one—the Lake Toba Supervolcano in Northern Sumatra, Indonesia—detonated 74,000 years ago. Releasing prodigious quantities of greenhouse gases—the same emissions that we are currently pumping into the atmosphere—it exterminated 99 percent of humankind, reducing a surprisingly wide variety of human species to two frail branches. Humanity's survival depended on as few as 1,000 breeding pairs for its survival. When one branch ended with the Neanderthal die-off, the sole surviving line became *Homo sapiens*. That massive explosion in the Sumatran Volcanic Front is now known as *Homo sapiens'* "genetic choke-point," the point at which human genetic diversity ended forever. Today, mitrochondrial geneticists can trace *Homo sapiens'* lineage back to a single Adam and a single Eve because of the Lake Toba Eruption. In a sense, *Homo sapiens* was born out of a supervolcanic eruption.

In A.D. 535 another supervolcano detonated in the Pacific Ring of Fire 20 miles northeast of Krakatoa, the massive volcano that shook world civilizations 1,300 years later. Devastating agriculture worldwide, this proto-Krakatoan eruption destroyed all the major civilizations in Europe, Arabia, and China. Obliterating European agriculture, it inaugurated the so-called Dark Ages. The droughts, which this global warming unleashed, ravaged countries and communities worldwide. Mexico's fabled

Toltec empire—ruled by the god-king, Quetzalcoatl and famed for its golden city of Tula—is only one example of a great civilization brought to its knees by global warming and its malevolent offspring, drought.

Again, that near-extinction event flooded the atmosphere with hothouse fumes and debris. Initially the volcanic particulates saturated the upper atmosphere. Darkening the sky, they blocked the warming sunlight and cooled the earth. When they came down, however, the greenhouse gases took over, heating the atmosphere. These greenhouse gases launched a 500-year heat wave, known now as "the Medieval Warm Period."

These supervolcanoes still pose an apocalyptic threat, and historically, they were decisive—perhaps even the predominating factor—in four out of the last five major extinction events.

"The past is dead," General Hagberg said. "We don't have to worry about that stuff anymore. Like you said, we haven't been hit with a species-threatening eruption in seventy-four thousand years, and that one threatened the species only because we were were so few and inhabited only two continents."

"Really?" Dr. Cardiff said with a small smirk. "Read."

The general and Bradford Chase reluctantly returned to her briefing paper.

Moreover, supervolcanoes are still alive and menace us. Active supervolcanoes are overdue to erupt in Italy, Asia, and the U.S. The Italians are so concerned, they are drilling a 2.5-mile hole into one of their active supervolcanoes—Campi Flegrei near Naples—in hopes of better understanding and monitoring the apocalyptic threat it poses. Indonesians continually monitor the Tambora megavolcano, which after erupting in 1815, destroyed much of the northern hemisphere's crops and livestock and turned 1816 into "the year without summer." America's Yellowstone supervolcanic caldera is the most dangerous of the three—far larger and far more deadly—and it has been bulging and overheating for decades. Web sites are dedicated to monitoring its rising caldera and its mounting surface temperatures. Statistically, it is also overdue to blow—at least when one charts on a graph its historical eruption cycles—and such eruptions are cyclical.

Revelation 8:7–13 predicts widespread wildfires, saying that one-third of the world's grass and trees will be destroyed. Globally unprecedented wildfires already plague the American Southwest, the Amazon rain forest, Australia, Europe, Asia, and Africa. Some experts have labeled the current period: "the Age of the Mega-Fire."

Revelation 16:8–9 says the sun will be "granted to scorch the men with fire. And the men were scorched with great heat." Not only is the planet facing record-setting increases in temperature, greenhouse emissions ultimate threaten the ozone layer, which protects us from the sun's ultraviolet rays. If global warming sufficiently degrades that protective ozone layer—and it is well on the way to doing precisely that—the penetrating ultraviolet rays will "scorch the men with fire . . . with great heat."

Revelation 8:7–13 also predicts the annihilation of all the planet's sea creatures, and *Homo sapiens* is doing its best to fulfill that prophecy. During the last half century—less than an eyeblink in the long history of mass extinctions—90 percent of all large fishes have vanished. During the next 30 years, one-third of all amphibians and one-quarter of all land mammals will face eradication, 90 percent of the lion population having already died off. *Homo sapiens* will have advertently or inadvertently exterminated over one-half of the planet's species by the century's end.

Calling this sixth extinction event "the Holocene Mass Extinction," scientists have dubbed it "the fastest extinction event in evolutionary history." Most mass extinctions take thousands, even millions of years to do their work. *Homo sapiens* is accomplishing its Holocene Extinction Event in one century.

Nuclear weapons are man-made stars exploding on the earth, and Revelation is filled with references to stellar fire razing the world. Revelation 8:7–13 describes pillars of fire, flaming mountains, and a blazing star obliterating the planet. The angel—whose face was the sun and whose feet were fiery pillars—conjures stellar fire, with which to incinerate the earth. Revelation 12:4 describes thousands of stars hurled at the earth. This divine conflagration turns the rivers and seas to blood, and at Hiroshima, the rivers and other bodies of water ran red with blood as burn victims plunged into the cooling waters and drowned. Even worse, the burn victims often learned to their horror that "the cooling waters" were stinging seawater, and they drowned with sea salt inflaming their wounds.

Many scientists believe that the most urgent threat is the one of nuclear terrorist attacks. Given our inability to contain the planet's nuclear bomb-fuel stockpiles, we are on the brink of that possibility becoming a reality.

As if summoning images of Revelation's stellar fire, nuclear weapons are miniature suns, exploding on the earth—man-made death stars, in point of fact—but while the press makes these weapons sound incomprehensibly complex and impossibly difficult to construct, fabricating and detonating a simple terrorist nuke is, in fact, far simpler than the media reports. If one terrorist drops a 100-pound, grapefruit-size chunk of bomb-grade Highly Enriched Uranium (HEU) from a height of six feet onto another 100-pound, grapefruit-size chunk, the two chunks will detonate with a yield of approximately half the Hiroshima bomb. Firing one ball of HEU into another HEU ball inside a section of old cannon barrel in the back of a panel truck in front of, say, the New York Stock Exchange will achieve a Hiroshima-style blast with far less HEU.

Moreover, acquiring the nuclear bomb-fuel is not prohibitively difficult. Nuclear bomb-fuel facilities in Russia—even in the United States—are shockingly insecure . . . especially if the terrorists can plant or coopt a trusted accomplice inside the facility. Many nuclear proliferation efforts are stunned that terrorists still have not nuked an American city.

General Hagberg was now visibly agitated. "Look, I know something about nuclear war. Yeah, sure, a nuke is apocalyptic to the city getting nuked, but a terrorist setting off bombs by hand is not a mass-destruction delivery system. Also acquiring nuclear bomb-fuel for more than fifteen or twenty bombs would be beyond the capability of today's terrorists."

"I can give you scenarios whereby the consequences are far worse than what you depict," Dr. Cardiff said. "Most experts don't expect sophisticated terrorists to focus exclusively on a single city when they set off their nukes."

"Read," President Raab said.

Even worse, some experts fear that a sophisticated terrorist group would spend years stealing and stockpiling enough nuclear bomb-fuel to produce six or eight terrorist nukes. Then the terrorists would not simply take out a single U.S. city but six or eight simultaneously.

Such attacks would engender so much rage and terror that one could easily imagine the victim's retaliation going global, particularly if it were a major nuclear power such as the U.S. or the EU. The natural impulse would be to eliminate all possible nuclear-terrorist enemies and their sponsors rather than risk further attacks.

Al Qaeda even envisions detonating a nuclear device in the Yellowstone supervolcano caldera. The consequent eruption would devastate most of the United States and Canada.

Revelation 9:13–18 describes a global war in which one-third of humanity is slaughtered. Without "the extinction pulse" of nuclear weapons, such carnage would be unimaginable.

Now Dr. Cardiff interrupted their reading. "The last page," she said, "is my gravest fear, perhaps because I spent my life in astrophysics, have worked at NASA, and am supposed to be doing something about this. Giant rocks from space are arguably the gravest threat of all and the one we do the least to prevent."

The men returned to their paper.

But what about real star fire—fire from space, not just man-made suns? Revelation warns us that stars will hammer the earth and is filled with references to stellar fire razing the earth. Revelation 8:7–13 describes columns of fire, blazing mountains, and a flaming star striking the earth. Revelation 12:4 describes thousands of stars hurled at the earth.

Asteroids and comets are frequently cited as the number-one species-killer. That an asteroid—or perhaps a comet—helped to exterminate the dinosaurs adds credence to this theory. More resilient than *Homo sapiens*, dinosauria ruled their world for over 180 million years and was easily the most indestructible species ever to dominate the globe. During that reign, they endured catastrophic destruction which humankind could never have survived. Massive volcanoes and seismic events were ripping their supercontinent, Pangaea, apart. Creating our current continents and seas, these megavolcanoes and colossal plate collisions, which helped to form them, drove these newly formed landmasses halfway across the oceans. Moreover, these spectacular volcanoes wreaked havoc on the dinosaurs' climate, flooding the dinosaurs' atmosphere with greenhouse gases.

Even so, massive volcanoes alone could not end the dinosaurs' reign. When the giant K-T rock hit the Yucatán coast 65 million years ago, it set the entire planet aflame and wiped these lords of evolution off the face of the earth, even exterminating those in the sea. The only dinosaurs to survive were those that dwelt in the air—those dinosaurs that today we call birds.

Species-killing asteroids and comets still seriously menace

the earth. NASA estimates that at least 20,000 of these massive species-threatening objects could hit the earth, and they detect near misses continually. Unfortunately, given NASA's lack of an asteroid-surveillance system, NASA fails to spot 25 percent of these species-menacing rocks until the last minute. Congress has mandated NASA to build and deploy surveillance systems, which would detect and alert the world to these earth-threatening rocks, but Congress has never allocated the funds to build the telescopes required to spot them. Many of these orbiting recon satellites would be inexpensive and easy to build—small six-inch-in-diameter spotting-scopes could be productively deployed in orbit. For $800 million, a system of NASA-deployed ground- and space-based telescopes could detect and chart 90 percent of these 20,000 earth-menacing asteroids and comets. Just a little smaller than the New Orleans Superdome, these rocks are defined as over 460 feet in diameter. To date, only 30 percent of them have been detected.

For $300 million, NASA could deploy a surveillance system that would detect, monitor, and chart those threatening asteroids and comets more than 1,000 feet across.

If NASA spotted and studied a true civilization-killing asteroid, they could send a probe to meet it far from earth and attach a transponder to its surface. If the signals proved it was a genuine apocalyptic threat, NASA could then mount an expedition that would deflect it from the earth's orbit.

So far, Congress has refused to fund these spotting systems, and NASA has done little to prepare us for the killer stars Revelation 8:7–13 and 12:4 say will obliterate us.

Dr. Cardiff looked up and saw that the men were all now on the last page—from her point of view, the most interesting of all.

The financial apocalypse.

Humanity's failure to invest money in catastrophe-prevention could ultimately be humanity's gravest apocalyptic failing.

One of Revelation's most devastating apocalypses is financial. In Revelation 13, "the Beast"—whom we often call "the Antichrist," even though Revelation does not use that epithet—controls humanity by exploiting its greed and extorting a fee for all financial transactions. Avarice so obsesses people that even after the world learns that financial rapacity will plunge the money-hungry into eternal lakes of fire, humanity refuses to repent, preferring to suffer eternal hellfire than give up its dream of ephemeral riches. Even when the angels scourge humanity in Revelation 16:9–11 with plagues of sores, blood, and fire, men "blaspheme God" instead of giving up their greed. The Bible constantly condemns that vice of vices: Adam and Eve are expelled from Eden for coveting and purloining God's apples. Judas betrays Christ for the sake of filthy lucre, and in Revelation, humankind burns eternally for its relentless rapacity.

Acquiring money to finance, produce, and sell essential goods and services is not evil but indispensable to the growth and survival of both civilizations and individuals. Creating financial schemes in which people produce nothing but profit solely off other people's money—often violating other people's property rights in the process—is, however, ultimately destructive. Yet such financial schemes are disproportionately responsible for the world's debt. Global derivative debt—which for the most part is a financial house of cards—is now well over $1.4 quadrillion.

Increasingly the world's major money markets are dedicated not to production but to spurious financial chicanery, the destructiveness of which confronts us at every turn. That the Beast of Revelation—whom we now refer to as "the Antichrist"—destroys humanity through apocalyptic avarice now seems both shockingly plausible and eerily contemporary.

The men put down their papers and looked up at her. "Gentlemen," Dr. Cardiff said, "Rider Number Four—the Pale

Horseman of the Apocalypse—unleashes hell's fury on earth. He embodies all the infernal horrors, which scientists now fear will hammer *Homo sapiens* into extinction. The Fourth Horseman's hellish whole will be infinitely greater than the sum of his species-killing parts. The late great science fiction writer, Robert Heinlein, believed that if *Homo sapiens* was to be obliterated, multiple apocalypses would have to hit the species within a finite time span, such as a single year. He called his hypothetical mass extinction 'Year of the Jackpot.' In a sense, the Fourth Horseman of the Apocalypse personifies Heinlein's apocalyptic 'Jackpot.' A potpourri of global catastrophes, this pale rider destroys *Homo sapiens* synergistically, all within a surprisingly short time frame.

"That is what our supercomputer foresees, and that is what Quetzalcoatl lived through, saw, and says will return to bite us in 2012, and that is what NASA's supercomputer and its PCSEG program concluded after they crunched all the data we fed in. They said our most likely scenario and end-game paralleled the catastrophes of Revelation."

"Our supercomputer and its software program," President Raab said, "argue that John on Patmos knew more than all our scientists put together."

"And that we are in the Age of the Antichrist?" Bradford Chase asked.

"And you think we need Quetzalcoatl's final prophecy to determine whether his early suspicions and our supercomputer are right?" General Hagberg asked.

"Yes," Dr. Cardiff said, "because the apocalyptic pulse that wiped out the Toltecs could well be cyclical, its wheel now turning to our time."

"Those chickens are returning to roost?" Bradford Chase asked.

"That's what PCSEG argued. And we have to find those final codices," Dr. Cardiff said, "to learn where those chickens are and what they are up to."

"Meaning, we have to find the girls," General Hagberg said. For once he wasn't sneering.

Staring at them silently, Dr. Cardiff nodded her head, once, then twice.

Taking her hand, President Raab said, "We'll find them, Cards. If we have to harrow hell for their lost souls, we will find them."

Monica Cardiff picked up her papers and stood. She looked at President Raab a long moment.

She gave him a silent nod.

She turned to the door, and walked out the room.

PART XIX

94

Before I left Tula, I bought a yellow dog and killed it, burying it with Axe so it would guide him through the hellish nightmares of Xibalba.

I didn't buy a dog for Sparrow, because I would be her guide. I loved her, and she had given her life for me. I would carry her heart through the Place of Fear and clear the path for her by pitting my strength against the servants of the Lords of Death.

I headed southeast out of Tula to find a mountain pass that would take me from the high Valley of Mexico down to the coast, where I could find passage on boats back to the land of my people.

From a ridge an hour's walk from the site of the ancient city, I looked back and saw warriors also leaving the city. Aztec warriors, following the trail I had taken, were leaving—warriors famous for their endurance and prowess.

I turned my back and kept walking, not worrying about them. There was enough rage in me to fight an entire army. And determination that made me willing to defy even the Underworld's gods. I had two treasures to safeguard: the essence of the woman I loved and the book of fate for the entire One-World.

Not even the gods would stop me. Once I carried Sparrow's heart through Xibala, she would find eternal peace—her soul would be turned to dust and scattered in a field of maize.

I owed that to her. But I would have done it even if she had not given her life for me. I would have done it for love.

I didn't sleep the first night. Not because I feared the pursuit but because I wasn't tired. Angry, bitter, even empty inside, but not tired.

By the next night I was calm enough to relax after a meal I purchased from a farmer's wife. I avoided caravans of porters. The dangers of banditry were not the same in the Aztec lands as in my own, and I didn't want the company.

I built a fire, and for the first time I opened the book of fate and read it by the dim, flickering light.

Some of what I read was already familiar to me—at the whim of the gods, the One-World had been destroyed four times before. The first time water from the great seas rose and covered the land; then fire from the sky scorched the world; next brimstone erupting from a great fire mountain blackened the air and sky; and finally a bitter cold came from the north and spread until it encased the entire world.

What I learned from the codex was that all civilizations rise and then fall when the gods tire of them. When societies fall, the people do not fade away but turn savagely on each other as food and water become scarce.

The codex revealed that besides the periodic growth and eclipse of nations, sometimes the gods physically disrupted the entire world as they did the previous four times.

The codex was not based upon what the Tula astronomers knew, but upon the knowledge of all the ages of the people in the One-World that the god-king Quetzalcoatl had gathered in his golden city. It was the knowledge of the peoples of the One-World that had been passed down in writing and stories around the cooking fires since the world began again. The knowledge of how the fifth world would end was contained in the codex. When it would end was calculated, and a Long Count Calendar was created as a warning for when the time would come.

The Long Count Calendar was straightforward like the Calendar Round. An integral part of our daily lives, the Calendar Round told farmers when to plant, kings when to go to war, and cities when to hold festivals.

But, the long calendar was based upon catastrophic events: It began the day the world was created for the fifth time after the gods had destroyed four previous times . . . and its final date was the year when the fifth destruction would take place.

I felt a great burden, knowing that I carried with me the revelation of the fate of people not yet born or even imagined.

95

The hills rose higher, turning into a great wall of mountains that could be crossed only by a narrow path that weaved back and forth until I reached a split between the shoulders of great peaks.

The farther my steps took me up the mountains, the colder it became. When I reached the top of the pass, tiny ice particles hung in the air and bit at my bare skin like voracious mosquitoes. My hands and feet first became numb and then felt as if they had been put into a fire and scorched.

I had never experienced extreme cold before. I was not even up to the snow that caps some of the tallest mountains surrounding the valley.

The wood, which had once lined the trail, had long been consumed by the fires of previous passersby, leaving me to eat cold tortillas and lay shivering on the cold ground. Until I felt the burn of wind that carried ice and snow, I had not been able to conceive the killing force of either the Great Cold that once destroyed the One-World, nor the House of Cold in Xibalba.

I now knew why the gods had created smoking fire mountains—the fuming, blazing pits in the mountains warmed the godly heavens.

The air grew warmer as I descended down the mountain and the terrain that went from barren rock to scrub trees and finally to thick jungle. By the time I reached the coastal plains, the air was as hot as my own land and much wetter. Even though our Mayan jungles in ordinary times get as much water from the rain god as this region, most of it slipped away to cenotes. In this coastal area, there were rivers flowing to the sea.

Coming down from the mountains and onto the shores of the Great Eastern Waters, these rivers brought me to the land of the Tlax-cala.

The Tlaxcala were enemies of the Aztecs who, while not completely conquered by them, were forced to provide tribute and sacrifice victims.

I had seen the Tlaxcalan ambassador humiliated in Montezuma's palace because the emperor was not pleased with the tribute.

When I reached the coast itself, with the incredible Great Eastern Waters laid out beyond, I heard frightening rumors: Light-skinned strangers had come on canoes the size of palaces, and the Tlaxcala had welcomed them as allies to war against the Aztecs.

The news staggered me. The invaders that the madman called Jeronimo claimed would destroy the One-World had arrived.

Going over the top of a hill, I saw the giant canoes in the bay below. Eleven ships sat in the bay, each the size of a small palace. Tlaxcalan canoes that each held a dozen men looked like mosquitoes next to a log.

I saw the warriors on land at a distance, hundreds of them, and they were truly warrior-gods capable of destroying worlds. The men wore clothes of a strange, silverlike material that glistened in the sun, the war uniforms that Jeronimo had called *steel armor*.

Some of them rode on giant deerlike beasts with great hooves that could crush a man.

I watched in horror and awe as one of the warrior-gods demonstrated their divine power to headmen of the Tlaxcala by firing what Jeronimo had called a musket and killing a vulture a thousand paces away, blowing the bird apart as it was hit.

And then I saw him, the man I had spoken to in Tulúm, Jeronimo de Aguilar. I heard from a Tlaxcalan that the leader of the warrior-gods had ransomed him.

Catching my eye, Jeronimo began to taunt me. "God has dispatched angels with swords of fire to rid you pagans of its false idols!" he shouted at me.

I ran and didn't look back.

"You can't run from it!" he yelled.

"Xibalba!" I shouted back.

I don't know if he understood. I don't even know why I said it. Perhaps I wanted him to know that hell would be better than what his people would do to our land.

PART XX

96

XIBALBA

I hear my name whispered.

The darkness in the House of Gloom swaddled me like a babe.

I knew from the many tales I've told about this darkest of stone houses that it is a labyrinth with many traps and only one path out.

The Hero Twins, Hunahpu and Xbalanque, were champions of *tlachco*, the game played with a rubber ball on a long, narrow court. They were tricked into descending to the Underworld to play on the personal court of the Death Lords of Xibalba. The two brothers hadn't realized that the Xibalbans would use a ball with razor-sharp obsidian blades that cut a player each time he hit it. However, the twins cleverly substituted another ball for the bladed one and went on to win the match.

When the bladed ball failed to kill the twins, the Lords forced them into accepting the challenges of the stone houses. They entered the House of Gloom, which was a dark, complex maze, with only one way out.

The Lords of Death's plan was to have the twins wander aimlessly until they were so weak from hunger and thirst that demons could ravage them.

From the hundreds of times I repeated the story, I knew the route the twins took through the labyrinth. Missing from the tales told around supper fires, however, was the thing I faced at the entrance to the stone house.

Something was there; I could sense it. Perhaps the priests who had fled the chaos above were coming down to hide in the dark and wait for a two-legged meal? The ghosts of those I had killed? Was the spirit of Flint Shield waiting to take back his heart?

I heard it before I saw it. When I moved closer and it took form in the shadows, the sweat on my back turned to ice.

I was staring not at a ghost but a great grotesque thing covered from head to foot in the skins of people. As wide as Axe, the beast had two heads and wore necklaces of ears and fingers and belts festooned with human heads. Parts of faces were patched on his head and the heads on his belt. The heads still had eyes. Pieces of the cheeks and the foreheads clung to the heads in patches. The noses and lips were pulled around both sides of the faces.

Whatever the thing was, it was insane with madness and hunger or it would not have challenged a man with an obsidian sword. Even worse, the creature split in two before my eyes, and I realized it was two monsters in hideous costumes. My first guess was the correct one—before me were priests that had once flayed the skin and ripped the hearts from people in the temple above, and were driven down into the caverns as mobs who couldn't find maize and beans, so sought out the flesh of their fellow men.

The two in front of me wielded clubs. Then more of the once-human creatures came out of the shadows. Armed with clubs and spears and rocks, they surrounded me on all sides. I let out a war cry and charged the two in front of me, lashing out with my sword, taking the arm off one of them at the elbow as he raised his club.

The other creature's club hammered my left shoulder and sent me staggering. A spear hit my back but fell off after biting into the flesh. My sword came back around and hit the club wielder on the side of its leg before the thing could swing again.

Another one jumped on my back and bit into my neck. I smashed its head with my sword hilt. Knocking it off my back, I swung at another, which was charging me, slicing open its abdomen, spilling its guts. Spinning, I sidestepped a spear thrust and caught the attacker on the side of its neck, severing its head from its shoulders.

I ran for the black void that was the House of Gloom, the head of the creature bouncing behind me, a whirlwind of weapons and screeches of rage coming from the demons behind me.

I was determined to complete my mission. I would lead Sparrow's spirit through this hell of hells and secure the codex. Only if I could safeguard both would my own soul ever find peace.

There was nothing left above to which I might return. That world was doomed, and I understood that while the codex had foretold its destruction, my life's annihilation had begun much earlier—when I killed the white jaguar.

As a collector and teller of my people's legends, I knew better than anyone what a proud and mighty civilization we had been. To see chaos reign and people turn on each other as food and water became scarce were not events I wanted to remember or tell.

I also realized why the beast I fought was a white jaguar, the holiest of all the One-World's creatures. The death of the sacred beast symbolized the death of our own benighted land and also defined my own quest: I was to shepherd and secret the book, which foretold—and some said determined—my world's extinction.

More than a messenger of death, I was to be the divine emissary of the One-World's final doom.

I had to and would find a secure sanctuary for that last and fateful book—the Dark Rift Codex.

PART XXI

97

"What you mean they got away?" Emilio Luis Carrizo—*el supremo patrón* of the Apachureros army—asked his adjutant, Raphael Morales. "We sent three hundred of our best men after them."

"*Sí,* and two hundred of them men no come back."

Carrizo stared out over the lush Chiapas rain forest two hundred hundred yards from his patio, teeming with teak, mahogany, and fragrant frangipani. A lanky, hard-boned man with a black, carefully trimmed goatee and ponytail, shiny as burnished ebony, dark hard-mean eyes and skin like *café con leche,* he poured another cup of coffee from the sterling silver carafe into his white bone-china cup, then added cream and sugar. He was dressed in light-blue trousers, auburn cowboy boots heeled with sterling rowels, and a white long-sleeved shirt hand-tailored for Carrizo in Singapore. Carrizo was especially particular about his shirts, insisting that they accentuate his prison gym muscles which he had so painstakingly acquired during his five-year bit in the Pelican Bay supermax.

"Say here they escape in a *federal* helicopter."

"Which we shoot down."

"*Sí,*" Morales said, studying the field report spread out on the table before him, "but the *puta*-bitch with the codex, we shoot her out of the chopper, drop one hundred and fifty feet into white-water rapids, get swept over three waterfalls and . . . *live*."

"We send twelve men after her."

Carrizo was now staring fiercely at his second in command. Bald as a tangerine, short, squat, and middle-aged, Morales had been with Carrizo a long time. Unlike his *patrón*, Morales favored flashier attire—shirts splashed with primary hues, scintillating with yellow and red, black and white. Baggy and voluminous, always worn outside his pants—in part to conceal the small arsenal of guns and knives he carried inside his belt.

Carrizo found Morales' taste in clothes . . . tasteless.

But long ago, Carrizo had stopped offering his subordinate sartorial counsel.

Fuck clothes.

He relied on Morales for other things.

Carrizo silently sighed. To the extent Carrizo trusted anyone, he trusted Morales. Unfortunately for Morales, Morales did not know this, and in point of fact, Carrizo did not truly trust him. He trusted no one. He trusted fear—only fear.

He knew Morales feared him 24/7, and he trusted the fact that Morales was and always would be afraid. Carrizo fixed him with his most menacing stare and said: "This report say they all dead. She kill all three?"

"Read the report again. Say they got mauled by animals. Skulls crushed, heads bit off, ripped to shreds by talons and fangs, even beaks. One *hijo de puta* live long enough to say they was wiped out by an eagle, a snake, a crocodile, and a jaguar—a white jaguar."

"He was hallucinating," Carrizo said.

"I no think so," Morales said. "They find eagle tracks and feathers all over the ground—eagle feathers in the men's blood. They also find jaguar and croc tracks and the winding snake trails is leaving b-e-e-g trails, mucho b-e-e-g. Like this thing ain't no grass snake. This thing, he be . . . *huge*."

"You sayin' a jaguar, a crocodile, an eagle, and an anaconda kill twelve of our men, and the *puta*-bitch escape again?" Carrizo's stare was hard enough to drill through diamonds.

Morales tried to meet Carrizo's diamond-grinding eyes. He couldn't. "Tha's what they say, *patrón*," Morales said sheepishly.

Carrizo continued to terrify him with those fathomless orbs. "You find th-e-e-s-e *puta*-slut, you get the fuckin' codex. You no find it, we got a problem, meaning *you* got a problem."

"*Patrón*, she disappear like smoke."

"Morales, no *puta*-gringas kill our hombres like she do'n walk away. We hunt them all down. We hurt and kill them all. You hear me? You hear me?"

"*Sí, patrón.*"

"You no find them, I decorate the trees out there"—he pointed at the lush rain forest on the far side of his lawn—"with the entrails of my *puta*-soldiers and their officers. 'Cause if the commanders no command, what good are they? You get my meaning, *Commander* Morales?"

Mostly it was the eyes that got to Morales.

The eyes.

Eyes blacker than the grave, blacker than the abyss.

Blazingly black, blacker than the dark between the stars—balefire incarnate.

"*Sí, patrón*," Morales said. Bowing slightly, he left his boss.

Sí, Carrizo thought, fear was a fearsome thing to see.

Glancing at his watch, he decided it was time to open the Maestro Dobel Extra-Anejo tequila, aged and distilled from ten-year-old blue agaves, each bottle labeled, numbered, and marketed with the name of the ranch where the agave was harvested. Cracking open the fresh bottle, he poured himself four inches, downed it, then poured four more.

Remembering the flicker of fear in Morales' eyes, he smiled.

Yes, fear was a fearful thing to see.

He sipped the second drink, content—then threw that one back as well.

98

OCOSINGO, CHIAPAS, MEXICO

Skeletons and skulls—just what I need, Coop thought.

The Day of the Dead festival—which she and Jack Phoenix walked into after getting off the Chiapus bus—was a solemn event to honor the deceased. With eerie candies in the shape of skulls and coffins, however, and with street vendors selling "walking" wooden skeleton puppets and death's-head candies, it was hardly solemn. "Ghoulish and ghastly" was how Cooper Jones saw it.

The sidewalks were crowded with people watching a religious procession coming down the street carrying candles in glass jars while behind them a stupendous skeleton towered over the festival on a parade float. People ate tacos and mangos on a stick bought from street vendors. Animated drunks laughed, argued, and talked in small groups, while she and Jack worked their way through the crowd with coteries of kids whirling about them continuously. On the run, dodging trouble, they had come to this city posing as tourists, and she hoped they could get lost in the crowded festival.

Situated between the Tropic of Cancer and the equator, Chiapas was, to denizens of the north, unbearably humid, its torrid tropical dampness clinging to Cooper Jones like a hot wet beach towel. Heavily dependent on agriculture, its people were mostly subsistence farmers, producing coffee, chocolate, cotton, and bananas as well as the standard staples of corn and beans.

It was also an Apachurero stronghold.

Well, at least, she knew *they* were on her trail. But what about the other guys? Who in the government was working with them? Whoever they were, their existence meant she and Jack were women and men without countries.

Coop stopped on the Ocosingo street and leaned against a building for support and pretended to be interested as a street vendor manipulated a skeleton puppet. Her head swirled, and her knees got weak each time the nightmare reality of her life sank in and set her nerve ends aflame.

"*No gracias*," Coop said, shaking her head as the vendor offered her the puppet.

She and Jack started walking again. She periodically glanced behind them—to see whether they were being followed—but she tried not to be too obvious about it. She also tried hard to keep from worrying.

She was failing miserably at it.

Were she out of danger and discussing the codices with Cards over a drink at their favorite watering hole, they would have found the implications of Quetzalcoatl's writings disturbing enough. But the apocalyptic portents implicit in the god-king's prophecies combined with the armed men on their back-trail—both Apachureros *and* government killers, she now feared—made their situation truly grim.

The Mayans, who had saved Jack, had also rescued his computer. When they found an Internet café she thought might be safe, she'd e-mail her rough translation of the latest codex to Cards.

She and Jack also had their sequence of blind Web sites by which they could contact Reets surreptitiously.

If she were still alive.

Belay that thought.

Reets is alive.

Reets has to be alive.

Jack still had four grand in his money belt. More than enough for them to buy provisions, guns, trail garb, and gear—they could then vanish back into the deserts and jungles of southern Mexico, where they would become just two more peons.

Somewhere along the line, they would reconnect with Reets, Graves, and Jamesy.

And recommence their search for what Coop hoped and prayed would be the final Quetzalcoatl codex.

They had to find it.

The god-king was indeed predicting the Year of the Apocalyptic Jackpot, all the calamities of Revelation rolled up into one.

The final codex defining the exact nature of this extinction event—the who, where, when, how, and why of Questzalcoatl's apocalypse—was indispensable to humankind . . . if the species had any hope of surviving the cataclysmic horrors to come.

They had to find it.

If they didn't, there'd be hell to pay.

Book of Revelation–style hell.

And then?

And then?

And then?

Day of the Dead, indeed.

Cooper Jones wasn't religious, but she instinctively, fearfully crossed herself.

May God have mercy on our souls.

99

Dr. Monica Cardiff stared at the three men sitting before her in the White House conference room. Usually, they fidgeted and studied the briefing papers from other meetings. Not now. President Raab had obviously told them of the nightmare to come.

"I suspect you know," Dr. Cardiff began, "that I received an e-mail from Cooper Jones. It came via a dozen or so blind Web sites, and I doubt we'll ever trace it back to its exact point of origin. Even if we did locate the spot from which she sent it, I doubt we'd find her. She's with Jack Phoenix, and they know those southern Mexican deserts and jungles like squirrels know trees. I'm sure they have already gone to ground."

"They sound a little paranoid, you ask me," General Hagberg said.

Dr. Cardiff's stare was hard enough to crack granite. "They have reason to fear us. Someone in our ranks has systematically ratted them out to the Apachureros. That we have not tracked the informant down by now is an outrage."

"I share your anger and your concern, Dr. Cardiff," President Raab said. "Please continue."

"Coop e-mailed me her rough translation of the new codex. It's not pretty."

"Let's hear it," said Bradford Chase.

Dr. Cardiff cleared her voice and began to read from the e-mail in front of her.

The White Jaguar will bring pervasive plague
Such as the One-World has never seen.
Blisters, boils, bloody feces, contiguous, ubiquitous sores,
Wounds so vast, the blinding blood cataracts out.

The Red Jaguar brings war like nothing the One-World
Has ever known—millions of men in arms,
The eternal war of all against all, slashing, stabbing,
Deep in gore, bathed in blood till the land screams
Till the rocks themselves cry out from rack and ruin,
From pain and rage, from terror and from truth.

The Black Jaguar brings drought, the streams, lakes,
Croplands, cities drying up. Famine sweeps the land
Like nothing the One-World has known. Women scream,
Children cry, men murder and rend, all devouring all,
Till nothing, no one, no living thing is . . . left.

Then comes the horror of Mixlan's hell. Through
The Dark Rift and the Underworld Road, from
The Black Abyss at the World Tree's root,
Hell's legions are freed, all the earthly woes
—Fire, earthquake, volcanic fury, the stars
Themselves crash down, locusts with stinging tails,
The planet splitting like a gourd, the lakes and rivers
Not soothing fluid but molten fire, brimming blood.

All is lost.
The One-World is lost.

The People lost.
The world lost.

Time shall end
And eternity close.

President Raab stared at Dr. Cardiff a long time, then spoke a single world: "Revelation."

"Four jaguars would have been the closest thing Quetzalcoatl could have conjured up that would have resembled Revelation's four horsemen. Other than that, his prophecy is essentially the same—right down to the jaguars' colors and the kinds of catastrophes Revelation describes."

"The supercomputer was right?" Bradford Chase asked. "The prophecy of Revelation is at hand?"

"The supercomputer and Quetzalcoatl concur," Dr. Cardiff said. "John on Patmos called the shot. It's Year of the Jackpot."

"And we're about to get jacked," Bradford Chase said.

"By an albino on horseback," General Hagberg muttered under his breath.

"Indeed, General," Dr. Cardiff said, sadly nodding her head. "The Pale Horseman is coming to call."